SWORDS OF ROME

By Christopher Lee Buckner

For my mother

For your love and support while writing this book

PART ONE

CHAPTER ONE

"Blood, Mago – I want blood on my sword!" Hannibal yelled as he turned to face his younger brother, Mago Barca. "Yet, my blade remains sheathed in its scabbard, unstained!" His mood had been bad for the past several weeks. The siege was not going well. This was made worse by the fact that his men's nerves seemed to be wavering with each day the city of Saguntum held, now over eight months. And, with each week that went by was another that Saguntum greatest ally, Rome might send its legions from Italy to Spain in defense of its treaty.

Hannibal wanted war with Rome, it was his eventual goal. But, he needed Saguntum and its supplies if he was going to make the crossing over the Alps and supply his forces once he was in Italy. More importantly, he needed the support of the nearby Gallic tribes, which watched eagerly at Hannibal's success or failure. If he won the siege than they – tens of thousands of fearsome barbarian tribesmen would flock to his cause. They, with his Spanish and Carthaginian forces would swarm like a locus horde. Yet, if he failed to take Saguntum his allies might turn against him, seeing weakness in his resolve and challenge his stronghold in Spain; New Carthage might fall. If that happened, how long before Rome followed and took what remained of Carthage's new territories in Spain or even the attacked the homeland?

"The city elders are weakened from starvation and thirst, brother. I doubt they could hold week longer. By then we might be able to present terms for their surrender," Mago tried as best he could to put a positive spin on their situation, but he knew his brother too well to know anything but absolute victory would satisfy his craving.

"Terms?!?" Hannibal rebuked. "I want those walls! I want the city fathers heads on spikes for their defiance! I want the grain and, not to mention, our men want the cunt and booty that awaits them in Saguntum!"

"Then, brother, barring an earthquake or an act of the gods, I doubt our intents or the wants of plunder and rape for our men will be enough to bring down Saguntum's walls."

Hannibal leered at his brother for a long while, not angrily, but focused as his mind was drawing up a plan of desperation. It was in these moments of crisis that Hannibal knew he was at his best – when his back was up against the wall that desperation gave birth to his greatest and most daring plans. His father Hamilcar, who had never lost a battle against Rome during the war in Sicily a generation ago, had taught him to never run from a superior foe: *It was only when faced with an rival that was larger, meaner and stronger than yourself did one truly understand your own worth,* he would say around the campfire.

"Get your men ready to storm the gates when I give the signal," Hannibal finally broke the long silence as he leaped down from his horse and pushed his way through the bodies of the gathering soldiers. Mago did not ask any questions as this was the reaction he was hoping to see from his brother. He looked around, noticing the prying eyes of dozens of men standing around him who had overheard the whole conversation.

Smiling wide, Mago drew his sword and held it up over the head of his horse.

"Well, do you want this fucking city or not!" Mago cried as loud as he could. His men roared as they raised their assorted blades to the sky, bashing iron against their shields, and bellowed murderous expectation. Saguntum was going to fall and everyone and everything in the city would be theirs for the taking.

Gisgo hadn't time to scream before an arrow plunged into his right eye socket. He had done his duty as one of Hannibal's bodyguards – giving his life so his general may live. Hannibal liked and respected the big Numidian who had first served with his father decades earlier. He had three sons back in Carthage and a dozen more bastard children here in Spain. Hannibal vowed that he would tell Gisgo story, about how he had died bravely in battle, even if the veteran never saw the man that took his life.

"Keep moving forward you dogs!" Hannibal barked as he urged the torrent of men all around him to push against the onslaught of arrows, slingshots and rocks being hurled from the stone walls. Hundreds were wounded as they bled on the ground, trampled by their comrades that refused to waver behind Hannibal's urging. They knew they had to reach the rampart and begin to scale the walls or more of them would be going to the underworld before the day was done. Hannibal, however, did not attend to be among them. He was determined even if he had to tear down Saguntum's walls with his fingernails, stone-by-stone, he would. To fail would mean certain death, either by his supporters here in Spain, or back home in Carthage where generals who failed in the field were often crucified outside the city walls.

Finally, within the mud-soaked grounded of blood and gore the first set of ladders rose to the rim of the stone walls. Archers from the ground did their best to insure they stayed in place as men made ready to scale them.

Gripping one hand tightly around the base of one ladder, his shield held firmly in the other hand, positioned above his head, Hannibal turned towards his army and cried out, "Follow me to glory! Saguntum shall be ours! The wine, the gold, and the cunt are ours for the taking!" His men bellowed with excitement as Hannibal was the first up the ladders, soon followed by dozens more men across the length of the southern wall.

The defenders held fast as they threw down a volley of arrows and stones. Men's heads caved in, and bodies feathered, but still they climbed with madding determination never before seen as Hannibal was the first to reach the top. He did not know if anyone had followed him. He had heard over the deafening roar some of those below him fall to their doom as their bodies were crushed by falling stones and well aimed slingshots. Regardless, he pressed forward and locked sights on the first man – a boy really that came within range of his sword.

Hannibal was no stranger to killing. He had taken his first life when he was eleven years old, and had trained to use a sword the moment he dropped the rattle. He was a Barca, a famed and feared family of Carthaginian warriors that knew nothing of defeat or dishonored. As the oldest son of Hamilcar – a man in his own right that was a terror to the Romans during the last war with the republic for control of Sicily, a great deal was expected of Hannibal. He was groomed from boyhood, like the kings of Sparta or Macedonia to take up his father's mantel and carry out his dream of a Mediterranean world dominated by Carthage, and not the upstart city-state of Rome. So far there had been one setback already with his home-state's capitulation during the last war, and the dishonor that followed the Mercenary Wars soon after when Carthage could not pay the armies it had paid to fight Rome, now turned against their mother state. Hannibal would restore his beloved city's status in the world – he would elevate it at any cost.

To think, Hannibal's father used say, *that Carthage is responsible for Rome existence. If it weren't for our help they would never have overthrown their old kings. Now, look what they've done to our great nation. We are but a shadow of our former glory. But, you, Hannibal, you and your brothers will reclaim Carthage's honor and restore our rightful place at the head of Mediterranean – as it should be.* Those words had echoed through Hannibal's head since he was a boy, more so now in the past year than ever before. However, he knew what he did now wasn't just for his father's memory, or for Carthaginian domination, but for himself as well. If he could do what kings and warlords, barbarians and Greeks could not do before – topple the Roman Republic, he would be a god made flesh – forever immortalized as one of the greatest generals of all-time – if not superior even to Hannibal's own idol, Alexander the Great.

The man that Hannibal sighted, a boy no more than fourteen who crewed the wall, holding a longbow in his hand, drawing arrow after arrow never saw Hannibal coming as he hurled himself over the wall. He was so focused on his duty that he only stopped firing when Hannibal's sword ripped through the soft flesh of the boy's neck in one effortless motion.

The second man that Hannibal sighted was another archer, older by a decade, only just barely managed to glimpse him before Hannibal drew his sword in a violent horizontal arch, which sliced across the man's face. The right eye socket exploded with gore as the eyeball ruptured as the impossibly sharp iron blade tore through flesh. The man screamed in pain before he stumbled forward. Those cries ended as he plunged over the edge of the wall and fell onto the collection of densely packed Spanish and Carthaginian soldiers down below.

Hannibal moved with blinding speed as he attacked once more a third opponent. By now the walls were choked with dying men as more of Hannibal's soldiers had joined him, fighting up and down the length of the narrow walkway that was set between two forty-foot stone towers.

A spear came in high towards Hannibal's head, but he managed to raise his shield just in time to parry the blow away. Striking low, Hannibal counter by jabbing his sword into the man's exposed right knee. Blood and bone jetted out from the wide wound as the man bellowed in agony before Hannibal rose back to his feet and rammed his shield as hard as he could against the man's broad chest.

As the defender fell to the ground, Hannibal stood over the lying man and rammed the bottom of his shield into the defender's mouth, shattering teeth as the layers of wood sliced all the way through the man's cheeks, nearly cleaving his head in two.

Hannibal winced in pain for a moment as he bore down on his teeth. A sword had slashed across his exposed flank, cutting deep in the fat of his back. Already he could feel his own blood gushing out, but thankfully his chain mail armor had saved his life or otherwise he would have been dead.

Turning sharply Hannibal drove his sword into the man's face that had just attacked him. His sword lodged between the defender's skull and the back of his head for a moment, causing Hannibal a great deal of difficulty in trying to pry his weapon free. It was then that he heard several heavily armed men come rushing behind him. He glanced back for a moment and saw infantry charging up a set of stone steps, hoping they could repel the attackers before the walls fell.

Hannibal was trapped. He was forced to release his attempts to retake his sword from the man he killed and turn to face the charging infantry. Raising his shield while holding it firmly against his shoulder, Hannibal screamed a battle cry before he charged. He threw all two-hundred and thirty pounds of weight, plus armor against the collection of infantry, driving his shield into the first man who gasped as the air was knocked out from his lungs on impact. Hannibal cursed under his breath as he was cut once, twice, and then three more times across the arm and legs – not deep enough to slow him down, but painful enough to sap what strength he had left.

With one final burst of energy Hannibal bellowed and murderous roar and pushed against his shield, throwing the dozen men that stood on the either side off of him, but in the process he lost hold of his only defense as it was stripped from his grip and cast aside.

Hannibal, his head dripping with crimson blood bore his teeth as he raised his fists. He would not fall so easily he vowed, but then before the first foot soldier could charge him, he was struck dead-center by a well-aimed spear throw.

The soldier staggered back as he fell into his comrades as several more spears were thrown from behind Hannibal easily found their mark.

Hannibal turned and saw his bodyguards and several Carthaginian soldiers come rushing towards him, crying out, "Save Hannibal! Defend the General!"

Ordax, one of Hannibal's Spanish-born bodyguards handed him a new sword as the remaining groups of infantry and archers on the wall were easily dealt with. Soon after, the only men on the south wall were Hannibal's, who raised their weapons to the sky and roared his name in one thunderous body, HANNIBAL! HANNIBAL! HANNIBAL!

"Do you want this city?!?" Hannibal bellowed joyfully.

"Yes!" Everyone roared.

"Then open the gates and take what is rightfully ours!"

Hannibal, with his bodyguards and a dozen other men charged down the stone steps. Most of Saguntum's defenders were in a blind panic at this point as they ran once it became clear the walls had fallen. A few officers, however, tried to form a phalanx and repel the invaders, but their efforts were not enough as Hannibal charged forward, his destination the southern gatehouse.

Most the men Hannibal cut down, he did so as they turned and fled, dropping their swords or spears, and even more foolish, their shields. Those that stood their ground died just as easily. As brave as these men might have been, they weren't warriors. The wealth that poured into Saguntum made its people fat and lazy, much like Romans. If this had been a Gallic stronghold, Hannibal knew he would have to fight to the last man to claim victory.

Hannibal's eyes open wide with surprise as a small trickle of a smile cracked in the corner of his mouth once he saw a well-dressed – well armored and armed officer he knew by the name of Ballista. What made this captain of the guard valuable beyond his rank, as it was Ballista that had marshaled Saguntum defense over the past eight months, was that he was also a Roman citizen, sent by his senate when Saguntum declared its loyalty to the republic some years ago. The man had been a constant annoyance for Hannibal as he had represented the city elders during the various negotiations over the past eight months. Stubbornly, Ballista had been confident in his defiance's, which had now collapsed all around him.

"Hannibal, you shit-eating dog, face me yourself, if you have the courage!" Ballista sneered with bitter distain as he held his ground, sword and shield at the ready with a dozen trusted men standing before the gatehouse, each refusing to move.

Hannibal grinned, "Finally, a Roman," he said under his breath. "The Roman is mine! Gut the rest," Hannibal then demanded as his men roared their excitement before they charged in a mad fury towards the waiting defenders.

Ballista squared himself as Hannibal neared him, yet not attacking. Hannibal could see not just from the man's age and many scars to his arms, but too from his form that the Roman was seasoned from many battles hard fought and won. A worthy adversary, or so Hannibal expected.

"I always knew you were a cunt, you barbarous dog," Ballista barked as he obviously hoped to break Hannibal's concentration and force him to attack ill-rationally, but Hannibal would not allow himself to be baited.

"You should have given me the city when you had the chance. It would have spared you a lot of pain, Roman," Hannibal added as he slowly advanced. He held no shield but wielded a heavier sword than Ballista, which placed him on the offensive as Ballista remained fixed behind the thick wooden layers of his blue painted shield, his gladius held low to the side – the tip just barely visible.

"Even if Saguntum falls, Rome will make you –"

Now! Hannibal thought as he lunged forward, attacking Ballista before he could finish his sentence, and despite his large size, the sudden outburst of speed and the fury of Hannibal's attack threw Ballista off-guard as he was forced to fall behind his shield for protection, which rattled horribly under Hannibal's assault.

The Roman captain barely managed to hold his ground. He did not seem used to such savagery in combat as Hannibal fought like a caged bear set loose upon the population, swinging his large iron sword as if it weighed nothing, causing thick chunks of wood to splinter free from Ballista's shield with each violent bash.

Ballista was driven back off of his feet as he tried desperately to keep his shield held firm. To lose it now would put him at a serious disadvantage as his shorter sword, good for thrusting, was not ideal against Hannibal's longer cavalry blade, which had several inches the length over his gladius. But, after a dozen devastating blows that made Ballista's arm feel as if every bone in it had been broken, he could not bear the onslaught further as his shield was finally knocked free.

Ballista screamed in agony as a bone in his wrist did indeed snap. His shield, now broken in three pieces splintered to the ground as it dropped into the mud-soaked ground. Before he could react Ballista only saw the blur of Hannibal's blade come racing toward his face. A moment later he felt the sharp sting as his flesh unzipped as the tip of the iron blade was drawn across his brow, down his nose, and tearing out a chunk of his right cheek.

Hannibal's strike had been done purposely. He did not attend to kill Ballista, not yet.

"You filthy whore!" Ballista spat a mouthful of blood, which landed against Hannibal's broad leg as he stood poised over him. "You think you've won a great victory here? You've accomplished nothing! Rome will see you crucified at the stake for this crime. I only hope you live long enough to see Carthage burn and its people sold into slavery before your end will come, dog!"

Hannibal smiled as drizzles of Ballista's blood dripped from his sword tip.

"It is Rome that will burn, and it is your senate that will lick the *shit* from my feet before I'm done. But, I'm afraid you won't be alive to see that day come to pass." Hannibal reached back, brining his sword high over his head before he plunged it down with all his might.

The heavy iron blade sliced into Ballista's head, splitting his skull like a burning stone drenched with water. Brain and bone mixed with hair and blood gushed over Hannibal as he held his sword firm for a long moment as he savored his kill – the first Roman he'd ever slain in battle. He knew with eager anticipation that Ballista only represented the first among many. Soon, even if it took years more Hannibal would build on his victory here and march across Gaul, over the Alps and into Italy. The people there would rise and join him to be free of the republic's yoke, and soon, with his will and the armies he shall raise in the coming years, gods willing the walls of Rome will be torn down and the arrogant people who think themselves superior to other men will bow before Hannibal, begging with their dying breath for his mercy.

The rest of Ballista's men were dealt with in short-order as Hannibal's guards slaughtered all those that stood firm against their overwhelming numbers. Within moments the first men stormed into the gatehouse, slaughtering those defenders still within before freeing the city gates from their chains.

The ground rumbled as Hannibal stood among the dead. A moment later as the southern gate opened his brother Mago and twenty riders charged into Saguntum, followed by hundreds more soldiers that ran in all directions, roaring with murder on the mind as they moved deeper into the city.

"Well done, brother. I'm sorry you left me so few to kill," Mago grinned as he stopped his horse near Hannibal, who looked almost unrecognizable as he was covered head –to-toe with the gore of his enemies.

"There are plenty more waiting to face our iron, brother. Do not let them wait much longer," Hannibal replied, Mago laughing hard as he reared his horse and ordered his men forward. The city was open to them and in a few hours, there would be no male left alive to defend it.

"Please general, I beg you!" the cries of the city-father were cut short as the axe blade sliced through the soft flesh of his neck, freeing his body of the burden of the man's head, which rolled carelessly onto the blood soaked ground before it was picked up by one of Hannibal's men, and tossed into the pile of two dozen other skulls that sat near the corner of the citadel walls. This same scene had been repeated two dozen times over the past hour as Hannibal, standing with his brother by his side, his drunken men surrounding him, stood with a wide smile as he watched his enemies fall before him, one by one.

The sun was still set high in the sky, beaming its blazing heat down upon the ruins of Saguntum, which burned as its streets and buildings were filled with the terrifying screams of women being raped, and men botched like pigs. The blood that had soaked Hannibal caked and dried like that of an erred lakebed as he took a long swig of wine before passing it to his brother.

"Ah, it was a hard fight – long and brutal, but you did it, my brother, you truly did it!" Mago bellowed as the warm honey wine drizzled down his gullet. "But, shouldn't we spare at least a few of these vermin to ransom to Rome?"

"No. Rome, and all those that hear of this victory will learn what it means to defy me, brother," Hannibal replied harshly as another man was dragged forth, an older man, fat, wearing a Roman toga, looking to be in his early sixties. He begged for his life as so many others had already, offering his captives all the riches they could ever hope to spend. Little did he know, Hannibal already had everything the man own, save for his life, which he was about to take momentarily.

"So what now? One victory does not make us conquers," Mago asked bitterly.

Hannibal snorted. Mago was the most pessimistic of his brothers. However, it was his realistic view of the world that made him valuable to Hannibal's campaigns. He wasn't interested in *ass-kissers* like that of a Roman consul.

"No, it does not. But, this victory will go a long way in subduing those Gallic tribes that stand in our way. Those that's weren't afraid of us will now back off, and those that will stand before us, we can pay off."

"And those that don't do either?" Mago asked.

Hannibal turned towards him. "We crush," he answered simply.

As the old man's head was taken and his body, which twitched violently, was dragged away, Hannibal reached out and took back the wine skin before taking a deep breath. "But, Rome is not Saguntum. It shall not prove as easy."

"Eight months is hardly easy," Mago commented, knowing full well that wasn't what his brother was speaking of.

"Indeed. There will be many more battles, harder fought that we will encounter, brother, and our men must be ready. I want only the strongest for this journey. The trek and

15

those we face along the path to Rome will weed out the weak. When we reach Italy, Rome will be facing an army the likes it has never seen before."

Mago smiled as he slapped his brother on the shoulder. "Then my brother, we have a lot of work to do before your war with Rome can begin. Maybe even year's worth before the first drop of Roman blood is spilled.

Hannibal smiled as his mind drifted to the days and months to come, perhaps even years, it did not matter how long it took as he was one step closer today to his goal than he had been yesterday. After a lifetime, his family's wraith was finally being turned where it was meant to be directed. Rome and all those that serve under its banner would bleed.

CHAPTER TWO

Gaius steadied his breathing to calm himself. He listened carefully as he stayed within the tall brown wheat that was almost ready for harvest. He couldn't hear anything save for the sounds of the wind as it blew across the seemingly endless field. A few geese flew overhead in perfect formation; their constant honking braking the pristine quiet momentarily as they passed high above. The only other sound was the thumping of his heart. And then, he heard a sudden rustling in the grass to his right.

Gaius held his breath as he gripped the hilt of his sword tighter, with the blade at the ready. After a few tense seconds the noise sounded again, nearer to his position; sweat dripped from his brow as he knelt on one knee.

He was as still as a cat ready to pounce its prey. No one could have seen him unless they stepped right on top of him. He had concealed himself well, as he had been trained. He hoped it would afford him an advantage over the man he had been eluding for several hours now.

His pursuer was good, and seemed determined to find him before the sun fell over the western sky, which was less than two hours from now. However, every time Gaius felt that he had lost him, the man showed his ugly face, having already chased him across this country with the aggression of a madman. It was a bitter rivalry that had been going on far too long. He wanted to find his hunter and defeat him, so he could be free. However, Gaius had a mission to complete that took priority over his own need for justice, so he waited patiently, looking for a way to circumvent his prey and reach his objective. But if he could achieve victory here, he would be free to carry out his duty without impediment.

The quiet rustling came again, nearer still. He readied his sword as rustling in the field was moments from revealing itself to him. Now he had the advantage and would do away with this villain.

"Got you!" Gaius cried out as he broke from her perch and dashed forward, parting the grass as he came out into a small clearing. His eyes opened wide as his sudden action startled a deer that had been chewing the weeds; its eye opening in a wide panic, frozen for a moment as it gazed at the frightful Roman. However, he did nothing as the deer took the opportunity and darted off quickly back the direction it had come.

Gaius took a deep breath and then letting it out with a sigh. His heart was pounding as the creature escaped, most certainly not the man that had tracked him for all these hours. His nerves were getting the best of him. He was tired of running. He needed to confront his pursuer now and deal with the villain before paranoia overtook him.

Wiping his brow with the sleeve of his shirt, he looked up at the bright overhead sun. In a few hours it would descend. Nightfall was not his ally as his mission was sensitive. He had only until the new-moon to finish it, which was drawing nearer.

He dared to rise a little bit. He could see a road not too far from his current position, which would take him to the compound that housed his objective.

My enemy might be watching the road, Gaius thought to himself as his tired mind pondered his options. *I've got to try. I would rather face my foe then continue to hide from him. If the Jupiter is with me, I might actually be able to ambush the tyrant.*

Staying as low as he could, Gaius carefully ran through the field towards a lone pine tree that stood on the outer edge of the dirt road. Stopping every few yards, he listened carefully for sounds that would indicate that he had been spotted. When he was certain he had remained undetected, he quickly raced over to the tree that loomed before him, well-concealed against the wide trunk of the century old pine, provided him with shade from the scorching heat of the sun.

Peering around its base to see if anyone was coming down the road, he saw no travelers. A part of him hoped that the hunter would be marching down the road so he may end this tiresome chase once and for all, but he saw no one.

Gaius felt a little more relaxed as he felt perhaps he had finally escaped the Greek who hunted him. He might now be able to complete the mission he had been given by his king, without having to fight his way to the prize, the wife of his brother Paris.

Determined that the way was clear, Gaius readied himself to break from the cover that hid him from prying eyes. As he prepared to dash out into the road he heard rustling of leaves above him. For a moment he thought it was a bird, nesting high within the thick branches, but then he heard a high-pitched scream, and knew that the sound was not that of birds.

Gaius barely managed to roll out of the path of his attacker as the man leaped down from the tree, plunging his sword into the dirt where Gaius had been standing.

Covered from head to toe in mud, Gaius rolled to his feet as the Greek quickly withdrew his sword and screamed like a wild animal, before attacking once again.

With a bloodlust in his eyes, he lunged forward in an attempt to impale Gaius with the thick blade of his curved sword. But just in time Gaius fainted to the right, dodging the Greek's violent attack. Before he was able to counter, however, the hunter swung upward with blinding speed.

Gaius backtracked, managing to stay on his feet as he slipped in the mud. He only now seemed to notice that the Greek warrior had dried mud on his arms and face, which was why he was able to hide in the tree, hidden within the shadows of the long branches – just waiting for him to make a mistake and drop his guard long enough to launch his surprise attack. A brilliant tactic he hated to admit.

The Greek warrior seemed to be the same age as Gaius, but two inches shorter. His build was slimmer and wiry, which gave him a slight edge when it came to speed, compared to the taller, more muscular Roman. Both men seemed equal with the blade in terms of their execution. However, Gaius was better trained and more controlled in his form, which allowed him to deflect each attack that came at him. The Greek was more violent and his more aggressive style made it difficult for Gaius to counter without considerable effort.

Gaius knew instinctively that if he kept this up for too long, the more crazed swordsman would overpower him. He needed a plan – enough time to take advantage of his attacker's weaknesses.

As Gaius blocked another powerful sword strike from the Greek, he noticed that the sun was starting to drop lower over the western sky. He didn't have much time left. His mission to save his brother's wife was too important to fail – for if he did, a kingdom would fall.

As his opponent leaped forward, Gaius rolled to his left. The Greek missed wide, which allowed Gaius to reach down and grab a fistful of mud, which he hurled at his attacker's face.

The Greek, already covered in dried mud, managed to raise his hand up in time to block the clump of dirt. But as he readied to attack once more, he saw that his target had fled, darting as quickly as he could across the road and back into the tall field.

"You coward!" the Greek warrior roared as he chased after Gaius, who disappeared before his eyes as the brown grass engulfed him.

Gaius ran as quickly as his tired legs could carry him. This country was his homeland – he had lived, worked and fought here that he knew it as well as his own hand. This he hoped would give him the advantage against the foreigner.

Quickly, Gaius ran around a large bolder that he knew stood several dozen yards down the side of the road. It was just barely large enough to conceal him from view, and perhaps provide the opportunity to set his own ambush.

Gripping his sword tightly, Gaius struggled to control his breathing as his heart raced. The chase had been exhilarating, despite being so near to death. A warrior was only at his peak when faced with his equal, or so he had been taught to believe. Only then could the true test of a warrior's mettle be proven, and if he survived, he would be greater for it.

Gaius heard the Greek approaching. The man no longer cared for stealth as he was slashing through the wheat with his blade.

"Show yourself you cowering girl!" The taunt might have worked in the past, but Gaius kept his nerve as he waited, ignoring the spiteful comments that the Greek bellowed.

As Gaius peeked over the top of the rock, planning to give the Greek what he was asking for, he steadied his breathing, opened his mind to his surroundings, and waited patiently.

Gaius felt a calming peace come over him. The kill was near, he knew, and soon he would be allowed to complete his mission and claim his reward from the honorable king – a prize that would make him a very rich and celebrated hero.

He readied as the Greek neared.

Gaius placed one hand around the hilt of his sword, while the other slowly inched over the top the of the rock, making sure he had a firm grip on the stone before leaping over; he couldn't afford to make any mistakes, not when he was so close.

The Greek turned abruptly as he heard Gaius' war cry, as he rose over the edge of the bolder and leaped with his sword held high over his head.

There was nothing the Greek warrior could do, he was completely defenseless, his eyes opening wide as he knew without a doubt that this would be the last thing he would ever see before the end came. However, death did not come as Gaius had planned. Instead of driving his sword through the Greek's chest, the mud that had yet to dry on his feed caused him to slip. There was nothing he could do as he fell, landing flat on his back, on the ground with a loud *thump.*

The Greek took advantage of the situation and ran forward. Gaius didn't have time to regain his footing before the sandaled heel of the Greek's foot crashed down onto his chest.

"A valiant effort my opponent, but alas it was a vain one. Now, you shall die," the Greek yelled as he drove his sword through Gaius' stomach.

He screamed as the blade was driven through the soft flesh of his belly, twisting as it tore through his entrails. It was not a quick or painless death, but slow and agonizing as the villain laughed, enjoying his victory, at last.

Death was not what troubled Gaius as he breathed his last, as his thought drifted to his failure to complete his vital mission, knowing that the kingdom he had sworn to protect would fall to the foreign hordes. It was bitter knowledge, worse than the agony he was in now.

The world grew dark as death overtook him. Then, as the Greek roared his victory, Gaius left this world as a defeated hero, slain by his enemy, who would now claim the greatest prize in the known world.

However, darkness did not linger as his eyes opened once more, and his lungs filled with fresh air. He tried to stand back to his feet but could not as the foot of his murderer was still firmly planted on his chest, keeping him pinned to the ground.

"I, Achilles, have defeated the powerful and mighty Hector of Troy. I am now the greatest warrior on the face of the Earth! No man can stand in the path of the great Achilles!"

Gaius tried to stand to his feet, but the would-be-Achilles pushed him back down onto the muddy ground – the same wide grin still evident on his face as he turned his attention to someone else.

"Now I shall claim my prize, my queen, Helen of Troy," Achilles said with a sinister smile as he stepped over Gaius' body, walking over to a girl that sat across the road, watching the whole ordeal with wide eyes and a bigger grin.

"Ewww!" the pretender who played the part of Helen of Troy cried out as she sat on the top of a wooden fence, swinging her legs back and forth.

"But you must marry me. I have defeated Hector for you," Achilles said as he stood before the younger girl who looked disgusted by the thought of marrying the warrior who walked towards her – his arms held wide to his side as he knelt down on one knee, waiting for her to run into his embrace.

The uncooperative Helen leaped down from the fence. As she hurried over toward Achilles, she pushed him out of the way, which forced him down onto his backside before she hurried over to Gaius, who finally managed to get back to his feet, tying to brush the drying mud off from his tunic and bare legs.

Throwing her arms around Gaius, the girl looked back at Achilles, the boy who was actually her brother, and proclaimed, "I choose Gaius as my husband. He is my hero and I shall marry him!" she cried out as she looked up into Gaius' boyish eyes with a wide smile on her young face.

Her grip on his leg was firm, not caring about the dirt that stuck to his body, as long as she had him in her arms.

"Hey! You can't do that. He is supposed to be Hector. And he is dead!" the pretender that played Achilles yelled with a frustrated expression, bitter as he watched once again his sister ruin his game.

"And besides, Helen is supposed to be in love with Paris," Gaius said as he looked down at the little girl.

"I can marry whoever I want!"

"No you can't, Julia!" Anthony, her older brother screamed. "You can't just go and change the story. Can't she, Gaius?"

Gaius looked down at Julia as she stared back up at him with her big, dark green eyes, seemingly asking him without words that he should agree with her and not her brother.

"It doesn't really matter, I guess. Pretty much everyone dies in the end," Gaius answered as diplomatically as he could – setting the historical facts straight.

"Well, that isn't very fun. Why can't we just change it?" Julia asked.

"Because, it isn't our story to change," he answered.

"Yeah, so strop trying to marry him already," Anthony said as he walked over to his sister and smacked her upside her head. Julia turned, yelling at her brother as she started to swing at him.

Gaius looked on, watching his two friends as they fought, as they normally did. For the moment, he was thankful that he was the only child in the family.

As Anthony and his younger sister fought in the middle of the road, Gaius looked over his shoulder and gazed upon the falling sun, which in fewer than two hours would be gone, ending his day with his two best friends.

He sighed as he had to start his way home. If he didn't, his father would be angry with him. He still felt the effects of the last time he had made the mistake of getting back home after nightfall.

"I have to go home before it is too dark," Gaius said, but he wasn't sure if his friends actually heard him, as Anthony, taller than his six year-old sister, was mocking her foolish attempts to beat him with her tiny fists.

Julia, while four years younger than her brother, held her own. She never backed down from a challenge, or let her brother bully her. So she would fight him, confront any attempt to demean her, especially when she was with Gaius. He figured that Julia felt she had to prove herself worthy to play with the boys, or risk being cast out if she should back down.

For all the talk and physical torment that Anthony committed against his sister, it was clear to Gaius that he loved and looked out for her as any good brother should. He simply wasn't accustomed to having to share his friends with a girl, who demanded daily to play with the two boys, namely because she desired to be around Gaius as much as she could.

Julia followed them day after day, like a little mascot as the two filled the afternoon with fantastical wonders, pretending to be warriors or acting out classical stories, as champions defending Greece from Troy, or the Persians, or battling the fearsome Cyclops, the Hydra, or the frightful snake-haired Medusa. On occasion the two found use for her, such as their need

24

for a girl to play the part of Helen of Troy. But, stubbornly, Julia was always more interested in the here and now – being around Gaius, and preferring that she, not an alter ego, be the object of his affections.

He found her cute, to say the least. She was an adorable young lady, even though she was half his age. She had a small, dainty body, groomed to someday be a proper Roman woman. Her hair smelled of scented oils and was curled in strands around her bangs. Her nails were painted different colors almost every day as she was tended by a dozen slaves, all women who acted like second mothers. But Julia didn't care about being a girl, trapped in her physical limitations. She liked being around the boys and playing their games. It might have proven an issue if her father was around more, but he spent most of his time in the city. Her mother was gone as well, having died during childbirth when Julia was born. Perhaps that was, as Gaius figured, why the two rich children of a Roman senator found common interest with a simple farm boy, as Gaius had lost his mother as well.

"I have to go home," Gaius called out again as he picked his wooden sword up off the ground; bashing it against the dirt road so he could dislodge some of the loose mud from the blade that meant to simulate a Roman *gladius*, the standard sword of Rome's infantry.

"I will walk with you," Anthony replied quickly as he let go of his sister, who was pushing against him with all her might. The act caused her to fall to the ground as Anthony turned and grabbed his own things that lay up against the fence; his wooden sword that was designed more in the fashion of a longer Greek blade made of cooper, a simple wool cloak and a small water skin.

"I will come as well," Julia eagerly said as she picked herself up off of the ground, already forgetting her skirmish with her brother.

"No! You go home, Julia. And take these with you," Anthony called out as he walked over and dropped his things into her arms.

"I want to come with you," she demanded as she dropped the items to the ground.

"Julia! Take these and go home – Now!" Anthony demanded once more, harshly, as he picked his things up and again pushed them into her arms. However, she continued to refuse as she crossed her arms, not giving him an inch.

Gaius smiled as he shook his head. He knew he had to intervene if this matter was going to be resolved within the time he had. These two could argue for hours if they were allowed to continue without interruption.

"Go home, Julia. I promise you and I can play a game, just the two of us, tomorrow," Gaius said calmly.

"Do you promise?" she asked.

"Have I ever broken a promise to you?"

She rushed over to Gaius and threw her arms around him, calling out, "I love you Gaius!" before she turned and hastily grabbed her brother's things and ran up the road, heading back in the direction of her own home. Technically, she was already home, as everything for miles in all directions was owned by their father.

"I guess you just need to know how to speak to women," Anthony commented.

"Maybe we should walk her home, before you and I leave," Gaius suggested.

"She will be fine. What could happen to her on my father's property?"

The land that was owned by Gaius' father wasn't anywhere close to the size of Anthony's. His land was simple, enough for a family to live on without due hardships. The property, as Gaius knew, had been reward given to his father after many faithful years of service to the republic. He had fought and nearly died in the last war that Rome fought with its oldest of enemies, the nation to the east, Carthage. Gaius did not the particulars of what happened, but his father had become a celebrated hero. For that, he was given this land, which now was overgrown with weeds, an unkempt field, and a home that was barely standing. Sometimes he was embarrassed to bring Anthony here as he came from a wealthy family who never knew what it was to want. The land that the two boys had played on was only the tip of Anthony's estate, which extended for thousands of square miles, and was attended to by five hundred slaves and workers, which tended to the fields, grounds and other profitable endeavors.

Anthony, however never said anything disrespectful about the state of Gaius' home. He always shred what was his, never asking for anything in return other than a good friend with whom he could act out their favorite adventures, such as the Battle of Troy, Hercules and his Twelve Trials, or Alexander the Great's conquest of Persia. Gaius had observed that Anthony had a hard time making friends because of his father's status within Rome, as one of its wealthiest citizens and leading members of the senate. Anthony knew plenty of boys who pretended to be his friend, but typically these friendships were born out of interest by the other boy's fathers, who sought influence and political or financial favors. Gaius, on the other hand, had no hidden agenda or dishonest intentions. As a result, while they had only known one another for little over a year, they had grown very close, almost brothers.

Julia on the other hand came along only a few months ago, when she was old enough to keep up with them. She was in a worse state than her brother. She had no friends to call her own, as most of her father's associates own daughters were either too old, or only had sons. Regardless, she enjoyed more boyish games than what was typically expected of young ladies.

Once she joined the two in their frequent adventures, her affection for Gaius grew. She had an obvious crush on him, and for a time, it bothered him, given his none experience with girls. However, he grew to accept Julia's less than vague hints about her desire to marry him, even though both barely understood what the concept entailed. Ultimately, he grew to like her as much as he did Anthony – his extended family of a sort.

The two boys continued their play as they neared Gaius' home, as they pitted their wooden swords against one another in a running, uphill battle, as the sun was nearly below the western horizon.

Anthony pretended he was a great swordsman. He loved tales of the blade and often imagined he was a master with it. Honestly, he was just a boy and his skills extended only to basic thrust and poor blocks. Gaius on the other hand, while no master was more practiced. His father showed him years ago how to handle and properly wield a sword – how to respect the weapon and use it if need be to protect himself. Because of this, he held back when playing. He didn't want to hurt Anthony's feelings by winning each bout, but he wasn't going to lose them all either. He made sure to keep their victories and defeats about even, and along the way, he showed Anthony a few useful tricks to improve s own form. The gesture was appreciated and made their games all the more enjoyable.

"So, did I tell you that I was going into the city in a few days?" Anthony spoke as he thrust his sword high, which was easily parried by Gaius.

"*The city*? You are going to Rome?"

"Yes. And I was wondering if you would like to accompany me? It is the last day of the games, and there is to be a festival in honor of Jupiter. My father said I could bring a friend along, if I so choose. And who better than you?"

Gaius couldn't help but smile at Anthony's words. For as long as he could remember he had dreamt of going to Rome, the capital of the republic – the greatest city on the face of the earth. It had always annoyed him greatly how close he lived to the city, yet had never been allowed to see Rome for himself.

"Yes, of course I would like to go. You know I do!" Gaius replied enthusiastically. "But…" a terrible thought suddenly entered his mind, which wiped the wide smile from his face.

"What is it?"

"My father – I would have to ask him, and I don't have to tell you what his feelings are about Rome," Gaius answered, his voice filled with doubt.

"I am sure you can convince him, if you try. But, let me know by tomorrow, will you? Good day, Gaius." Anthony patted Gaius on the shoulder as he turned and raced down the hill, heading back towards his father's lands; swinging at the overgrown weeds with his sword as his mind was still trapped in the body of classical heroes.

Gaius felt a knot begin to form in the pit of his stomach. The prospect of having to convince his father in letting him go was daunting, and as he neared his front door, he began running through his mind what words he would use that might better his chances. But none came to mind as he reached his house.

Gaius reached for the old and warn wooden handle that led into his home. He took a deep breath before he pulled down the latch and opened the door. He had just gotten home by the expected time, but as he entered he could clearly see that his father was nowhere in sight, which brought a faint sense of relief as he latched the door shut, and then putting his things by his bed, which was set against the far left corner of the small home.

Gaius scrunched his nose as he smelled what was cooking over the small fireplace directly in front of the door. A large cast-iron pot sat over the medium-burning flame. The contents inside: a brown gloppy mess, which he was all too familiar with eating over the past two years, was boiling over. He didn't wait for his father to come back before he reached on top of the fireplace and pulled down one of the two bowls and spoons that rested above.

Stirring the stew, which made him turn his head slightly from the smell, Gaius finally scooped out a large portion for and spooned it into his bowl, before walking over to the long table that sat on the opposite side of the room, and took one of the stools.

The stew smelled worse than it actually tasted, but after having to swallow the slop nearly every day for two years, since his mother's passing, he was beyond tolerant of it by now.

It was a shade of brown; thick and had a foul odor that reminded him of a dead rabbit he found last year behind the barn, which had been decomposing for a week. Inside there was cuts of rough beef, various vegetables and some other stuff he had never been able to identify, nor was he sure that he wanted to.

Gaius grabbed a hearty piece of bread, tearing it free from the loaf and dipped it into the bowl. As he took his first bite, as he always did, he plugged his nose with one hand, while scoping a spoonful into his mouth with the other. Then soon after, he poured himself a cup of water from a clay jug that sat in the center of the table, and gulped it down in one sitting, before pouring another cup. He repeated this process for the first five minutes, eating as quickly as he could, both because he was hungry, and out of nervousness about what he was going to say to his father when he returned. A part of him wished he might get to bed sooner so that he could avoid the conversation altogether. But he had promised Anthony that he would see what his father said about the subject of going to Rome.

Gaius heard the latch on the front door as his father stepped inside, carrying a stack full of logs in one arm, and a heavy iron axe in his other.

He glanced back at his father, Julius, as he set the logs down by the fire – sweat dripping down from his brow as he then walked over to the fireplace and readied his own bowl of stew.

Julius was a tall, muscular man, taller and bigger than most Roman men, which was contributed to the family's Gallic ancestry. He had tanned skin that glistened with perspiration. His hair, even though he had been out of the legions for going on eleven years, was still trimmed neatly, low and tight around the ears and neck. His left eye was partly clouded, which obscured his vision, and while his exterior was rough, no one save for Gaius knew that inside, his body was failing him.

As he sat across from Gaius and shoved a spoonful of stew into his mouth, a number of deep scars that ran along his thick muscular arms shined neatly in the low flickering candlelight, symbols of the many battles he fought and lived through during his youth with the legions.

Julius moaned for a brief moment, a sound that Gaius was familiar with. He was in almost constant pain, with few days free from the daily torment. While it bothered him a great deal, he was not about to voice his discomfort to anyone beyond a few groans and moans. Gaius did not know what ailed him precisely, only that his continuing problems must have been the reason why he left the legions a decade earlier.

It was not uncommon for Julius to wake in the middle of the night, haunted by dreams of his past deeds and torments suffered. Two years prior Gaius' mother would have been there to calm him, but since her passing, things had only gotten worse.

A few nights ago, Gaius caught his father rummaging through the large footlocker that he kept under his bed. Inside was his gear, the effects and weapons of a Roman soldier. He noticed, as he watched him, hidden in the shadows of the moonless night that he seemed most interested in the crest that was engraved on the chest plate of his armor. Later, when he was certain his father was gone for the day, tending to the grounds, Gaius snuck a peek inside the footlocker and saw what his father had been staring at so intensely. The plate was engraved with an ivory wolf's head. The craftsmanship was beautiful, and it must have been worth a small fortune; enough, if sold, to rebuild the house and replant the fields, yet it remained locked away, carefully wrapped in a silk cloth.

Whatever it's meaning to his father, Gaius had yet to ask. Since then, ever so often, he would sneak another peek; rub his fingers over the extremely detailed image of the white wolf, and wonder what it must have been like for his father to have worn the armor into battle. He would never dare ask him about his military past. Some mysterious were best kept under the bed.

Gaius put his spoon down before he took a deep breath, and then spoke.

"Father, I would like to ask you something."

"What?" Julius asked with a grunt as he chewed.

"My friend, Anthony, has asked me to accompany him to Rome in two days. There is a festival in the city and he said that I could come, if you agreed."

"Anthony?" Julius seemed to ponder the name for a moment before he spoke again. "That is Maximus Titus Varro' son?" he then asked as pulled out a small bone from between his teeth.

"Yes father. We are friends. We have been for some time now," Gaius answered, knowing he had mentioned Anthony's name numerous times – A futile effort. He had better luck speaking to and getting a reaction from a stone wall.

Julius never raised his eyes from his food as he shoved another hefty spoonful into his mouth before he answered, scraping the bowl clean as he spoke.

"No. There is too much work that is needed around here for you to run off and play in the city."

"But father...I can do all my chores before I leave. And besides, I won't be gone longer than a day and half, two days maximum. I promise," Gaius pleaded as he moved his still full bowl aside, and stared at his father, who hardly acknowledged what he was asking.

"Rome is not a place for a boy of your age, Gaius."

"But father, I will be thirteen in two months – almost a man. And I won't be alone. Anthony's slaves will be with us the entire time, and his father as well."

Julius finally looked up and stared long and hard, clearly growing frustrated by his son's unwillingness to drop the matter, even though he already given his answer.

"I said no, and that is final, Gaius. I will hear no more on this subject. Is that understood?" He waited for Gaius to answer, which he did after a long pause. "Yes father."

There was an awkward break between the father and son as Julius stared at Gaius in silence for a moment longer, watching him swirling his spoon around the edges of the stew, clearly disappointed, but not seemingly expecting otherwise.

"And besides, I need you here."

"Of course, father," Gaius added before his father was finished speaking.

"There is someone coming in a few days – someone that I want you to meet. It is important that you be here."

"Who is coming, father?" Gaius asked, just a little bit curious, but not enough to really care as he kept his head low, still playing with his food as his disappointed thoughts drifted endlessly. He wasn't looking forward to telling Anthony that he couldn't go with him to Rome.

"He is an old friend of mine. He has come a very long way, just to see you," Julius finished.

"Me? Why?" Gaius' interest was finally piqued as he looked up at his father, waiting for him to answer. However, Julius sat still for a long while, seemly contemplating what he was going to say.

"Because..." The two were silent for nearly a full minute as Julius froze before he could complete his sentence. There was much that he seemed to want to say as he gazed into Gaius' eyes, but for some reason he held his tongue and returned to the previous subject.

"A day and half, you say, maybe two?"

Gaius' eyes opened wider with the sudden, unexpected words that seemly flew out from his father's mouth.

"Yes father. I would be back by week's end, just after midday. I promise!"

"Rome is a dangerous place. I expect you to keep that in mind and return home once this festival has ended. I will hold Varro responsible if you do not. Is that understood, Gaius?"

Gaius did not need to answer as he leaped from his stool and ran over to his father, throwing his arms around him, hugging him with all his might that his small arms could manage.

"Oh thank you, father. I promise that I will do double my normal chores before I leave," Gaius said enthusiastically while still holding onto his father.

"That you will, boy. You had better finish eating and get yourself to bed, so you may start bright and early."

"Of course father. I will!" But sleep would be allusive for Gaius for the next two nights, as his thoughts would be focused on the wonders and sights he was bound to see. Never did forty-eight hours seem so far away.

CHAPTER THREE

Gaius looked on in amazement as the vast crowds of people passed, nearly cramming into every square inch of the streets of Rome. Never before had he seen so many people in one place before, the very thought that this many souls could exist in the world was a new concept to his young mind. There were people of so many different sizes, colors and races. Men, women and even children walked and ran like chariot racers through the narrow streets and alleyways. Rome truly was a wonder to behold. Clearly, as his young eyes shifted from one sight to the next, his father's words about this city not being a place for someone his age was misleading, as he saw many boys and girls, some younger than he, running through the streets without care.

The many voices rose like a choir of sound, making it impossible to make out a single person among so many. The street corners were lined with shops that sold goods from all corners of the republic: spices and silks from the east, wheat and jewels from the south, and rare stones and crafts from the north, it would take a lifetime to see it all – an entire world he knew nothing about. He thought for a moment he may never want to go home again.

Gaius and Anthony ran like wild horses through the dense crowds that hardly paid attention to them. They joined other groups of boys from time to time, until their attention was turned to new attractions, from jesters performing feats of magic in the streets, to puppeteers and actors putting on shows on large and elaborately made stages. The volley of cheers and laughter constantly pointed them to new wonders.

Gaius noticed that Julia wasn't able to take part in the boy's games as she was held firmly by her body slave, who had been charged with watching all three children. However, the boys easily distracted the slave as they continued their exploration of the city.

Julia tried many times to break free and join them, but once the four rounded one street corner she managed to chase after Gaius, who attention was turned to a large gathering of people.

Standing shoulder-to-shoulder, seemingly mesmerized by a spectacle beyond, pushing through the adults he worked his way to the front of the pack. What he saw both scared and excited him. In the center of a large forum, a small circus of sorts had been set up where dozens of street performers leaped into the air, twisting and bending in ways that shocked and amazed the onlookers. But it was the wild animals that captivated the peoples focus.

A burly man stood before the crowd on a stage. His voice billowed, easily heard over the crowd of hundreds of onlookers. Behind him, Gaius noticed a series of large cages, most of which were covered with thick, red cloaks. The sounds and shifting shadows behind the covered cages sparked their imagination as the beastmaster enticed the crowd, describing creatures from all corners of the known world; that no one would ever forget what they saw this day.

"Beware the Man-Ape!" The beastmaster proclaimed as his assists revealed a cage which held a dozen small creatures that looked like hairy children gone mad, screaming and chewing at their iron bars that held them.

"Behold a beast so powerful that he could tear your head clear off of your shoulders!" he bellowed at the top of his lungs as another, even larger cage was uncovered, revealing a bear, which roared loudly, bearing its two-inch fangs, which caused more than a few of the onlookers to step back in near panic.

"But none compare to the power of the next exhibit. A monstrous animal worshiped and hunted by the kings of the heathen savages of the East."

Julia ran up to Gaius after finding him among the crowd where she wrapped her arms around his, as the new cage was wheeled before the two. He smiled down at her as his attention was turned from the cage for a moment as her soft hands cuddled his. She gleamed up at him, her dark hair reflecting in the high sunlight as her smiled widen.

Inside the cage Gaius could see a shadowy silhouette pacing back and forth. He felt his heart beat faster with anticipation as both he and Julia stood focused on the attraction. The beastmaster smiled at the two children, namely Julia as he gripped his chubby fingers over the red cloth.

"This one especially likes the taste of little child," the beastmaster proclaimed in a low voice, his dirty, gapped teeth smiling down at the pair. And then, with one hard yank of the thick cloak that covered the cage, he revealed to everyone the animal trapped within – one that many had heard of, but never seen with their own eyes.

Within the cage, the iron bars seemed barely strong enough to hold the beast back, was an old silver mane lion, whose claws lashed out through the gaps between the bars, stopping short just a few feet from Gaius and Julia, causing her to scream out in panic as she ducked behind Gaius for protecting, shivering horribly.

"Beware the king of the dark Eastern lands!" the beastmaster proclaimed over the frightened crowd, which couldn't help but take a few steps back as the iron bars hardly seemed capable of keeping the powerful cat at bay.

Gaius stepped in front of Julia as she shivered behind him, both her hands tightly gripping his arms. He could feel her heavy panicked breathing against his back as he stood firm. If the lion should break free, he could not stop it from tearing through them. Regardless, he stood before her and would protect her no matter what.

The old lion had numerous scars running across its face, roared again with so much force that even the beastmaster seemed a bit nervous as he stepped a few extra feet away from the cage. With just a nod to his men, the beastmaster directed them to control the animal as they placed pokers into the cage to invoke its rage and attention.

"In just a few short hours, this king of all beasts will be unleashed in the arena. If you want a show, be there to see this, the most powerful predator let loose against the Republic's greatest collection of gladiators every assembled. And I warn you, it has a taste for human flesh," the beastmaster bellowed as he promoted the gladiator games located just beyond the outer walls of the city.

"Now, come one, come all, I have much more too show you. See wonders never before seen by Roman eyes!" The beastmaster directed the attention of the crowd to other sights, less violent animal attractions, but just as exotic: elephants and giraffes from Africa, prized horses and tamed bears from Hispania and Gaul, as well as rhinos, monkeys and exotic birds from all corners of the Roman Republic. Each animal was symbolic of Rome's growing power over the natural world, and all Rome's citizens reveled in that knowledge.

As the crowd parted, Gaius heard Julia's name called several times. She, on the other hand didn't seem to notice at first as she stayed behind him, still holding his hand.

"Are they gone?" she asked Gaius, tears still rolling down her swollen cheeks.

"They are," Gaius answered as the lion's cage was wheeled out of the forum once it had been covered once more.

Gaius turned to Julia and knelt down so he could wipe away her tears. "Don't worry, little flower, I can protect you," he said with a soothing voice. She smiled at him, throwing her arms around his broad shoulder and said, "I believe you."

"Julia!" the body slave said as she reached down and took hold of her arm, pulling her away from Gaius. "I've been looking for you. Don't you ever run off like that again! The master will have my hide if something were to happen to you. Do you understand?"

"There was a big cat," Julia told the slave as she was pulled away from the forum.

"Yes, of course, and a lady such as you have no business being around such horrid creatures. Now come, we shall find your father and forget about the filthy animals you saw. Come Gaius. Do not linger."

Gaius was about to follow as Julia and her slave left the forum, but as he looked back one more time, he saw a new series of cages that had been hidden by the ones the beastmaster had been showing.

He stepped forward as his eyes looked at one cage in particular, housing five wolves that paced back and forth in the twenty-by-twenty cell. However, as he looked closer he noticed that one of the wolves, one that was entirely white stood, seemingly staring right at him, calm as it was knelt down on its hind legs. His eyes were fixated on the white wolf, for it looked eerily like the ivory wolf he seen on his father's breast plate, hidden inside the footlocker.

Their eyes, boy and wolf, both blue, locked. Gaius found himself walking closer to the cage, wanting to see the white creature in more detail. However, as he neared a hand reached down and stopped him from approaching further.

"Whoa, boy, you don't want to get to close. Most of these animals haven't been fed in days. We need to keep them starving for the games, or the show won't be as entertaining for the mob," a large bald man with a thick eastern accent said.

"What?" Gaius asked, looking up as if he had come out of a daze.

"I said for the games. We starve them or else they want eat the slaves and criminals sacrificed for the mob. So, just stay away from them, boy, and be gone with yourself."

As Gaius looked back toward the cage, to his surprise he only saw four wolves. The white one was gone, leaving only the four hungry canines that paced back and forth.

"Sir," Gaius called out. The man turned back around and glanced down at Gaius, who indicated towards the wolf cage with puzzled eyes.

"Where is the white one – the white wolf that was there moments ago?"

The man looked puzzled.

"The white wolf, sir. You couldn't have missed it," Gaius added.

"A white one," the man laughed. "Boy, if I had a white wolf I could make a fortune on it. Do you really think I would put it in the arena with the rest of these filthy beasts? Now, be gone with you. A white one," the man couldn't stop laughing as he turned and went back to his work.

Gaius wondered for a moment if his eyes had been playing tricks with him. However, as Anthony called his name, demanding that he hurry and rejoin them, he let the incident escape his thoughts for the time being. There was still so much more to see and do before the festival was concluded.

The long, hot day was finally drawing to a close. The excitement in the city had died down some. As the sun was set to go down in a few short hours, other nightly activities would take root that the more innocent daily enjoyments that had occupied Gaius' mind were at an end. Now Gaius and Anthony were with Varro, Anthony's father, but unlike earlier in the day, they were bored stiff as they waited for Varro to stop talking and drinking with his friends. They were standing outside a large wooden arena that had been built for the festival, just outside the city walls, where the gladiator games were being held. Not too long the group would be heading back into the city to Varro' estate, to bed for the night before they left early the next morning to head back to the country. But apparently they had come to the arena to see the final bout of the day, to see a gladiator that had been the main gossip of the event.

Anthony begged his father to allow him and Gaius to see the famed gladiator matches, but he had refused time and time again. Instead, Varro had allowed the boys to see the arena and the holding pins for the gladiators, who were displayed like the animals in the forum, free for the crowd to mock, admire and fear. Now, Varro stood near a wine stand talking to his associates, while Gaius and Anthony waited, listening to the cheers and jubilation inside the arena walls, wishing they could see the real action.

Anthony tried to occupy his mind by kicking stone, or throwing them at his father's slaves, who pretended to enjoy it and attempted to doge his playful tosses; Gaius was more interested in listening in on Varro' conversation, or at least as well as he could as their topic was beyond his understanding.

The men that stood around a tall table, drinking heavily, wore the same colored, white, elaborately made togas or tunics. Varro', however, had a long gold band sewn into his fabric, signifying that he was a senior member of the senate.

A heavyset man who seemed to drinking his weight had been doing most of the talking, between long swigs of his wine, which spilled from time to time on his tunic. It seemed to Gaius that this man, who was named Marcus, was perhaps the most obnoxious adult he had ever heard, as his voice easily carried over the other men. It was impossible not to listen to what he was saying since his bellowing speech carried easily.

"All that I am stating is that those damn desert pigs think that they have the right to rule the entire world. First, we allow them to lay claim to Spain, then they side with pirates that attack our ships on a daily basis, and now this, attacking our settlements in Southern Gaul. It is virtually impossible for an honest man to make a living these days with all these disruption in trade. By the gods, did we not win the war the first time around?"

"An honest man in Rome, HA!" the youngest of the group laughed as he took a drink. "If you find one, please let me known. And besides, what would you have us do, Marcus, send our legions to Spain and forcefully remove the Carthaginians? They have a right to exist as much as you or I."

"Precisely my young Maximus; we should send our legions to Spain and wipe them out, and then onto Africa next. Better this be a Roman world than a Carthaginian one," Marcus bellowed, believing that Maximus was agreeing with him, as he heard only what he wanted to hear.

"And whose son's shall we send to fight this war, Marcus, perhaps yours?" Maximus added; his words were forceful and growing angrier.

"Calm yourself, nephew," Varro spoke as he placed his hand onto the young senator's shoulders. "No one is talking about starting a war. Rome has had her fill of bloodshed after the last one. However, these recent acts serve to bait Rome into action."

"I don't know, Varro. This new leader in Spain; what is his name? He seems a determined man, even more so than his father was," Nero spoke next.

"Pig slop! They are all savages. What could they do to the Republic that they haven't already tried? I still say we march north and deal with this Hannibal now, before he becomes more trouble," Marcus commented as he poured another cup of wine into his goblet.

"It is so easy for you to make such thoughtless decisions, isn't it? You may think of them as savages, but look what we nearly lost in the last war. How many ships did we lose, huh? Was it a thousand, or five thousand? And how many souls died with their bellies spilled open, rotting in the sun, fifty thousand, a hundred? You tell me, my dear friend. If we are to survive the next one, we must start thinking differently," Maximus argued, but his words were falling on deaf ears.

"Thinking differently isn't what has made the Republic as powerful as it is. It is through force of arms, and that is what is needed to take care of our enemies," Marcus raised his cup, speaking louder as if he was addressing the whole senate.

"And fatten your purse too, I take it?"

"Please, Maximus, we all grow rich from war and trade. You included, my young friend," Nero rebuked.

"Perhaps, but I will not sacrifice the lives of my children to filled my purse with more coins."

"Hah! That is what I love about you my young nephew. You are so dramatic that I believe sometimes you missed your true calling as an actor; if only you didn't have such a brilliant mind," Varro said, almost mockingly, but speaking the truth.

"I speak what is in my heart, uncle," Maximus replied.

"That is understandable. But, I speak from experience, if you want to survive the game of politics, you'll have to do more than carry your heart on your sleeve. All the passion in the world will not save you if you make too many enemies in the house. At least the Carthaginians will give you an honorable death in battle," Varro added as he spoke firmly.

"Is that a threat of some kind?" Maximus asked sharply.

"Of course not, I speak only from my own experiences. I wouldn't be standing here having this entertaining conversation with you now if I hadn't learned how to play the game. You would do well to learn it too, quickly, because I see great things in store for you. However," Varro learned in closer, "One day you may have to abandon your conscience if you want to speak for the people and make the hard decisions that will shape the course of history."

"I am afraid that, uncle may be too high a price to pay," Maximus exclaimed.

Varro only smiled. The two stared at one another as Marcus continued on, changing the subject to other topics relevant to the senate. Gaius on the other-hand grew bored listening to the four men speaking of matters that his young mind could not comprehend. So, his attention turned to the shops that lined both side of the street which led to the arena.

Most of the stores were ordinary. They sold mostly food and drink, which due to the heat had kept them busy in the late hours. A few shops sold various items of expensive taste: rugs, jewels, and pottery, clothing, gold and silver trinkets, to the wealthy patrons of the games.

As he surveyed his surroundings, one stand in particular caught his attention. It wasn't as well kept as the rest. It stood at the end of the block, towards a back alley that shaded much of the stand in shadow.

Unlike the other stores, the owner did not try to entice every passerby to look at his merchandise, or make exaggerated proclamations that his items were the finest in Rome. Instead, the storekeeper sat, keeping his eyes forward as he smoked a long, curved pipe.

Anthony, who had grown bored with his own games followed Gaius as he broke from the adults and crossed through the crowd, making his way over to the small stand.

Once he drew closer, Gaius saw that the stand seemed to sell all sorts of medallions, each of them of artistic quality. He looked across the trinkets that lay stretched out before him on the table, or hanging off from the poles that held the stop up. They came in all shapes, sizes and substances, such as gold, silver, wood and clay. Symbols of various Greek and Roman gods, historical figures, heroes of old, and creatures of fantasy, representing dozens of cultures: Greek, Persian, Egyptian, Gallic and Roman adorned the medallions.

Anthony fumbled through them, picking one up, and then setting it back down. He didn't seem as interested in them as Gaius. The old man said nothing as he sat, legs crossed, smoking his pipe, watching the boys. And then Gaius' eyes caught sight of one medallion in particular. It wasn't made of fine metal or engraved with gold, silver or ivory. The object was simple, round and made of hardened clay. But it was the image of the white wolf engraved on it, which fixed his attention.

Gaius' eyes fixated on it, taking in every detail as he stared into the animal's unblinking eyes, as it were the same wolf he had seen earlier in the forum – in fact, he was sure that it was the same beast, down to the last detail.

As he was about to touch it, the old man spoke abruptly.

"Ah, so your eyes gaze upon Lupus? Good choice, young Roman."

"Excuse me?" Gaius asked as he pulled his hand back.

The old man stood to his feet, propping himself up with the help of a thick cane that looked as if it was from an uncarved tree branch. He limped over toward Gaius, keeping his eyes on him and not taking notice of Antony, who took a step back.

"That is Lupus, the She-Wolf – mother of Rome," the old man spoke again as he reached out and picked up the medallion, holding it for Gaius to see more closely.

"Here, take it," he urged it closer for Gaius to hold as he continued.

"It is said, those who are drawn to Lupus are protected by her; that they have a destiny. You do know her story, don't you, young master?"

Gaius looked over at Anthony who stood next to him, also looking down at the medallion that Gaius now held in his palms. "No sir, I do not believe that I do. Could you tell us?" Gaius answered.

"Of course. A strong Roman boy such as you should certainly know the story of our city, and our protector," the old man replied with a wide smile.

"Then please tell us, sir," Gaius asked eagerly.

The old man smiled as he stood a little taller. Still, as he began, his words were directed towards Gaius even though Anthony's own attention was interested in the tale.

"Well, our story begins a long time ago, many generations now past, with the fall of a great king who was removed from his throne by his brother, Amulius. The king's daughter, Rhea Silvia, was forced by her uncle to become a Vestal Virgin, which meant she was forbidden from bearing children. If she were, then they could claim right to the throne, as heirs to the true king. However, the god of war, Mars, came down from the heavens and took interest in Rhea Silvia. He saw greatness in her and knew that she would bear him not one powerful son, but two, both of whom would carry his banner and build a new nation that would honor him unlike any before."

The old man paused, the boys hanging on his every word.

"I will spare your young minds the more intimate details of that night, but by winter's end, the young and very beautiful Rhea Silvia indeed carried two children, as Mars had foreseen; two sons that she named Romulus and Remus upon their births. However, when the usurper discovered the infant boys, he had Rhea Silvia murdered and the brothers cast down the Tiber River. But the Fates had other plans for the twins as they were found by Rome's guardian mother, on this very spot."

"Lupus?" Gaius interrupted.

45

"Yes. Lupus was a wise wolf, with white fur, blue eyes and touched by the gods. Instead of devouring them as any beast would, she took pity on the infant brothers and suckled them until they were strong. She cared for them for many months until she found a kind famer by the name of Faustulus. Lupus left the boys with him, but was always nearby to watch out for them. When the time came, and the boys had grown into men, Mars returned and told the brothers of their destiny. They would raise an army and marched to overthrow their cruel uncle that left them for dead, and retake the throne of their grandfather. The war was long and bloody, but the gods themselves favored the brothers, giving them knowledge, strength, courage and patience to win back their kingdom. When the war was finally over, the brothers sought to build a new kingdom, one that would honor their father, Mars, and the She-Wolf that had saved them from a certain death."

The old man held out his hands and directed them to all corners of the city.

"They picked a place on the spot that they had first been discovered by Lupus, where seven hills rose up and overlooked the land. It was here that the brothers laid down the first stones of Rome, and began our history."

"And the Republic was formed?" Gaius asked.

"Oh, the birth of our Republic would take many more bloody years to come to pass. That is another story entirely, young Roman."

"And what became of the two brothers, Romulus and Remus?" Anthony asked.

"Romulus killed his brother and then proclaimed himself the sole king of Rome," Varro, who walked up behind the boys, answered before the old man could say anything.

"Is it true?" Gaius asked as he turned and looked up into the eyes of the old man.

"I'm afraid that is true, young master."

"Father, I want this medallion," Anthony said as he took the clay medallion of Lupus out from Gaius' hand, holding it up for his father to see.

"There are far better ones than that, my son," Varro said as he looked down at the clay medallion that his son held up for him to buy, unimpressed by its simple design.

"But it is the only one of Lupus. I want it, father, please," Anthony pleaded.

"Very well," Varro agreed as he took a few coins from his pocket and tossed them down in front of the old man, not caring if he overpaid.

"Thank you, sir," the old man replied as he scooped up the coins, biting down on the silver to make sure it was pure. Anthony, with the medallion in hand, walked away from the stand with his father as they head towards the arena.

Gaius watched his friend leave, as Anthony held the medallion up, admiring it before placing the string around his neck, where the medallion rested on his chest.

"Do not fear, Gaius, Lupus watches over you, even now."

"What did you say?" Gaius asked as he turned sharply back to the old man, but the man had already sat back down, closing his eyes and continued to smoke his pipe, as if nothing in the past several minutes hadn't ever transpired.

Gaius did not ask his question again as he heard Anthony call his name, wanting him to hurry and rejoin them.

He glanced back at the old man one more time, thinking back on his story a second before he finally ran off and rejoined his friends.

CHAPTER FOUR

Dust drifted down from the rafters as thousands of people cheered and roared at the spectacle that was being displayed for their entertainment. Unfortunately for Gaius and Anthony, Varro would not allow the boys to go into the arena, much less see the matches that were being held. They were so close that the clash of weapons could easily be heard over the roar of the audience that it drove both boys mad with anticipation.

Gaius watched as Anthony tried to get his father's attention. Varro was standing with the men he had been speaking with outside, plus half a dozen other associates. From what he could tell, the men were placing bets on the upcoming bout, the *Primus*, which normally would be held midday, but had been moved to the evening to signal the end of the festival.

Anthony's efforts to convince his father to allow him and Gaius see the fights were ignored. He wanted to see the gladiators fight as much if not more than Gaius, so he was rather persistent in his endeavor. Gaius, however, was content with taking in his surroundings, enjoying yet another sight of Rome he had never seen before.

The arena was one of the largest ever built. It was only temporary, constructed for these games, and would be torn down when the Festival of Jupiter was concluded. But the spectacle was worth remembering. It easily seated over a thousand spectators. Hundreds more could watch the day's events standing if they could find room. Elegant marble statues of classical Greek, Etruscan and Roman figures stood in every archway, set between enormous arches that stood the height of five men. More food and drink stalls were set inside the arena. Hundreds more men, mostly slaves, toiled below the floor, tending to the beasts, other slaves and prisoners that were to be executed, and the needs of the gladiators; and while the games were nearly over, that fact did not slow the day's work.

People of all classes, from the poorest Roman citizen to the noble senators and aristocrats, walked shoulder to shoulder through the winding halls, most carrying food or drink in one hand, and their coins in the other. Perhaps bigger than the bouts outside on the arena floor, were the bets being made inside. The spectators eagerly placed coins on their favorite gladiators, or how many slaves and criminals would be devoured by the starving animals in the allowed time. The wagers were varied from a few coins, to a fist full of gold, to the deeds to entire estates. Gaius noticed that the upcoming bout seemed to receive the most attention, as he heard the name *Calfax* spoke frequently since he had been watching and listening to those around him.

"Come Varro, come. The match is going to start soon," Marcus, the fat man that had been latched to Varro like a pet all day, eagerly said. He was like a child who squirmed wanting seeing his favorite hero in person.

"I want to come, father!" Anthony demanded once again, but even as his father was quite literally being pulled away by his friends, he turned and demanded that he and Gaius stay where they were, calling back, "I shall return shortly. Remain where you are. Is that understood?"

"This is unfair!" Anthony blurted out as he crossed his arms, watching as the crowd swallowed his father from view.

"What can we do about it?" Gaius shrugged as he stood next to Anthony.

Anthony's eyes widen as he watched several slaves head down a flight of stairs.

"Come with me. I know where we can get the best seats in the arena." Anthony grabbed Gaius by his hand and led him towards where the slaves had gone.

"Where are we going?" Gaius demanded as he nearly tripped trying to keep up with Anthony.

"Do you want to see the match or not?" Anthony yelled back, increasing his speed with each step.

"Of course I do, but you father said that we were to stay where he left us."

"Bah! We will see the match and return before he knows we were gone." Already the two boys could see the growing light that cast down on the arena floor, as they ran through the tunnels.

A few minutes later, the boys found what they were looking for as they ran over to a large, closed iron gate that looked over the arena floor. They latched onto the gaps between the bars and lifted themselves up a few steps so they could get a better look. It was, from their point of view, quite possibly the best seat in the house as they were right on the ground-floor, which at the moment was being circled by three horse-drawn carts, while men in the rear of the wagons tossed fresh loafs of bread into the crowd while a dozen men were quickly sweeping the sand, leveling it for the next bout.

Gaius released any reservations he had a few minutes ago. Now, he looked out at the arena with his mouth open, gazing up at the row upon row of seats, filled with people that cheered as the three carts tossed their goods to them; a sea of fingers eagerly grabbing for anything that was thrown towards them. When the carts emptied, they departed through one of the side gates, leaving the arena floor empty once more.

Gaius and Anthony noticed a man with rosy cheeks and a curly bright-red wig step on top of a large podium, and raised his flabby arms as he signaled for the crowd to be silent. After a few minutes, the mob finally did begin to settle as the editor of the games started to speak. Through the oval arena, his broad voice carried like the wind.

"My fellow Romans, esteemed senators, honored guests, and freedmen, I welcome you to the Games of Jupiter!" The editor paused and allowed the crowd to roar once more, as he nodded his thanks to the audience as their praise was directed towards him.

"This week we have seen blood, death and great warriors live and die. Now, I promise you that the final bout of this grand celebration will be one for the ages. Each of you here today shall remember this battle for as long as you shall live. You will one day speak to your grandchildren about it," the editor boasted joyously, drawing out with his words the magnitude of the final battle. "Without further ado, Rome is proud to present to you, your challengers from the House of Brutus!"

Across from Gaius and Anthony, one of the gates similar to the one they were now hanging from opened up. Seconds later, as the crowd began to roar, throwing down flower petals that fluttered like rain, five men, bigger than any Gaius had ever seen, emerged from the darkness and stepped out into the arena; arms help up as the crowd cheered furiously for them.

Anthony roared too, as loud as his lungs could muster, but Gaius own mouth stayed closed as he studied each of the men, who stood in the center of the arena, in a perfect half circle waiting for their opponent to enter.

The five men, three white, two black-skinned, carried an array of weapons: spears, short Spanish swords, a trident, and small shields that cupped their hands. Two of the gladiators wore large fish-bowl helmets that concealed their faces from view. One of the black-skinned men wore a tight formfitting helmet; while the other dark-skinned man, as well as one of the white men had their heads exposed, wrapped simply by a long brightly colored cloth, clear for all in the audience to see their scarred but still youthful faces.

Their powerful, well-toned bodies glistened in the falling sun as they stood proud, taking in the endless admiration from the audience who cheered each of their names. They knew what the next match meant, that unlike most gladiator bouts, this one would be fought to the death. Yet, they waited, absorbing the energy from the crowd, ready and willing to do what was demanded of them for the pleasure of the mob.

"Now, for our main attraction!" the editor called out as the loud as he could; arms raised as the eyes of thousands turned back towards him. "The man you have all come here to see. The greatest warrior to walk the Earth since the time of Achilles, Hector, Heracles or Cincinnatus; a man who knows no fear; a man who has defeated a thousand men across the whole of the Republic; a man who needs no introduction – I give you, Calfax of Sparta!"

The announcer's words were easily drowned as the crowd erupted into a thunderous applause that shook the grandstands like an earthquake. Gaius saw a few of the spectators faint as the big Spartan stepped out into the arena and took his position between the five other men, who quickly circled Calfax.

Anthony, while he didn't know who Calfax was, was so swept up in the excitement that he cheered as loud as the audience, or at least tried. Even this low to the arena floor, Gaius could barely hear his friend's joyful admiration for the gladiator.

The gladiator Calfax wore a tight fitting Spartan helmet, made of bronze, which was topped with a bright red feathered crest. He was bare-chested; his torso and arms lined with hundreds of scars that stood out even more with the oils that had been rubbed over his body and muscles before he stepped into the arena. In his hand he carried two swords, no shield. One sword was curved, a falcate, while the other blade was a short dagger, about half the length of the other.

Once the crowd began to die down, each of the gladiators looked up towards the fat editor of the games. He was seated with several other men and women of notice, each dressed in expensive clothing and adorn with jewels and gold. Gaius recognized Varro among them too. He figured they were the financiers of the games, so were awarded the best seats.

Gaius turned his attention back towards the gladiators as each of them spoke the oath, *"We who are about to die, salute you."*

It took Gaius a few moments to realize that Calfax was going to be squaring off against the five gladiators on his own. And as the five men lowered their weapons, staring with focused attention on the lone Spartan, the crowd once again erupted into a frenzy of excitement.

Gaius felt his mouth dry as he watched, never taking his eyes off of Calfax, who stood, seemingly unconcerned. He kept his focus forward, on one of the dark-skinned gladiators who carried the trident, which he twirled, readied to attack any second.

Gaius looked down at Anthony, who seemed to be climbing the bars as high as they would take him. He was yelling with the crowd as his eyes were fixated on the six men who were nearly close enough that the two boys could smell their sweat. And then, as Gaius turned, the first strike came, suddenly and without warning.

Gaius felt his heart skip a beat as he watched one of the white-skinned gladiators charge from behind Calfax, who shifted his stance just slightly as the first opponent lunged at him. That man's thrust missed, coming just a few inches from piercing the Spartan's back.

Calfax struck down with his right blade, which cut deep into the man's right arm.

The man, who wore no helmet, screamed, however, his cries of pain were silenced a fraction of a second later as Calfax stepped quickly to the side and struck with his dagger, tearing through the nape of the man's neck, severing his spinal cord before the tip of the blade tore through the front of his throat.

Blood squirted from the wound like a fountain of red water, which sent the crowd roaring as Calfax drew first blood, with amazing speed and ferocity.

Gaius glanced toward Anthony once he realized his friend's cheers had suddenly stopped. What he saw now was a pale-faced young boy bent over near the corner of the gate, vomiting up everything the two had eaten before the fight.

As he turned back around to the arena floor, Calfax ran his dagger through the stomach of the second dark-skinned man. His entrails spilled out from his gut, which the gladiator tried in vain to keep inside his body. But Calfax ran behind him before he thrust his blade in between the man's shoulders, silencing his screaming.

A sword came at Calfax's head as his back was turned momentarily. Sensing that the strike was coming, he ducked just in time as the blade sliced across the red crest of his helmet.

Calfax sliced his sword across the man's knee before he dropped hard onto the ground, clutching his wound as tendons were easily cleaved.

As Calfax rose back to his feet, he drove his bloodied dagger into the man's face, sticking him through the left eye, where he kept the blade.

Gaius continued to watch as the remaining two gladiators struggled to overpower the veteran, who, despite his age was as nimble as a cat. A moment later, another man, the largest in size and height went down from another series of savage blows from Calfax, who drove the edge of his sword across the man's throat.

The last gladiator, the dark-skinned man that carried the trident lunged forward, hoping to catch the Spartan off guard. As before, Calfax's uncanny sense of the battlefield did not fail him as he weaved away from the heavy iron tips of the trident.

The crowd released more of their building rage of excitement as Calfax swung down with his sword, cleaving into the dark-skinned man's exposed wrist. The sword, now duller than it had been did not cut all the way through the bone, but on the second strike, the hand separated from the man's body, hanging loosely by a narrow strip of skin.

The dark-skinned man screamed in agony as he lost his grip on his weapon. The audience went wild with anticipation as Calfax stood poised before the quivering gladiator as a stream of hot piss ran down his leg.

Gaius was close enough to hear the dark-skinned man begging for his life, or so he assumed. He spoke a dialect that he'd never heard before, but regardless, Calfax held no mercy for the man that cradled his severed hand in his other.

Calfax swung, the tip of his sword sliced across the dark-skinned man's throat. Blood squirted out, splashing over Calfax's body like rain as he stood where he was, looking down at the defeated man, who choked on his own blood. It was not a quick death as the dark-skinned man's agony lasted several more painful moments before finally Calfax raised his sword, and plunged it down into the man's gullet, ending him finally.

Gaius did not blink, not once as he watched Calfax claim his victory. He did not enjoy the show, not like he thought he would, but he wasn't mortified by it either, unlike Anthony.

As the cheering crowd stood to their feet, Calfax removed his helmet, allowing the adoring audience, and Gaius to see his bald, scarred and one-eyed face clearly for the first time.

Flowers drifted down across the arena floor as the mob showered Calfax with their admiration, respect and fear of a man who was impossibly powerful and deadly. He did not seem, however, to care for the affection that was being bestowed on him. He looked down at the dead that lie on the floor; the thick pools of blood and guts, mixed with flesh and bone covered the sandy floor of the arena, showered by the beauty of the flowers turned Calfax's stomach. And then Calfax turned his gaze toward Gaius.

For a moment their eyes locked, and for the first time Gaius truly felt fear as he looked into the single good eye of the man he had watched kill so easily, and without mercy.

As Calfax flared at him, he saw nothing but hatred in his soulless eye, that if he could, the Spartan would kill every Roman, man, woman and child. No matter how much applause he might receive, even now, as his name was hailed, Calfax was a slave.

He finally pulled his gaze away from Gaius, turning once the far gate was opened, allowing him to leave the arena as several men rushed out with hooks in hand to drag the bodies back inside. A moment later the fat editor of the games returned to his podium and began his closing statements to the adoring crowds.

By now, Gaius had lost interest in hearing anything more. He stepped away from the barred gate and turned his attention towards Anthony, who sat with his back up against a wooden support beam, clutching his stomach with both hands.

"Is it over?" Anthony asked as he looked up at Gaius.

"Yes, it is over," Gaius replied as he reached down and lifted his friend to his feet. "We had better get you cleaned before your father sees you like this, or it will be both of our backsides that feel his wrath."

Anthony nodded as he and Gaius left, having seen what it was they wanted to see. Now, both just wanted to forget what they'd witnessed and salvage their day before they had to head back to the country, leaving the wonders of Rome behind.

CHAPTER FIVE

The summer sun was high as Gaius, along with Anthony and Julia walked along the crumbling stone wall that led up to his modest home. The same slave that had watched over the trio during their time in Rome was with them now, escorting Gaius home as Varro had ordered.

Gaius was returning about the time that his father had instructed him before he left for the city. While he wished his time in Rome could have lasted longer, he did not want to overextend his experience quite yet. Now, with his head swelled with memories of the past two days, he regretted having to leave so soon when he was just starting to see all the wonders the capital had to offer.

The trip was everything he had hoped it would be. The sights that he saw were beyond words. He and Anthony talked long into the afternoon, and stayed up late each night reliving what they had enjoyed together. Even though Anthony had been to Rome many times in the past, this seemed to be the most memorable for him as of yet. Neither boy, however, spoke of what they witnessed yesterday in the arena, after the fight, where the gladiator Calfax defeated five other men. Gaius managed to get Anthony cleaned up so that when Varro returned, he found the two boys right where he left them. Anthony had still been reeling from his ordeal when Varro first saw his son, but Gaius explained to him that Anthony wasn't feeling well, from the long day and the heat. That was enough to end the questioning. Still, for himself, what he had seen continued to replay in his mind – every lethal blow seen in perfect detail, the smell of blood, the screams of the gladiators as they died horrifically.

Gaius had seen death before, mostly animals he and his father hunted in north. He had even seen a man die once; well, a man that was still a boy, only three years older than he was now.

A season ago, Julius had been called north by a former soldier friend to help hunt down a pack of wolves that had been terrorizing the local farmers. Since leaving the military his father had taken on dozens of such jobs. However, this was the first job he had taken since Gaius' mother had died, and with no one else to look after him, Julius decided to bring him along; a journey Gaius had looked forward to as much as he had for Rome.

On the third day of the hunt, after they had come back with four dead wolves, their pelts hanging over the side of one riderless horse, a boy named Claudius, the son of Julius' friend fell suddenly from his horse as it was spooked by a snake that lay near the side of the road.

Gaius remembered watching the boy's horse rear up, throwing Claudius off its back. He had no chance to recover, it all happened so quickly that when he hit the ground, his head cracked open against a rock. Claudius was gone, just like that.

He remembered watching the boy's father cry to the heavens, smashing the snake to little pieces of bloodied flesh, even slicing the horse's throat for it panicking. Yet, like yesterday, Gaius stood, watching, not mortified by seeing the boys' brain and blood splattered across the dusty road. He had assumed that after his mother's long-suffering illness that anything related to death would ever bother him again, and so far, it hadn't.

The fates were strange beings, his father had once said. One moment a boy was with his father chasing down wolves, riding home to celebrate, and the next moment his ashes were being spread across the earth after a quick and pointless end.

Gaius hoped that like those five gladiators, he might be able to see his death coming, and perhaps be able to fight to prolong his life. Staring death down, shaking a fist in its face, that was how he hoped he would go, not meaningless because a snake just had to lay in the road and spooked a young mare.

For the moment, Gaius tried to block the memories of what he had seen yesterday and years before, and enjoy the time he had now with his friends.

Julia ran up beside Gaius and pushed into his hands several flowers that she had plucked from the side of the road.

"For crying out loud, would you leave him alone already!" Anthony blurted as he reached to smack his sister, but she ran off, giggling as she darted behind the older woman who followed them closely.

Gaius smiled as he couldn't help but smell the flowers he now held in his hand. He looked back at Julia who was fast at work once more, as she filled her hands yet again with another arrangement of summer flowers, lost in her own little world.

"Gosh! She can be such as pain in the ass," Anthony moaned.

"It's okay, really, I don't mind at all. She is in her own world without a care." Gaius looked back at Julia, enjoying her carefree exploration of his lands, not carrying about the sorry state it was in. Something about her spirit always seemed to lift his. He hoped she stayed this way, innocent and fearless. He couldn't help but wonder what the future might hold for the two of them as they grew older. He found himself thinking more and more about that with each new day, a question that was starting to haunt him that at times, he was eager to grow so he may have his answer: would her affection always be this strong toward him, or would it lessen as her world revealed more to her than a simple farm boy could ever provide.

"Hey, it looks like you have some company," Anthony commented as he looked up towards Gaius' home, which finally came into view.

Gaius had to put his hand over his brow so he could see through the bright glare of the sun. Indeed, he saw two horses standing outside, each one packed with enough supplies to last a week.

"I wonder who it could be," Anthony pondered as he and Gaius quickened their pace.

"I do not know. We don't typically get many visitors," Gaius replied, curious, as he kept his eyes ahead. It was just then that he recalled his father, when last he saw him mentioning that someone was coming on this day, and for whatever reason, he insisted in him meeting the stranger.

As the three friends came nearer to the small home, Gaius could see that the horses had been branded with the seal of the sixth legion, with a second brand under it that read, *S.P.Q.R.* The larger of the two was brown and looked as if it could carry a heavy individual wearing full armor and kit. The second horse was also brown, only lighter and smaller, more a horse for someone Gaius' age.

Anthony and Julia remained with their slave as Gaius approached his front door. He couldn't shack the bad feeling that was brewing in the pit of his stomach. And then, as Gaius went to reach for the door handle, it was pulled open before he could reach it.

Gaius stumbled back, eyes wide as a large man stood before him, seemingly not noticing the boy who had to tilt his head; eyes panicked as Gaius squared himself, fist clenched into a tight ball.

The burly man was about the age of Gaius' father, only a bit larger and with a thick grayish beard. He wore a lion-skinned cloak over his shoulders; its paws dropped down over his chest which was covered with a loose-fitting, brown leather armor chest plate, which bore the same engraving of the white wolf that Gaius had seen several times. It was, however, what was in the man's hand that scared him the most, a small dagger.

As the stranger finally looked down, Gaius could see a long scar that ran from the top of his brow and ending just above his cheekbone. It seemed recent, and gave him a menacing appearance.

At first the man's expression hardened, his stare cold as he studied the boy that was standing before him, and then he spoke.

"You don't look like much. I expected you to be bigger by now," the man said in a deep and raspy voice.

Gaius could smell the scent of cheap wine coming off of the man's breath as he spoke.

"I guess it could be worse. You could have taken after your father," the old soldier then laughed as his expression suddenly changed to a friendly grin.

The man raised his knife to his other hand and sliced a piece of dried beef, before putting the meat into his mouth and began to chew; still with a big grin as he continued to take in Gaius, who still stood like a statue.

"Very funny coming from someone with a face like yours," Julius spoke from behind the old soldier, which too sounded as if he had been drinking all day.

Julius stepped out, moving the other man aside so he may stand in the doorway. His hand was placed on the stranger's shoulder as he looked down at Gaius with a big, uncharacteristic smile that reached from ear to ear.

"Gaius, I would like you to meet an old friend of mine, Legate of the Six Legion, Claudius Augustus Valerius. He and I are old friends."

"You said that already," Valerius mused. "And actually, I have met you once before, lad. Only then you were too young to remember me as you were just a little nip, still suckling on your mother's breast."

Gaius' face hardened, not liking the picture that formed in his head as Valerius knelt down and extended his hand. But he refused to take it.

"Now don't be rude, Gaius," his father spoke.

Gaius hesitated for a moment, but then obeyed his father and reluctantly accepted Valerius' gesture of friendship. As he took the legate's wrist, he tried as best he could to make sure his grip was tight, but compared to the veteran, he might as well been a bug standing next to a bear.

"Well, we need to fatten him up, put some muscles on him and hair on his chest before we can call him a soldier," Valerius chuckled as he stood to his feet

"He comes from fine Gallic stock," Julius added.

"That he does," Valerius laughed as he tapped Julius' shoulder, stepping aside as he walked over to his horse.

"Well old friend, I will be waiting out here. Take all the time you need."

"Are you leaving?" Gaius asked a bit rudely, but neither his father nor Valerius took notice of it.

"Come inside, Gaius. There is something very important that I need to talk to you about."

"What about my friends?" Gaius asked, sounding more than a bit nervous.

"They can remain out here. Come now." Julius placed his hand on Gaius' shoulder and urged him into the house, before closing the door. Both Anthony and Julia looked on with concern, but they weren't leaving as both settled in for the wait.

Gaius watched as his father cleared the table, moving aside several empty wine jugs, before pulling the stool out.

"Sit down, son. There is something that I need to talk to you about."

"Father?" Gaius spoke nervously, but he did what he was asked as Julius move to the other side of the table and took his normal seat.

"Who is the man outside, father?" Gaius spoke first as Julius interlocked his fingers, looking unsure about how to being their discussion.

"He is a Roman soldier, commander of the Six Legion, my former legion when I served the Republic. We fought together during the last war and many before, and as I said, he is a dear friend of mine."

"I do not recall you ever speaking of him before this day," Gaius noted.

"I know, and that is my fault. But believe me, son, I trust no one more in this world, aside from yourself, than I do Valerius. He is as close to me as blood and, well..." Julius paused as he tipped over one of the wine jugs, seeing that it was empty.

"Why is he here? Is he just visiting then?" Gaius asked, but he knew it wasn't that simple. Otherwise his father wouldn't be acting the way he was.

"No, I asked him to come here some weeks ago. I've... I have come to a very difficult decision that concerns you, Gaius."

"What is it?"

"You see, Gaius...Damn, I wish this was easier to say."

"Just tell me, please." Tears were already beginning to form under Gaius' eyes as he eagerly waited to hear what troubled his father so much that he held his tongue, afraid to speak.

"I'm dying, Gaius. I don't know how else to say it."

Gaius' eyes opened wide as tears began to fall, rolling down the side of his cheeks. Flashes of his mother's passing flooded his mind, seeing her so sickly, waiting, and even wishing the gods would take her just so he didn't have to see her suffer much longer. He knew what his father said was the truth, his heart told him. He had known for a long time: his father's difficulties sleeping, his apparent weakness, his headaches and fainting spells, but he prayed to the gods that it would pass. Clearly, Julius knew it would not.

"Why? You can't be. You just can't...Why do you say such a terrible thing?" Gaius balled.

"I'm sorry, son. I don't know how else to tell you. The gods have deemed it fit that my time on the earth comes to its conclusion. I don't know when, exactly, but I do know it will be sooner than either of us wants it to be. I won't be able to take care of you, and you're still too young to take care of yourself. I have to look out for your safety and try to insure you have a future."

Julius stood from his stool and walked over to Gaius, dropping down to one knee and tried to look his son in the eyes, but Gaius turned his head away, not wanting to let his father see him cry.

"There is nothing that can be done. I'm grateful for the time that I was allowed. I should have died a long time ago. It was only by the grace of the gods that I survived this long, to find a woman I loved, and for her to give me a son I care so much for, even if I've failed to express it as much as I should have."

Gaius lowered his head as he couldn't control himself. He wanted to be strong and not cry, but his father's words ran through him like knives, more painful than anything since his mother's passing.

"I'm sorry, son, there was so much that I wanted to teach you. So much that I wanted to show you. We've had so little time and I fear that I was not always the father that you needed me to be, not since your mother left this world. But I won't leave you alone, not ever. That man outside, Valerius, he will watch over you like you were his own. He will do this because we are close as any two men can be without being brothers by blood. He will teach you everything you need to know; how to survive in this world. He will guide you down the path of honor; you will become a great warrior who will stand for his country, and one day, a long time from now, you will lead men who you will pass the knowledge you've learned, as Valerius will you."

Julius placed the palm of his hand on Gaius' face, turning it towards him so he could look into his son's eyes.

"I know you want to stay with me – I can see that in your eyes. But I will not allow you to watch me die, Gaius. Your destiny lies elsewhere, even if you can't entirely understand why I am doing this now. But you will understand, someday. You will understand the gift that I'm giving you. You will have a life, a purpose and be able to stand for something greater than ourselves. Will you be strong for me, Gaius?"

He tried to hold back his already flowing tears just for a moment as he looked into his father's own saddened eyes, and answer him.

He did not want to agree. He did not want to leave him alone to die. He did not want to start down the path that his father and Valerius wanted. Gaius fought to stand and tell his father that he refused what he was saying, and that he would stand by his side until the end.

However, as Gaius looked at his father, he could see the pain that he was in, and that deep down, while he did not want Gaius to leave, he knew it was for the best.

Gaius rubbed his tears from his eyes and wiped his cheeks, before he found the courage to answer.

"I understand, father. I promise I will not let you down."

"That's my boy. Now, come, I want to show you something."

Gaius watched as his father walked over to his bed, which was on the far side of the small house. Gaius soon joined him.

"I know you have seen these before, when I wasn't around," Julius confronted Gaius with a grin. "Now I want you to know what they are."

Gaius sat by his father's side as he opened the trunk and removed the thin sheet that lay on top of the items inside. Most of the things were ignored, but it was the chest plate with the ivory white wolf that Julius held up.

"This is the crest of the Sixth Legion, the Wolves of Rome," Julius began as he rubbed his hand across the face of the wolf, which stood in the center of the expensive armor, surrounding by fig leaves of silver, with smaller depictions of wolves running in a pack on each breast.

"I was their chief centurion, and they were my family. I would have done anything to protect them, and they would me. We were defenders of the Republic, willing servants of Rome, but most of all, we fought to protect those we left at home. Very few of the old guard is left, save for myself and Valerius. He trains young men such as you to become the next generation of Wolves. Because of that, the Sixth Legion is unique. They aren't comprised of farmers or seasonal soldiers, but men that have sworn a lifelong oath to keep our Republic safe."

"But, I thought Rome had no standing army," Gaius asked. He had studied a lot about warfare, mostly so he could make his games with Anthony more entertaining.

Julius smiled. "True, to a point, but Rome is always at war in one form or another. We've only just united the whole of Italy, and before that a year did not go by that we weren't at some one's throat. But, the Sixth, they, as I have already said, are unique. They are kept ready in the south to protect the Republic's interests, and prepared at a moment's notice to march anywhere the Senate might deem necessary," Julius explained. "For the most part, however, Valerius keeps the legion filled at less than half strength, around a thousand men. More are added as needed."

Julius handed the armor over to Gaius, urging him to take it from him, which he did.

He had held it many times, but now, after hearing what his father had said, it never seemed heavier than it did now as his shacking arms struggled to kept it in his possession.

"You are too young to be a soldier now, but soon, when you come of age this armor will be yours to wear. With it you will carry a huge burden, and the honor of our family. The Sixth will become your new home, its men your brothers, and Valerius your guardian to take my place."

Gaius looked over at his father with a heavy heart as he fought to hold back his tears.

"Watch out for them, your men, your family – your pack, and they will protect you from the evils of this world."

Gaius stared down at the image of the wolf, which looked much like the one he saw in the forum in Rome. Why, he couldn't understand but for some reason this animal was looking out for him, as the old shopkeeper had said.

Gaius cradled the armor close to his chest as he embraced the destiny his father had set him down. He swore to make him proud; he would become a great warrior as his father was before him, but today, he just wanted to be a twelve year old boy that was saying goodbye to everything he'd known.

Gaius fell into Julius' arms as for the first time in his life the man embraced his son and cried with him. They would remain together for several more hours as Julius would tell more tales about the contents of the chest, gifts that he was giving to his son for the journey that was to come.

CHAPTER SIX

Gaius stood before the front door, his hand resting on the latch, not yet finding the courage to pull it open. Two hours had passed quicker than he would have liked. There was so much more that he wanted to say to his father, but his mind had drawn a blank as his emotions overtook him. Now, it was time to go, and before him stood the first independent act he had to master.

"It is okay, Gaius," Julius said as he rested his hand over his son's, urging him to pull the door open.

His hand shook terrible but with his father's encouragement, he finally pulled the door open, revealing the setting sun, and to his surprise, Anthony and Julia still waiting for him.

"Gaius!" Julia called out as she rushed over to him with her brother a step behind her. Right away the young girl's eyes could see that something was wrong.

"Where are you going?" Anthony asked with haste as he saw his friend holding a large bag filled with his personal belongings, his father holding another bag over his shoulder.

Gaius could not answer as his eyes were gazed downward. He still had difficulty understanding himself what was happening.

"Are you leaving, Gaius?" Julia asked as she stood next to her brother, who held tightly onto her hand.

"He is," Julius answered for his son; resting his hand down on Gaius' shoulder, trying to support him as best he could.

"Why?" Anthony demanded as his voice showed signs of a quiver.

"I have to," Gaius finally spoke.

"But why? "I don't understand," Julia asked, tears falling from her eyes.

"I just have to!" Gaius replied sharply, not really meaning to sound so harsh.

Julia let go of her brother and stepped in front of Gaius, looking up at him with tearful eyes as she struggled to understand the sudden turn of events.

"Don't you like me anymore? Did I do something to upset you that might be causing you to leave?" she pleaded.

Gaius could not answer. A part of him wanted to yell at her, tell her that he didn't like her anymore. Certainly it would have made more sense to her if he had. But words could not form.

"Young Gaius has made a very brave decision. He has chosen to serve the people of Rome so that he may protect little girls such as yourself," Valerius broke the awkward silence as he stepped beside Gaius and answered Julia's question.

"When will he be back?" she asked.

"When he has finished his training," Valerius answered.

"When will that be?" Anthony then asked, he too having trouble keeping his emotions back.

"I'm afraid it will be some years," Julius spoke as he handed Gaius' bags over to Valerius, who then strapped them to the smaller of the two horses.

"I don't want you to go, Gaius!" Julia cried as she rushed forward and wrapped her arms around him as tightly as she could manage, tears rolled down Gaius' chest as she buried her face into his tunic.

Gaius held her for a while as she replied, "I don't want you to go!"

Gaius straightened himself and sucked back his own tears, before he pulled Julia away from him, still holding onto her shoulders, but now gazing lovingly into her deep eyes.

"I have to go. I have to become strong. If I don't, I won't be able to protect you from the monsters of the world, like I promised. I swear to you, Julia, one day I will come back for you. Do you believe me?"

Julia wiped the snot from her nose as she replied, "Do you promise?"

"I swear it – I swear it with all my heart that I will come back for you, and we'll never be parted again."

"But you'll forget me."

Gaius hugged Julia tightly as she again wrapped her arms around him.

"No. I could never forget you, Julia."

"I love you, Gaius," she whispered, only loud enough for him to hear.

"I love you too."

Anthony stood next to his sister, removing the clay medallion of the She-Wolf Lupus. Carefully, he snapped the token in two halves before handing the top piece to Gaius, for him to take.

"Here, so you shall remember me. We will always be brothers, as long as each of us has a piece of the medallion. Don't forget that, okay."

"I won't forget," Gaius answered as he placed the broken medallion around his neck, letting the top half of Lupus' head rest on his chest where he vowed to never take it off.

Anthony took his sister's hand and guided her back to where they had been resting. The body slave took the still crying Julia into her arms, wrapping a shawl around the girl while she comforted her.

"I'm proud of you, Gaius. Today you have taken your first step to becoming a man. Never forget those that we leave behind, for they are the ones you'll fight for when the time comes," Julius said as he knelt down before Gaius, speaking to him with a clear, proud voice.

"I won't forget, father. I promise."

Gaius hugged his father for the last time before Julius forced himself to let go.

"You train him well, Valerius."

"I will, old friend. I will see you in the next life," Valerius said as he extended his hand for Julius to take.

"Take your time getting there." Julius grabbed his oldest friend and embraced him, before the two men parted quickly, not wanting to prolong their separation any longer.

"Come lad, we have a lot of road to cover before we reach the legion barracks," Valerius said as he escorted Gaius over to his horse, helping him up onto the back of the smaller mare, before he leaped onto his own.

As the two of them turned and started down the dirt road, heading south, Julia ran behind Gaius for several paces crying out, "Don't forget me, Gaius! Don't forget your promise! I will be waiting for you, I promise you! I love you, Gaius!"

He smiled down at her, watching her until she disappeared over the horizon as the falling sun soon crossed under the western sky, ending the last day of his old life.

CHAPTER SEVEN

The Senate of Carthage

North Africa

Two large gold-plated doors that led into the Carthaginian senate swung open once the visitors from Rome were announced to the gathering of politicians, foreign delegates and the nobility of Carthage. The glare of the sun, blistering hot, filled the chamber that seated over three hundred representatives, who had gathered to meet emissaries from Rome. These men waited eagerly; most, if not all, with apprehension and contempt that filled their hearts. The last time representatives from Rome stepped foot in the Carthaginian senate, was to accept their surrender to Rome. Now, as the collective audience took a deep breath, they looked on as five men, each dressed in pristine white togas, stepped through the open doors after two days sailing, and walked without breaking stride toward the gathering of men that would hear what Rome demanded of them.

Each senator waited in silence, in anticipation. Only the rhythmic tapping of the representatives of Rome shoes could be heard as they crossed the marble floor to see the leader of the Carthaginian senate.

Finally the leader of the group, a tall, well-built man, clearly the equestrian class, with short close-cut black hair, dark eyes and a stern glare nodded his head to the leader of the Carthaginian senate. His name was Quintus Fabius. He was a former tribune in the Roman army and now appointed chief envoy by his senate to deliver a message to Carthage, in hopes of preventing another war.

Each of his four aides stood poised behind Quintus. They each were soldiers - purposefully big and intimidating, as if they carried the might of the Roman army on their shoulders.

"Senators," Quintus began, not waiting to be formally introduced or spoken too. His voice carried high, easily heard from all corners of the senate chambers, as all who listened, paid attention to him and his words with great and worrisome interest.

"I have come to you with great urgency. It would appear that this house has allowed one of its generals to run astray." Quintus' opening statement was designed to sound purposely mocking. More than a few of the Carthaginian senators snorted their contempt at his acquisition.

"Three months ago, a general by the name of Hannibal Barca, birthed out of New Carthage in Hispania, raised an army and laid siege to the settlement of Saguntum, a Roman ally." His voice rose higher on that last statement Quintus directed his gaze around the room.

"Three weeks ago Saguntum fell to Hannibal's forces, and now Rome has learned that the rogue Hannibal has unified a number of barbarian tribes within Gaul, and is planning his march across the Alps even as I speak, with the clear intentions of invading Italy."

A number of Carthaginian senators began to openly voice their belay in the accusations that Quintus was making.

"Where is your proof?!? Yelled one man, but Quintus ignored him and all others that demanded the same.

"Rome," Quintus' voice rose even higher, "will not tolerate this act of open aggression against our allies and our people. If this Senate does not act now and forcefully remove the renegade Hannibal of his command, and present him to the Roman Senate so he may face punishment, his actions, and the unwillingness of this Senate will be considered an act of war."

Quintus stretched out his words, putting extra pause on the word *war*, so that his warnings would resonate deeply with the men who had gathered to hear his demands.

Quintus lowered both of his hands down to his sides and filled them with the folds of his toga, before raising it higher, as if he was offering the cloth to the senators. He paused for a moment longer, allowing his confusing gesture to be seen by all in the chambers before he continued.

"In my folds, Rome brings you either peace or war. Which do you choose?"

The Carthaginians seemed puzzled as a chorus of voices rose up, most of them outraged by the proposal and the seemly theatrical gesture by Quintus.

The leader of the senate rose from to his feet, fixing his dark gaze on Quintus as he gave his reply. Like many of his fellow representatives, he donned a thick curled black beard that made him distinctly alien to the five trimmed Romans that stood before him.

He raised his right hand, palm held out, and urged his members to be silent for a moment as he gave his answer.

"Which do you prefer?" the senator seemed like he was going to say more, but before he could; Quintus dropped his folds and tilted his head in a respectful manner.

"Then we choose war. This, the Senate, the People and Rome accept," and then Quintus and his four burly bodyguards turned abruptly, walking with haste out of the Carthaginian senate even though a number of the senators, including their leader urged them to return so that negotiations could continue. Other senators, however, accepted Rome's statement and rallied for war as the chambers erupted into frenzy.

Quintus glanced back one last time as the senators and other Carthaginians present at the brief assembly were at each other's throats. Some accepting Rome's offer for war, while others demanded that they sue for peace, at any cost. This told Quintus all he needed to know. Carthage was not ready for a prolonged conflict, and more than likely would not send aid to Hannibal. The rouge would be alone and easily dealt with when and if he crossed the Alps. And., at the very least he would be bogged down for a number of years, perhaps even a decade without help from home before he could actually threaten Rome directly. No matter, Quintus knew Rome would be back here, in these chambers, with Hannibal's head on a pike. With him, Carthage would knee before Rome and her legions.

The republic's destiny was at hand.

*   *   *

Gaius stared into the fire and watched the flames dance with no particular interest, as the embers from the newly placed log burned bright into the night sky. It had been four days since he had left his father, and the only life he had ever known. He understood the reasons why he was forced to leave; still, a part of him wished he could see his father and friends one last time. So much needed to be said, but so little actually had been spoken. Now, he found himself in the company of a stranger.

Valerius had served with his father long ago, during Rome's last war with a nation called Carthage. He learned that fact but knew little else since neither of them had said more than a dozen words to one another since they had set out on their long journey. He knew that Valerius was talking him to some kind of camp, one where he trained other young men to serve the republic, the home of the Sixth Legion. But what new life awaited him, he knew nothing about, or if he could properly prepare himself for what was to come in the weeks and months.

Becoming a soldier, a warrior of Rome had been one of his boyhood dreams, ever since he discovered his father's armor, he dreamed about glorious adventures in faraway countries; fight barbarian hordes, and defending the values of Rome. But now, too soon had the obligation been thrust upon him that he doubted his ability to overcome the trials that would be waiting for him when he reached his final destination.

Valerius stroked the fire. For four days the two had been heading south, and while they were never far from a town, every night they camped under the stars. Gaius did not mind this; he was accustomed to sleeping outdoors, which was comforting for him since it was something he and his father had done many times. Tonight, they sat under a tall tree that had twisted and weathered braches, which protected the pair from the light rain that was beginning to fall.

Rested up against the tree, Gaius glanced over at the breast plate that Valerius had worn. It too bore the same engraving of the white wolf, only in a different style, but serving the same meaning.

Gaius noted that both his father and Valerius seemed to coven the crest a great deal. Even when they spoke of the Sixth Legion, their words were filled with respect and joy, like two proud fathers. Gaius wondered what it all meant. Would he also come to cherish the Sixth as they had – his new family, his brothers? How would he know if he was going to like the life that was being forced on him? His mind was vexed with these questions and many more – too many uncertainties. He hated not knowing what to expect. He disliked surprises, and more so feared his own lingering doubts. Fear was terrible and it had sunk its teeth into him. What should happen to him if he failed? What if he was a terrible soldier? He had nothing to his name but what was strapped to the horse.

What would become of me? Gaius shivered at the thought.

"Are you cold?" Valerius broke the awkward silence as he noticed Gaius rubbing his arms as he huddled near the fire.

"Not really," he lied.

Valerius smiled as he reached behind him and tossed Gaius his lion-skinned cloak. Gaius eagerly wrapped the warm fur around him, enjoying the soft feel of the hide, which lifted his spirits a bit higher.

"You should try spending a winter in north of the Po Valley. Some nights, it seems you have to light the whole damn forest on fire to stay warm. Hell, we couldn't burry our dead some nights," Valerius commented as she continued to stroke the raging fire that sat between he and Gaius.

Gaius did not reply, which Valerius sighed at, seemly hoping his attempt at humor would break the tension between he and Gaius.

"You should eat something. You're practically skin and bones."

"I am not hungry, thank you," Gaius replied as a nearly full bowl of stew sat near his feet. The food wasn't bad, and in fact, it was very much the same that his father had made every night since his mother passed from this world.

As thunder clapped in the distance, Gaius glanced over at Valerius, who continued playing with the smoldering logs in the fire. It was then that Gaius seemed to recognize that the old soldier's mind was lost, as if the gravity of what was asked of him was weighing heavily on his mind. It was then that Gaius realized, that while he had lost a father, Valerius had lost someone special to him as well, and it was out of love that he had decided to take Gaius under his wing – a last act of friendship.

Taking a deep breath, Gaius spoke. "How long did you know my father?"

An uneasy grin appeared on Valerius' face as he continued to play with the fire, more so out of distraction than necessity.

"Well, I was a few years older than you when I first met your father. Back then we both joined the Sixth during one of the wars with the Samnite. We, I was young and stupid back then, full of unfounded confidence. I was a big lad, already skilled with the sword, hailing from wealthy roots. I believed I deserved better position just because I thought I was better than anyone else. But your father, he challenged me, put me in my place more than a few times; showed me that to be a good leader, I had to be a better follower."

Valerius smiled at the memories of his youth.

Gaius leaned in closer, listening carefully to every word the legate said.

"So, you two were friends then, from the start?" Gaius asked.

Valerius laughed with a bellowing roar.

"Oh no, dear boy, your father and I were bitter rivals from the very start. I hated his guts from the moment I first laid eyes on him. So pious, confident, and like I, remarkable skilled."

Gaius looked more than a little surprised to hear Valerius' statement, which was spoken with all honesty.

"What do you mean?" Gaius asked as his smile disappeared.

"I and your father challenged each other daily, in anything and everything you could imagine, just to see who the better was: who was better with the sword, spear, and the better horsemen, boxing, wrestling, eating, and even who could lay the most women." Valerius winked with the last comment and added, "I must admit that I always came out on top with the woman," he finished with an odd grin that Gaius failed to comprehend.

Valerius continued, "Many times our daily challenges came to violent blows. We would fight until one of us couldn't get up, or until the centurions beat us over the backsides with their vine-canes; bloodied, bruised and even a broken bone or two from time to time. It did not matter as long as one of us proved who the better was. But with all that said, our spirited contests made both of us the best amongst the Sixth."

"And then you became friends, from your contests?"

"Oh no, we became even greater rivals."

"Then what changed? What made you two brothers in the end?"

"War – namely Rome's conflict fought with Carthage, many years before you were born." Valerius tossed another log onto the fire, which sparked and crackled as the heat of the flamed engulfed it.

"Carthage?" Gaius' mind drifted. It was not the first time he had heard of the unseen and unlearned country before. While Rome had seemly won its war against Carthage, it seemed many Romans still feared Carthage, or at least another war with them.

"Rome has many enemies that would see our Republic torn down, our walls crumbled, our temples burned and our loved ones sold into slavery, but no nation equals Carthage."

"Where are they?" Gaius asked.

"Africa, to the west of Egypt and Numidia. They aren't too different than us, in many ways: similar government, similar heritage, similar customs, yet, we two couldn't be more different either. Both Carthage and Rome seek to control the Mediterranean, but they have a superior navy and trade than we, at least they did before the war."

"Is that why Rome went to war with Carthage?"

"Who can guess: land, wealth, greed, or two fat men who couldn't come to an understanding. All I know is, young men like your father and I were called to service, to fight and to kill men we've never met or seen until then. The *why* wasn't important when we fought to stay alive."

"So the war made you friends, finally?" Gaius asked.

"Yes, it did," Valerius smiled, as Gaius seemly cheered up in knowing that his father hadn't damned him to one of his enemies.

"You see, Gaius, all those years your father and I fought one another, made both of us strong men, better than most. We quickly realized that alone we were powerful men, but when we were together, we were nearly unstoppable. We lost many friends during the war, most we trained with our entire adult life, but always we were there for each other – he protecting my back, and I his.

Gaius smiled at the thought of seeing in his mind, his father in his prime, battling wave after wave of enemy barbarians with Valerius by his side. What a sight the two must have been, true heroes of Rome; champions like those he acted with Anthony.

The two were silent for a moment as Valerius' own thoughts drifted to his youth with Julius and their many adventures together. And then after several quiet minutes he broke the silence, his voice now low and somber as he felt compelled to confess the truth to Gaius.

"I have something that I need to tell you – something that I think is important for you to know before we continue forward."

Gaius could read the change in mood as Valerius stared at him with daunting eyes that showed the slightest hint of reservation behind them.

"What is it?" Gaius asked.

Valerius took a deep breath, and then spoke." I am the reason your father is dying – the reason he had to give you away. It is entirely my fault that you were forced to leave your old life behind, and those you called your friends."

Gaius' eyes opened wide as he struggled for words, but managed to utter, "What...What do you mean it is your fault? I don't understand."

Valerius hesitated as he dropped his head low, not wanting to look into Gaius' innocent eyes, as he stared with confusion at the confession.

Taking a deep breath he began: "The war was nearing its conclusion. Our cohort was on patrol. We had been camped in Sicily for nearly a year, and had tamed most of the tribes that were loyal to Carthage, so we did not expect anything to come. But they did, from the hill like raving madmen. We held our ground against several charges as the bastards bashed into our shields times and time again, until finally they broke. But your father, who was chief centurion of the cohort, did not fall for the trap. He ordered our forces to hold their ground, but I, foolishly disobeyed. By century advanced, determined to slaughter the cunts to the last man, but it was then when we were at our most vulnerable that they hit us from either side. With the hills around us we couldn't form proper ranks, so my century was being slaughtered almost to the last man."

Valerius' words were growing angrier as he detailed the encounter, becoming more animated as he went into further description about the fighting that followed the ambush.

Gaius hung on his every word as he inched himself closer to Valerius. He tried to imagine what the old veteran must have been like, young and strong as he battled the horde of bloodthirsty Carthaginians and their allies.

"Eventually most of my men ran back to our primary line, which was now beginning to pull out under the threat of being encircled by a superior force, a wise choice on your father's part. Me, on the other hand was lost in my rage. I stood my ground as my men withered all around me, holding my own against any bastard that challenged me. However, even I in my youth wasn't Mars; I'm shameful to admit now."

"What did you do? How did you survive?"

"The whore-son's had me surrounding, at least twenty of them, and despite the bodies that lay around my feet, they weren't fearful of the Roman officer who stood defiant. They teased me, using their spears to slow me, taking pot-shots when they could – pierce my leg, my arm and my hip. I was done for, either then or later when they took me prisoner, but then I heard your father's war cry as he charged down the field on top a horse. Where he got one I can't imagine, but he looked like the god Apollo coming to my rescue."

"Wow! Apollo?" Gaius mused with a wide grin.

"Oh yes, my boy. He charged into the Carthaginian ranks, killing at least three of them before I regained my wits and finished off another pair."

Valerius paused for a moment as he took a deep breath.

"But, one of the bastards tossed a spear, which tripped the horse. Your father was thrown from it, landing on his head. He lived and seemed no worse of ware, but he cracked his helmet straight now its seam. Blood gushed from a deep gash to his head, but strangely, he did not seemed phased by it at all. He charged at the remaining soldiers, crazed with madness, killing, I dare say, more than I. Those who stood alive ran off, giving your father and I time to escape the battlefield."

"Then he saved you?"

"Yes, but with a price. As we were leaving, several miles safely from their territory, your father collapsed and would not wake up for a very long time. I carried him back to our legion camp and got him the help he needed. For a while I wasn't sure he would ever wake up again, but he did, and again, probably thanks to his hard head, he seemed okay."

"I don't understand," Gaius asked as he now sat right next to Valerius, trying to wrap his young mind around what was being said.

"Well, you see lad, there are many injuries you can sustain on the battlefield that will end you slowly over time, but those taken to the head can be the worse – worse than death, for it will kill you over a lifetime. You may be fine for years even, but then one day, everything is different; your body won't work anymore, you may have fits of the limb, cold sweats, raging temperatures, and much worse. A powerful man, such as your father can become as frail as a small boy, I'm afraid. And while your father would not show it to you, he knew that his time was growing ever shorter. He wanted to spare you from seeing him fall – overtaken by this old wound, one that I'm responsible for."

Valerius lowered his head, his voice filled with regret as his somber words ran deep through Gaius' heart.

"If it weren't for me and my action, your father would still be alive. He would be able to raise you, teach you what is needed to become a man, and allow you to make your own choice as to what to do with your life. I've robbed him of his life, but so too I've done the same for you."

Valerius looked down at Gaius and rested his hand on the boy's shoulder as he continued.

"Gaius, I will understand if, someday you seek to avenge your father's fate. I am at fault and it is your right as his son. I deserve no less." Valerius' words were sincere.

Gaius did not say anything for what seemed like a long time. He didn't know how to respond. He knew it was in his right to take action against the man who was to become his teacher – the man that would train him to be a soldier, to kill. Yet, Gaius looked up at Valerius with different eyes, not filled with hatred for what the old soldier had told him, but a sense of understanding that was beyond his years.

Gaius shook his head, "No. My father told me once, shortly after my mother left this world that we can't question the will of the gods. We are not wise enough to understand their plan for us, and that we have to accept that each day that we live, is a gift. What he did for you, he did out of love. It is no excuse for why he had to come to your rescues, but he would have done it regardless, even if he knew what the outcome would have been. I believe he never blamed you, and therefore, I have no need to hold any grudge against you for your part in what happened."

Valerius managed a smile. It was obvious that he did not feel right about the mistake he made, but he admired the young man for his wisdom nevertheless.

"I don't think I could kill," Gaius suddenly stated after a short silence. The image of Calfax came to him: the way he killed, so meaninglessly, without mercy or feeling for those he cut down. A part of him wondered if that was his future now, to be trained to fight other men, and to take pride in the act of killing – to allow vanity to confuse him as it had Valerius in his youth.

Valerius shook his head. "It is never easy. As a soldier, you might be...you will be called to do so, to protect yourself and the men under your command."

"What do I do when I'm faced with the chose?

"It is different for each man. You will learn things that you can't understand now, skills that will give you the tools you'll need to protect yourself, and hopefully prepare you for the day when you'll be faced with your life, or another's. But, nothing I teach you will make it easier. When the time does come, it will be up to you to take action, or die. It really is as simple as that. I would, however, suggest that you always keep in your heart the memories of those you are fighting for. It will make it that much easier in the end."

"Julia, and Anthony," Gaius muttered to himself before he gazed up into the old soldier's eyes. "How do I know I will ever be strong enough, when that day comes?"

"You, my young ward, have more courage and strength than you know. I can see great things in you, as I saw long ago in your father. I know you will one day be valiant, greater than your father and I."

Valerius took a swig of water before he placed his arm around Gaius' shoulder, deciding that it was best that he change the subject to something more entertaining for the lad.

"Did your father ever tell you how he met your mother?"

"No, he did not," Gaius replied as his ears perked up with renewed interested.

"Oh, wonderful; let me indulge you then. As it so happened, when your father was back in our camp, after his rescue of me, it was your mother who nursed him back to health when he finally woke up from his long slumber."

"Really, she did? Why was she in the camp?" Gaius asked with a wide smile.

"Well, as I'm sure you already know, your mother was quite a talented healer. But too, she was a strikingly beautiful woman; some think your father acted through most of his recovery just to be around her longer. Many of the men, including myself had desired her, but it was your father that won her heart. Even still, I never saw what she saw in that big lug, but the two ultimately fell in love. But, there was one big problem that stood between their union."

"What was that?"

Valerius looked down at Gaius and spoke softly as he answered, "Your mother was a slave."

"A slave?!?" he gasped, truly shocked by the revelation.

"Yes, I'm afraid so. She belonged to our camp prefect, and since she was beautiful, and a talented healer, the prefect was not willing to part with her. Yet, that fact did not stop your father from approaching him and requesting that the prefect sign her over to him – he even offered to buy her."

"What happened?"

"I'm getting there," Valerius laughed. "Well, by the time your father woke up and started his romance with your mother, word gotten out about your father's heroics on the battlefield, how he saved a certain promising officer with strong family connections, myself, from a hundred rampaging Carthaginians – or was it two hundred? I forget. Needless to say, your father was a real hero of Rome. The prefect offered him anything he wanted, promotion, money, other slaves, land and more, but it was only your mother that he desired. Not wanting to lose face in front of his men, the prefect agreed to sign ownership of your mother over to Julius."

"Then what happened," Gaius asked eagerly.

"Well, you're here aren't you," Valerius chuckled.

"That isn't what I mean. What happened next? Did they marry?"

"Well, your mother was now the property of your father, and he could have forced her to do anything he wanted. But, the first thing he did was give your mother her freedom. I tried to talk him out of it. I believed she would run the moment she was a freed woman, but to my surprise, she remained and agreed to marry your father. A few years later the war finally ended. Your father was awarded land for his bravery before he eventually left the army and retired to his property, where you grew up."

Valerius' smile widen as he admitted a hard truth to himself. "I must confess, while I've enjoyed my life, wealth, privilege and the chance to train many fine young men, I have always envied your father greatly. He found true love, something that is precious, and something that so few men actually manage to find."

"I never knew any of this," Gaius commented as his thoughts drifted.

"I suspect they never wanted you to know, not now anyways."

Gaius smiled as he looked up at his new friend, "Thank you, Valerius."

The veteran just smiled.

"You should hear about our exploits in Africa, your father and I. Now those were some harry days," Valerius bellowed with a funny grin.

"Please tell me."

Gaius stood taller as his stare fixed on Valerius as he began another story. For the rest of the night and the days that would follow, the apprehension between the two had left. They had bonded, overcoming the fear that lingered between the two. Now, from this moment on, Gaius was not fearful of what lie before him. He knew he could trust the old soldier as much as his father had, and for the first time, was excited by the adventure he was about to embark on.

CHAPTER EIGHT

The smell of fresh wheat that was a few days from being harvested filled Gaius' nose. He loved that smell, the scent of life and hard work. It reminded him of home and the life he left behind, now seven days ago.

He and Valerius were now on the southern tip of Italy, heading toward the Sixth Legion's barracks, which the old veteran commanded. It had been two days and nights since they had talked by the camp fire, sharing the stories of Valerius past, which included tales of Gaius' mother and father.

He had been afraid of the older man when he first saw him, but now neither one of them was uncomfortable with each other's presence. They had become fast friends as they shared a common interest and love for Gaius' family.

Valerius had told more stories about his and Julius' exploits in their youth, and Gaius had listened to each one with keen interest. He figured that, given time, that he would have his own story to tell, one that would equal his father's. But at the same time, the tales of his father's deeds made him lonely. He had never felt altogether comfortable around his father – he had been closer to his mother, but since her passing the small house had been empty and cold, even though the two men shared it together. The only release Gaius had was when he was with Anthony and Julia. At least with them he could be a child, living life as he should, not troubled by the worries of men.

He missed his friends greatly. He wondered what they might be doing now, without him. So too his mind thought terrible things; he nearly convinced himself that they would forget about him in time, maybe even within a few months. It saddened him greatly, but no matter what his mind told him, his heart reassured him that he was doing this to fulfill his promise to Julia. He would grow strong, confident and skilled in new trades that he could protect her and keep her safe. From what, it did not matter, and for now those thoughts kept him moving forward.

The field came into view as Gaius and Valerius rode over a hill, the sounds of their horses' hooves clopping in a soothing pattern mixed with the joyful sounds, the singing birds and casual conversations of the workers in the fields as they readied the harvest. The sun was high and pleasantly warm. Gaius' eyes widened as saw children running to and fro, playing in and around the fields, their mother's warning them every few minutes to stay where they could be seen. Hundreds of men and women walked casually down the narrow paved road with bushels of already gathered wheat on their backs, or carried in horse-drawn carts.

In the distance he could make out the outline of the legion barracks, which was surrounded by a high wooden wall. Further still were hints of a small town.

A number of workers acknowledged Valerius, calling out greetings as the two rode slowly passed them. Gaius could see on the old veteran's face that he enjoyed the small pleasantries as he sparked short conversations with a number of the men, asking about their families, knowing many of them by their names.

"Are these people your slaves?" Gaius' head was on a swivel as he took in every detail, sight and sounds, feeling that he was on a grand adventure.

Valerius chuckled as he glanced back with a thin smile.

"No, these men and women are all freeborn. I pay them to work the field. We share in the bounty; my men are fed and clothed while the workers sell the goods in the town or export elsewhere. It is a simple arrangement that works for both parties. It is about balance, Gaius."

"Balance?" Gaius asked confused. It seemed to be a lot of work to him for so little reward.

"Yes. Look at them. Look at each of their faces. Are those the faces of slaves?"

"But Rome has many slaves."

"Indeed, it was built on the backs of slaves. Countless generations of people, both from our own piece of the world and from lands not even seen by my own eyes have lived under the crack of a whip. Even today, without them the whole system would cease to exist, and the Republic would crumble."

"Then why don't you own them. It would be cheaper, and your bounty larger?"

"True, I suppose. But easier isn't always cheaper, no less is it honorable; men who work honestly, knowing that their labor is its own reward, will work that much better. A slave has no choice; work or suffer the consequences. Besides, less than a century ago these people were all Greek, enemies of Rome. If I were to treat them as such, our legion would not be enough to hold back their wraith. To treat them as equals, while not citizens of the state, we keep the peace while still maintaining Rome's presences."

"I don't really understand," Gaius admitted. He had seen slavery his entire life. Once, in a fit of anger about having to do his chores, when all he wanted to do was go outside and play, he suggested to his father that they should get a slave or two. At the time he was sure they could afford it. Anthony and Julia had many slaves, all of whom rushed to please their master and their friend. He didn't see anything wrong with it: if Rome's foundation was based on it, what could be wrong?

Valerius glanced back and looked at Gaius, seemingly amused by his confused expression as he tried to wrap his head around Valerius' reasoning.

"You may not understand yet, Gaius, but I've seen much of the world. There is too much suffering and pain, much of it caused by Rome. I swore a long time ago that I would not add to it if it could be avoided. I would rather starve and have my men be without than force another to tend to our needs."

"Then Rome is wrong for its practices?" Gaius asked.

"I don't know, Gaius. I'm but a simple soldier. It is not for us to question centuries of tradition, but that doesn't mean we have to follow every one either. You'll have to make your own mind up one day. I love our Republic. I love what it stands for, what it could someday become, but it is far from perfect."

Valerius stopped his horse and turned back, facing Gaius, who also came to a stop. The legion barracks were in full view now; its gates wide open, the sentries on post as dozens of people came and went through the entrance. The whole placed seemed daunting, impossibly huge to Gaius' young eyes. Thousands of men, most much older, stronger and more skilled than he lived there, it was literally a whole new world he knew nothing about that he was frightened to move another step forward and cross the threshold.

"Gaius," Valerius begun, his voice firm, his eyes fixed. "What favor I may have shown you over the past few days has to end right here. I loved your father and I promised him that I would take care of you, but you have to understand that once we go through those gates, I am your legate and your teacher, and nothing more. I will treat you no different than I would any of my other men, regardless of whose blood flows through your veins. Do you understand, Gaius?"

He didn't answer right away as he took one long look around, absorbing his surroundings, watching the people, listening to the wind, and thinking back to everything he left behind. Honestly, he did not know if he was ready for this.

But then the faces of Anthony and Julia flashed across his mind. He remembered the promise he made to her, and the brotherhood that he and Anthony had formed. He recalled his father's words to him before they left the house, retelling in his mind the importance of the armor plate that was strapped to Gaius' horse, and the legacy that it carried. He knew his childhood was over. He understood that much was going to be asked of him. He too knew it was his choice to ride through those gates.

With a heavy sigh, Gaius answered. "Yes. I am ready."

Valerius nodded as he turned his horse back and continued towards the barracks of the Sixth Legion.

Gaius glanced over his shoulder, staring for a long while to the north. A part of him was saying his goodbyes to where he came from. He wondered at this moment when he might return, if he ever would.

When the time was right, Gaius whispered, "Goodbye," to his old life and kicked his horse, urging it forward to his new home.

CHAPTER NINE

"Ten years, brother, ten long years and there it is," Mago said to his brother Hannibal as they stood shoulder-to-shoulder on horseback.

It was cold, more so than Hannibal had thought possible. Before him stood the peak of the Alps, which loomed like a monolithic wall that blocked him from his destiny. On the other side lies his bitter enemy, who for ten years since his sacking of Saguntum has stood beyond his reach, beckoning him with their arrogance and contempt for the rest of the world, to be vanquished. But, his senate at home had nearly hampered Hannibal's plans to carry out his father's dream of seeing Rome kneeling before Carthage. They, when Rome had sent its emissaries to Carthage a decade ago, broke under their threats. Since then, at a constant state of war with Rome, they had not turned Hannibal over to the republic as demanded, but neither did the home-country support his efforts to start war on Rome. As such, Hannibal had to build on his own successes – form alliances on his own from captured or mined gold from Spain, and forge new friendships through victory over the Gallic barbarians that stood in his way. Now, all that stood before him was the mountains – a natural barrier that had kept the Italian peninsula protected for generations from invading armies by land.

Further in the rear both Hannibal and Mago's attention was diverted by the noise from his war-elephants, which, despite their fearsome sizes and bravery were not adept for the cold climate of Europe. The creatures seemed to be in constant agony, four having already died as the army climbed higher – and yet, they hadn't even begun the march into the actual Alps as of yet.

"How many do you think will make it?" Mago asked.

"Not enough," Hannibal answered.

"I was referring to the men, not the beasts."

Hannibal starred at his brother for a long moment before he answered. Already, he had begun this journey from Spain in the spring with fifty-five thousand men, and due to barbarian attacks and disease he had lost eight thousand. But, he knew there would be many more to come – a whole lot more. The bitter, relentless cold, the brutal environment, and those Gallic tribes that call the Alps their home would make sure that tens of thousands of Hannibal's men would not live through the crossing.

"It does not matter, brother. Those that die are weak. I want only the strongest men for this campaign," Hannibal answered sharply.

"And if I am among the dead, brother?" Mago asked seriously.

Hannibal leered at Mago for a moment. He knew that Mago knew best to not try and draw sympathy from Hannibal. He loved his brother as much as he should, but he loved his dream of a conquered Rome with more passion than any thousand siblings.

"Do not test me, brother. We will need the strongest to challenge Rome's legions – not weak men that can't survive cold. That pertains to my family as well, Mago. Now, signal for the march to begin. I will wait no longer – rain or snow," Hannibal remarked as he kicked his horse, which galloped down the long formation of Carthaginian allied soldiers that had joined Hannibal's endeavor.

"As you command, brother."

*   *   *

Muscle and flesh collided with a loud *thump* as dust and sand was kicked up, mixing with the sweat that poured off of the two men who battled one another in a grueling match for dominance. Grunting, they fought for the best position to gain the advantage over the other. These two had fought like mountain goats as their large arms and equally large bodies locked

98

tightly before each man broke, staring intensely at each other as they breathed heavily. And then with a powerful yell, the two collided once again with so much force that it that they found it difficult to maintain their footing in the white sand.

Neither man showed the slightest hint of weakness. Back and forth they fought - breaking and colliding and countering the other's moves and locks, until finally, one gave in to the other's overwhelming strength.

One competitor was a giant of a man. He had short black hair that was cut close to his skull. His muscles, nearly as large as melons, were covered in sweat, which rolled in between the rippling folds of his arms, back and shoulders. His legs seemed as if they had been forged in fire, crafted from the finest iron, impossible to break.

The second man was shorter by a good eight inches. With short close-cropped blonde hair, this man's body was no less defined then the larger of the two. The height, however, was something the shorter man was having difficulties overcoming. He continually struggled to position his body in the stance that would allow him to overpower the larger man.

His youthful face was covered in sweat and showed the agony he was in as he began to lose any advantage he might have had when the two first locked together.

With an angry grunt of frustration, his grip slipped, just slightly. That, unfortunately, was all the large man needed as he grabbed hold of his opponent's wrist; twisting it until he broke the smaller man's hold entirely.

In one painful pull, the taller man lifted his opponent up and over his head before slamming him squarely onto his back.

Sand kicked up into the musty air as the defeated man lay still on his back, eyes closed, his entire body racked with pain. This had been the fourth time this afternoon he was put down so hard.

Opening his eyes, the sun glaring down, the defeated man lifted himself back to his feet as the victorious opponent laughed at his sorry and tired state. He wasn't alone as half a dozen men too joined the jubilation.

"Gods be dammed!" yelled the defeated man as he wiped sand off of his bare-chested body.

"You don't give yourself enough time to find the right moment to strike. You act too fast, Maurus," Gaius stated with a grin as he tried not to join his comrades in their amusement of his friend's continuous defeat.

"It isn't fair, Agrippa is the size of a horse," Maurus complained, which was nearly true.

"Since when does size matter?" Gaius replied.

"Oh, this coming from someone who is six-foot two. I, on the other hand am only good for chasing rats under the kitchen table," Maurus joked at his own expense as he again took to the center of the sand-cover arena, squaring off against Agrippa once more.

"You are pretty good at chasing rats, Maurus," Agrippa said with a humorous grin.

Once again, the two young soldiers faced one another.

Gaius stood off to the side – his arms crossed as he watched the two with careful eyes.

This day, like most, Gaius was overseeing the daily practice and training of his century. Two dozen other legionnaires, most of whom the same age as he, pitted against one another as they wrestled inside the large rectangular pit.

Each man fought in the nude, as they trained for three hours without rest. Already, as the day was just beginning, they still had another hour to go before they would move to another exercise.

Gaius did not join them this day as he, a senior officer and already most skilled among the group, watched and passed along his advice in order to help improve the soldiers skills, most of them new, having joined the Sixth Legion less than a year ago.

Most of his attention was, however, kept on Maurus and Agrippa.

Gaius raised his fist into the air and held it there for a few moments, before he quickly dropped it towards the mat.

Once he had given the indication for Maurus and Agrippa to begin, he stood back and careful studied Maurus, who rushed in and tried to quickly overpower the larger man.

With a thunderous clap of naked flesh, the two Romans collided. Each man's hand and arms violently fought as they reached for the best position to gain the early advantage. The sweat coming off their skin made their grip that much more difficult.

Maurus was considerable faster, and a damn good fighter. He normally took the first step in the battle, outpacing the slower and more cumbersome Agrippa. The problem was, Maurus tried too hard. Instead of using his strengths and natural gifts to bring the larger man down, he fought tooth and nail to muscle Agrippa onto his back.

While Maurus could defeat most men easily, he could not understand the concept of fighting a larger opponent. In his mind he had already lost before the bout had begun.

For over three minutes, the two fought. As before, Maurus would make the wrong move as he continued to attempt to overpower Agrippa.

Taking advantage of his size and strength, Agrippa allowed Maurus to make a fatal mistake, and then counter the error, always resulting in him flipping the young Roman onto his back, ending the bout.

With another loud *thump*, Maurus was thrown down, losing yet again where he was breathing heavily and refusing to get up.

"Are you dead?" Gaius asked as he stood over his downed friend.

"Yes, now leave me be and let the vultures have my flesh and bones," Maurus replied as he stared up at the slow-moving clouds.

"Good. Now get back up and start again." Gaius grabbed Maurus' wrist, lifting him back to his feet.

"I hate this sport. I do not wish to do it any longer. I am paid to carry a sword and shield, not fight bare-assed in the sand," Maurus complained.

"You will be thankful you know how to fight when you've lost your sword, and fighting a Greek hoplite in battle, hand-to-hand," Gaius commented with a smile.

Maurus grinned as he wiped away a trickle of blood from the corner of his mouth.

"Like a boy-loving Greek could ever disarm me."

"You might be surprised; the Greeks did invent this sport, and were once masters of the world."

"They don't have much to show for it now, do they?" Maurus slowly stepped back into the pit, falling into a fighting stance as he again stood across from Agrippa, lowering himself down into a three-quarter stance.

"I am Greek decent," Agrippa commented.

"I thought you from this neck of the woods, old boy?" Maurus mused.

Gaius smiled.

"Nearly everyone in the south of Italy is Greek decent. If only you showed as much care to history as you do your body hair, you may be a bloody legate by now. Now, let's try to show some improvement before dinner, shall we?" Gaius joked as he dropped his fist for the two to begin.

Once more the two young Romans collided, but this time Gaius' attention was turned elsewhere as messenger rode into the compound and galloped towards Valerius' office.

This rider had been the third one this week and while the contents of what they carried was private, everyone in the camp, including Gaius, had some idea what the fuss was about.

There were rumors spreading across the countryside that trouble was coming from the north. A Carthaginian general was moving fifty thousand men down through the Alps, and would enter Italy in a few weeks.

Gaius was now twenty-three, and he felt he was ready to defend Rome if word came from the senate that the republic was going to war. He had studied hard, harder than most in the legion and thought himself ready as any veteran in the Sixth Legion.

He still recalled the promise he made to his father the day he left home with Valerius: he had vowed to make the man proud and do his very best to be a proper soldier like his father was, and to this day, from the moment he walked through the camp gates, he had done everything that had been asked of him.

While he legally couldn't join the legion until he was sixteen, he spent those first three years in Valerius' shadow, learning and watching the old legate's every move. When his training began Gaius found he had a natural talent in many forms of warfare. He easily bested men twice his age in numerous forms of soldiering: wrestling, swordsmanship, horsemanship, boxing, and most important, tactics, strategy and command. Because of these skills he was made an optio when he was seventeen – greatly due to his ability to also read and write. Two years later he was made a junior centurion and giving command of his own century. Currently, Valerius had him assigned to the first cohort of the legion, where his promotion continued to climb. The old man seemly wanted Gaius to stay near him as he came of age, grooming him to perhaps one day take command of the legion itself.

He knew that Valerius had great faith in him, and would one day entrust him to lead the Wolves. That was an honor that both excited and scared Gaius greatly, most of all because he could not imagine living to see a day that Valerius did not command this legion.

Gaius' thoughts return to his duties as he heard another loud *thump*, as a body hit the mat.

Taking a deep breath, without having to turn his head to see who lay on his back, he called out, "Again. And do try to win a match while we're still young, Maurus."

Later that evening Gaius walked into Valerius' office and stood quietly at attention, standing in the doorway as he waited to be called forward.

He watched his old mentor pack several maps into a stack of satchels, assisted by two young aides who rushed around quickly from shelve to shelve.

Ten years ago when he first met Valerius, he seemed as frightening as a titan. Gone now was the burly, haze-eyed brute that donned a thick grey beard. Replaced, Valerius had in him the fire of a teenager.

He was clean-shaven, although there were still some streaks of grey running through his short hair, and a few extra lines under his eyes. He moved and acted with a renewed sense of purpose, which gave Gaius hints about why he had been summoned.

The legate's eyes were locked on one map. From Gaius' vantage, it seemed to be a detailed map of northern Italy. The two aides, no more than fourteen, rummaged through the shelves that were filled with other documents. They were busy sorting, collecting and categorizing them into small travel bags that would be moved with Valerius' command. Gaius smiled as the boys glanced over at him. It wasn't too long ago when he was in their shoes, doing errands for Valerius or the other officers of the legion. The work was tedious and thankless, but they were learning important lessons, even if they hadn't realized it yet.

One of the aides, a young dark-haired boy fumbled as he was carrying an arm full of documents, most of which seemed to be dealing with the payroll for the legion.

The papers rained down onto the floor, turning Valerius' attention away from his work.

"Dammit, boy! Pick those up and be more mindful of what you are doing, or by the gods, I'll send you back to the whore of a mother of yours," Valerius yelled.

"Yes, legate, sir. I apologize," the boy repeated several times over as he franticly dropped to his knees and quickly collected the papers.

"Centurion," Valerius said without even raising his head to look at Gaius. "I want the first cohort ready to march first thing in the morning. Have them in full kit and enough rations for two weeks."

"It will be done, sir," Gaius responded obediently.

He did not move or say anything more even thought it was clear those were all the orders Valerius wanted to issue at the moment.

Valerius lifted his gaze; his eyes showing signs that the old Roman hadn't slept for a full day now.

"Is there something else on your mind, Centurion Gaius?"

"Yes sir, if I may ask. What is our destination?" Gaius quickly replied without hesitation. Even though he and Valerius showed each other the proper formalities that was expected of any legionnaire, they still had an easy relationship with one another that Gaius knew he could ask anything of the legate and probably get an answer.

"You may ask, but that does not mean you will get an answer." Valerius leered at Gaius with cold eyes, a stare that would have made other officers nervous, but Gaius held his ground with an unmoved expression. He was as eager, if not more so than anyone else to know what was going on. War, was, after all what these men had trained for their entire lives.

Valerius snorted.

"The Senate is having a special session in four days. My presence has been requested in Rome, and the legion placed on standby," he finally answered.

"Then it is true, we are going to war with Carthage?" Gaius asked, his question shared by the whole legion, who waited eagerly to hear if the rumors spreading were true or not.

"It is not for me to decide such things, lad. However, if I were a betting man, I would say we are. It was bound to happen sooner or later," Valerius answered with an unwavering reply. While he would never say it, Gaius could see in the legate's actions that he was excited as well. He'd been stagnate for too long – away from a real fight for years, with only hunting pirates and putting down tiny Greek rebellions to occupy his decades since the last war with Carthage.

Gaius tried to hold back his smile, managing only a faint grin.

"Then, if I may inquiry further, sir. Why only one cohort? Won't the rest of the Sixth be needed if up north if Hannibal is crossing the Alps?"

Valerius stared at Gaius, knowing full well he had not mentioned the particulars of the message or what is transpiring in the Alps as they spoke. But, as he fought to hold back his smile, he knew that Gaius was smarter than he had ever been, and had deduced that knowledge from careful observation.

"The Senate is fearful of a possible Carthaginian naval invasion of either Sicily or southern Italy. If that is to happen, than the Sixth needs to be on call and ready to respond the moment the first whore-sons set foot on our territory."

"Even if the fight is in the north?" Gaius asked, sounding disappointed.

"Other legions will be levied. We have our orders, centurion. Now, if there isn't anything else that is pondering your young mind, carry out my orders and have the first cohort ready to move by sunrise. You are dismissed."

"Yes, sir," Gaius saluted before he turned and quickly left Valerius' office, keeping his smile from being too obvious, only with difficulty.

As he walked outside, Gaius saw Maurus was already waiting for him before he quickly ran over, a big cheerful grin on his face.

"Well?" Maurus eager asked.

"Well what?"

"You know what I mean. Are we going to war or not?"

"My word, Maurus, I think you should see the medicos. You look terrible," Gaius observed as the deep bruises on his friend's face had swollen to large purple welts. He hated to think what the rest of his body looked like by now, but the young soldier shrugged it off, too excited by the news that Gaius was withholding.

"Forget that. Just answer my original question: *are we going to war*?"

Gaius chuckled, "Yes, or so it would seem. The first cohort is heading for Rome tomorrow, and the rest of the legion is on standby, until further orders are giving. So, it would appear the rumors are true, for once, the enemy is coming to our home, and we're going to stop them."

Maurus couldn't hold back his cheer as he beat his fists into the sky, hollering at the top of his lungs.

"Oh, such wonderful news. Finally, those Carthaginian bastards will fill the iron of the Wolves once again. And off too Rome, how grand, you'll get to see home again, my dear friend."

Gaius' smile hardened sudden as Maurus' words resonated deeply through his mind. It had not dawned on him until now – *home*, he would be going home.

"I will not keep you, my friend. I will go tell the boys the news. I doubt, however, very many of us will be getting much sleep tonight."

Maurus ran off, still joyful as he quickly spread the news across the whole camp. For Gaius, however, the excitement of the moment had escaped him as he walked toward one of the larger structures in the camp, needing to be alone so he may be with his own thoughts a moment longer.

Grabbing a lantern that hung on the wall near the entrance of the stables, Gaius walked down the narrow path that was centered between two rows of holding pins that housed the army's horses. When he reached the one he was moving toward, Gaius opened the gate where his horse, a black coated stallion, which he named Apollo, raised his head with interest as Gaius stepped inside, hanging the light on the wall.

The horse lifted his ears and nodded his head as Gaius ran his hand along Apollo's neck.

"Hello, my friend, guess what?" Gaius spoke softly.

Apollo, whom Gaius had named in honor of his father, recalling the story that Valerius had told him ten years ago near the camp fire, about his father's bravery, of course did not respond as he nudged his master, indicating that he wanted Gaius to continue rubbing his neck.

"We are going to Rome," Gaius finished, his voice still low. In the distance, he could hear the beginnings of celebration as word had spread quickly about the prospects of going to war.

Most of the legion was young – legionaries from sixteen to twenty-two, with a few hundred older veterans, yet few who saw action during the last war. So, with excitement, the Sixth was eager to prove itself in doing what it had been trained for, glorious war. Gaius' mind was, however, trapped in the past. It hadn't dawned on him that he would be going home, back to Rome until Maurus had said as such. Now, his thoughts plagued him with memories of Anthony and Julia, who had never been far from his mind.

Sometimes he could go weeks, even months without thinking about them over the past ten years. But, there were days, such as this one that he couldn't stop his restless mind from recalling them, however, it was his fears that consumed them – the chance that he may actually get to see them again.

"I wonder what they are like now. Anthony was only a year younger than me – how he must have grown. And his sister, Julia – I've told you about her, haven't I?" Gaius mussed.

Again, Apollo failed to reply.

"She must be sixteen now. I wonder what has become of her, how beautiful she must be now, nearly a woman – a Roman lady."

Gaius felt silly, not because he was speaking with his horse, but at the memories of the girl he only remembered as a frightened child that had cried in his arms when he left home.

"I wonder if she even remembers me. So much time has gone by. I'm not so different, am I?" Apollo lifted his head, staring at Gaius with his big brown eyes. "I am being silly, aren't I? We were children, and she was much younger than I. Our time together was brief, less than a year. How can I expect either of them to recall a distant friend they hardly knew?"

Gaius knew that he could not expect their memories of him to be as cherished as his. They had lives of their own; years to make new friends, to fall in and out of love. He couldn't help but feel selfish and arrogant to think that he meant as much to them as they did to him.

"I should not worry about such things, should I? We might be going to war soon. I've trained and I've excelled at becoming a soldier. I have a duty to my men and to my country, and yet, I can't stop thinking of them – of her."

Gaius put his head down on his horse's neck, rubbing its fur with his hand as he asked his last question.

"Tell me, Apollo, am I a fool for being in love with a dream?"

Gaius waited, but Apollo only made a faint noise that was either disagreement, or a statement that he was indeed a fool. Which it was, he could only guess.

"Thanks, you are a lot of help, you know that," Gaius smiled as he went back to brushing his horse. Outside, the camp made preparations for war. What would come next filled Gaius' young mind with all sorts of possibilities. At the very least, he would get the chance to see Rome again. He wondered how much the city had grown since his last visit.

In three days time, he would know.

CHAPTER TEN

A harsh wind cut through the city just as thick gray clouds opened and unleashed their captive water, which seemed to fall like buckets down onto the sooty paved streets.

The rain beaded off Gaius' red cloak as if it was in retreat the moment it touched him. The discomfort wasn't enough to impair the joy that he felt, to be back in the grand city he had only visited once in his youth. Nothing about Rome seemed to have changed from last he remembered; running through the streets as a boy, enjoying all the wonders his young mind hadn't experienced before. Only now, his perspective was different as he looked at his city with older eyes.

He wore full armor, the same dark leather plate that his father had given him ten years ago, when he left home for the Sixth Legion. A long red cape draped down from his shoulders and wrapped around the hindquarters of his horse. Apollo, himself, trotted in a slow rhythmic pattern as if the animal believed he was on parade; the hooves of Valerius' steed, who rode beside Gaius, echoed down the crowded streets, causing all who stood before them to step aside as they headed towards the great forum, in the heart of the city, and while not customary to ride horses in the city, Valerius wanted to reach the senate without pause.

A week ago Gaius had been frightened by the prospect of returning to Rome. Now, he could hardly contain his excitement as he caught himself talking in every sight and sound, with the same enthusiasm he had when he was twelve.

Valerius, on the other hand did not have any interest in the city, and in fact, he loath it. Gaius knew the old Roman well enough to know that he preferred the open country to the artificial stone and wooden structures and narrow streets of the city. He might defend Rome to his last breath, but walking through it was another matter.

Valerius kept his attention forward. A tight-ridged expression that Gaius had lovingly become used to over the years was present on his weathered face. It was painfully clear that he wanted to hurry and get to the senate, and be done with his duty, and off to join the campaign.

Gaius tried his best to follow his mentor's example. He rode tall atop his horse and gripped the reins firmly; chin held high like an officer on display. Even the continuing annoyance of the dripping water from the brim of his helmet was ignored. Still, despite his best efforts, he found that his attention continued to drift from one sight to the next as it had done when he was younger.

The streets, even with the heavy rainfall, were filled with hundreds of people who shopped or ate at the numerous stands that lined the busy corners. There seemed to be a pub or brothel on every block, Gaius noted, and not a single one seemed short of business.

One brothel caught his gaze as he rode by. It was quite elegant, made from white stone and freshly painted red wood. Out front stood several beautiful women who chatted to each other, or enticed only the wealthiest of men to enter their establishment, with wooing comments of great pleasures and wondrous exploitations of the flesh they won't soon forget.

The women wore silk dresses that were cut low around their breasts, and had slits that showed their long and shapely legs. They adorned themselves with a wide assortment of jewels in their ears and or around their necks. Most wore bright colored wigs of red, blonde, black or other assorted colors that weren't natural to the female body. However, most engaging about them was their odor; their exotic perfume carried over the street, drawing any man to them like a Sirens' call.

One woman caught Gaius' eye in particular. She was an extremely beautiful young lady with long, waist-length black hair. Her skin was tanned and seemed softer then a bed of feathers as long lashes, heavy with black mascara wrapped around her piercing eyes, giving her an exotic, foreign look.

She watched Gaius as he rode past her, never taking her eyes off the young officer.

He smiled at her with a boyish grin, which she returned pleasantly.

So focused on this woman, Gaius veered his horse into Valerius' own animal as both horses neighed and nipped at each other. This quickly brought Gaius' attention from his fantasy as he corrected his error.

Valerius looked oddly at him, not saying a word as Gaius quietly voiced his apologies.

Valerius grunted his reply, knowing all too well what had caught his young officer's eye.

Looking back over his shoulder Gaius saw the exotic woman giggling with the girls that stood with her, before she glanced back over towards him, still with a big smile on her face.

He continued to watch her until his vision was obstructed by the dense crowds, disappointed. He suddenly realized that some things were indeed quite different than the last time he was in the city – things his eyes couldn't have appreciated ten years ago, now served only to pique his curiosity as he wondered what other hidden gems Rome held tucked away.

Slowly, the narrow streets began to open as they rode into the great Forum of Rome, which house the senate, the Temple of Jupiter and other assorted government and religious buildings.

The forum was filled with thousands of people as dozens of small shops had been set up where merchants sold items from all across the Mediterranean and beyond: rugs from Persia, silk from Africa, Slaves from all corners of the known world, each auctioned in open markets as hundreds of buyers eagerly placed bets on the best bodies, strongest men, youngest boys or shapely women.

In the distance Gaius could see a large wooden structure that housed an open theater. Currently a play was being shown to the crowd of adults and children that laughed and jeered at the performance of a strange looking man, who wore a multi-colored dress and white painted face. He carried an over-sized shield and sword. His hair was colored gold and was curled. Top his head was an unpleasant helmet that was adorned with large white feathers. In his crotch, hung a huge fake penis that the actor frequently waved and pointed towards the audience, drawing waves of cheers and laughter from them; its meaning completely lost on Gaius as he watched from afar.

Two bare-breasted women ran around the stage as a very short man, only as tall as a small boy, perused them with his hands held out, trying to grab them from behind.

The tiny man was dressed in the fashion of a Persian king, dark clothing with long black curled hair and a thick beard. He acted like a clown as he chased the two women, who screamed out until finally, the gold-locked man stepped between them, and smacked the short king over his head with the fake sword, and then poked him with his oversized penis as the little man fell.

The king dropped to his knees and began to plead for his life. The hero, however, stood over him and waved his prop over the defeated man's head.

The crowd loved all of it even though not a word had been uttered on stage, but soon Gaius began to recognize some of the similarities in the play as the story of Alexander the Greats conquest of the Persian Empire.

He smiled even though he felt that the historic interpretation of the actors was terribly wrong.

"The people don't seem to be too concerned about the prospect of war," Gaius commented to Valerius as the two stepped down from their horses once they reached the Roman senate.

"Bah. War is only an inconvenience to most of these people. Nothing that would actually affect their mood; and besides, most the dying will come from the allies anyways," Valerius snarled.

Gaius looked up at the senate. The large structure that hosed the power behind the republic wasn't entirely what he was expecting, as the Curia wasn't grand or set high upon a hill like the Acropolis in Greece. It looked more like a large house, built in a simple fashion, set against some of the most important structures in Rome. It was painted red and purple and adorned with flowers. Banners of the republic draped down the side of the building, while the two large heavy wooden doors that led into the senate were currently wide open, indicating that session was in order and any citizen was technically invited to listen to the hearings, although, most did not bother or dared to step foot inside.

Still, Gaius did not let his imagination overshadow the importance of the building. He knew inside were the most powerful men in Rome – those that commanded the loyalty of the people and the army, governed the provinces, and ensured that Rome's light shined the brightest in the world. And, while the senate did not make or pass the laws, their collective voices helped shape the course of Rome's future.

Gaius was so intrigued by the senate building that he failed to notice what greeted him.

Along the base of the walls was a row of beggars, many of whose hands were stretched out as they pleaded for coins from the numerous citizens passing by.

The wretched souls looked as if they had just crawled out from their own graves, and took residence in front of the symbol of power. Their clothing was a mix of tattered rags and patch-work of other garments and as Gaius came closer to them, their smell was unbearable, which was made worse by the rain.

Most of the men, far too sad and miserable to look at, seemed to be living ghosts, their faces pale and hair matted. All of them looked older than their true age would have testified to.

Their wary eyes stared up at Gaius as he was force to walk passed them in order to reach the senate doors. A few of the beggars raised their hands out towards him, asking without words for a few coins. Gaius, feeling sick from their smell, ignored them as he held his breath and continued up the steps.

As he reached the senate doors, he let out a gasp and breathed in fresh air. Even now, he was still able to smell their filth. It made him want to throw up. He was ashamed that a man could let their lives fall to such ruin that he wished they would just go away, swept down the gutters like the trash, carried off by the rain water.

Gaius was about to speak to Valerius, who he assumed was still with him; no doubt having to also hold his breath and hurriedly climb the senate steps to avoid the beggars. However, when he looked back Valerius was nowhere to be seen.

And then Gaius saw him, strangely standing at the base of the steps talking to several of the beggars, seemly asking a pair of men questions.

Gaius couldn't hear what was being said, not over the rain and the chorus of voices that carried over the forum. A moment later he watched as Valerius reached to his belt, removing a small leather bag that was attached to his waist, before tossing it, along with its contents of silver to the three men.

Gaius was dumbfounded as he watched the beggars rise to their feet, shake Valerius' hand before they ran off, pushing through the bodies of citizens before disappearing from view.

"Who were those men? Did you know them?" Gaius asked as Valerius climbed the steps and joined him.

"I do not know. Just soldiers, like you and I."

"What? Are you serious?" Gaius asked, the shock on his face evident as he looked back down at the beggars, studying them with careful attention. A number of them were indeed wearing the red tunics, although now badly faded and stained, of the legion.

"It is a disgrace that they have allowed themselves to fall so far." Gaius spat as his eyes drifted away from the former legionnaires and back towards Valerius.

"Do not fault them, Gaius. Not ever man was made to serve the legions, or has the body and mind to come home, after living through and seeing what most men will never experience."

"Regardless, what makes you think they won't spend the money you gave them on drink and women?" Gaius asked.

"I don't know, and I do not care. It is no longer my money," Valerius replied plainly.

"A waste of coin if you ask me," Gaius commented rudely.

"Then it is a good thing I did not ask for your permission." Valerius' tone was controlled, not holding Gaius' empty words too heart, but he was firm nonetheless.

"Come; stop straining yourself on matters your young mind can't possibly understand right now. You've yet to see a senatorial session. Wait until it has concluded, then your outlook on Roman life will be even more distorted than it is now."

Gaius did not reply as he stared at Valerius with a questionable expression before the legate of the Sixth escorted him inside.

Inside three hundred senators sat tightly, shoulder-to-shoulder on two sets of elevated stone benches. Their combined voices echoed over the marble and limestone chamber as they debated without pause about Rome's most pressing issues, which were numerous, beyond that of the approaching army, led by Hannibal.

Two seats sat in the center of the chamber. There, the two co-consuls would have sat, but on this day only Consul Gaius Flaminius was present as his counterpart was out of the city.

The chamber was well lit; the sweat smell of the oil that burned filled the room as Gaius and Valerius walked quietly, making sure not to interrupt the proceedings. Several other officers also stood towards the back, where they listened quietly.

As Gaius spend the next couple hours listening, the day's proceedings had been filled with debates on taxes, shipping and trade issues with several Greek states, piracy, plague, grain shortages in distant territories, and of course, finally, Hannibal and his alliance of barbarian northerners making their way down across the Alps.

Speaking now was an older senator that looked to be in his late sixties. He held the folds of his toga in one hand, while the other he brandished violently in the air as he spoke, dramatically.

"The destruction of Saguntum by the Carthaginian, Hannibal ten years ago was a clear sign that his government, which has already refused our demands for justice, has always been seeking war with the Republic," the senator named Quintus spoke loud enough for all to hear him. Numerous senators added their angry voices to his claims as he continued once the roars lessened.

"Now, reports tell us that Hannibal has amassed an army of fifty thousand, many of whom are Gallic barbarians that have sworn their service to him, as long as he promises them Rome. Hannibal's intentions are very clear: with his army, he will threaten the whole of Italy once he has completed his journey across the Alps, and yet, this Senate will do nothing in response to this act of aggression!"

"We sent an envoy to Carthage, numerous times since Saguntum's fall," one senator spoke up, trying to defend the actions of those that did not support the call for war.

"And they continually refused our demands for peace, have they not?" Quintus asked which was followed by an uproar of anger.

"We offered them peace, and they refused it," another man proclaimed.

"We must still try to continue with peace talks. The actions of Hannibal are not the desires of Carthage. Even they have acknowledged this much to us."

"Yet, they support him!" a voice called out.

"We cannot hold a whole country accountable for the actions of one man. If this Senate declares war on Carthage, a war we are in no position to fight right now, then our enemies, those nearer to us, will act. It is the continuing conflicts in Greece and Macedonia that we need to focus our attention on, not some renegade general and his band of barbarian followers," Liberius announced, but quickly his cautious words were drowned out by the supporters for war.

"You only care about your grain shipments, and not the honor of your country, Liberius!" Senator Appius yelled as he challenged his colleague's loyalty to Rome; his words caused another outburst between the two factions.

"We cannot ignore the threats from Greece, nor can we deny that the Carthaginians have brought war to our lands once again," a new voice stood as he tried to be the voice of reason.

"Agreed!" yelled both factions, as each believed the words were in support of their point of view.

Consul Flaminius raised his hands, begging for his fellow representatives to be silent as he rose to his feet.

"Nobel senators, I do not wish war with Carthage. The last conflict our two nations shared was bloody, and cost the lives of many of our finest men. It is true that the protection of our grain shipments from Greece and the East take priority over the threat that Hannibal poses."

Numerous hecklers erupted as those that support the cause for war responded to what the consul was saying.

Flaminius again raised his hands and asked for silence.

"However, this act of aggression by a single man cannot go unpunished."

Cheers replaced the negative jeers as the volume in the chambers rose higher.

"If our enemies see that Rome takes no action to defend our allies, and punish those responsible for defying the Republic's laws, then we as a nation would have proven that we are not up to the task of crushing even the tiniest insect, or protecting our friends. For this, Hannibal and his barbarian horde must be crushed, and Carthage, taught a lesson it shall never forget!"

The sound of applause and cheering was deafening as three hundred senators stood to their feet in support of Flaminius. Even those that had been opposed to war quickly reconsidered their position; it would not be patriotic to stand against the consul.

"I will send word for Consul Publius Cornelius Scipio raise an army and march them north, and cut Hannibal's advance into our territories," Flaminius proclaimed. "Once Scipio has dealt with this unprovoked aggression, we shall send Hannibal's head back to his country!"

For several minutes the senate commemorated Flaminius' call for war. Already the bloodlust within the house was beginning to boil and would soon reach the streets outside where thousands of citizens and freedmen would eagerly be waiting to hear the news.

The prospect of such a large war was frightening to Gaius, and yet exciting. He was young and had trained for such a day. But as he looked over towards Valerius, expecting the old general to be beaming with excitement, his mentor's face was blank, and his eyes filled with concern and disappointment.

"How many legions will be sent?" a senator cried out.

"Hannibal is but one man with an army of barbarians. We do not need to combine our legions to deal with him. So, we shall leave this victory to Scipio and his men, as they are already nearer to the border, and have more experience in dealing with the Gauls than anyone in this room," Flaminius replied as he sat back down.

"Only one legion? Are you mad?" a chorus of voices spoke up, but their concerns were drowned by the overwhelming supporters.

"Bah, he just wants Scipio out of Rome. The bloody fool cares nothing about stopping Hannibal. If there was glory in it, he would be leading the army himself," Valerius mumbled quietly to himself.

Gaius stared nervously over at him, seeing that a number of the other officers too agreed with the veteran's statement. They had marched with the men to Rome, expecting to be called upon to confront Hannibal, now it seems they weren't needed, or were going to be sent elsewhere to protect wealthy men's purses.

After a few closing statements from other senators, they began to exit into the forum, where crowds had formed at the steps of the senate, waiting to hear about the day's proceedings.

Gaius remained with Valerius as he spoke to his colleagues, expressing their concern privately to each other. Already it seemed they were planning their own strategy in case the worst should happen, and Hannibal breaks through Scipio's legion. For the moment, at least, the Sixth would be staying put, which disappointed Gaius more than he figured it would.

Gaius' attention was turned as he heard his named suddenly called among the crowd of senators and advisors that had gathered, speaking openly among themselves.

At first he did not recognize the man that called his name, as he stepped through the crowd, a joyful, surprised expressing on his face, and spoke again.

"Gaius? By Jupiter's beard, is that really you?"

"Anthony?" Gaius questioned before he too recognized his boyhood friend.

Anthony stopped before Gaius, holding him in his hands as he looked taller, larger man over in careful detail; the smile on his face was ear-to-ear.

"Look at you. You really did it. A real, honest to gods' soldier of Rome," Anthony said with a prideful voice as he embraced Gaius.

"And you, a senator of all things."

Anthony laughed. "Hardly; I'm too young. I leave that to my father, but I do, someday, have to follow in his footsteps, so it seems. So all I do is sit quietly and let him do all the talking, like a good puppet. I never get to take part in all the excitement. However, it is a start, I suppose."

While the two friends were nearly the same age, they couldn't have grown more different. Anthony was a head shorter than Gaius. He had a thin build, smaller in size by a considerable margin to the well-toned and muscular Gaius. His face was more youthful, with soft skin. His build was lanky, a body pleasing to most young women. Clearly he hadn't seen a hard day's work in his life as he was unblemished by the heat of the sun or the crack of a centurion's vine-cane.

"The senate can't be that bad, can it?" Gaius asked.

"Ah, my friend, I'm afraid that the Rome we grew up dreaming of is a far lesser thing than we imagined. This city is harsh, and so is its politics. Take what you heard today. What our dear consular said is only the tip of the spear. He will hang Scipio out to dry – if he fails, he loses favor, allowing Flaminius to take the glory when he marches his own army north to stop Hannibal. But if Scipio wins, then he doesn't receive as much praise: he only crushed a rogue general and his band of barbarians, and Flaminius still stands tall as he moves against Carthage. Regardless, he gets what he wants at the expense of our men."

Anthony leaned closer to Gaius and whispered, "Truthfully, almost everyone here is my age. Politics does terrible things to a man's youth. It is a very slow and painful death," Anthony laughed.

Gaius managed a false smile. He was beginning to see that Rome, the eternal city of light he'd grown up believing in, was indeed becoming something else entirely. There were harsh realities that his eyes had opened up to this day, as Rome seemed a city of horrible contradictions.

"You are in position to make change, are you not?" Gaius asked.

"Perhaps, someday; however, as I said, politics is a game, a rather difficult and dangerous one too. I have to play it by its rules or risk being swallowed up by it. I must admit, I envy you, my friend. At least your enemies won't slit your throat while you sleep." Anthony's words were friendly, but Gaius could hear in the undertone the unfortunate truth.

"Anthony! Come, it is time we leave," one of the older senators called out.

Anthony turned to face his father, his face beaming with excitement.

"Father, come over here and see who has graced us with his presence."

Varro looked puzzled for a moment, not sure whom he was looking at as he walked over and stood next to his son. But then he recalled the young man that stood before him, as his eyes widen with genuine admiration.

"Young Gaius, is that really you?"

"Senator Varro, I am pleased to see you are doing well, sir."

"Well, look at you, an officer in Rome's legions, and one of Valerius' Wolves too. Well done, my boy."

"I am honored to serve Rome, and the Sixth Legion, sir."

"As you should be, he is famed and respected, even among us older senators. I'll tell you what, I'm having a get-together with a few friends at my city estate, and I would be honored if you could attend this evening as my guest."

"Yes, that would be a brilliant idea, father," Anthony eagerly spoke.

"Oh, I don't know. I wouldn't wish to impose. We are only in the city for a short while," Gaius replied, as he wasn't sure he was ready for this sudden reunion.

Anthony leaned closer to him and spoke softly into Gaius' ear.

"Julia will be there. I know for a fact that she will be very excited to see you again, after so many years apart."

Gaius' posture suddenly changed at hearing Anthony speak of his sister. His mind worked out what his answer would be as he wanted, needed to see her again. However, the prospect also frightened him terribly. Nevertheless, he gave his answer with a warm smile.

"Then, I will make the effort to come."

"Excellent. Until tonight," Varro said before he turned and rejoined his fellow senators.

"I think he likes you better than me," Anthony jokingly commented as he placed his hand on Gaius' shoulder. "Unfortunately, I have too much boring work that needs taken care of, and so little time to do it. So, I must take my leave, old friend. Tonight, around six, the same house we stayed in during our first trip to Rome as boys. You do remember where it is, don't you?" Anthony asked.

"I think I can manage," Gaius replied warmly.

"Wonderful. Until tonight," Anthony turned and quickly rejoined his father as they exited the senate, along with a dozen other men behind them.

"Until tonight," Gaius replied with a soft voice. He took a deep breath, already birds swirled in his stomach at the thought of seeing Julia again. Already ideas to find excuses to escape the dinner ran through his mind. Regardless, however, he knew he wanted to see her, despite his fears, so he would do what was asked of him and man-up. What was the worst that could happen – she'd grown fat?

CHAPTER ELEVEN

The night air was cool and had a pleasant aroma of fresh rainfall, which for the time had washed the filth from the city, at least on the surface; in the morning, the smell of trash and excrement would return.

Gaius walked down one of the countless mazes that made up the streets of Rome. The night was dark, which made every step a careful one. A few torches lit his path, but they did not help his journey much. While he was a stranger to these streets, he did not have much trouble finding his destination. Varro' estate stood along a stretch of road that was dominated by numerous wealthy homes and businesses. Currently, he was less than two blocks from the gates.

He did not entirely feel comfortable about being out alone. While the streets of Rome were relatively safe during the day, at night, it was a different story. These narrow corridors were famous for hunters that emerged after dawn. Muggers and rape gangs preyed on the unsuspecting. A few hurried footsteps and peering eyes from within the surrounding darkness would from time to time catch Gaius' attention. Most of them were harmless, but every few blocks or so he could hear ominous whispers from the shadows.

He wore no armor of any kind but only a long red cloak, which signaled him to be a soldier. This for the most part was what kept those prying eyes away from him, if any of the men behind those stares had other intentions, and if there was trouble, Gaius kept his right hand firmly on the hilt of his sword, which hung loosely down beside his hip. A small dagger also was kept behind his back, both of which he was more than comfortable using if he needed them.

There was a part of him, as he neared the estate of Senator Varro that wanted to be attack. He was young and had trained for years in the art of warfare and single combat. However, Gaius had never had the opportunity to truly test his abilities outside of training, nor had he killed a man since joining the Sixth. But that didn't mean that Gaius was a stranger to death. In ten years since joining the legion he had witnessed a number of accidences and fights that ended in one or more men dead. He, himself had been cut a number of times that if not attended to by the camp doctor, he would have bled to death.

As it would stand, no one dared challenge him this night as the gates to Varro' home came in sight.

After Gaius knocked on the hard wooden gate, a small hinged door opened and allowed an old man's eyes to peer out.

"Announce yourself stranger," the man demanded.

"I am Centurion Lucius Gaius," a sense of pride filled his words. "I am here by invitation from Anthony, son of this manor and senator of Rome."

When he finished his address, the small door closed with a hard *thud* as the old man backed away. A moment later Gaius listened as the sounds of heavy iron bars were removed from behind the gate, before it swung open, just enough for Gaius to enter.

Standing behind the gate stood a short man, bowing his head slightly as Gaius stepped inside.

"Greetings, and welcome Master Gaius; Master Anthony is expecting you. If you would please follow me, I will take you to him with haste," the old servant now said with the utmost respect.

Gaius followed the slave through the courtyard. To his right he noticed several stables that currently held four horses of expensive breeding. Two boys tended to the animals, taking the moment to glance behind them and stare at the soldier who walked through the yard.

Slave living quarters were set to the far left of the high stone wall that surrounded the whole property. The estate, like many in the city was built like a small fortress, meant to keep people in as much as out.

Six guards patrolled the grounds. One man, whom had a long scar running across his face, kept his eyes on Gaius as he stood in front of the main entrance. The men were big and burly, meant to intimidate on sight. Gaius noted that the man by the door had a brand on his inner right arm, indicating that he once was a gladiator; a normal practice by Rome's wealthy elite to hire the famed champions of the arena as bodyguards.

The slave then turned before leading Gaius further inside, and held out his hands, palms up. "I will require you to relinquish your weapons, sir."

Gaius was hesitant for a moment, but the slave's old eyes were firm as he did not budge from his posture.

Gaius did as he was asked, first removing his sword from his waste, and then pulling his dagger out from behind his belt before handing each over to the slave carefully.

The man's expression returned to his normal cheerful demeanor as he turned and handed the weapons over to a female slave that stood by the doorway.

"Thank you, sir. You are free to enter. Master Anthony is expecting you and should greet you shortly."

"What of the lady of the house?" Gaius asked.

The old man smiled oddly, as if he was in on some privet joke.

"Lady Julia is present."

Gaius nodded as he stepped over the threshold, glancing back for a moment as the slave went back outside to man the gate, probably waiting for the rest of the guests to arrive.

The air was warm and comfortable as opposed to the stiff breeze outside, and while Gaius had been in the house once before, ten years ago he was still easily impressed with the elaborate and tasteful décor of the interior, which seemed to have been remodeled, perhaps several times over since he last walked through these halls.

Gold-capped columns were placed throughout the large interior that received all guests. The cleanliness was heavenly as the stone marble floor gleamed brilliantly from the numerous torches that cast their flickering light across the open spaces. Opulent furniture, tables and statues were scattered throughout the front room, while a low-lying marble pool, touched with floating flower peddles center the floor.

Along the far wall, leading into another set of rooms were the death masks of generations past, decadents of Anthony and Julia's family. Gold and copper bowls of fresh fruit, and scented oils filled the room with a sweet aroma that swirled around Gaius, begging him to enter further.

"Gaius!" Anthony called out as he turned the corner, where a cheerful chorus of voices could be heard behind him. A big smile quickly formed on his face as he raced over towards his waiting guest.

"It does my heart wonders to see my brother back in Rome," Anthony exclaimed with a beaming smile as he embraced Gaius; a full cup of wine in one hand, which he was careful to hold away from Gaius' fine red cloak.

"It is good to see you as well, my brother," Gaius replied.   Anthony stood back and shook his head, amused as he looked Gaius over, taking in every detail as if his eyes could barely believe what he was seeing.

"I still cannot get over seeing you like this. How can this be the boy that I beat at every turn with our wooden swords?" Anthony laughed with a delightful grin.

"Oh, your memory is deluded with fantasy, my friend. I do recall that I won more than my share of engagements," Gaius smiled.

Anthony laughed again as he clapped his arms around Gaius once more, unable to hold back his excitement to see his friend finally after ten years apart.

"I think that military stew has clouded your mind," Anthony added.

"Then perhaps we can test our skills again and renew our contest."

"I would welcome the challenge. Come, you must regale me with the many marvelous adventures you've been on since last we saw one another," Anthony said as he escorted Gaius further into the house, leading him to where the other party-goers were gathered.

"There isn't much to tell, I'm afraid. I eat, I sleep, I train and then I repeat it all the next morning."

"Oh come now, I'm certain there is more to a soldier's life than that. The details of your womanly conquests alone must be worthy of tales written by Homer."

Gaius couldn't help but burst out laughing at the serious tone in Anthony's voice.

"Well, I suppose it would be worthy of a poem or two. There were the Brutus sisters a few winters ago."

The two old friends continued to talk before Anthony led Gaius to the arboretum, where a dozen men and their wives and daughters were gathered, talking, drinking and eating small morsels of fruit and nuts. But before Anthony took Gaius further, he stopped him and looked his friend over, seemingly looking for something.

"What is it?" Gaius asked.

"Oh, nothing; I'm just trying to see if you've brought a knife. After more than an hour with this crowd you're bound to want to slice your wrists open," Anthony mused with a somber tone.

"It cannot be that serious, can it?" Gaius asked with a puzzled expression.

"Trust me. Drink as much as you can, or kill yourself now. These are my father's friends, either by choice or by purse."

Gaius managed a cheerful smile, wondering how much of his friend's words were genuine.

"Gentlemen, I would like to welcome our new arrival, the finest soldier in Rome, Centurion of the famed Wolves of Rome, Lucius Gaius, and my oldest and dearest friend I might add," Anthony announced with beaming pride as he escorted Gaius, presenting him before the gathering guest of his father.

"Rome's greatest soldier, eh?"

"Well, behind you that is," Anthony smiled as he nodded towards his relative, Fabius Maximus.

"Sir, it is pleasure to see you again," Gaius said as he extended his hand, greeting his superior.

"Oh, have we met before this evening?" Fabius asked, trying to place Gaius' face.

"Apologies, sir. You visited the camp of the Sixth Legion a number of years ago, and we spoke only briefly that day."

Fabius laughed.

"I'm sorry, but I can't say that I recall such a day. I do tend to see many of our legion barracks. Regardless, it is always a pleasure to be introduced to our next generation of officers. I'm sure you are making your legion proud and Rome as well."

"I do my best, sir. And thank you."

Anthony took a big swig of his wine before he moved to the next group of guests, introducing Gaius to each of them. All personal friends and or patrons to his father, they greeted Gaius with pleasant smiles, most of which seemed false as they had little care to know one of Anthony's friends in detail. Regardless, Gaius kept his smile firm.

Gaius wasn't introduced to the group of women who sat together, further down from the men; most of whom were younger or the same age as he. They were the wives, daughters and concubines of Varro' guests, most very beautiful and dressed in expensive dresses, adorn with jewels, silver or gold.

Many of the young ladies eyed Gaius with curious expression as they seemly sized the young and handsome Roman officer up; wanting to remember his face, for future interest.

As Anthony had been introducing Gaius to the party guests, his eyes had been secretly scanning each of the women's faces, looking to see if he could identify Julia among them. He had no idea what she might look like. He barely recalled her face as it was. Ten years was a long time, and she would be sixteen now, a woman, so any one of the females at the party could have been her as far as he knew.

As Gaius was standing, facing away from the main entrance, Anthony directed his gaze behind him as another guest arrived. With a careful glance, Anthony said without words for Gaius to turn around, which he carefully did, not knowing what to expect.

Gaius could smell the wonderful scent of perfume before he turned and saw who was standing behind him. The rose oil swirled around him like a storm at sea, demanding that he take notice of the person wearing it. And as he turned, the woman that he had dreamt of every night for ten years was standing before him.

It took no effort for Gaius to recognize Julia as she stood in the entranceway, poised as all eyes turned towards her.

He paused, suddenly feeling at a loss for words, staring for a long while, completely dumbfounded as to what he should say to her.

Gaius had imagined her many times over the years – his imagination running wild as to what she might look like. He had pictured wonderful images, and horrid ones as well as those that were unrealistic; whatever his mind needed to do to keep his heart in check. However, even he could never have believed that the little frightened girl who cried in his arms the day he left home could have grown into the vision of beauty that stood before him.

Her hair was long, nearly down to her waist and was as black as a moonless sky, glistening against the torchlight, which reflected the oils that coated the finely woven braids and curls. Strands of her curled hair hung freely over her youthful face. Her lips were rose red and glittered with sparkles of gold dust. Julia's arms were bare, as her neckline was exposed as long purple silk dress that glided along the marble floor dropped loosely off of her shoulders.

In her hands a beautiful shawl was held carefully. Gold and other jewels hung from her ears and neck, as well as wrapped around her forearm and wrists.

Julia moved as if she had been born an Egyptian queen. Her presence brought everyone's attention to her as she entered the arboretum.

Gaius stood, still without words as her piercing eyes stared at him for a long while. She then took the first step towards him, extending her hand, waiting for him to take it and kiss the top of her palm.

He felt the softness of her flesh against his rough hands as he held her palm carefully, smiling with a silly grin. She, on the other hand stared at him with the same mild-tone expression.

"I am unsure what to say," Gaius finally spoke as he stood a few inches before her.

"Introductions would be the customary thing to say in this situation," Julia's words were polite, but said with an unfamiliar tone. Her voice carried like a lady, one that was confident and commanded respect from those that stood before her. She was a Roman woman now and not the little girl that Gaius had remembered so vividly.

Gaius' heart sank to the floor as he stared at her for a long while, silent before he did as she had said.

"My lady, I am Centurion Lucius Gaius." His words felt heavy as they came from his mouth. He kissed the top of her hand carefully, but Julia's stare was expressionless, stern and unforgiving, showing no hints of familiarity.

Julia managed a faint smiled before she stepped away and greeted her father and the rest of the guests.

Gaius was confused as he glanced back towards Anthony, who too seemed unsure by his sister's strange attitude. Gaius wondered if all his worries had proven true: had she forgotten him? What a bloody fool he had been. What did he expect – her to leap into his arms and cry out his name?

He lowered himself into his seat next to Anthony as Julia joined the other women who quickly sparked their own conversations, focusing on the gossip of Rome.

Gaius felt like a fool. Julia wasn't the same person he remembered. She wasn't the little girl that hung on his every move like a lost puppy. She was sixteen and a proper Roman woman ready to take her place among the social elite of the republic's upper class where memories playing in the fields with a farmer's boy, pretending to be a princess who waited for her brave hero to come to her rescue, were in the past – games for children.

Gaius wished he hadn't come. A part of him wanted to get up right then and leave. He could find any number of excuses to justify his absence, but he knew it wasn't right for Anthony. He wanted to spend time with him as much as he desired to see Julia. So instead, Gaius took a long swig from his wine and decided to stay.

As Varro and his guest continued with their conversations, loosing track of time before diner was to be served, Gaius did the best he could to pretend he was interested in what the men were say. From time to time he and Anthony would share a few comments, but it was mostly Anthony that was involved in the conversations, taking his father's points of view more than expressing his own ideas on the topics.

He still couldn't help drift his eyes over to Julia when he thought no one was looking. He admired how beautiful she had become, and how well she commanded those around her as all the women hung off of her like extensions of her jewelry.

And then, as he was about to turn his attention back to the guests, as the girls started laughing about something Gaius hadn't been able to make out, Julia slowly turned her gazes towards him, first only with her eyes, then she slightly tilted her head and locked onto his stare.

As Gaius looked at Julia, for only an instant her whole demeanor changed as her alluring eyes widen, strangely seeming to change back to the girl he remembered, as if a spark had been ignited. She showed a hint of nervousness, which was shared equally with Gaius as a small smile crept across her face.

With faintest of gestures, Julia mumbled a polite and familiar *hello* to Gaius, ending with a loving grin that she tried best she could to hold back, but failing.

Gaius replied her privet greeting before Julia was forced to turn her attention back to the other women, as they asked her a question, which she eagerly answered before the group erupted into giggling once again.

Gaius' spirits lifted in that instant as Julia's stare lingered again, as the two caught one another in each other's eyes when the opportunity presented itself.

She has not forgotten me, Gaius thought to himself, joyful by his own words. He longed to be by her now, to share in her words, yet, after ten years he was so close, but still distance separated them, as did proper edict.

He would wait, he decided. He had this long already.

CHAPTER TWELVE

The wine flowed freely, as did the discourse as Varro and two dozen of his guests sat around a long marble table, which at the moment was covered with the fifth course, which comprised of an assortment of pastries, rich and sweet breads, and a dozen varieties of fruits and nuts, served with an endless flow of hot, cold or honey wine.

Slaves moved in between the guests, refilling silver goblets. Plates were removed when they were emptied, and then filled again as everyone ate until they were full. A number of the guests, to Gaius' dismay, vomited into copper buckets that were set next to them; an acceptable act, done so they could expel their meal and then quickly refill their bellies with more delights as if this was the last meal they were ever going to eat again.

The main course had consisted of assorted soups, spices and wild game such as duck, boar, quail and fish, all mixed with vegetables, breads and sweets that Gaius had never seen, much less tasted. It had been the best meal of his life, and unlike the guests, he wasn't about to expel the contents of his stomach until nature took its course. Consequently, he wasn't able to try everything that covered the table.

Varro sat at the head, as the guests were seated by their importance along each side. It had been the senator that carried most of the conversations, as Varro had an unlimited roll of topics which to bring up at any moment. These interests drifted across many subjects, from catching up on personal and family business, to politics of the senate, and what internal and foreign troubles were plaguing the republic. More recent, talk had shifted to the rogue Carthaginian general, Hannibal and his seemingly madman's determination to crush Rome entirely on his own.

Hannibal's name had been echoed all day through the streets, since the senate had declared its intention to march against him. Most of the men in the room were old enough to remember the last war Rome fought with Carthage, and more so, Hannibal's father who stood undefeated as he controlled the island of Sicily – sweeping aside one legion after another that dared set foot on its shores. Haunted memories troubled many men, namely those that stood to lose the most if Hannibal became as troublesome as his father had been.

Most vocal had been Fabius Maximus, who despite the growing, annoyed stares from his uncle continued to bring Hannibal up at the dinner table.

Fabius was a military man, raised to lead men into battle. He clearly wanted to be north with Scipio's legion as it moved to intercept Hannibal, yet, here he was, stuck with his uncle in Rome due to family obligations. Gaius could see the raging storm that brewed behind his eyes, but Varro treated him like a child, using his authority as master of the house to continuously denounce what his nephew tried to argue.

Gaius found it uncomfortable to watch Fabius squirm in his seat as if some insect had been chewing away at his backside since dinner started. He clearly needed to be heard, wanted to reach out to these men, men who had it in their capability to make changes that could protect Rome, but acted powerless when faced with threats that stood to topple everything men for generations had sworn to uphold.

As Gaius listened to the ongoing conversations, it seemed to him that Varro was positioning himself to take control of the senate. If that was a good or bad thing, he did not know. However, it seemed that everyone around the table, and many more businessmen and senators unseen stood to gain a great deal with Varro' rise to power.

"How can any of you sit here today eating my uncle's food and act like the world isn't going mad?" Fabius interjected, bringing the previous topic of conversation to a halt as he blurted his statement out with a slight slur in his voice.

"There is no need for theatrics, Fabius," Varro spoke up.

"I'm afraid there is, uncle. When will each of you wake up and see what is staring us in the face? We act as if nothing can touch our city, yet, expect that all of our enemies will bend to our every demand. And now, when one man stands to challenge Rome with an army of northern barbarians, you simulate a fiction that we aren't in danger," Fabius added as he stood angrily to his feet.

"Sit down, nephew. Was it not I that called upon the Senate to take action first?" Varro defended as his tone rose with annoyance. By now all of his guests had ended their privet conversations and had turned their gaze to the front of the table with keen interest.

"You might have been, but why is the Senate turning against Carthage, demanding, not requesting, that they deal with Hannibal on their own?" Fabius paused briefly, but he did not allow Varro to reply. "He went against them as much as he is challenging Rome. Yet, instead of standing with Carthage, we shift the blame for Hannibal's actions to them, which will very likely lead the Republic to war on two fronts, and that if our enemies in Greece and Macedonia don't take advantage of this conflict and rise up against Rome as well. What will you do then, uncle, when our legions are stretched beyond reason? How will the Senate protect its people?"

"We cannot make peace with Carthage anymore than we can a wild dog," Varro cried out, his anger starting to get the better of him.

"It is easy for you to see them as lesser, isn't it? Then tell me, dear uncle, how will you explain you position to the crying widows and mother of our dead legionnaires as their blood is spilled not on just our own soil, but on lands distant from home?"

"Because they are lesser than us, dear Fabius," a new voice added to the argument.

Gaius directed his attention towards the man that sat next to Julia; closer than he would have liked. He recalled his brief introduction with him earlier in the evening as a man by the name of Paullus.

The name was not unfamiliar upon introduction. He was a powerful figure, more so than even Varro, wealthy, respectable and hailing from an influential family that had served the Rome for generations. Most notably Paullus had spent much of his time in Greece with his four legions, putting down one rebellion after another. These acts had made him a celebrated man.

However, it was not these details that concerned Gaius, more so the frequent stares and subdual gestures, and hidden whispers he made to Julia that had kept Gaius on edge all night.

Julia played her role, laughing and smiling at him with affection when called for. Right now, it was how Paullus had gently rested his hand down on hers' with an uneasy familiarity that went beyond simple friendship.

"If Hannibal wishes, let him cross the Alps. The legion under Scipio's authority will crush him and his horde like we would a slave rebellion. It will serve as a reminder to all those who dare stand before Rome's destiny," Paullus commented as he finished a cup of wine.

"If you are that confident in our legions, why are your men staying in Greece?" Fabius asked.

"Please, my good friend. There is no glory in crushing Hannibal and his rabble. Those spoils are for older men, well past their prime, men such as Scipio," Paullus snorted.

"I would hardly call fifty thousand men a rabble," Anthony commented, which brought a sharp gaze from his father.

"A few thousand Gauls, nothing more - No lesser beings on the face of the earth," Varro quickly commented to weakening his son's hasty statement.

"Do remember your history, father. It was those blue-skinned dirt worshipers that sacked Rome," Anthony quickly shot back.

Varro looked across his table as a number of mummers from his guests filled his ears.

"That was a long time ago, when Rome and the Republic was weaker. I would not show any faith in Hannibal's ability to maintain his alliance with the Gallic tribes for very long. They are as likely to rip his throat out as they are ours." Varro tried to salvage the debate and ease his guests' mind, but still it was easy to note that many at his table were becoming uneasy about the topic as the wine and food had stopped.

"And we Romans are so superior that we, in such a short time are faced with another invasion?" Fabius added.

"Oh, come now!" Varro blurted out as he finally lost his sense. "You cannot honestly believe what you are saying." Varro slammed his fist against the surface of his table, which drew everyone's attention to him. "No army of Carthage or barbarians can topple this government or its legion, regardless what some may say at my table. Rome is strong, and this emboldened, delusional Hannibal will soon be nothing more than a footnote in our history when we are done with him!" Varro asserted.

There was silence for a moment as Varro looked around the table. He could plainly see that it was starting to weight on his guest that the night might be lost.

Gaius noticed that Varro had a desperate glare in his eyes. He needed to find someone that would agree with him, beyond those he already had in his pocket. It was then, to Gaius' concern that Varro settled his eyes on him.

"And what about you, Gaius, what does our younger generation think?" Varro directed his gaze down to his son, "that has proper training and experience in matters of warfare has to say about these matters that face our great Republic?"

Gaius swallowed hard as he suddenly wished he had a shell in which he could hide in, as everyone's attention was turned towards him, as if he had the wisdom to ease their troubled minds and instill confidence in Rome's abilities to handle the current crisis.

Taking a deep breath, Gaius wasn't sure what he could say. Truthfully, beyond the simple facts that every common citizen knew, he understood little about Hannibal and his bloodlust against Rome. He hardly had enough time to think on the matter, not with so many other concerns that kept his troubled thoughts preoccupied.

Gaius decided it was best he play it safe.

"Well, Senator, the luxury of being a soldier is, you don't have to have any political views. I merely fight who I'm told without question as to why."

Varro was silent for an awkward moment before he burst into laughter, which was soon copied by a number of his guests.

"Well, lad, with men such you, Rome is certainly safe."

Gaius forced a shrewd smile as he took a sip of his drink. He knew that was what Varro expected him to say, to follow his superiors' authority without question, and blindly walk through the gates of Hades if instructed.

It was then that Gaius looked into Julia's eyes as she stared at him with disappointment, and suddenly he felt ashamed. He had lied, and she knew it, somehow. He had his own mind and his own opinions, but he allowed the pressure of those he precieved to be superior to him clouds his thoughts, and Julia saw threw him.

Gaius coughed, which drew Varro and his guests attention back towards him.

"However, Senator, if I may continue," Gaius interjected. "Those are the thoughts of what is expected of a simple soldier. But, I am a centurion in Rome's legions, and a citizen of this Republic. I know the truth isn't as simple as we all wish to make it seem. A soldier works in facts, and the simple fact is Hannibal has armed a combined force that numbers well over anything Rome has faced in two generations. We are the sons of the veterans that knew this enemy, we have heard their stories and because of that, I know one thing above all: no matter what you wish to call them, so that your words can give you comfort, they are not weak, nor should we ever underestimate them. Carthage has a culture as old as ours, and like us they will not allow a foreign power to dictate how they grow and expand. If we are to mend the damage between our two nations, then those that lead us need to make more effort to reach a compromise that doesn't risk the lives of more Roman men. Or, I fear we will face the dire consequences of our failure to be responsible to those citizens that place their trust in us."

Varro laughed, attempting to break the tension in the room as the whole table went silent.

"Mend how? We offered them peace and the bastards spat in our faces."

Gaius noticed Fabius' sneer at Varro hasty comment.

"To my understanding," Gaius began before anyone could speak first. "The Senate demanded that Carthage bend to our will and do something about Hannibal, regardless of the fact that they had no control over him. Perhaps it is us that should have bowed to reason and found a solution for both our nations, so that we might have resolved this crisis before it has gotten this far."

Gaius looked around the table, gazing in each of the guests' eyes as he continued. He could see their doubts as if they were shrouds covering their heads.

"We are alone in the world, with fewer friends than enemies, whether or not you want to see that. If this city is to survive, then it is in you, Senator, that we must find the means, to either grow stronger by building a lasting union with those we think lesser, or we will perish from this earth, as a people and nation – never to have been remembered unless told by those that have enslaved us."

"And what should we do about men like Hannibal?" Paullus asked. To even Gaius' surprise the man seemed keenly interested in what he had to say, as opposed to Varro' who face had turned bright red.

"Do no misread my words, gentlemen. I am a patriot first and foremost. I love Rome and the Republic that we have built more than my own life, and I would gladly lay it down to keep Rome and those I love safe," Gaius directed the final part of his sentence towards Julia, who smiled as she hung on his every word. "Hannibal must be stopped, that I agree with completely. I only asked that we think about, have we giving this man reason to hate us?"

"Well said, centurion," Julia broke the silence as she raised her cup to him, which was soon followed by Paullus and a number of other guests; Varro wasn't among them.

Gaius remained silent during their acclaim, taking a deep breath as he looked at Julia, who smiled at him. He knew it was time for him to make his departure. He wasn't sure if he could stomach the night much longer.

Gaius cleared his throat as he stood to his feet. "Unfortunately Senator, I'm afraid that I must take my leave before the hour grows too late. My men have a great deal to do before the week is over."

Varro stood to his feet, managing a false smile as he nodded respectfully," Thank you for coming, Centurion." Gaius noted the small hint of annoyance in Varro address. He took no offense to it. He needed this night to be over with. "And thank you for the wonderful evening, and the insightful conversation.

Anthony stood from his chair, deciding to walk Gaius to the exit as Varro' guests' quickly found new topics to explore, as the room once again filled with conversation.

As Anthony escorted Gaius out to the courtyard, he suddenly burst into laughter.

Gaius too joined his friend, even though he tried his best to hold back his enjoyment of the moment.

"By the gods, I think you put the fear Pluto in them. I never thought I would live to see my father speechless. Oh, if only there was a way to capture that moment and replay it over and over," Anthony chuckled as he held his stomach.

"I did not mean to offend."

"Please, it was wonderful. Do not let those old goats bring you down. You spoke you mind, as you should have. My father surrounds himself with puppets that don't think for themselves, all but Fabius and Paullus, I must say."

Paullus, Gaius thought to himself, still trying to figure the man out.

Anthony placed both his hands down onto Gaius' shoulder; his smile beaming as he stood before his friend.

"Honestly, it does my heart wonders to see you well, my dear brother. I have enjoyed this reunion, and await our next gathering."

"As I," Gaius replied honestly. It was hard for him to think about why his fears had taken hold of him so strongly. Anthony, while older than the boy he remembered, was still young and carefree – still untainted with the burdens that weigh most Roman men down.

"Perhaps in a week's time, if you aren't too busy soldiering, we can explore the city and its many wondrous treats that were forbidden to us in our youth."

"I would enjoy that very much. But, you will have to pay, I'm only a poor soldier, after all," Gaius joked, which brought about more laughter shared between the two friends.

"I shall bring my purse and make certain that it is filled with plenty of coin." Anthony hugged Gaius one last time before he turned and headed back into the house. A moment later, Gaius watched as Julia stepped out from the doorway and stood on the patio.

It was colder outside than it had been when Gaius first arrived, so Julia was wrapped with a fur cloak that draped well past her feet.

Anthony gazed up at his sister with joyful eyes. "You be gentle with our boy now," he smirked. She only grinned before he left her alone.

"Are you leaving so suddenly, without saying goodbye to me?" Julia asked as she walked carefully down the steps, before moving towards Gaius, who stood, taking in every detail of her as she neared him.

"I wouldn't think of it. I was hoping we would get the chance to speak tonight, just the two of us," Gaius answered.

"Oh really. Was there anything in particular you desired to talk about?" Her stare was alluring, nearly overpowering Gaius, who had to hold back with every fiber of his being to not reach out and grab her, wanting with all his heart to taste her seductive lips.

"I..." his mind drew a blank. He had had countless conversations with her in his mind over the past ten years. There, within the recesses' of his thoughts he was in control, without fear and able to formulate the words of poets to describe his longing for her, and how her presence gave him strength to carry on when he felt most alone, however, Julia stepped within inches of Gaius, placing the tip of her index finger against his lips, forcing him to remain silent as she stared deeply into his eyes. She did not break from her probe, seemly looking through him, searching for something that wasn't on the surface, but still within Gaius.

"What is it?" Gaius broke the awkward silence as he touched Julia's hand, feeling her soft skin against his rough fingers as he pulled her reach away from his face.

"Nothing," she mussed with a wide grin. "I am merely looking for that boy I knew – the one that vowed to protect me with his body and heart." She beamed - her touch, presence and voice leaching into Gaius that he was without thought or words – awestruck by this woman as if the goddess Athena had come from the heavens and stood before him now.

Gaius swallowed. "Am I so different now?" he asked nervously as he rested his hand over hers.

"No," she smiled. "And yes. But you are he. I knew it the moment I saw you – those same eyes that shine the goodness of your heart that I've longed to see once again."

"I'm pleased that I haven't disappointed you," Gaius replied, barely able to form a cohesive thought.

"I on the other hand, must be quite different. I imagine you pictured me astray – fat, with hideous skin and matted hair," she giggled.

"At times, perhaps I might have imagined that fiction. But, you are nothing that I could have dreamt." She stared at him with curious eyes as Gaius took a deep breath. "You are beyond any beauty I've ever seen – a goddess statue made real," Gaius caressed her cheek, memorizing her every feature.

Julia blushed, noticeable even in the cold. She then eagerly took his hand and pulled him over towards the stables, "Come with me. I want to show you something."

"What is it?" he asked as he followed without hesitation.

"*Hush*, you shall see in due time."

Julia signaled for one of her slaves to bring two horses over to her and Gaius.

He noticed, a boy no more than twelve years old escorted two horses to them that the animals were already prepared for riding. It seemed to him that she had planned this encounter, when she was able to escape her father's party and be alone with him without fear of interruption.

Gaius ran his hand over the horse he was given, feeling the soft hair's of the animal's mane between his fingers. It was an expensive horse, and elegant, not the bulky steeds that were drafted in the legions.

Taking the reins, Gaius pulled himself up onto the horse's back, quickly easing into a comfortable sitting position. He was surprised the animal did not voice any discomfort. It felt odd for him to not be on Apollo's.

Julia mounted her horse with the assistance of a slave. As she positioned her thighs over the mare's back, she glanced over towards Gaius who rode next to her, both waiting as the gates were swung open.

"It can be dangerous for a lady to ride this late at night," Gaius commented as he stayed a few paces behind her, knowing that she would be leading him through the city, and to whatever destination she had in mind for the two.

"Then it is a good thing I have my protector with me. Do try to keep up, soldier," she smiled before kicking her horse, which reared back slightly before bursting into a full gallop and rounding the corner once outside the gate.

Gaius spurred his horse forward and as he took raced down the paved streets, their two animals' hoofs echoing through the night as Julia led Gaius towards the western gate. Where she was taking him, he did not care. He was lost in the moment.

CHAPTER THIRTEEN

The empty abyss of the hollow doorway loomed before Gaius, who feared to move forward as he rested several feet from the entranceway to his boyhood house. The home, if it could be called that was barely standing. Most of the roof had caved in, and part of the west wall had fallen, scattering bricks over the weeds and waist-high grass that'd grown between the foundations; the only life came from a cluster of roosting birds that had nested between the broken beams.

Gaius had almost forgotten about his home. He hardly thought about it and had never planned on returning, yet, here he was now, standing before the threshold, afraid to go inside.

Julia was stagnant behind him, just out of arms reach. She hadn't told Gaius about her plans to bring him to his home when they left the city behind them several hours ago. They rode through the darkness, guided by the full moon. Her heart, like his had raced with excitement, and she hated believing she had deceived him. But she felt that she needed to bring him her, to lift some of the burden she knew he carried on his back, for leaving his father and her behind ten years ago.

"It is okay, Gaius. I'm right here," Julia spoke softly to him as she rested her hand down on his shoulder.

He wanted to feel angry with her. He wasn't ready for this, but as he turned and glanced back, he could see the concern in her eyes as she urged him forward.

Gaius took the first careful step towards the propped door, moving it aside and resting it against the side of the doorframe quietly, as if he was afraid that someone might hear him.

Brushing aside cobwebs, he entered, with Julia close by.

There was enough moonlight to see by, which cast through the broken roof and gaping holes above. The illumination revealed nothing of interest as no furnishings besides a single bed and a long table were present, both of the wooden frames having long ago rotted and covered with moss from prolonged exposure.

There were no personal effects whatsoever. Gaius didn't much care. There was nothing of value regardless – everything that had been his father had given him when he left to join the Sixth Legion.

Gaius clenched his fists as memories of his childhood filled his mind: that last night eating with his father at the table, begging to be allowed to go to Rome with Anthony. The bed which held the footlocker, and the fireplace that cooked the tasteless military stew, and the occasional fits of anger and laugher shared between his father and mother, when she was still alive.

Gaius was silent for a long time as his eyes drifted lazily from corner to corner, seemly expecting to find something. And then he spoke, low and without turning towards Julia, who remained fixed behind him, still standing between the broken doorframes.

"When did he die, my father?" Gaius whispered as he focused his attention towards the bed.

"Some years after you left. He hung in there for a long while, still," she answered carefully.

"Then he died alone. I imagine the animals took his corpse eventually. He never would have asked for help from anyone, even till the end," Gaius spoke bitterly. He should have been there, he had always told himself.

"No, he did not die alone," Julia replied. Grabbing Gaius' hand she pulled him out of the house. "Come with me, I wish to show you something," she urged him.

Gaius was reluctant at first. Earlier this night he followed her without question, and this was where she brought him. Why, he wasn't so sure, or keen on asking. He was still trying to take in this realization.

Julia led Gaius around the house, beyond the barn, which was little more than a pile of rotted wood that had long ago collapsed, and out into the horribly overgrown field that had once blossomed wheat. In the distance, cast by the bright moon and starry night sky loomed a lone tree that stood at the summit of a slopping hill, which over-looked the whole property from a high vantage point.

Julia felt a slight hesitation as she was forced to stop, once she realized that Gaius had slowed his pace.

"It is okay, trust me, please," she said in a low tone, easing Gaius along, now with more care.

Gaius knew what lie at the top of hill, and at the base of the century old cypress tree. He had seldom gone there, not since his father placed his mother cold body into the earth.

Gaius' eyes widen for a moment as he saw two marked gravestones at the foot of the tree. One he knew belonged to his mother. It had been her people's custom to be buried, and not burned like Romans. His father had honored that, but upon closer expecting of the second slab of stone, Gaius read his father's name.

Gaius stared at Julia with a puzzled expression. She answered his question before he ever uttered a word. "He asked to be laid to rest with your mother, not to be cremated, but to honor her Celtic traditions and be buried in the soil."

"How..." Gaius struggled for words, "did he get up here. He would have never asked for help, from anyone."

Julia fought back a laugh as she smiled at the memory. "No, he would not have asked for help, and never did. But, he did not have too. Anthony and I took care of him until the end. And when that day came, we prepared his body, dug the earth, and brought him to rest with your mother."

Gaius was dumbfounded by Julia's confession.

"He demanded that we leave him alone once you left." Julia's smile widen from the memories that she shared with Gaius. "Every day he cursed Anthony and I when we volunteered to cook, clean, tend to the grounds, whatever he needed done and wasn't able to do for himself. At first he chased us off with a club, cursing our names, but each day we came back. And when he wasn't able to get out of bed, as his condition worsened, we did what needed to be done so he may live the remainder of his days in comfort."

"Why would you do this?" Gaius asked as he stepped closer to Julia and carefully took her hand and placed it in his.

She smiled at him, gazing into his eyes as she squeezed his hand tightly.

"Because, we loved you...I, *love* you. It was the only way that my brother and I could show it." Julia rested her palm against Gaius' cheek as she said her next words carefully. "You took an oath, for me, Gaius. How could I not do something for you in return?"

Gaius turned his sight away from her embrace and stared down at his parent's graves.

"As I grew older," Julia continued, "your father would break down as he became accustom to our company. While Anthony was at the market, selling what he grew on your land, Julius confided to me how proud he was of you, and excited in knowing the man you would someday grow to become. When I asked about you, as I often did, he painted me a vivid picture, who you were, what you were like, and who you would become. I knew without having to try that it was you standing in my father's house. I had seen your face my whole life," she rubbed her hand carefully across Gaius' cheeks, staring up at him with unconditional love.

"I was terrified that you would have forgotten me," Gaius confessed. "I did not want to come back, and I hoped to the gods that I would never see you again – better to remember you as you were than who you might have become."

"Why?" Julia asked.

"We were only children, you far younger than I. Our lives were fantasy and fiction. How could I continue to love a girl I hardly knew, no less, you I?"

Julia smiled as she moved closer.

"Those fictions, as you call it, were the only reality my brother and I had. Our lives are laid out for us from the moment we were born, to the day we die. You freed us with your games and your stories. We could never do enough to thank you for that. You gave us a freedom we could never have attained on our own. You've allowed me to see the world through your eyes, Gaius."

Gaius grew somber as he lowered his head.

"I'm afraid the reality isn't the truth we believed, Julia. Rome, this Republic, it isn't what I thought it was. It corrupted, rotting and ignorant to the reality of our world. I feel, Julia that I'm fighting to defend a fantasy that only exists in my mind. Rome isn't what I once thought it was, not after what I've seen and heard over the past couple days."

Julia shook her head fiercely, grabbing his hand once more and pulling him down the hill as quickly as their legs could carry them.

"Where are we going now?" Gaius asked with a hint of annoyance.

"Just be quiet and follow me. I will show you the Rome you dream of, Gaius, one that even my father and his flock can't take away from you," she cried back as they raced towards their horses and again rode out into the night.

Gaius knew that Julia was leading him back towards Rome, but they had left the road some miles back and were riding through the country, now for over an hour, but still heading in the direction of the city.

Moments earlier Julia leapt from her horse and urged Gaius as the two climbed a steep hill. She reached the summit first, turning back, staring down at Gaius as he reluctantly followed.

"Look, Gaius, look upon your dream – the dream that is Rome!" she called as he reached the top of the hill.

Gaius' eyes widen when he looked upon Rome, the whole city stretched out before him, for as far as he could see. The fires from the countless millions of torches flickered behind the tall stone walls that encompassed Rome, shining brightly like a sea of stars that rolled with the seven hills.

The water of the Tiber River glistened in the full light of the moon as lone ship drifted lazily downriver, heading out toward sea.

A flock of birds flying south as winter's breath moved from the mountains...

The sight was the most magnificent thing Gaius had ever seen. It was peaceful, clean and absent the blight and rot he'd seen since arriving; Rome, indeed seemed like a beacon of civilization, order and the rule of law that was absent throughout much of the world, that he was a loss for words to properly express what he was seeing.

"This is your Rome, Gaius, the city you've given you life to defend. It is the symbol to all men that we can reach beyond our standing, and strive to better ourselves," Julia voiced with pride as she stood by Gaius' side. "It is not perfect, however. There are men who seek to twist the dream of Rome for their own ambitions. There are those who go without, dying each day on its streets, and our system is far from perfect, but it is the best the world has to offer, because we, the people of the Republic have choices in how we govern ourselves."

Julia looked up at Gaius, drawing his gaze down towards her as she gently caressed his cheek with her hand.

"Men like you, Gaius, are the keepers of the dream. You fight to ensure that our flame never dies, to protect our greatest ambitions from those that would destroy everything we have, and might still achieve."

Time seemed to stop for Gaius as he stared into Julia's deep eyes. Just being this close to her was overpowering that he couldn't hold back his feelings any longer, nor could she as Gaius wrapped his arms around her thin waste, and embraced her with ten years worth of building passion.

He wanted to hold onto her forever, never to let her fall through his fingers as they kissed for a long while, each intimately enjoying the taste of the other's lips against their own. However, after a while, Julia pulled back suddenly, forcing herself to turn away from him, as if she was ashamed.

Tears began to form under her eyes as Gaius looked on with concern. "Julia?" he spoke nervously as he rested his hands on her shoulders.

"I love you, Gaius. I always have, and I always will," she whispered with a heavy heart that seemed as if it was tearing apart within the walls of her chest.

"Then what is wrong?" he asked.

"It is, Paullus," she finally admitted, pausing between words with a heavy sigh. "We are to be wed in the summer. I have no choice or say in the matter. It is the desire of my father. With Paullus' support and money, my father will rise higher within the Senate, as will my soon-to-be husband. They have the chance to create one of Rome's strongest unions, now and for generations to come, beginning with myself as the prize."

Julia turned sharply, driving her face into his chest where tears ran down his tunic, soaking the fabric as she wept.

"This is ridiculous!" she cried out, still holding tightly onto him, who held her with careful embrace. "My life is to be in ruin for politics, not love. Paullus has money, power and an army, he can give me anything my heart could ever desire, but not the one thing it wants the most, and that is you. I don't know what to do."

Julia was angry, her words resentful and bitter. She obviously wanted to hate her father, but seemly could not bring herself to say it. It was the way the world was, they both knew it: as daughter to Varro, she had her obligations and it was within his right to do what he wanted with her – marry her to whomever he desired, her heart only got in the way.

Gaius pulled Julia back so he may look into her eyes, and said, "I feel as if I have waited my whole life for this moment. There hasn't been a day that has gone by that I haven't thought about you. I have prayed to the gods many times for just one chance to tell you how I've felt – just one chance to confess that I love you. But, I cannot change what we are or what the fates have in store for us. All I know is, right now, we have this moment, which no one can take away from us."

Gaius held his stare for a while as his words sunk into her heart, which brought a faint smile to her face as he continued, "I've loved you for so long, Julia, and I will continue to do so for many years to come. Nothing will ever change that, not as long as the sun rises and falls...I will love you with my whole heart."

Julia leaned close and kissed Gaius once more, softly.

They treasured their shared feelings, staying the rest of the night at top the hill that overlooked Rome. They wanted their time together to last for all ages to come. This was their moment and the affairs of their lives could wait a little while longer.

CHAPTER FOURTEEN

The screams of the dying beast carried over the battlefield, adding to those of the thousands of men wounded and dying, which littered the ground with limbs, entrails and flesh, saturated in pools of crimson blood and glinting metal of iron and armor.

Hannibal's attention was not focused on the dying Romans, which his men eagerly dispatched from this world with joyful purpose. Instead his gaze fell upon one of his elephants, which had been speared numerous times in the belly, which now lay on its side, riving in agony as it stomach had been sliced open, pilling entrails across the snow-covered field.

The smell was horrific, but its dying cries were worse as with each shallow breath it took, the trunk sprayed misty blood from its nostrils, which showered down on the warriors who tried to put the creature out of its misery. However, its thrashing made it difficult for the dark-skinned hunters to finish the beast off.

Hannibal sighed with a worried heart as that elephant was the last he brought with him across the Alp, a dozen already having died during the long and cold journey, the remainder killed by Roman spears. He had once hoped they would have made a greater difference in his campaign, perhaps lasting another two or three battles.

He watched with unblinking eyes as a Numidian hunter carefully crept towards the elephant's head, with a spear raised, ready to strike.

With one powerful thrust, the deed was done as the spear tip burst through the animal's eye socket, rupturing through its iris, and tearing all the way into the elephant's brain. A fraction of a second later the animal stopped moving.

One of the lead hunters ordered his men to begin harvesting the elephant's meat, which could still be used, and another group to remove the long tusks, which could be sold.

Other cries of agony also carried over the battlefield, but they weren't ended with as much care or concern as Hannibal watched his Celtic allies, perhaps too eagerly, walk among the wounded Romans, torturing them by hacking off limps, appendages, or gentile while the men attached to them were still breathing. The already dead were plundered of any wealth they might have carried: iron, coins or trinkets were prized among the barbarians.

Hannibal detested the methods of his allies. His enemies, even if they were the hated Romans, deserved better treatment - better a quick end with a spear through the heart than the sadistic pleasure the northern tribes took in murdering their hated continental neighbors. But Hannibal wouldn't dare say a thing. While he would never allow his Carthaginian warriors to act as the Gauls, he needed the barbarians more than he cared to admit. They had only joined his crusade at the promise of treasure, glory and blood. Without them, this war would end before he ever came within view of Rome's city walls.

Regardless, Hannibal expected more from Rome. The battle that followed his crossing of the Alps was not what he expected or had heard of from his father's stories, of the bravery, cunning and skillful art of warfare and famous Roman discipline that won them many battle in the past, including the war with his mother country, Carthage many decades earlier.

His opponent, Hannibal knew was more capable than this. Co-Consul of Rome, Scipio the Elder was already renowned for past glories against Carthage, pirates and rebellions across the republic. Yet, and with great disappointment, a stray arrow, fired from afar had struck the consul in the early minutes of the battle. With Scipio out of action, the Romans soon lost heart as their officers, outnumbered were soon overwhelmed. What followed would be utter slaughter.

Scipio's body hadn't been found, and Hannibal doubted it would be. Early reports told him that the general was taken by his son, who shared the same name, off the battlefield and was now heading back to Rome. The body of a consul of Rome could have gone a long way to bolster Hannibal's ranks, no less the moral of his tired and hungry men. Regardless, he knew this victory would due for the mean time. He was now footed in Italy, and soon Rome would know that they had underestimated him.

More would come – legions upon legions would be sent against the invaders. Hannibal knew he would soon be outnumbered, and more than likely many of his barbarian allies would run and return to their homes, once their thirst for blood had been satisfied and their backs loaded with as much Roman gold they could carry. Yet, Hannibal did not fear what was to come. He had not set out on this campaign without considerable planning. This war was not one of shortsighted ambition. It would be long and grueling and he would have to sacrifice everything if he was to achieve his ultimate goals in the end.

Hannibal's attention was turned as Braca, a trusted friend that commanded the Numidian cavalry who rode towards him. He was dependable friend, one now that Hannibal had to turn to as he had sent his brother Mago back to New Carthage to ensure that his supplies from Spain to Italy could not be cut.

"My General," Braca spoke as he pulled his horse alongside Hannibal. "My riders have been combing the Roman dead, but we have yet to find the body of Scipio among the fallen. I believe the Romans are taking him back to their city. At best, they might have several hours on us."

"And what about the consular's staff?"

Braca shook his head as he answered, "Taken from the field. But, we did find the play chests. We could give pursuit for the staff if you wish."

Hannibal thought on the matter a moment longer, scratching the rough stubble on his chin as he took a drink from his water skin. He wanted the staff as much as he would have liked Scipio's body. They meant nothing in terms of value, but the Romans and his allies, both were powerful symbols that he could use to rally more to his cause. However, with a heavy sigh, Hannibal knew what he must do.

"Do not worry yourself longer. We have to consolidate our position here until the rest of our troops and supplies come down from the mountain."

"And what of these...creatures?" Braca asked sarcastically as he glanced over his shoulder, directing his words toward the Gauls that looted and murdered the Roman dead and wounded; the wounded cries continued to carry over the battlefield as they were gutted alive.

"I do not trust them. How do we know they won't head back north, now that they have their victory over a Roman consul, and enough wealth to keep them drunk through the next two winters?"

Hannibal took a deep breath. He had pondered the same question for hours now. He knew the Gallic tribes weren't dependable. They had only joined him for glory and wealth, both of which he'd already brought them. Unfortunately he needed them. While he loathed them more than the Romans, if they stood against him it would be impossible for him to secure enough supplies from Spain to continue his campaign in Italy.

"I suspect they will remain loyal, for the meantime. There are a number of settlements south of us, and more than a few of the chieftains have expressed interest in sacking them," Hannibal answered.

"And you agree with this? We will need Italian settlements to stand with us against Rome," Braca's words were like ice as his distain boiled through each word he uttered.

"I do not have much of a choice, not at this moment," Hannibal shot back. He wasn't angry by Braca's words, but at the realization of hard truths. His war was against Rome, not the Italian people, yet it was they who would suffer the most. It sickened Hannibal. Most of the northern settlements that would fall prey to his horde were once, a century ago part of greater Gaul, until the republic came and conquered them, unifying all of Italy under Rome's banner. But those barbarians with him did not see distant kin, but only weakness, a prey easily crushed and sacked for their unquenchable thirst for blood.

"No, we must continue as planned," Hannibal reiterated as he collected his wayward thoughts. "Ready your men. Once *they've* finished toying with the Romans, I will give word to march to our next objective."

"As you command, my General," Barca nodded before he turned his horse and began to trot off.

"Barca!" Hannibal called out. The officer stopped and turned his head, "Steady your heart and mind, and remember why we are here. It will only get worse from this point forward."

With a heavy heart, Barca nodded his understanding and rode off.

"Victory or defeat, I am set upon my course, "Hannibal uttered to himself as he turned his attention back to the battlefield. "Send me your legions, Rome...Send them all."

PART TWO

CHAPTER FIFTEEN

Gaius lowered his head and allowed the sweet aroma of Julia's scent to swirl around him, drawing him nearer to her as he took a deep breath, inhaling her essence. Julia was in his arms as they sat on the river's edge, several miles west of Rome's gates. A brisk, but tapered wind blew across the water's edge as they sat, arm in arm, looking over the horizon, watching as the last vestiges of leaves fall from the surrounding trees.

They had spent as much time together as they could over the past week; every free moment either could spare. They found any excuse, both real and fictional, to escape their duties before they would find one another outside the city gates and venture out into the wilderness. There they would spend hours together until the sun went down, leaving promises for another day of passionate lovemaking and long quiet afternoons together.

These had been the best days of Gaius' life. He never wanted them to end, and even though he knew that Julia's pending marriage loomed, they never spoke of it. Right now, each day was a gift, and both wanted to appreciate it to the fullest.

Julia ran her hand over Gaius' arm, wrapped loosely around her shoulder and chest. She wore only a loose sheet, draped from her shoulders, hanging low. One hand was gently placed over the top of her right breast.

Gaius was bare chested, his firm muscles, earned after ten years of training pressed against the smooth flesh of her bare back, where Julia's long black hair was tangled mess; strands of the curly bands rose up with each cool breeze, fluttering across Gaius' face.

She pressed herself nearer to his body, so that she may share his warmth.

They said nothing to one another. They hardly had to speak to fill the endless hours. Each other's touch, their smell and sight was all either needed or wanted. Both had, however, shared quite a lot about one another – stories told to no one else. They were living in the moment as only two young lovers could, with no thought of the future and the obligations that both had to Rome, family and the senate. If they pretended hard enough, with only the slow current of the moving water in front of them and the sounds of the calm wind against the bare branches of the trees, they could have lost themselves in time, as if they were the only two souls left on earth.

Julia tilted her head back and stared up at Gaius for a moment. She raised her hand and rubbed her palm against the rough fuzz on his cheek, admiring the man he had become. Yet beyond the strong body, a few scars and more hair, his eyes were as she remembered – proud, calm, strong and loving. When she looked up at him, she was taken back ten years when she was but a child. Then, as now, she looked at Gaius and saw courage and strength. She had always felt safe with him, and while one might cast off her affections for him as a child's crush on an older boy, she knew then, like she knew now that her feelings for him were very real.

Julia loved him and that love had grown.

Gaius knew without her having to say it, he could see the passion in her smile, in her endless gaze as she stared at him, and in her touch. He wondered if this was what it was like when his father had first seen his mother. He prayed to the gods that they give him the chance to give to Julia the same love and affection that his father had shown to his mother, now years past.

He knew, with her in his arms, he could do anything. However, he was a practical man. Julia was a dreamer; she always had been, while Gaius was stuck in the here and now. While he did not say it, when she looked at him like she was now, when anything seemed possible, the truth of his reality caught up with him. It wasn't enough for him to have her now – her body and her heart. He needed her like he needed to breath, and the thought that in a few months, another man would have her, nearly brought tears of rage to his eyes.

"What troubles you?" Julia asked, as she could see the sudden shift in his expression, as faint as it was.

She turned all the way around; the thin silk sheet falling off from her shoulders, revealing her naked body as she repositioned herself, now sitting in front of him as she wrapped her legs around his waist.

Gaius lowered his hands and held Julia firmly by her waist as she rested both of her arms over his shoulders, firmly fixing her gaze into his.

"Do I not make you happy, my love?" she asked with a sweet smile as she ran her hand through his close-cropped hair.

"More than I have words for," he answered, trying as hard as he could to hide his true thoughts. But she was like an oracle, able to read his mind – knowing his darkest fears and lingering doubts.

"You are concerned about Paullus? It is he that takes your thoughts from my loving embrace, isn't it?"

Gaius felt ashamed as he grabbed the sheet that lie on the grass, and tried to wrap it back around Julia. When he attempted, she pushed his efforts away.

"Gaius," she began to say as she rested both her hands on his cheeks. "I love you, and nothing or no one will ever come between us. Say the words and I will leave Rome and my father behind, to be with you. We can run, go elsewhere: to the south, onto Sicily, or to the east, toward Greece, perhaps even beyond, deeper into the Hellistic world. You only have to utter the words." Her words were spoken with honesty and without concern.

Gaius knew that if he should say the words, she would do as he wished without a second's hesitation. But, still the lingering doubts remained at the knowledge of taking her away, what it would mean for them when Varro hunted for them.

The prospect of fleeing across the republic, traveling to shores beyond their wildest imagination, it was exciting, even Gaius had to admit to himself. But, he knew it was a foolish dream of two very young and naïve individuals in love.

"Julia, the world doesn't work that way. All because we desire it, that doesn't mean we can just get up and leave everything behind. Your father and Paullus would track us to the ends of the earth. And I couldn't betray Anthony's friendship either," Gaius spoke with a painful heart, more so at the sudden sadness that crept through Julia's eyes.

"My brother knows what you mean to me. I do not hide my secrets from him, Gaius." She tried to fight his argument, but could see right away that there was no changing his mind.

"Even so –"Gaius turned his head, afraid to speak what he had been thinking. "It does not change the reality of our situation. I am a soldier of the Republic, Julia. Do you know what that means to me?"

She stared at him puzzled, but Gaius did not give her the chance to answer his question before he continued.

"I took an oath to defend Rome with my life; to serve the Senate, and to lead those men under my care. That is not something that I can turn my back on, not for anyone, not even for you."

"Then do not turn against your oath," Julia blurted out with frustration. She sat shivering in his arms, but not from the growing chill of the late evening, but in knowing what the end result of their conversation would lead to.

"Julia, I can't love a married woman either." Gaius' words were like ice picks through her chest. "I can't hide in the shadows and wait to steal you away when opportunity presents. If we were found out, it would be the death of both of us, literally."

Julia tried to speak again, to debunk what Gaius was saying, but he spoke sooner than she could.

"And even if we aren't discovered, in time, you will bare Paullus children. What place would I have then in your life? Do you think I would be low enough to still seek you – to tear your family apart?"

"What are you saying, Gaius?" her words trailed off as tears formed in her eyes. She suddenly felt very exposed as she broke away from him and reached down, wrapping the sheet around her naked body.

"I don't know. I know that I won't betray my oath, and I can't stop loving you, but –"he struggled for words, desperately trying to find the right sentence that might ease her mind. He felt like he was betraying his love for her that she might believe that he loved her for her body, there was no other need for her. He hoped she didn't feel so. He could never use her and just throw her away. But he was pulled between his honor and his passion for her.

"I'm just…" he never got to finished his sentence when their attention was turned east, down the river and toward the bridge that led back to the city.

There was a strange, distant noise which he recognized as the rhythmic marching of soldiers, followed by the trumpets of Scipio's legion as they returned from the north.

"The legion is back!" Gaius said enthusiastically as he stood to his feet.

"This early?" Julia asked as she too stood to her feet, wrapping herself in the sheet as she stood next to Gaius.

"Something is wrong," he noted as the trumpet call weren't that of a victorious army, but a warning to any along the road to move aside and allow the legion to pass unimpaired. Even this far Gaius could hear that the marching was sporadic and ragged, not the orderly movement of a legion.

"I have to see what is going on," he said as he bent down and grabbed his clothes. Julia quickly did the same before the two headed back towards Rome.

It did not take them long to reach the stone bridge that crossed over a narrow patch of the river, which led to the northern gate of the city. For the moment the troubled conversation that he and Julia shared escaped their thoughts as both hurried along the river's path. And then when the two saw the legion, both paused with horrid looks as they witnessed the sorry state of the army.

The soldiers that had been sent north to confront Hannibal were broken. Most of the men, marching in a loose formation, were dirtied, tired and bloodied, with blood-soaked bandages over their limbs and heads. Those that still carried weapons were slumped oddly over their shoulders or dragged along the stone-paved road without care, while their armor was a mixture of chainmail, leather and tunic, all covered with week's worth of mud and spackled with dried blood. Even the horses the officers rode seemed short of breath as many of them had deep gashes across their powerful bodies. The wounds had been hastily filled with mud so that the animals didn't bleed to death, but a number still bled from their noses, indicating that their serious injuries were indeed taken its toll.

A wagon-train followed the legion. The foul odor of the rotting bodies and congealed blood forced Julia to turn her head. The living that was too wounded to walk under their own strength had been forced to ride with the dead.

As Gaius looked into the legionaries' eyes, almost all of them as young as he, they stared dully out into space; more than a few clutched arms or legs that had been amputated after the battle.

"Soldier!" Gaius called as he drew the attention of one young man who seemed no worse for wear beyond a few cuts to his face and arm. "Tell me what happened to your legion?"

The soldier shifted his tired gaze over towards Gaius as he neared him, but did not break stride.

"Hannibal, sir – the bastard cut us to pieces after we lost Scipio."

"What? The consul is dead?" Gaius asked as he kept pace with the young man.

"Yes. He was killed quickly, before the first hour of the battle. Those left in charge weren't able to organize a proper defense. Hannibal tore through us with his damn elephants and cavalry, like we were cattle. It all fell apart after that."

"By the gods," Gaius uttered to himself as he stopped, allowing Julia to catch up to him, as the surviving legionaries moved towards the safety of the city.

"What is going on, Gaius?" Julia asked as she didn't comprehend what she was seeing. She saw that a number of other citizens had also gathered along the road. Already a number of women stood on the road's edge, weeping as they fell to their knees, calling out for their sons or husbands. It was enough to bring tears to her eyes as she watched, powerless to do anything.

"I have to get back to the barracks." Gaius grabbed hold of Julia and urged her forward as they quickened their pace, heading in a different direction than the defeated army, but still back to Rome.

CHAPTER SIXTEEN

Gaius stood in the rear, surrounded on each side by a collection of officers: five optios and five centurions, as well as a tribune and a single prefect. All were in Valerius' command tent, where he had summoned his commanders to assemble. He watched carefully to the men as they spoke among themselves and to Valerius. By now, everyone in Rome was aware of the fate of Scipio's legion, and the auxiliaries sent north to stop Hannibal.

Rumors had spread quickly through the city. Some said that Hannibal was marching on Rome, while others still stated that Scipio was alive somewhere, wounded but still breathing. More extreme gossip implied that along with Hannibal's attack in the north, Carthage had landed an expedition force in the south, which moved to link with Hannibal and his barbarian hordes, which were in the process of ravaging the countryside, hoping to starve or panic Rome into submission.

The only real truth that mattered to Gaius at the moment was that a Roman legion under the command of a decorated officer had been soundly defeated in the field. With this knowledge, Gaius like the rest of his fellow officers wanted to know what the Sixth Legion was going to do; would the senate final call the rest north.

Finally the flap to the tent was pulled back where sunlight filled the interior for a moment as all eyes turned; their voices falling silent as Valerius entered and stood before his officers.

Valerius took a deep breath once he was certain all eyes and ears were fixed on him. "Consul Scipio is dead," he spoke. A moan filled the space that occupied the gathering officers, which was quickly followed by a chorus of questions.

Valerius raised his hand, silencing them.

"Early reports indicate that at least twenty-three hundred men are dead, missing or wounded, not counting those that deserted Scipio's legion before its return to Rome. Most of the legion commanders, including Scipio, were killed, or are also missing. The Senate has not received any ransom demands for those captive –"

"Because, they're all fucking dead and likely put the bloody sword by those savages!" Centurion Marco cried out, interrupting Valerius' report. His statement was supported by all the officers in the tent as they jeered their frustration.

"And what is the bloody Senate going to do this time? Sit on their collective asses, and wait for Hannibal and his horde to encircle Rome?" Tribune Titus demanded to know.

Valerius raised his hands once more as a wave of angry roars drowned his words before he could utter a single word.

"I have just come from a special session of the Senate. Newly appointed Consul Titus Sempronius Longus has pledged to the soldiers of Rome, and its people that he will not let the atrocities in the north go unpunished. He has dedicated himself to leading a larger force, which is to march north by week's end." Valerius paused for a moment as his men soaked up the building anticipation of what they hoped he was going to say next. "And, I'm grateful to tell each of you that the Sixth Legion will once again mark its name in the history of our Republic, with another victory, once Hannibal and his rogue army is crushed beneath our heels!"

Valerius' words brought a wave of cheerful excitement that echoed beyond the walls of the command tent, as his officers bellowed with glee at the prospects of avenging their falling brothers, and taking part in the coming campaign to punish Hannibal for crossing iron with the republic.

Gaius cheered, but he was more reserved than they. He had never seen a battle no less took part in one, and commanded men – one hundred souls, whose very lives rested on his decisions.

"Listen!" Valerius cried as he raised his hands once again, signaling for his men to be still while he continued. "While I have already dispatched riders to send word for the rest of the Sixth to march north, the consul will be moving from Rome before our brothers can join us."

"More glory for us then!" Cried one of the older centurions, a man Gaius barely knew by the name of Sempronius.

Valerius laughed as he spoke again. "Now, it isn't all good news. Since we are under-strength, we will be charged with guarding the auxiliary cohorts."

A chorus of moans erupted from the officers.

"So," Valerius continued once the groaning from his men subsided. "I'm afraid we will be babysitting the rear, at least until we draw Hannibal out for a fight. I do, however," Valerius raised his finger high into the air, "promise plenty of glory for you when the battle comes. So, I want each century to be ready at a moment's notices. Make sure your men are kitted, feed and ready when word comes from the consul. If he is wise, he will wait for the rest of the Sixth, and other legions to arrive before going north, but politicians I'm afraid, aren't known for their keen intellect."

The wave of laughter brought a smile to Valerius' face as his men's excitement for the coming campaign was as he hoped.

"Alright then, what are you waiting for, Hannibal to come to us? Get out there and make sure the cohort is ready - dismissed!" Valerius gave his final order as each officer, beaming with joy turned and stepped from the tent, save for Gaius, who Valerius called before he left with his fellow officers.

Gaius stood at attention as he watched Valerius moved around his desk and sat down, where he ironed his fingers together, staring up at him with a displeased expression that sent shivers up Gaius' spine.

"You have not been in the camp much, have you?" Valerius asked, his question sounding more like a statement of fact than a query.

"I apologies, sir, I have been –"

"Preoccupied with the daughter of one of Rome's leading senators," Valerius interrupted, filling in Gaius' words.

Gaius stood frozen, trying as hard as he could to think of something that might excuse him, but he knew it was best that he not bother trying to cover his ass.

"Yes, sir. Julia is her name. You met her once, ten years ago."

"I don't give a damn who she is, Centurion!" Valerius shouted as he rose to his feet. His voice was colder than Gaius had ever heard him speak before.

"Do you know who her soon-to-be-husband is?" Valerius demanded.

"Yes sir, I have met him," Gaius replied with a heavy heart. The lump in his throat felt like an apple trying to expel itself.

"Well, I will assume you are unaware of who he is, but if not, let me tell you: he is one, if not the most powerful man in Rome. His family alone holds more weight in the senate than any hundred men. And his wealth could buy ten legions if he so wanted. We need him to win this war, regardless of what that twit consul thinks – this conflict will not end with Hannibal's demise. So, I would very much not like to see Paullus preoccupied with having to hunt you down and impaling that pretty young head of yours on a pike, because one of my best officers couldn't keep his cock in his pants, sleeping with a man's betrothed!"

"I love her, sir!" Gaius blurted, falling from his careful attention stance, as he momentarily forgot his place and whom he was speaking too. "But," Gaius began again before Valerius could respond to his statement. "I'm not ignorant to the facts, sir, despite what you might think. I do not plan to see her further, romantically, which was decided before current events unfolded." It was painfully hard for Gaius to say his last sentence. He loved Julia with all his heart, and it pained him more than anything to think of telling her what he had just said to Valerius.

Valerius took a deep breath as he sat down. His expression changed as he looked up at his young pupil with concern.

"I do not envy your position, Gaius. I know you love this girl. I know what she has meant to you over the past ten years, since I took you away from your home. But I know too what Rome is like. In a better world, there would be nothing standing between your happiness. But, this isn't a perfect world, or is it a perfect system, and unfortunately, people born into your class vs. hers; there is very little room for love."

"I understood, sir," Gaius replied with a heavy heart as his head sunk lower.

"I wish you did understand, but you will. Both of you are very young and stupid," Valerius smirked at his own comment, as he was lost in his own youth for a moment. "I do not pretend to know what the future might have in store for the two of you, but I do know what the present demands, and she isn't part of it. Your place is here, with me, with your men. No matter what might happen in the coming campaign, you cannot forget the oath you took to serve and defend the people of Rome. Victory or defeat, this war won't be over as quickly as the politicians want the plebs to think. I need you levelheaded and ready to carry my banner onto the field. Are you ready for that, Gaius?"

Gaius straightened himself to full attention as he answered, "I am, sir!"

"Then make ready your men. And Gaius, do not let me down."

Outside, Gaius stopped before Valerius' tent and took a deep breath. He felt like he had been holding his breath the entire time. He knew his mentor's words were truthful and only spoken out of love and concern. Regardless, his words ran deep, piercing flesh like knives.

Gaius knew what he had to do – what he was ordered to do, but that didn't mean he wanted to do it.

For the first time, just for an instant, he wished this wasn't his life. He wished he hadn't taken the oath. Even now the thought of running with Julia, as she had suggested ran through his mind. Certainly, she would be safer elsewhere then here, if the war turned against Rome's favor. They could be together and create some kind of life, living someplace far from their responsibilities. But, those thoughts were fleeting as Gaius knew what had to be done.

CHAPTER SEVENTEEN

Gaius stood nervously in the garden as he stared down at what had been a rose bed, which was now bare, as frost covered the weathered vines that wouldn't bloom again for months. It was bitter cold as a harsh winter storm had rolled across the countryside in the days following Scipio's defeat. Since then, a new army had been assembled. It would be commanded by another seasoned veteran of the previous war with Carthage, Co-Consul Sempronius, who was determined to win himself a great victory; elections were coming in a few weeks, so he hastily readied twenty-five thousand men of arms to respond to the incursion.

But Gaius' mind had been elsewhere since his talk with Valerius. He had to make a choice, as he ran through his head all the possible things he could say to Julia to ease what needed to be said.

Gaius reached down and touched the last blooming rose. The petals were a dark shade of red, almost black, as the last vestiges of life were seeping out from the flower. Two petals fell effortlessly from his gentle touch, drifting slowly to the ground before they were eventually captured by a brisk wind, which carried away more withered flowers into the gloomy sky.

"Gaius?" Julia called as she stepped into the garden behind her home, within the walls of Rome.

He turned slowly to meet her.

As usual, she took his breath away. In the mid afternoon sun, even with the cold and grey skies, she was perfectly captured by the sun's warming gaze.

She wore a long fur coat, which she had just put on before stepping outside from the warmth of her home. Underneath, Gaius could see a blue gown with a low neckline, showing the expensive jewels that adorned her neck, before she pulled the high collar up and tightened it.

"What are you doing here?" she asked as she rushed over to him, taking both of his hands in hers as she spoke more softly, "I wasn't' expecting to see you until tomorrow morning."

"I had to come today and tell you –"Gaius fumbled with the words for just a moment, captivated by her large dark eyes, which stared up at him eagerly.

"What is it?" Her voice shook as she seemed to dread the reason for his sudden visit.

Gaius glanced behind Julia, seeing only a few slaves as they walked back and forth inside, going about their work.

Julia looked back as well, but quickly turned her gaze to Gaius and asked again, "What is it, my love? Speak to me."

"This..." Gaius struggled as he pulled away from her.

"*This*, what?" she questioned with worried expression.

"*Us*, Julia, we can't keep doing this! As much as it pains me, I can't see you anymore this way." Gaius spoke quietly, still afraid that someone might be near enough to overhear. "We cannot continue to live in this fantasy, this fiction we've created for ourselves."

Tears formed in Julia's eyes as she stepped closer to him, but he held out his arms, keeping her at a distance as if her touch would force him to change his mind and resend his hurtful words.

"I love you, Gaius, and you love me," she pleaded.

"It is not a question of love, Julia. I love you more than you could possibly know. I would do anything for you; face any punishment or torment, whatever it took to keep you safe. I promised I would protect you, and I will never resent that oath. But we can't be anything more than friends. The world simply doesn't work the way we want it to."

"Gaius –"Julia uttered painfully as she tuned from him, unable to control her tears. She was ashamed to let him see her this way, so she covered her face with her hands and tried to finish what she wanted to say.

"I do not love Paullus. I do not care why my father has arranged my marriage with him. I will refuse it and confess my love for you. He will understand, they both will," she cried out, not carrying who overheard her, but even her own words did not sound certain as Gaius stepped closer, forcing her to turn and face him.

"Neither of us can afford to be so naïve, Julia. We have too much to lose."

"I do not care about all of this," she cried out as she flung her hands out.

Gaius took Julia's hands and held them in his as he spoke quietly.

"It is not your wealth or my position that we stand to lose," he told her.

Julia's tear-filled eyes opened wide with the sudden realization of what he implied.

"My father would never..."

Gaius shook his head.

"Perhaps, or perhaps not, but no matter, we have betrayed his trust. Even if he took no stand against us, Paullus would, and if it wasn't our lives that he demanded for the embarrassment, he could hold your father accountable for betraying his word in promising his daughter to him. He could ruin your whole family."

Julia tried, wanted to rebuke him. She desired to insist that Paullus was not that kind of man, but Gaius didn't have to know him intimately to understand that Paullus cared for her deeply.

Gaius wondered if the arrangement in taking Julia's hand in marriage wasn't just a play to join two powerful families. Perhaps the man actually loved Julia as much as he. A man like that could be unpredictable, most of all one that had the means to reshape Rome, no less the lives of two individuals.

"I do not like this, Julia. I do not wish this. I want you. I want you by my side for as long as I live. I wish we were different people, not obligated by our duties, to even be slaves, perhaps, free to love one another without reserve. But, it isn't so. Our world and our place in it, is not that simple."

Gaius reached for Julia, taken hold of her as she lowered her head, resting it against his chest.

"I will love you forever, for as long as I draw breath. My heart will always beat for you and you alone. But, I cannot give you anything more." Those were the last words Gaius spoke to Julia, as she pulled away from him.

He watched her as she stepped through the threshold and back into her house. She turned only once; tears filling her eyes as she looked out to him. He wanted to say more, but there was nothing else to be said. Nothing could ease the suffering that they were both going through, so he left her, wondering if he would ever see her again...If she would forgive him?

CHAPTER EIGHTEEN

Snow drifted in thick clumps between the Roman lines, which advanced along the banks of the nearly frozen Trebia River. Even with the bitter cold and long marches, Gaius' thoughts continued to drift back to Julia, and the last day he saw her, now six weeks past. He doubted the memories of that day would ever leave his troubled mind – how he wished he could have had a second chance to speak different words to Julia, to better make her understand that he wasn't abandoning her, or that he didn't love her with all his heart, but what had been said was done, and nothing could remove the stain.

Gaius was now occupied with the duties he had been trained to carry out. But, unlike the rest of his cohort, who were excited by be given the chance to avenge their falling brothers, he felt like a corpse, still breathing, but dead inside. The joy and anticipation of the coming battle did not echo in his heart. However, for weeks now, Hannibal continued to elude his pursuers despite attempts to draw him out into a pitched battle. The legions under the command of Consul Sempronius were close to him, nipping at Hannibal's heels, but with their numbers, superior to the Carthaginians, the legions move slower, allowing the barbarian rogue to stay one step ahead of Sempronius.

Sempronius' legions marched from one burnt-out settlement to another, engaging stray units, mostly Hannibal's Gallic allies that were more interested in plunder than warfare. But Hannibal's seasoned troops - his Carthaginian, Spanish and Numidian allies remained hidden, utilizing the trees and worsening weather as cover. This frustrated the legions, which were growing tired and complacent, most of all the impulsive Sempronius; and now the bitter cold nights were beginning to sap the legions fighting spirit.

Gaius watched the army arrayed far ahead of him. He feared Sempronius' eagerness to end the war might be a price to high to pay if things kept going the way they were, a sentiment shared by many officers.

As Gaius marched near the rear of the Roman formation, which moved slowly down the embankment of the Trebia River, his mind still drifted back to Julia. He knew it was wrong to continue to think about her, so he struggled to keep focused with each step he took. Perhaps, a lingering fantasy that continued to picture in his mind, he could win enough honors in the coming battle that he could go back to Rome and demand that Varro present Julia to him as a prize, much like his own father had won his mother in the previous war with Carthage. But that fantasy was an illusion, which angered him and made his already cold and restless nights all the more tiresome. It affected his duties as he was quick to anger, snapping at his men when their discipline lapsed for only a moment. He did not like the person that these feelings created. He did not know how to deal with them, but he soldiered on nonetheless, hoping the pain would go away.

Gaius' thoughts returned to the reality as his foot kicked over a small stone that rolled down into the cold water.

The pace was unbearably slow, made worse by the snow that blinded the army's advance. Ahead, Gaius could see through the fog the main formation of Sempronius' lines. They were only two men across, not ideal for a quick defensive formation if an attack should come from the trees. There was no other choice, however, as the riverbank and the sloping hills, surrounded by thick forest, had forced the legion to travel in a long line.

Gaius glanced for a moment over his shoulder, seeing Valerius, who rode on horseback a few paces behind. His old mentor did not look happy. Gaius had never seen him more on edge as he silently cursed Sempronius' impatience, despite his warnings that legions should not advance in this manner.

Earlier in the morning the consul had summoned all his senior officers to his tent. The legions had been attacked daily since it had camped some miles from their current position days before as Hannibal's dark-skinned horsemen continued to harass the army's extensive supply lines, and each time Sempronius sent out his cavalry to confront the Numidians, they broke and retreated. This had frustrated the consul to no end. Now, Sempronius was driven by madness as he was determined to find Hannibal and crush his ragged army once and for all, even if it put his whole army at risk.

Gaius knew the moment that he laid eyes on Sempronius this morning that the mad was deathly sick, and clearly not thinking straight. He was running a high fever; however that fact did not stop him from planning his next move despite the urging of Valerius and a number of other legates.

Sempronius wanted, needed to confront Hannibal, not for the sake of defeating the man, but to return him to his former standing in the eyes of the Roman people and the senate. He was not the most popular figure in politics, commonly known to all those living in Rome. He spent half of his time in Sicily, or in Greece, attending to private affairs in regard to his vast land-holdings and businesses. This made him an easy target for his opponents in the senate, namely senators such as Varro, who challenged Sempronius on his priorities and conventions to the Roman people. He had only been made co-consul out of desperation after Scipio's death because of his previous experience dealing with Carthage and the Gauls north of the Po River. Other than that, the senate would have been content to let him rot somewhere else if there had been a more able man – one that was that actually cared about confronting Hannibal. This battle, despite his early victory was still not one that most senior commander's saw important for their notice – not enough fame or glory to be had, but, enough for Sempronius.

Several paces ahead of Gaius, he heard one of the legion prefect's call-back, demanding that the rear guard, which comprised of the first cohort of the Sixth Legion and two cohorts of auxiliary troops to maintain the pace, as it seemed to be falling back from the main body.

"Bloody fool should get his ass back here and see if he can keep this pace up," grumbled Valerius, which even Gaius, heard from where he was standing.

Gaius looked out towards the looming trees as visibility was becoming especially difficult as the snowfall picked up, coming down in violent sheets. He directed his gaze up towards the looming trees for no particular reason. It was nearly impossible to see anything beyond the faint outline of the forest, but then, for only a moment he caught sight of something standing out among the trees, staring right toward him: a white wolf.

Everything was eerily quiet for a moment, as if the world, the army, and his surroundings faded away until only he and the wolf, which stared at Gaius with unblinking eyes, remained.

Gaius felt himself reaching up to his chest, before placing his right hand over the spot where he wore the broken half of the clay medallion that Anthony had given him ten years ago.

The wolf and the medallion, all seemed familiar, as if he had seen this same animal before.

"Lupus?" Gaius whispered softly, and then all at once the noise of twenty thousand men marching rushed back as he blinked, and then the wolf was gone.

Gaius looked over his shoulder to see if anyone else had seen what he had, but those behind kept marching forward, like he, unaware of what was in the trees.

Gaius looked back to the trees, which were nearly impossible to see by now. The wolf was gone, as if it was never there. It was then that a horrible thought accrued to him, one that sent shivers of panic up his spine.

Gaius sudden broke from his formation to the dismay of those around him, and rushed back towards Valerius, who halted his horse, seemly ready to bark at Gaius for breaking rank, but Gaius never allowed Valerius a word as he spoke frantically.

"Valerius, we have to stop the army, now!"

"What are you babbling about, boy?" Valerius asked, confused and angry at the same time. In front of him the first cohort of the Sixth stopped, which forced the long column of auxiliaries to also end their march. Quickly, murmurs queried from man-to-man, all the way down the ranks.

"We have to stop the army, now, or we are all dead, Valerius. You have to believe me," Gaius pleaded; his own words filled with terror, which quickly caused panic among the other men that were close enough to overhear him.

"An ambush?" Valerius pondered as his eyes began to scan the trees, seeing nothing but snow falling, and the ever consuming white haze that was obstructing his visibility.

"I don't know. I wish I did, but I feel –"Gaius did not know what to say, or how to say what he'd seen. "I just know if we keep going, something terrible is going to happen to us. We have to warn Sempronius to turn us back, or to form ranks, something before he marches us to our graves."

"Damn it, boy," Valerius lowered himself, speaking firmly. "Don't you think I know this is foolhardy? But there is nothing that can be done. We have to keep pressing forward until we reach the far side of the embankment, to open ground. If we stop now, or pull back, we are doomed regardless."

"Then we have to form ranks, now, and make a stand. We may still have a chance." Gaius reached out and placed his hand on Valerius' shoe, squeezing it; his eyes still opened wide with fear. "Please, Valerius, you have to trust me."

The legate seemed ready to kick Gaius aside, perhaps even order one of his officers to take him into custody, but then, suddenly, after staring into Gaius' eyes for a long while, his own expression changed.

"By the gods," Valerius cursed under his breath. "Lepidus!" he then called out. A moment later one of his junior officers ran forward and saluted, awaiting his orders. "Hurry to Sempronius, at once, and inform him that I'm holding the march. There might be a risk of attack from the trees, and that, I'd advise him to do the same. Now go!"

"At once, Legate," the young man replied as he ran on the outer edge of the formation, quickly disappearing into the mist and snow.

Valerius looked down at Gaius and spoke as he turned his horse, facing the trees now. "You'd better be right about this, or more than our careers will be over."

"I pray that I'm wrong," Gaius replied.

Valerius sneered as he cried out, "Form ranks." Each man did so, turning to face the trees, the only way an attack could come, and joined their shields together, creating an unbreakable wall.

Gaius had rejoined his men as well, taking his spot among them. His breathing quickened as he tried not to relieve himself, even though he was shaking terrible, and not because of the cold.

Silence fell as the group of fifteen hundred plus Romans waited, listening for any hint that an attack was coming.

The trees were the only logical place for an ambush. With the river to their backs, some men standing in ankle-deep water, they waited. And then as the first ten minutes drifted by, the only sounds that could be heard was the breathing of men and animals.

The running that Valerius sent forward came back into view, racing past Gaius, before he stopped before Valerius, who remained on horseback.

"Sir, Consul Sempronius demands that we rejoin the rest of the column, or, as he said, he'll have your head," the runner relayed Sempronius' instructions.

Valerius glanced down at Gaius, who stood in formation several dozen paces to his right, and stared at the young centurion.

For a moment Gaius feared that Valerius would do as he was instructed, but then, the old veteran turned his focused back to the runner and said, "Return to the Consul and inform him that I'm holding position, until I'm confident that an attack is not eminent. And, that I advice him to do the same – form ranks and look towards the trees."

The runner looked nervous, clearly afraid to repeat to Sempronius what Valerius had told him.

"Do as you are ordered, soldier," Valerius ordered with a firm, but understanding tone.

"Yes, sir." the massager ran off, again disappearing in the thick haze before he was gone from sight.

Gaius took a deep breath. He knew if the boy should return, more than likely it would be with a detachment of soldiers to relive Valerius of his command. All Gaius could do was glance back up at him, giving him worried eyes, mumbling his gratitude for believing him. Valerius did not reply, but held his position.

"You're risking the legate's live, Gaius. Are you a fool?" Agrippa muttered under his breath. The big man stood to Gaius' left, and at glance Gaius could see that his sentiment was shared by the rest of the men in his century as the stood uneasy, nor for threat of ambush, but for what Sempronius might do when he turned his men around and removed their commander from the Sixth.

"I'm not doing this because –"Gaius' words were broken when his and every man's attention was turned suddenly to the trees, as a strait of drums and horns blew, echoing, knocking snow from barren branches.

Gaius' heart skipped a beat as the roars of thousands of bloodthirsty men cried out, yet unseen, but clearly heard, as if a powerful beast of unimaginable size dwelled within the forest.

"Hold formations and ready javelins!" Gaius heard Valerius bellow at the top of his lungs. His orders were repeated by each centurion up and down the formation, including Gaius, who had to lick his dry lips twice before he could repeat the command to his century.

A moment later a swirl of whistling sounds blew through the trees. Most of the men, too young to know what the terrible warning was, were unprepared as hundreds of arrows impacted against their shields and armor. A moment later, when the last shot had struck its mark, a chorus of moans rang as men struck by the sharp projectiles, shrieked in horror as they were hit.

Gaius turned abruptly as he heard one of his men go down. No arrows had struck his shield, but as he looked down, he saw that one of them had torn through Agrippa's throat.

The man whizzed violently as his hands reached up to his neck, trying desperately to stop his own blood from gushing out through the hole in his throat.

Blood bubbled from Agrippa's neck. No one could help him even though a number of men called out his name, or cried out for the doctor to rush to his aide, but with the impossible gap between the men and the river, no one could get to Agrippa in time, as if it would have help, before he choked on his own blood.

Gaius was in near panic as he looked back towards the trees. Only now did it seem the weather was lifting, as if the attackers had the power to control nature.

He gazed upon thousands of murderous savages, many of them bare-chested, painted with bold blue patterns on their bodies – others covered in head-to-toe in the furs of wild animals. They bashed their assortment of weapons against their small wooden shields, as they bellowed loudly in their barbaric tongue.

Gaius was panicked by the sight of the demon-men, all of whom seemed larger than the greatest gladiator in the arena. He wanted desperately to run, even risk freezing in the river, as long as he escaped. And as he glanced around him, seeing the same fear in his men's eyes, Gaius knew he had to take charge. He was a centurion and the Wolves never turned their backside to the enemy.

"Hold your formation and wait for these bastards to come to us!" Gaius yelled as loud as he could, surprised even by his own voice and the renewed confidence in it.

"We are Wolves, and these men are only sheep. Show them what Roman iron can do!" he added, which brought a joyful boom from his men as they cried out his sentiment, challenging the Gauls to test them.

Further commands from other centurions and lesser officers carried across the whole Roman formation, as the Sixth and its escorted auxiliaries knew what their duty was. They had all trained for war, young and old alike, and while individually a Roman was lesser to a Gaul in a straight fight, as one, they were a machine created for one purpose, and that was to destroy anything that was before it.

Another volley of arrows shot from the trees, only this time the Romans were prepared for the attack, as hardly a whimper was heard from the lines, as arrow struck harden shield, deflecting harmlessly to the snow-covered ground.

And then, with one last monstrous war cry, thousands of Gauls charged down the steep embankment.

Gaius waited, his eyes just over the brim of his shield, holding firm as his grip on his shield with one hand was strong, equaled by his hold on the hilt of his sword. He could hear, feel and see the breaths of the men beside and behind him, as the soldiers of the Sixth waited for the oncoming charge, which rolled down the hill like a juggernaut, bent on one task alone - to spill Roman blood.

CHAPTER NINETEEN

"Pilums, loose!" Gaius cried out, as seconds later the men behind him unleashed their devastating iron-tipped spears at the charging Gauls.

Screams of barbarian foreigners blossomed as the triangle-shaped tips of the javelins tore through flesh and bone, wood and armor alike as hundreds of men were struck by the heavy Roman weapons.

There was no time for a second volley to be ordered. On open ground, the Romans might have gotten three or four attempts to weaken the enemy formation, but with the narrow terrain and rushing river behind them, it did not take long before the first wave of Gallic warriors collided against the Roman shields, like water against rock.

Gaius had never felt such power before as dozens of screaming, spitting, and enraged men fell against his shield. He and the whole line slid several inches back as the hard-packed snow was quickly being chewed into mud. But, the line held as the shield wall, proven time and time again in battle, could not be broken, regardless of the determination of the opponents.

"Push them back!" Gaius bellowed, unsure if his voice could be heard by his men. But as instructed, the men to the rear pushed against the men in front of them. A moment later the minuscule ground the Gauls had gained, was again reclaimed.

Gaius had often wondered if his training would indeed become second nature to him. He had heard stories from the veterans that a soldier acts on instinct, loosing himself in the battle as a strange sense of calming peace overtook them. Others had said the opposite - battle was chaotic, frantic and loud, that a man, regardless of how many years he had to his name, was an enraged beast, hacking and slashing to stay alive, and that all the Roman discipline counted for shit.

Gaius found that the former was true, at least for him. The fear and panic that had gripped him moments ago had seemly vanished. He responded as if his actions were not his own as ten years worth of drilling – the memory of Centurion Quintus' vine-cane against his back, pushed Gaius forward. Lost in to himself, his mind hardly recognized the first man he killed.

The moment came quickly and unceremoniously. A screaming Gaul with long brown hair, matted and caked with dirt and grit, a bright painted face, rotting teeth and thick wooly beard, the barbarian could have been twenty, but looked decades older under so much hair. He had squared himself against Gaius' shield, pashing his small axe, which he held in his right hand – a tiny wooden shield in the other. He cursed Gaius in his native language, which Gaius understood enough of the Celtic tongue from his father's teachings years before.

The barbarian tried desperately to get his axe-head over the brim of Gaius' shield, wailing frantically, but Gaius was taller and protected by the well-crafted iron helmet that covered his head, and the wide shield he held tightly in his grip.

The act of killing the man came quickly, within the first few seconds after the Gallic horde had crashed headlong into the Roman formation, as Gaius rose up, peeking for just an instant over the top of his shield, and struck.

The short Roman sword, a *gladius* was a perfect weapon in Gaius' trained eyes. While it wasn't too good at slashing or bashing at an opponent, it was perfect for thrusting. Its narrow, but sturdy iron blade rested comfortably in his striking arm, precisely balanced. The ivory grip, showing wealth beyond Gaius' station once belonged to his father – the engravings of the pack of wolves, carried the lineage of the Sixth Legion.

As the Gallic warrior screamed, his deep blue eyes blazing with rage, Gaius thrust his sword neatly over the brim of his shield, and plunged the tip into the man's mouth. His expression changed suddenly with the realization that, despite his many years as a proud warrior, and the victories he must have achieved, meant nothing when his end came quickly, and without proper challenge.

Gaius felt the faint resistance as his sword struck flesh. He pushed with little effort, forcing the blade, now caked with blood and little pieces of flesh, out the nap of the man's neck.

Gaius withdrew his sword a fraction of a second later, pulling with it a spray of crimson mist and teeth. The whole action lasted less than a fraction of a second before Gaius ducked his head back down under his shield, trusting his capable helmet to keep him safe from a counter attack.

The Gaul's feet buckled out from under him. He was dead without another sound uttered. It did not take but a second before a new opponent took up position, as a taller barbarian drove his sword down toward Gaius' head. The shield took the brunt of the attack, denting where the hard iron blade struck, which forced Gaius' to lose his position for a moment as his shield dropped a few inches.

The second Gaul was worse than the first: massive broad shoulders, extending down into muscles that seemed forged in fire. This man had blonde hair, better cut and a neatly trimmed beard, which was braded. He too was bare-chested; something that marveled Gaius as he and many Romans didn't seem able to adjust to the bitter cold. The man's chest featured a looping blue marking, extending from the left shoulder and wrapping down around his back. He wielded no shield, only the long two-handed iron sword, which he raised over his head and drove it down once more, like a huntsman rooting a tree.

Gaius, even as large, young and strong as he, faulted for a moment when his shield received the blow. His arm which held it, felt like mush under the assault, but he again managed to hold his position.

Gaius reached his sword up once again as the large barbarian pulled back to attack once more. However, his aim was not true as the blade only cut across the man's left cheek – deeply, drawing a torrent of blood, but not enough to sway the man from rethinking his attack.

Once more a third blow came, a bit more off centered, which did nothing to compromise Gaius' defense. But now, the man used the length of his weapon to his advantage, pulling back far enough that Gaius could not strike again with his gladius.

He did not have too as the large Gaul was struck dead center by a javelin, which was tossed by the legionnaire behind Gaius, when opportunity presented itself.

The Gaul looked dumbfounded for a moment, and then his eyes filled with a sudden rush of anger as he grabbed the wooden shaft of the javelin, and forcefully tried to remove it. This caused him obvious pain, more than any man seemed capable of dealing with. But, despite the man's strength, the triangle-shaped iron head could not be easily pulled from his flesh, as only the loose wooden base broke free.

Regardless of the two foot iron shaft sticking out from his chest, the Gaul roared with unequaled anguish as he charged forward – blood already beginning to seep from the corner of his mouth.

Gaius did not wait for the man to bore down on him. He plunged his sword forward. Its tip caught the man's throat, tearing easily through the soft flesh.

Gaius twisted the blade as he had been trained, before he withdrew it. The gash widen with the action, drilling a hole through the man's neck as blood oozed like water from a spick.

Still, even with the killing blow, the Gaul attempted to advance, but now as life-given blood poured from his wounds, his strength left his arms as the heavy sword fell to the rocky ground.

Gaius attacked again, slashing this time. The bloodied tip of his sword sliced across the barbarian's face, carving across his right cheek in an upward arch, tearing through his noise and rupturing his left eye, before it cut through the white bone of the man's skull.

Even before his body dropped to the ground, another man' took his place. Gaius could hardly fathom the relentless onslaught. His men, his cohort and the auxiliaries they protected were in formation, ready for the attack. And despite early loses, they held firm. But, he couldn't imagine what the rest of the legions were going through. Sempronius obviously had not heeded Valerius' warnings of a possible ambush. Unable to form ranks and properly defend their position, even the well trained Roman discipline could do nothing against the brutality of the Gallic horde. Man-for-man the barbarians from the north were stronger fighters: raised from childhood to be warriors and hunters. They knew no fear, and welcomed death. The Roman's, most weren't seasoned soldiers, nor was their commitment completely given to the legions. They were called upon by the senate: farmers, freedmen, craftsmen, fishermen, poor and the rich alike. Gaius and the Sixth, among a few other legions across the republic, practiced soldiering as their livelihood. But even still, unlike the restless tribesmen from the north, warfare was not a daily exercise for the men of Rome. Like Gaius, the majority were untested and unprepared for the reality of war, no less facing an enemy that craved their lives – coveting every head as a trophy.

Gaius felt a wetness growing around his feet. At first he feared that the river might have risen, but upon careful glance downward, he saw that much of the snow had turned bright red as blood pooled from the hundreds of bodies that fell before the Roman wall. It drizzled into the water behind the Roman lines and joining the clear stream, which soon ran crimson as the first signs of Roman dead floated downriver.

Gaius reacted again, this time feeling a sharp sting against the side of his brow. Something grazed him, what it was, he did not know. In response, he instinctively thrust his sword forward blindly. Once more he felt the touch of human flesh against the cold iron of his sword, and again he pushed, sending the tip deeper into whoever had wondered before the gladius.

He lost track of time. Had minutes gone by, or hours? There was no way of telling. But his arms and legs began to strain. He was as fit as any man could be, and he was still young, in his prime, yet, he felt old and tired as the weight of his sword and shield soon began to feel like raw iron ore. It was then in the back of his mind he thought he heard the sound of a loud whistle, which blew in a preordain pattern.

Without even thinking, before his mind processed what the call meant, the moment a hand touched his right shoulder Gaius withdrew from his guarded stance, and turned his body as the man behind him rushed forward. This action was repeated by every Roman soldier that held the frontline, which were replaced by the man behind them.

Gaius collapsed to his knees as he was pulled to the back of the formation, as did many other legionnaires, who ignored the cold rushing water, which provided the only solid ground for them to rest on without fear of attack.

Gaius' body looked as if he had been working in a butchers shop after fresh game had been brought in. His head and lower half, from his knees to his feet were plastered in bright red, which dripped from the brim of his helmet. It was only then that he seemed to notice the fowl coppery taste of Gallic blood that has washed into his mouth. He couldn't help but swallow it during the battle, which now he threw up, which included everything he had ate this morning. He was not alone in this action as dozens of other soldiers did the same.

It was then that a boy ran up to him – another dozen dispatched to other soldiers. Each of them carried water-skins, which they handed to the legionnaires that had been retired from the frontline.

Gaius took several long swigs, spiting the first mouthful out as he tried to rinse the taste of blood from his throat, to no avail.

He stared down for just a moment at the boy, no older than fourteen. He was a servant of the legion; destine to wear the armor in a few short years, if he lived long enough. The lad's face, ripe with youthfulness, bared eyes of terror and panic. But the boy did his duty where he was asked without question. Gaius couldn't help but pity him for having to see this day, so young, but he figured it was best to get it over with now than later; at least he would know what to expect when he took up the shield and sword.

By now some sense had returned as Gaius turned and looked upon his cohort, which continued to fight. The clattering of swords and the cries of wounded and dying men filled the pristine morning. He collected himself, quickly falling back in line behind the ranks. He would yell encouragements to the men before him, barking orders of support, and issuing men to plug holes where dead Romans eventually fell. And then, how much time, he did not know, he was back in the front as the ranks continued to shift, to allow rested men to again reform the shield wall – fighting the ceaseless wave of barbarian Gauls.

By this time, Gaius' actions were mechanical. The fear he felt when the battle started was drowned out by his will to survive. Eventually, the ground became littered with fallen Gauls, which further waves of attackers were finding it increasingly difficult to advance through.

Another whistle blew, but this wasn't a signal for Gaius to be replaced, but orders from the commander to advance. Now, the barbarians seemed lessened, their formation now tattered and unformulaic as their numbers had dwindled. Those who still fought weren't as brazened as their seasoned warriors that fell against the Romans when the fighting had begun. Now, stricken by fear, they began to panic as the Roman line advanced with deadly rhythm. Those that did not flee, attempting to run back up the slippery slope, which was now caked in churned mud, were cut down without mercy by the machine that moved effortlessly towards them, while those wounded on the ground were either trampled to death by the steady Roman march, or impaled where they lie.

When Gaius could go no further, as the rise in the landscape prevented him for advancing, the only vestiges of enemy warriors that remained, fled into the trees, protected by the layers of mist and snow, which still drifted lazily down over the battlefield.

A cheer ran throughout the Roman formation, but any sentiments of victory were quickly dashed as fighting could still be heard further upstream. Gaius knew, without having to see it that the men under the command of Sempronius were being slaughtered. The river of blood that flowed behind him was evidence of the massacre.

A horn blew, not Gallic, but Roman as the call for retreat was signaled from Gaius' cohort. Soon, officers began ordering everyone back into ranks, and the wounded Romans collected while there was a lull in the fighting.

It was then that Gaius saw Valerius, still alive, thank the gods. He, like every legionnaire was covered in blood. He too had sustain a number of cuts, as fresh blood drizzled from a gash to the old veteran's upper left arm, and a small nick to his neck. In the bank of the river, nearly submerged in bloody water, Gaius saw Valerius' horse, dead, with numerous spears and arrows sticking out from its body. He was amazed that the legate had survived at all, as he was the obvious target of the Gauls, as was any officer of note.

"Valerius, what of Sempronius?!?" Gaius called out as he moved to join the legate, who rallied his men to make a quick and effective retreat.

"There is nothing I can do for the fool. He's damned this army. I've got to save what I can," Valerius replied. Gaius wasn't even sure if the old man recognized him with all the blood and filth that covered him, believing he was just speaking to any number of centurions that were under his command.

"Let me take a detachment and force our way to him. The consul might still be alive," Gaius suggested, determined to salvage the day anyway he could. He was perhaps too young to recognize defeat, despite the number of barbarian dead that coated the earth around him. While the Sixth had found some measure of victory, it was a pinprick against the mammoth that had trapped his countrymen this day.

"The battle is lost, and so will we if we don't take advantage of this moment and pull back, now!" Valerius reiterated.

Valerius grabbed hold of Gaius' shoulder, pulling him closer to him and spoke, "There will be other days that we can avenge our fallen. But this is not one of them. Now, form you men and cover our withdraw!"

Gaius did not argue further. He did as he was ordered; grabbing those he could find that still had enough fight left in them to stand if challenged. But thankfully, those Gauls that had lived soon realized that the Romans upstream offered less resistance.

CHAPTER TWENTY

Gaius stared without blinking as several bodies floated by him as he knelt down on the edge of the partly frozen Trebia River. The bodies hadn't stopped drifting down stream even though the battle had ended five hours ago. Only now did the clear water seem to be restored, as for a long while it ran bright red. Still, trickles of the crimson gore drizzled downstream from time-to-time. Now, however, the quiet stillness of country had returned.

This army, what was left of it, was broken. Now, behind enemy lines, within their own country, what remained of Sempronius' legions had to move quickly, gathering what survivors they could find, and mustering what was left of the supplies before marching south, back towards Rome. The future was uncertain, more so now than it had been before. Hannibal had won a great victory, not against one legion, fought on equal terms on the field, but against a superior force, outsmarted, ambushed and slaughtered like no force Rome had ever assembled before. Now, what was Rome to do? How would the people react? How far would Hannibal go, now?

Gaius rubbed his hands in the water as he had continued to do so for the past twenty minutes, watching the dead drift by. His hands and much of the rest of him was clean of the blood that had been spilled during the battle. He had survived, and had taken lives, for the first time. His mind, however, was *not* trapped on what he had done, but what he had heard, seen and experienced: screaming, terror, the sound of flesh and blood, and the horror in a man's eye when he felt death's grip, and the feeling – the almost too easy act of pushing iron through a man's body. But, the most troubling thought that haunting him now was, why had he been spared? If it had not been for the image of the white wolf, and the warning he concluded from it, he would have shared the same fate as those legions under Sempronius' command.

Why had no one else seen it? Why couldn't it have shown itself to Sempronius? The damn fool. Why me?

The snow crackling under someone's foot indicated to Gaius that someone was walking up behind him. A moment later, the voice of Valerius told him who it was.

"We'll be moving soon," Valerius said. There was no real reason why he needed to come down to the river personally, not when any number of runners could have done the job, but Valerius' voice echoed a deep question, one which he wasn't sure how to ask, *how did you save us?*

Gaius did not give Valerius a reply, or showed that he was listening, even though there was no way he could not hear him. His attention was still fixed on the bodies that drifted down the river, most of them Roma, but barbarian Gauls as well.

Valerius sighed as he stepped closer.

"Whether you want to see it or not, you saved a lot of lives today, Gaius."

Gaius tilted his head up, looking over his shoulder toward Valerius and replied, "I did not save enough."

Gaius threw a rock into the river, breaking a chuck of ice from the edge as he stood back to his feet.

"Why didn't that fool listen to me, you, or any of his officers? We shouldn't have been on the banks of the river? We shouldn't have been marching in the storm? Sempronius is a bloody fool," Gaius remarked bitterly.

"Sempronius was a fool – he is dead."

Gaius just glanced at Valerius.

"We found his body, or what was left of it, along with the other ranking officers, each missing their heads," Valerius reported.

"Too bad Sempronius only had one life to give," Gaius utter with a viper's tongue. "And how many of our brothers did he take with him?" he then asked.

"By my estimate, at least fifteen to twenty thousand."

"What will we do now?" Gaius pondered; a question more for himself than in regard to Rome.

Valerius stood beside him, resting his hand on Gaius' shoulder as he joined him, watching the sadden sight of his comrades drift by.

"I am proud of you, Gaius. You fought well, but more importantly, you listened to your gut, regardless of the consequences. Those are merits for a true leader, one who seeks the wellbeing of his men, and not attaining glory; a rare virtue, I'm saddened to say."

Gaius just looked over at his mentor's tired eyes. He did not know what to tell him, about what he had seen, and why it compelled him to demand the army to halt. Even he did not understand it, and he doubted he ever would.

"Was it enough?" Gaius asked, his question pertaining to many things.

"We shall see. But, Rome is not out of this fight, just yet. I assure you that much. In the mean time, I have a new task I need of you and your century."

"What do you request of me, sir?" Gaius asked as he was starting to regain himself.

"Come, we have planning that is needed."

CHAPTER TWENTY-ONE

Eleven days after the Battle of Trebia

The migration of five thousand people marched over the countryside as they tried as best they could to avoid any of the main roads or settlements in the region. This collection of bodies wasn't an army, nor was it heading north to confront the invaders, no, these people were innocent civilians: men, women and children driven from their homes, and forced to flee for their lives.

It was Gaius' responsibility to protect them.

He watched them carefully as they walked, rode or be carried in carts across the cold, snow-covered earth that offered little in the way of fresh game or dry wood to build fires at night. Their destination was Rome, Capua, or any other heavily populated city in the republic that could shelter them until the threat of Hannibal and his horde passed.

The people were a ragged collection. Most were on the verge of starvation, half probably wouldn't make it to their destination before they froze to death as the nights had gotten colder. But, they had no hope. Hannibal's tribes had ransacked the northern country, pillaging, murdering, and raping. This was done even though envoys from Hannibal had promised sanctuary to any Italian settlements that stood with him against Rome, or offered his army shelter and food. But, even those too afraid to stand against him, were terrorized by the barbarians, who cared little for Hannibal's promises. They were here to claim what they wanted, earned in blood.

Gaius and his century of a hundred men had spent the better part of the past two weeks, since Trebia protecting those he could as they moved away from the conflict zones. When able, he chased down rogue elements of Hannibal's army and put them to the sword when opportunity presented itself. However, his primary orders were to avoid contact with the enemy, and to remain off the main roads leading to Rome.

His men, tired and hungry as well, had only enough for themselves, and were wary of this struggle already. Rome would be a welcome sight for them as well; relief from the death that surrounded them every day, at least for the moment.

Two days ago, Gaius got word from a rider sent by Valerius that he, along with the survivors from Trebia had linked up with a new army sent by Rome, which included the rest of the Sixth Legion. They, forty thousand strong, under the command of Gaius Flaminius, moved to find Hannibal. Gaius wanted to reach Rome, rest and regroup before his century rejoined their commander.

Storm clouds filled the sky, moving in fast from the north and sweeping down across the country like a blanket of death. As rain began to pour, it brought renewed misery to the refugees. While still midday, already the sun struggled to cast its light down on the land.

As lightening streaked across the sky, Gaius noticed three riders racing towards him, Maurus leading them. He had sent him out two days ago to scout ahead, and wasn't expecting him back for another day, not unless he found trouble that called for Gaius' attention.

"Gaius," Maurus cried out as he stopped his horse before Gaius' own. "Smoke beyond the horizon, big, but not large enough to be caused naturally, I fear."

"There are no settlements or villages in this region," Gaius pondered.

"None that I'm aware of, but, I fear we may both be mistaking."

Gaius knew he should ignore the warning, or at the very least, redirect the refugees. His men were not fit for another confrontation, nor could they risk drawing a large raiding party towards the civilians. There would be nothing his lone century could do to prevent their slaughter. He knew, however that he wasn't ready to allow another massacre to happen, not if he could prevent it.

With a heavy heart, weighed down by the burden of command, he said, "I want twelve of our best riders and swordsmen. Bring them to me, and then you'll lead us to the fires."

"Is it wise?" Maurus asked, not for fear of battle, but to be the voice of reason in case Gaius was acting foolish.

"Another two days and the civilians will reach Rome. If the barbarians have come this far south from the frontier, we at least have to know, or risk attack to our rear," Gaius confirmed his reasoning, which brought a welcome smile from Maurus, who quickly rode off to carry out his orders.

What little sunlight managed to break through the heavy clouds had vanished as it descended under the western horizon two hours ago. The darkness provided Gaius and his men enough cover to reach the outer walls of a large estate, unseen, which was big enough that it most likely belonged to a wealthy citizen, perhaps even a senator; the high walls that encircled the property, however, didn't allow Gaius to see beyond the walls to what was inside.

The fire that had consumed the estate had nearly burnt itself out, which had survived hours, despite the heavy rain, since the smoke was first seen by Roman scouts. Still, embers burned in spots where the flames had been the hottest.

Gaius slowly worked his way along the outer walls towards the front gate. A few bodies lay outside and on top the walls. None of them were dead Carthaginian or Gauls, Gaius noted, but slaves and hired guards, each of whom had tried to defend their master's home. So far, beyond the few dead, he did not notice much else – nothing that would have indicated that there was some sort of siege, or that the estate had been breached from the outside.

The heavy iron gates were swung open, which didn't look as if they had been battered down, but left as if someone had had pulled them open from the inside. This conundrum peeked Gaius' attention as he and his men worked their way to what he hoped would be answers.

Gaius led the first part, six men, including him. Maurus commanded the second group, which hurried over to the opposite side of the entrance and took positions alongside the wall.

None of his men wore armor or carried shields. The Romans carried only their swords and daggers, and had made sure to muddy their faces before striking toward the estate, where they left their horses on the other side of a low hill, with one man guarding.

Gaius took a deep breath as he peeked around the corner, fixing his eyes beyond the open gateway. He saw a few more bodies hacked to death; one lying in the middle of the entrance about twenty paces from him, another two slumped up against the walls, their bodies covered with blood as their heads were brutally mutilated rested a few inches from their owners.

With the few fires that still burned, Gaius saw nothing else – no one alive that was. He decided it was time for him and his men to advance.

Taken a deep breath, Gaius hesitated for a moment. He did not like this and wasn't altogether sure he was prepared to face whatever might be beyond these walls. He wondered for just a moment if he was ever going to get used to death.

Putting caution behind him, Gaius darted around the bend and ran down the gateway, his men quickly falling behind.

An overturned blackened cart was his destination. Gaius threw his back up against it, half expecting to hear a sentry call out once he was spotted, soon followed by a volley of arrows or spears. But there was no sound beyond the slight dripping of water, and sizzling as it cooled the smoldering embers of the burnt-out buildings.

The rest of the Romans hurried into the courtyard and also took cover; their swords held at the ready as their eyes and ears scanned the surroundings for any sign of movement. Like Gaius they too saw nothing, or had been seen.

Gaius looked for Maurus, finding him knelt down behind a stack of wet logs. He quickly gave him a silent hand signal, ordering him and the rest of the Romans to move quickly and spread out, and begin their search of the area for signs of life, or the attackers.

Maurus nodded his reply as he passed along Gaius' instructions to those men around him. A moment later, everyone moved from their cover, hurrying as fast, and as carefully as they could. While they hadn't been seen yet, that did not mean there wasn't still a presence in the compound.

Gaius chose to begin his search of a long building that looked as if it had served as a storehouse. It was one of the few that were still standing, even though signs of a fire were still present.

He moved by himself, wanting his men to cover as much ground as quickly as possible.

There was a short flight of stairs leading into the storehouse, which were partly burnt, but still sturdy enough to support his weight. The two doors were left wide open, a long dark abyss greeting him as he ventured into the structure.

A streak of lightning momentarily illuminated the dark interior, causing Gaius to jump at his own shadow. The light, however, did illustrate that the building had indeed been a warehouse. But where normally stacks of crates, jugs, sacks of grain and other assortments should have been, the storehouse was mostly empty. There were signs, however, that what had been inside was taken, and with haste as trails of spilled grain and flower covered the wooden floors.

Gaius saw nothing or no one that would raise his alarm, but as he continued deeper into the building, he noticed a far room, most likely an office of a sort where the quartermaster would have kept a tally on the goods kept inside the building, before being sold.

Inside the office there was still a fire burning, not enraged that it threatened the whole structure, but still enough that it provided enough light for Gaius to notice that the room, unlike the storehouse, wasn't empty.

There was no way for Gaius to be stealthy as he approached, which unnerved him even more as his feet scratched against the spilled contents that would have stacked the building's walls, or the increasing creaking the floorboards made with each careful step. Yet, as he drew nearer, he noticed what appeared to be legs sticking out in front of the doorway. Upon seeing them Gaius called out, "I'm a Roman officer, do not be alarmed. If you have a weapon, lower it now!" He spoke the last part of his sentence with more authority, or as much as his shacking nerves could allow. But still, there was no movement or reply.

Gaius was about to call out again, but he decided against it as he came closer to the open door. Only then as he came within sight of the pair of legs did he notice how small the feet were, like that of a child.

"Do not be afraid, I'm a Roman –"Gaius froze as he gasped upon walking into the office.

In the flickering light of the flames he saw two girls, lying next to one another, their clothes torn to shred, eyes wide open, and limbs covered with their own blood. Their throats had been cut, and their legs were spread wide, telling Gaius all he needed to know. Whoever had sacked this estate showed no mercy, not even for the very young.

Gaius fixed his eyes on the girls, one of whom had half of her body burnt to a crisp.

His back dropped against the side of the doorway as the sword in his hand felt too heavy to carry any longer.

He couldn't help but tear at the sight as he studied it, unable to turn away, but wanting too badly. It was only when he heard his name called out by Maurus did he pull away from the sight.

"What is it?" he asked, not allowing Maurus to cross the threshold.

"We found no signs of attackers, only tracks leading outside. I don't' suspect the assault happened from out there, but from within."

"What else?" Gaius asked. He could feel that Maurus was holding something back.

"We..." he struggled to say. "You should see for yourself."

Gaius tried not to look back inside the small room, forcing himself to pull his gaze from the carnage and replied, "Lead the way." What greeted him next was worse.

Moments later, Gaius stood in the center courtyard, surround by his men who each looked down at the collection of thirty bodies, most of whom were slaves, and others that weren't, including children. Everyone had been executed, heads cut off, limbs hacked, or throats slit. The women were all naked, having clearly been rapped before they too were murdered and left face-down in the mud.

The bodies that held Gaius attention now were different. Each had been knelt down on their knees, hands tied behind their backs. There was one woman, middle aged, four children, and one man, his age impossible to determine as he had been set on fire.

"I would wager that he is the owner of this estate," Maurus reported as he had pieced together what information her could figure. "And I think they would be his children and wife, more than likely."

"Looks like he was forced to watch them slaughtered before they set him on fire," Gaius concluded.

"Why do you say that?" Maurus asked.

Gaius just glanced back at him, "Why else take the time to set this up if they were simply to kill him first."

"Then who could have done this?" Maurus pondered.

Gaius pulled his dagger out from his belt and knelt down behind the burnt man. He carefully cut his bond; thankfully, the man's corpse remained knelling. Gaius then proceeded to cut a ring that was attached to one of his fingers.

When the bone snapped, Gaius wiggled the ring free. It was solid gold and engraved.

"Strange, you would think the ring would have melted when this poor fool was set ablaze," Maurus commented.

"That is because it was placed on his hand after he was killed, and the fires died away," Gaius had realized.

"Why would they do that? The things got to be worth some money, and everything else of value is gone, as far as we can tell."

"Because, they wanted us to know who he was," Gaius pointed out as he stood back to his feet, examine the ring more carefully – seeing that it was inscribed.

"Decima Felix Titus," Gaius read.

"Titus," Maurus' eyes widen. "He was a gladiator promoter. He ran one of the finest schools in all of Rome. I've seen a few of his games. Last years' Games of Jupiter, wow! What a show," Maurus commented as the name was quite familiar to him.

Gaius pocked the ring as he turned to face Maurus.

"I want all the bodies to be burnt and giving proper burial rights, slaves included."

"Do we really have the time for that?" Maurus asked, as he clearly wasn't looking forward to the grim work.

"Do as I have ordered," Gaius replied as he turned, looking around the compound a moment longer before he decided on his course.

"Alright lads, you heard the Centurion, on with it," Maurus spoke to men, once he realized that Gaius was continuing his own investigation.

Gaius pulled a wooden beam out from the doorway that led down into what he assumed was the holding pen for the men that had committed the murder of Titus and his family. He was in the rear of the compound, near an area that was surrounded by a large iron fence and several smaller buildings, each of which was still standing, undamaged by the fires. A few more bodies lied before Gaius' path, each of them guards he assumed, their weapons and armor stripped from their corpse.

Gaius walked down a set of stairs, heading into what looked to be a kitchen and holding pins for animals and men. The stench down below was horrible, nearly causing him to wish he hadn't decided to venture further. Blood spray lie on the ground; more men must have died during the escape, but their bodies not left behind for whatever reason.

Food that had been cooking had boiled over in a large copper pot, some kind of terrible porridge, brown with unidentifiable cuts of beef and other mixings.

Soon he found what he was expecting, several dozen cells, each with their heavy wooden doors pulled open. Again, there were more signs of blood as some of the men: slaves of another sort had died trying to escape. Inside were stray and dirty stained beds, with a bucket for shit and piss in the corner. The walls were layered with scratching, piled on top of one another for decades, written by the various men kept imprisoned within the walls.

Later Gaius left the cells and the kitchen area and ventured through the training yard. There were a few dozen wooden post and human-sized mannequins placed within the muddied sand covered courtyard. Each wooden figure was horribly scared with repeated sword strikes, training designed to hone a man's skill with the sword, something Gaius was all too familiar with.

Another building stood across the far side of the yard, its doors had been ripped clear off the hinges. A couple more bodies lay outside and within. These men looked as if they had been beaten to death with bare hands, as their faces and skulls had been caved in, reducing their flesh to a bloody pulp; and once again, these men like those Gaius had already found, lie naked, the cloths on their backs and weapons in hand taken from their lifeless bodies.

Inside the small structure were several tables and racks, each of which would have been filled with armor and weapons. Now, however, the room was bare of even the smallest of scraps, save for one object, which had seemly been purposely left behind, resting on the center table, facing the door, as if it meant to greet anyone that walked inside.

Gaius moved closer to the helmet, half expecting there to be a head still inside it, or at least, for someone to leap out from the shadows and attack. Yet, like everywhere else, there were no signs of life.

Gaius knelt down and stared long and hard at the helmet. He knew it was an old fashion Greek style, Spartan to be exact. It was cast of bronze, which had been polished to a perfect shine – its deep dark holes where eyes would have been, staring unblinking. A bright red featured crest rose from the top of the helmet, ending in a long tail that was carefully spread across the length of the table.

For a moment Gaius did not act indifferent to the helmet. But then, it hit him in a flash of memory. The uncommon headpiece of the fearsome Spartan warriors was worn by one man in the arena – a man he had only seen once in his life. And with that memory, the fear, the bloodlust and rage of him flooding through Gaius' mind, resurfacing haunting feelings he wished would have remained buried in the depths of his conscious.

"Calfax..." Gaius uttered to himself, as if saying the man's name would suddenly make him appear.

It was then that Gaius realized the helmet was left behind on purpose, and placed in this spot for a reason. It was a sign – a warning to all Romans that Calfax was free – having broken his bonds that had held him for gods knew how long. And now, he was out there, free to spread his hatred to any that were unfortunate to cross him. And with the old Spartan champion, he had with him a band of gladiators.

In that moment, the war took on a whole new meaning for Gaius. Hannibal had not just invaded Roman providence and jeopardized the republic; he had inadvertently released a monster upon the Roman people.

CHAPTER TWENTY-TWO

Lake Trasimene

Valerius thrust his sword, plunging it deep into the stomach of a Carthaginian soldier that had charged him, screaming in his native language like a mad man, consumed with rages. He growled as he clawed at Valerius' face even as the sword tore into his guts, spilling them out onto the blood-soaked grass. He struggled for a moment as the man's nails dug under Valerius' eyes, almost blinding him. The warrior was cursing him that much the veteran could understand, but it did not matter as he pulled upward on his gladius until the blade tore under the man's rib cage, piercing his heart.

The grip of the dead man loosened as Valerius pushed him to the ground. Quickly, yet again he was forced to defend himself as another man rushed forward.

Even as Valerius drove the tip of his sword through the man's face, the cries of battle filled his ears, which were logged with sprayed blood that drizzled from head, soaking him in the vial gore. Dozens of his men were dying by the minute, faster than they could kill the enemy. Once again, the Romans were the prey, fallen headlong into another ambush set by Hannibal – the very thought sent chills coursing through the legate's body.

How could this have happened again?

It was hard to see beyond a few paces, as a thick fog hovered over the shores of Lake Trasimene. It was cold too as the long winter seemed to not want to give way to the warmth of spring. This only served to make the battle harder as the bitter nip of the morning air seeped into Valerius' old bones, stiffening his reactions and ability to think.

Valerius' sword again struck home, boring into the top of a man's skull, but as more enemy warriors fell to him, more continued to come. It was only with decades of honed skills earned in countless battles that the veteran was able to hold out as long as he had.

Valerius grabbed hold of the man he had just killed, and pushed him at a Gallic barbarian that swung a two handled axe.

Valerius ceased the advantage quickly as the dead warrior collided with the Gaul. His sword was still stuck in the Carthaginian's skull, so he was forced to pull his dagger out from his belt.

Dashing forward, Valerius forced the blade into the Gaul's right eye, twisting the blade so that he may open the wound deeper.

The man screamed in agony as his eyeball ruptured, thick gore and blood spraying out from the socket as Valerius withdrew the dagger.

Before the Gaul could recover, Valerius thrust the dagger into his opponent's throat, before yanking it with all his strength to the right, tearing the iron across the man's neck, severing his jugular.

Blood sprayed out across the battlefield showering Valerius in the crimson mist before he quickly retrieved his sword from the other's man's skull.

"Romans!" Valerius roared as high as his powerful lungs could bear, "Form ranks around me, on the double!" he ordered, hoping that the dozen still standing could hear him. While they were still engaged in their own struggles, his orders were carried out as quickly as they could be heard.

Valerius was enraged, as once again, due to the ignorance of another general, this time Gaius Flaminius, the army had fallen into another trap set by Hannibal.

After the Battle of Trebia River, Valerius had taken the survivors and joined the four new legions that Flaminius had formed, and marched north to avenger those slain in the previous two engagements. But, just like before, under Sempronius' command, Flaminius was fooled into chasing after Hannibal, who used the terrain and weather to his advantage. With fewer men, Hannibal was able to move faster, and Flaminius, under greater pressure from the senate to defeat the rogue, rushed headlong into another situation he couldn't handle.

The attack plan had been brilliant, Valerius hated to admit as even he did not see the strategy beforehand until it was too late.

Hannibal lured Flaminius to the banks of Lake Trasimene. With the water to their backs, surrounded on all sides by hills, Hannibal's army waited in the woods, using the fog that rolled across the lake during the early morning hours to blind the Romans to his movements.

Flaminius believed he had Hannibal trapped, however, as he had seemly set camp in clear sight upon a nearby hill. But, Hannibal had set torches around the camp, giving the impression that he was where he wasn't.

The attack came early, at the break of first light. While the Romans still looked towards Hannibal's supposed camp, a safe distance away, he struck on three fronts. So fast and devastating was the strike that the Romans weren't able to get into proper formation to meet the ambush.

This was not the battle the legions were trained to fight. They were a well oiled machine of mechanized warfare. As a whole, they were nearly unbeatable, and Hannibal was smart enough to know that. Using the savage fighting skills of his own men, and those of his barbarian allies, man-to-man, save for the most experienced and capable, such as Valerius, the Roman soldiers weren't the equal to their opponents, not in this compactly.

Valerius wanted to order the retreat two hours ago, but even now, the voice of Flaminius could be heard as he his battle horns continued to blow, blinding giving ill-fated orders to his broken legions. However, few Romans fought under his guidance now, as they battled for their lives and not to seek some measure of victory. But the only means of escape was, either to push through Hannibal's lines, or attempt crossing the lake. Those men most capable of swimming had stripped themselves of their kit and armor, but nearly iced over, few men could make it to the other shore alive, as the banks of the lake were already timing with Roman dead.

Sometime later, as Valerius had gathered several hundred men to him, a blood smeared lad came rushing up to him, pushing his way between his tightly packed comrades and cried out, "Legate Valerius! I seek Legate Valerius!"

"I am here, boy!" Valerius called back, unable to see who called his name quite yet until the man pushed his way between two soldiers.

"Sir, Flaminius is dead, as well as his command staff and much of his legion. I was giving orders by Prefect Varo to seek you out, and to receive orders, if you were still alive that is," the young soldier puffed between long and deep breaths.

"What is the status of the his legion, or any for that matter?" Valerius demanded to know, forced to raise his voice as more barbarians poured against the shield wall his men had managed to form.

"We are near collapse. Two other legions and the auxiliary are already overwhelmed, beyond salvation. Do we stand and fight to the end, sir?" the boy asked, almost expecting that Valerius would demand such a foolish course – better to die brave than to return to Rome in shame.

"Don't be so damn foolish. Order whoever is still in command of the legion to join with the Sixth, if they can manage. We are going to make a break, and just maybe take a few more of these bastards with us as we do. Perhaps we can use this damn fog to our advantage as well, before it lifts with the higher sun." Valerius knew that not everyone was going to be saved. He was going to have to order that a full cohort would have to be left behind to hold the line. Their fates would be certain, but it had to be done for the rest of his legion, and what was left of Flaminius' to break through the Carthaginian formations and make for safety.

"Wouldn't it be best that we try for the lake, sir?" the boy asked.

"Boy, how well can you swim?"

"Not very well, sir."

"Then don't be a bloody fool. Now, be gone with my orders, and be quick about it."

"Sir!" the legionnaire saluted, and then turned, pushing his way back through his comrades and out of sight once more.

Valerius turned and retook his position among his men as he bellowed, "Hold these bastards a little more, lads. Make each barbarian filth rue the day they ever dared leaving their shit lands and trample Rome!" His words were meant with a joyful cheer from the Sixth, who fought harder than they had ever been asked before. Even if this was to be his final moments, he knew he would go to his ancestors proud of his boys. Still, it was not the glorious end he had pictured. Not knowing the fate of the war, no less Rome, if he should die, troubled him greatly.

"May the gods be with you, Gaius, for they aren't with us now," Valerius uttered under his breath as he watched a large formation of Numidian horsemen come charging toward his formation. He doubted suddenly that he would ever see Gaius again.

CHAPTER TWENTY-THREE

Gaius pushed his way through the gathering crowd that stood outside the west gate of Rome, which had been sealed shout, guarded by a century of city cohorts that forbade entrance. For the thousands of refugees that had fled to the city seeking refuge, this had caused panic.

The chorus of voices cried out, demanding that they be allowed into the city. This same scene was repeated at each of the city gates, some more violent as the people had been standing outside, undefended and exposed to the elements for days, at least what Gaius had heard since his arrival an hour prior.

Gaius hadn't expected to see this many people. He and his men had just returned, crossing over the Tiber River a day ago. Now, after Rome had promised its citizens protection, the city was closed. He had noticed the white smoke that billowed from within the walls when he first arrived as if dozens, if not hundreds, of buildings had been set ablaze. Why, he hoped to find out soon.

As he and his century forced their way towards the gate, the mob swarmed them. His men had to form a defensive line around Gaius, holding their shields up and basing away any that dared to challenge them, blocking thousands of fingers that were reaching for Gaius once they realized he was an officer, and could, perhaps, get them access to the city, or worse, held for ransom.

The peoples' collective voices cried out, demanding that he help them, stating they were hungry, that they had come to Rome for protection, and that it was the senate's duty to allow them entrance. There were so many that Gaius could barely make out a single person, all screaming and yelling, some throwing rocks as their madness was swelling, moments from bursting.

"Get back you bloody fools! No entry I said, on orders of the Senate!" bellowed one Roman soldier behind the sealed gate as he pushed with the blunted end of his spear through the iron bars, striking one elderly man in the face.

"What is going on here?!?" Gaius roared as his men pushed away the people that hung to the gate.

"What in Hades are you doing out there?" the soldier asked with a dumbfounded expression on his blank face. "There aren't supposed to be any more men outside the city walls. Didn't you get your orders properly?"

"Are you touched?!? Open the bloody gates and allow us in before this crowd has our heads!" Gaius demanded as rocks, clumps of mud and other assorted garbage was thrown at his men with increasing ferocity.

"At once, sir - Open the gates!"

Two dozen guards rallied to the gate and took up formation, interlocking their shields together, ready to repel anyone that dared follow Gaius and his men through.

Gaius' men were barely able to hold back the rushing mob that ceased opportunity once they saw the gates were rising, as hundreds of bodies pressed forward.

"Forward, quickly!" Gaius yelled as he and his men rushed into the city.

Several dozen people took advantage and ran forward as well, forcing their way through. Their efforts were cut short as the city cohorts attacked them, beating anyone they grabbed with clubs before pushing them back outside. The larger mass of people met with the Roman formation once Gaius and his century were safe. They bashed blunted swords against their shields as they carefully marched.

Some of the bravery men challenged the approaching Romans, urging those behind them to try their best to overwhelm the guards, but most, fearful of bruise and broken bones, after watching other refugees beaten down, decided against heeding the encouragement from those in front.

Moments later, the savage beating of already sickly and starving refugees began as the city guards easily manhandled the mob back outside the gates, before the heavy iron bars came crashing down. Those that were still trapped inside, were rustled to the ground, their foreheads bloodied, arms broken, crying out in pain as they were dragged away.

"What the hell is going on here? Why are the gates sealed and these people forced to suffer beyond our walls?" Gaius demanded between heavy breaths.

"I apologies, sir but two day ago the Senate declared martial law, recalling all soldiers beyond the walls back into the city, and the gates to be sealed until further notice. I wasn't aware that any of our men were left outside during the recall," the guard captain reported.

"We've only just returned from the north. Now tell me, why would the Senate do such a thing as forbade these people entrance to the city? Do you know what they have already endured? For crying out loud, man, there are thousands left on the road leading to Rome, dead, food for the birds." Gaius could not hold back his disgust. He had promised those he escorted that Rome would be haven for them, that the senate would embrace them and bandage their wounds. Yet, the sight upon reaching the city, and the fowl stench within Rome's walls, made him sick to his stomach.

"I am sorry, sir. But after the riots, which left much of the city in ruins, the Senate did what it felt was best."

"Why then do the people riot?" Gaius asked, dreading what his gut was telling him. Rumors had already reached him, which he prayed to the gods couldn't be true. But, from the sorrowfully stare from the guard captain he knew the truth before a word was uttered.

"Trasimene, sir - Flaminius' legions, all of them, to the last man – they are gone – thirty thousand men, just gone."

"My word..." Gaius could hardly contain himself. He felt week in the knees, his mind struggling to comprehend what his ears were hearing. *So many men...The Sixth...Valerius, all gone,*

"What about survivors?" Gaius asked.

The guard captain scratched his head, seemingly trying to remember.

"There have been a few trickling in, here and there. But the Carthaginians have been hunting them down, slaughtering them like wild game, or so I've heard. Needless to say, when word reached the mob, well, they acted like anyone would, I suppose. They rioted, nearly burning down the Senate House. Damn near a quarter of the city went up in flames. Those few days, well, I'm glad you weren't here to see it, sir. I don't enjoy putting the sword to our people, but, orders are orders."

The guard captain sighed heavily as he spoke again.

"Will there be anything else, sir?"

"No. Thank you. Carry on," Gaius answered. The captain saluted and then rushed off, barking orders to his men as they continued to hold back the mass of people beyond the gates. Gaius hoped, but knew it was wishful thinking that this same scene wasn't repeated at every entrance to Rome.

"Well, what do we do now," Maurus asked, having overheard the entire conversation.

Gaius wasn't too sure. He had been hoping to rejoin Valerius and Sixth Legion up north, but that was obviously out of the question now. At the moment, however, only one other person came to his mind.

"I need more answer as to what is going on. Come, gather the men, we march, now," Gaius replied.

The streets were nearly empty save for a few citizens who ran, with fear as they saw Gaius and his men marching down the narrow road. It was eerie, he was used to the volume of business and trade that normally occupied every block, but what greeted him were empty stands and boarded up windows. Soldiers were everywhere, patrolling with orders to take anyone into custody that were out passed the curfew, or looting those shops that were abandon or burnt-out.

Gaius understood the reasoning behind the riots well enough. Two armies sent north, tens of thousands of men and two consuls, dead, left to freeze in waning winter months before the thaw. The mob wanted answers as to why their fathers and sons would never come home – what was the senate going to do, and how would it protect Rome from Hannibal, who was fast become a man of mythical standing. But the sights that Gaius saw now, the stacks of dead, piled up like winter logs on carts, the smell of lingering death and burnt wood, and the sense of sorrow and hopelessness was overpowering. Rome felt like a blotted corpse – a defeated city, and Hannibal wasn't even within sight of its walls.

For the moment, Gaius' only concern was checking on his friends. He prayed every step he made that Anthony and Julia were safe. Had they left Rome before the riots, or had they endured? These questions plagued him without end until finally, he saw his destination as he and his men rounded the block, and turned down the street that led to Varro' estate.

Gaius' eyes opened wide as instinctively his right hand fell to the hilt of his sword, when he saw two dozen men, armed, standing around the home of Anthony and Julia. With them were several more slaves as they moved an assortment of furnishing, statues and other personal items into horse-drawn wagons.

"Looters, you suspect?" Maurus asked as he saw Gaius' sudden reaction.

"I do not know. But they don't look too friendly. Stand ready on my mark. I don't want to give them a moment to act if this should turn bad."

"Never fear, my friend, we have the numbers," Maurus mussed.

"Numbers haven't worked so far in our favor," Gaius added.

The steady marching of his men quickly drew the attention of the armed men around the home of Senator Varro. Their leader, a tall broad shouldered man, shaved head and numerous scars, most likely a former gladiator, rested his hand on his sword, watching with careful attention as Gaius and his century came closer.

Many of the big man's men weren't as seasoned, or ready for a fight. Some seemed panic by the sight of a hundred Romans marching towards them, but still, more than a few stood ready to fight if one was called for.

"I am Centurion Lucius Gaius of the Sixth Legion," Gaius called out with a firm and commanding voice, one that showed nothing of his apprehension. "And I am looking for the master of this house, or his children."

The leader of the gang sneered as he stood firmly between Gaius and the entrance to the house. Smoothly, not quickly, he drew his sword, but held it down in a relaxed position. Gaius in return did not order his men to draw their weapons, even though many of his boys were edgy to draw their iron.

"You can look, Centurion Lucius Gaius, but you cannot see," the gang leader replied with a strong hint of distaste in his voice.

It was then that Gaius wondered if these men weren't here to rob Varro' home, but hired to protect it. If so, a hundred Roman soldiers marching toward the front gate could be seen as an act to arrest Varro, who would be paying these men to keep him safe. So, Gaius eased himself, controlling his next words so not to sound too threatening, but still remained firmed in his determination to get through those gates.

"I am *not* here to harm the senator or his family. I seek an audience with them, to ensure that they are safe. Now, kindly move aside before bloodshed is required," the threat was purposeful, which got the reaction he was hoping from a number of the opponents as they seemed to shiver at the prospect of fighting well trained soldiers.

The gang leader smiled as he leveled his sword, aiming its point at Gaius. This action caused nearly all of his men, those most eager for a fight, and not fearful of Roman soldiers, to also draw their weapons.

There was nothing Gaius could do to stop his men from responding, as a hundred swords were pulled, save for his own. He did not want blood to be shed, but he doubted words were going to work against this man either.

"The senator has all the protection he needs. Now, be gone with you, before I carve my name in your pretty young face."

The threat was implied, and Gaius knew this man would not allow him to say another word before a sword came at his head. There was only one course for him to take right now – he needed to see Anthony and Julia – he promised to keep her safe, and a gang of thugs weren't going to stop him from keeping that oath.

As Gaius was about to draw his sword, a voice called out, drawing everyone's attention away from the conflict.

"Enough! Stop this madness, at once! Move aside you bloody fool, now I say!"

Gaius realized it was Anthony's voice before he saw his friend push his way between the hired goons.

"By the grace of Jupiter almighty, Gaius, you're alive!" Anthony cried out as he rushed over and embraced his old friend, throwing his arms around him without holding back his joyful emotions.

"What is happening here, Anthony?" Gaius demanded as he nodded his question toward the big lug that stood before him.

Anthony glanced back and leered at the gang, unable to hold back his anger.

"Lower you damn weapons, I command you! Who do you think you are raising swords against a Roman officer?!?"

"We are only doing the job your father paid us to do," the gang leader replied, but he did as he was told as he retreated his weapon, but clearly unpleased about Anthony's tone of voice.

"Ignore them, Gaius, they are goons hired by my father to safeguard our home and us from the rioters – mindless dogs, nothing more. Come, bring your men inside." Anthony waved his hand violently at the gang leader as if he was shooing a fly from his path, before he led Gaius and his century into the courtyard of his father's home.

"Bring water, and food for these men, at once!" Anthony demanded to a group of slaves that had been busy moving furnisher out from the house. They dropped what they were doing and ran off, gathering more help as they carried out Anthony's demands without question.

"What is going on here, Anthony?" Gaius asked.

Anthony sighed deeply as the first group of slaves brought back buckets of water and fresh baked bread. Maurus took command as he directed the men to corners of the large courtyard, while issuing twenty men to stand watch by the front entrance, clearly none-too-trusting of the gang that stood guard beyond the walls.

"My father, he is running, like many noblemen have done over the past few days. He is packing our stuff and moving us to our country estate where we can be better protected, or so he would hope."

"You are no safer out there, not with Hannibal and his horde running about, unopposed," Gaius commented.

"I know, but there seems no place safe, regardless. He acts out of fear, nothing more."

"It is that bad?" Gaius asked.

"I'm afraid it is worse," Anthony shook his head. "Once word reached the city about Flaminius' death and the defeat of his army, the people demanded answers from the Senate. But, those old fools had no answers to give. Some ran, fleeing for their own estates, or heading elsewhere out of Italy. The people, well, they just went mad."

Anthony closed his eyes as he recalled what he had seen.

"By the gods, Gaius, our own soldiers were slaughtering people in the streets, in droves. I barely escaped the madness myself."

"Then, the Senate must call more legions from the frontier to safeguard Rome," Gaius spoke, more demanding, as if he was in the senate addressing its members.

"It is not that simply, I'm afraid. While the Senate is taken Hannibal serious now, the bloody Macedonians have started a rebellion. What capable legions we have in Greece are forced to remain there to safeguard our settlements there, and our grain shipments, or else we all starve, Hannibal or no Hannibal."

By now, Anthony had led Gaius into his home. To his amazement, the place, which had been pristine upon his first visit months before, was sorry, as the floors were filthy, caked with layers of muddy footprints. Most of the furnisher was gone, as well as the potted plants, marble statues, the family death masks that dominated the far wall, and even the gold tiling had been removed from the floor.

Anthony sat down on one of the few chairs that remained in the house, as a slave brought him a cup of honey wine. Gaius on the other hand refused his drink, and chose to remain standing as he tried to wrap his mind around the information he had learned in the past hour.

"Then we must do something. We must reform the legions from the survivors, draft new soldiers from the country, hell, and even empty the dungeons if we must. With winter nearly over, we won't have much time before Hannibal has enough supplies to launch his full offensive on Rome," Gaius spoke, nearly yelling as if he expected it was within Anthony's doing to carry out the suggesting he was making.

"And then what? Who will lead them into battle? We don't' have an affective government right now. New consuls' must be voted into office. And then what, lead the new legions to their slaughter? I'm afraid it isn't as simple as you may wish it to be so, my friend." Anthony rubbed his index finger to his brow, before he took several long swings of his wine.

"You mean well, my friend, I know. But you haven't been in Rome to know the whole picture," Anthony added.

"No, I've been out there, bleeding for Rome," Gaius shot back.

Anthony couldn't help but smile.

"Oh, how I wish we had ten thousand men just like you, Gaius. We could conquer the world if we tried."

"I'm only interested in saving the Republic," Gaius replied.

"As am I. But until someone steps up for the task, I'm afraid there is little that can be done right now but wait and let the river take us where it may."

Gaius finally sat down, and then took a long, deep breath before letting it out. As he ran his palm through is growing hair, it was only when he pulled it back that he noticed the grit and filth from his scalp.

"I've seen things, Anthony, you wouldn't believe, and I'm not speaking of the battles or the men I've killed," Gaius' words trailed when he said, *killed*, as if he had only just then understood that he had taken lives – men who might be fathers, doing what they believed was right.

Anthony lessened carefully as Gaius continued.

"The men that fight for Hannibal, his barbarians, and..." Gaius did not know how to form the right words for what he'd seen at the estate further north, now a full week past. "The things they've done to our people – women, children, even the fucking slaves, you couldn't believe if I told you."

"The Senate has heard the reports," Anthony added.

"Not like this," Gaius' words fell silent as he pulled out from his purse that hung around his waist the ring he pulled from the charred corpse of Decima Felix Titus, where he held the small object tightly in his hand.

After a long pause, Gaius' thoughts returned from the lingering horrors he had seen. He turned his attention back towards Anthony and spoke with an unfamiliar firm tone.

"The Senate may be filled with cowards, and you may even want to surrender," Gaius directed his angry words at Anthony, speaking to him as if he represented the whole senate. "But, I've lost too many good friends to allow what I've seen done to our people to go unpunished." Gaius stood to his feet, clinching his fists shut once he tossed the gold ring of Titus to Anthony, who caught it, unknowing why Gaius had giving it to him.

"You need to understand, Hannibal doesn't want to defeat Rome or topple the Republic, but he desires to destroy us, all of us, so that our names may never be spoken again, for all history. I fear that even Carthage won't be able to pull him back."

"You cannot make this war personal, Gaius," Anthony said as he struggled to understand what his friend had gone through.

"Tell that to those people beyond our city gates, or the widows and orphans of our fallen brothers."

Gaius was about to leave when he stopped, as he saw Julia standing in the doorway, blocking his exit.

She had just walked in, and dropped the package she had been carrying, as apples rolled across the dirty floor. Her eyes quickly began to water as she first uttered, "Gaius," before she cried out his name once more, and rushed over to him, throwing herself into his waiting arms.

CHAPTER TWENTY-FOUR

"Gaius, I thought," Julia swallowed hard as she struggled for words, "I thought you were dead." She held him tightly, refusing to let him go. The smell of the oils in her black hair rose around him, covering the months of death, battle and exhaustion that shrouded him like a heavy cloak. He hadn't realized how much he longed for her, to feel her warm and loving embrace again. In light of what had happened over the past few months, his last words to her before he set off for the north, were meaningless.

"I am alive, Julia," Gaius replied with a soft voice.

Julia stood back, staring up at him with swollen eyes. Carefully, Gaius wiped away her fallen tears, which left behind a streak of filth across her cheek.

"When I heard about Sempronius, and then Flaminius, I feared the worst." She threw herself back into his arms. Gaius could hear the beating of her heart against his chest, even though his armor.

A part of him felt guilty as she hadn't been in his thoughts as much as he would have liked over the months. Now she was in his loving embrace again, and he realized she was what he needed to allow the weight of his burden to lift, just for a moment. He wanted to say so much to her, to confess his endless love and affection, and resend everything he had last said, but Gaius held his tongue, as he feared what it might unleash.

Gaius' attention was turned away from Julia for a moment as he heard the voice of a man, as he entered into the house, soon followed by the footsteps of several individuals as they came into the room that Gaius, Julia and Anthony occupied.

When the voice became clear, Julia pulled suddenly away from Gaius' hold, and quickly wiped her face of tears, but could do nothing about the redness under her lids.

A moment later Gaius recognized Paullus as he entered, with him, trailing close behind were two other men, bodyguards it seemed from their close military haircuts, and burly build.

"Ah, there you are Anthony," Paullus spoke, but held his words when he saw Julia's sorrowful expression. Concern quickly filled his eyes as he stepped toward her, holding out his hand so that he may caress her face.

"What is the matter, my dear?" Paullus asked, concerned.

Julia managed her best smile, replying with a soft giggle as she answered, "Oh, it is tears of joyful glee, my love, for my old friend Gaius has returned from the dead, it would seem."

Paullus stared at Gaius for a moment, seemly trying to place his face. A moment later he smiled, either recognizing the young officer, or pretending he did.

"That is wonderful. You were with Flaminius, I presume, with the rest of your legion?" Paullus asked.

"No sir, I was with Sempronius at Trebia. I was tasked with another assignment after the battle, so I missed the battle at Lake Trasimene, I'm sorry to say," Gaius replied as respectfully as he could. It was obvious how uncomfortable he and Julia were at the moment, and a part of him could not help but be angry at her sudden shift, from loving embrace to cold distant friendship.

"Then it is a fortunate thing you were not with that fool Flaminius, I must say."

"It is as bad as they say?" Gaius asked.

Paullus glanced back at his men for a moment, seemingly telling them with his stare to remain where they stood, before he placed his hand onto Gaius' shoulder, leading him nearer to the wall where he lowered his voice and spoke.

"It is much worse than they say." Paullus thought for a moment as he looked up at Gaius with a renewed sense of familiarity. "That night at Varro' entertaining dinner, I was impressed at your honesty. While he might soon be my father-in-law, the man can be a dreadful boar, made worse by his lapdogs. So, please, Gaius, share with me some more honesty. Tell me, what is your opinion of our people – how do they fare after the most recent defeat?"

Gaius was taken aback by Paullus' personal question, one that he didn't quite feel he was privileged to answer giving his status and position among men like Paullus. However, he would not lie either, so with a heavy sigh, he gave his answer.

"Dreadful, I'm sorry to say. We are broken, and on the verge of defeat. The men have very little heart left, and the people don't trust that our leaders or army can protect them. And Hannibal, he is no fool. He knows us better than we know ourselves, and I doubt regardless of what force we can manage against him, will do much good if we don't completely rethink our approach to this war – namely, the thinking of our leaders, as each disaster could have been avoided if it weren't for narrow-sighted, ambitious men."

Gaius felt nervous by the long silence shared between Paullus and him, when he finished his brief statement. If the man so wished, Paullus could have him sent to the farthest corners of the republic on a whim, or perhaps worse. He did not dare to understand what game the senior was playing, political or otherwise. So, he waited for Paullus' reaction.

Paullus turned and glanced momentarily at Julia, who stood by with the best smile she could manage, even though Gaius could see she was also nervous.

"You are right, my dove, he is quite the officer. It is shameful that Rome does not have more like him." Paullus smiled as if a wonderful thought crept into his mind, as he turned back and continued speaking with Gaius.

"Those men, outside, they are yours, correct?" Paullus asked.

"They are mine – the Second Century of the First Cohort, Sixth Legion. I'm afraid that at the moment they are what remain of the Wolves, I'm sad to assume," Gaius replied, wondering where the question was leading.

"Very well, Centurion. I would very much appreciate if you camp your men on the Fields of Mars. I would like them to join the city guards and what ruminant of the legions we have left that have already trickled back to Rome over the past couple days. I do believe that some of the Sixth are with them, perhaps you Legate is among them."

"I would hope so, sir," Gaius beamed, he wasn't aware that survivors of the Sixth were back in the city.

"Regardless, I would like you take command of what men we have left if Valerius has indeed joined his ancestors. I will have them folded into the Sixth under your watch as Camp Prefect," Paullus added with a slight grin.

"Prefect, sir! I'm honored, but, wouldn't that have to be approved by the consuls, which from my understanding, we are short two?" Gaius asked, truly shocked by Paullus' statement. He hadn't dreamed he could attain such rank, at least without another ten years of service, and even then, to be a prefect of Rome.

"Then, it is a good thing the Senate has used its emergency powers to appoint me as Consul of Rome," Paullus said, which surprised everyone in the room. He turned and looked over at Anthony, who had remained silent, sitting down on the couch, enjoying his cup of wine. "And, you father has been given the seat of Co-Consul, which is why I've come bearing such wondrous news. Where is he? I do hope he hasn't fled the city quite yet," the sarcasm was thick in Paullus' tone, but Anthony did not seemed offended as he stood from his seat and answered.

"No, he is still here. He is in his study at the moment," Anthony replied.

"Well, please be a lad and fetch him for me."

Gaius couldn't help but notice the tone in Paullus' voice when he addressed Anthony, as if he was just a child, even though he was only a year younger than Gaius.

Anthony did as he asked, first nodding his respect to Gaius, glad to see his friend well and safe, before he turned and went to retrieve Varro.

Paullus turned back toward Gaius. "And as for you, I'll grant you the temporary title of Prefect, until the proper documents can be drafted and approved, with all rights, status and privileges accustom. Do you approve, Prefect Gaius?"

232

"It is, sir, an honor," Gaius replied, failing to find the right words. "There is one concern, that isn't regarding my men, but the civilians. I've invested quite a lot of time and energy in ensuring their safety. But when we arrived to the gates of Rome, I found them locked, forbidding our people entrance and protection."

Paullus sighed heavily, lowering his head just a bit as he replied.

"Yes, an unfortunate thing to happen, one which I did not approve of. You can rest easy, Gaius that the first order I will issue is for the gates to be opened and martial law lifted. We must try to put this shameful past behind us, and move forward."

Paullus rested his hand on Gaius' shoulder, speaking to him with bolster, as if he was addressing the people.

"I will raise new legions that will not falter under wrongful leadership as our previous commands had demonstrated. You and I, Gaius, we will march north once more to avenge the terrible costs that our brothers have already paid. When we do, Hannibal will tremble with fear at such a sight. We shall, with his demise, rid Rome of his disease, and usher in a new dawn for the Republic."

Gaius could not say anything, but only manage a false smile. He had heard similar statements before, and while he doubted that Paullus was as naïve and ignorant as the previous two consuls, Gaius knew that Paullus had not faced Hannibal, had not seen what the man was capable of. Yes, Rome would recover, but too, Hannibal would be waiting for whatever the senate sent against him.

Paullus turned and faced Julia, now focusing his attention on her as he stepped before her, taking both hands in his and speaking with a loving voice.

"When this messy business is over, my lady, we shall be wed. Together, we will see our child grow in a new era, one safe from men like Hannibal and his ilk."

Julia managed her best smile and replied, "I look forward to such a wondrous time...my love." Her eyes couldn't help but drift toward Gaius. Paullus seemed to notice as an

233

uncomfortable silence filled the room. Thankfully, a moment later Varro entered, drawing Paullus' attention away, as he moved to tell his soon to be father-in-law the news.

"Gaius..." Julia struggled to say in a low whisper, but there was nothing she could do as he abruptly turned.

"I have to see my men to camp," he said, unable to look her in the face.

"Gaius, please," she pleaded silently, grabbing hold of his arm, forcing him to stop. But, he refused to look back at her.

"I...I..." Her mouth could not form words even though her heart was screaming out.

Gaius saved her from having to speak.

"I have to go. Goodbye, Julia." And then he was gone.

CHAPTER TWENTY-FIVE

The snow had begun to melt as the welcome warmth of spring finally arrived, and with it, renewed hope for the people of the republic. As the ranks of those men able to take up arms and fight for their freedom swelled outside the walls of Rome, the sense of invulnerability began to take hold of the peoples' hearts and minds. But for Gaius, Prefect and acting commander of the steadily growing Sixth Legion, his nights had been restless for weeks now as he tossed in bed, his mind too far gone for it to stay grounded, as he pondered too many issues that plagued him: his new rank and the responsibility that came with training hundreds of new recruits, most having never lifted a sword, no less used it. The impending campaign and the fear of again facing Hannibal in the field, but most of all, Julia and what had happened between the two of them when last he saw her.

His fantasy did not cloud reality. Gaius knew there was nothing he could do, and any words shared between Julia and he only made things worse between them. He could win glory in battle a hundred times over, and still not attain her. But he was not the problem, it was her.

Julia was a woman, and property of her father. Her heart played no role in how she was used, and simply, Paullus offered more for Varro's rise than Gaius ever could.

The guilt that he felt went towards Paullus as well. The man was good, and truly did seem to love Julia, despite Gaius' wanting otherwise. The man had entrusted him, and even bestowed an uncommon confidence in their relationship, one which Gaius found himself appreciating more than he would have cared to believe. So, Gaius sulked – depressed, not sleeping and hardly eating as if the whole world was crashing down around him. He knew he had no right, and thought about Maurus' word when he shared some of his feelings, *"there are plenty of fish in the sea. And being of rank, you'll have your pick of the best ones when this war is done."*

While his words were cliché, Gaius felt, having heard it a hundred times to love-sick men, he wondered if they were true. Was there another woman out there for him that would heal his broken heart?

NO! Gaius exclaimed with a fury, as he tossed his blanket to the floor.

Gaius grew bored of his inability to sleep, so he stood from his bunk, got dressed and decided to take a walk through the camp. Outside, the moon hung at its highest point. The nights had grown warmer, but still, there was a cold nip in the air, which forced Gaius to pull his cloak tighter around his shoulders.

The camp held almost four thousand men, almost all of them under his command. More recruits were being conscripted daily from Italian settlements and other providences loyal to Rome. Gaius had to admit that he was impressed that a new army could be raised so quickly. Of course, it was glory or vengeance that most of the new soldiers sought - their allegiance came from Paullus' wealth, which, alongside the senate had funding far more legions than the republic had ever fielded before.

Most of those men and young boys drafted into the legion were asleep within their goat-skinned tents. A few soldiers were gathered around fires, talking among themselves, sharing drink and stories with the veteran who had survived Trebia and Trasimene, or the riots that engulfed the city after.

While there had been a time that Gaius recognized nearly every man in the Sixth, now, as he looked into the faces of the men around their fires, he found it hard to place them. So many of his friends were gone now, and the war hadn't even reached a year yet. Many of those he would lead into battle were young, sixteen or seventeen, others a bit older; so desperate the recruitment had been that retired veterans had been promised a hefty ransom and promotion if they should reenlist. Gaius looked to some of these men now to guide the young, while he and his own veterans attempted to make them prime for battle. However, it troubled him more that the best men, the seasoned legions were still overseas, fighting in Greece, Macedonia and Africa. The senate, under the guidance of Paullus and Varro had convinced the mob that recalling them was not needed. While it was true that protecting the republic's interests beyond Rome's borders was important, it was more likely, as rumors had persisted that the two consuls sought to build their own armies, and in return, shaping their destiny.

If victorious, some wondered, or feared, how far the two men might rise once the threat had passed.

As Gaius wondered aimlessly toward the front gate of the camp, his attention was focused on one soldier that sat alone as he rubbed his hands over a dim fire. There was nothing of particular interest about the man – a boy really, other than the fact that he looked ridiculous in his oversized tunic.

His leather belt was fastened as tightly as it could, with a few extra notches carved into it so that the buckle could seal properly.

His arms and legs were nearly bare of hair, as was his chest and chin. His features were that of a boy, one that seemed barely fourteen, if not younger. His wide brown eyes stared without purpose at the dancing flames, as if his mind was elsewhere, perhaps home, wherever that might be.

"You should be asleep, soldier," Gaius broke the dim quiet of the moon-filled night.

The boy seemed taken aback suddenly as he hadn't seemed to notice Gaius standing a few paces before him.

As he focused his sight, waiting for his natural night vision to aid him, the boy sudden rose to his feet once his mind recalled Gaius' face, and more importantly, his rank.

"Prefect! Sir!" the boy saluted without hesitation as he tried as best he could to seem taller and broader across the shoulders, as he puffed out his chest.

"The hour is late, and a soldier wakes early," Gaius added as he came closer, before holding his hands out and embraced the rising heat of the fire.

"Yes, sir, but I was unable to sleep, so I thought I would come outside and sharpen my sword."

Gaius glanced to the boy's side, seeing that his gladius rested against the side of a log that the boy had used for a bench. Near it was a wet-stone.

"Are you having difficulty sleeping, or are the lads giving you trouble?" Gaius asked as the boy stood at ease.

"No sir. I find my accommodations acceptable, as well as my comrades."

"Then, you are expecting an attack?" Gaius mused with a grin.

"No sir. I merely thought it best to keep vigil, sir."

Gaius couldn't help but chuckle at the boy's eagerness. He clearly wanted to play the part of a soldier, well enough, but it was a terrible sight that he did not look the part.

"How old are you?" Gaius asked.

The boy hesitated for a moment. There was no denying his age, but the lad seemed to fear the answer, as if Gaius might cast him out of the army, or give him a lesser job. Yet, his young age and respect for Gaius' rank did not give him the maturity to learn to lie, so he answered truthfully.

"Fourteen, sir. But, I will be fifteen in three months."

"You could be dead in three months," Gaius added, which forced the boy to swallow hard.

"I could be dead tomorrow, or the next day, or twenty years from now, sir. Death claims all of us, eventually," the boy spoke, attempting to sound sure.

"Very true. What is your name?" Gaius asked.

"Cato, sir."

"And where are you from, Cato?"

"Tarentum, sir."

"You are a long way from home, Cato."

Cato's eyes drifted ever so slightly, as if he was recalling the home he left behind, which was to the south, along the coast, on the southern foot of Italy.

"Tarentum's ports are important to the Republic. You should be home with the garrisons protecting Rome's interests," Gaius commented after a short pause. "Why bother coming all this way, certainly your parents must miss you."

"I have no family to speak of," Cato stated.

"Then, what did you do, who did you stay with?" Gaius asked.

"I was a clerk's apprentice, working at the docks."

"Then a boy of some talent and intelligence, then?"

"Not really, sir. I was never very good at counting. The master..." It was then that Cato realized that he said too much, which caused Gaius to perk up at the notion the boy had just alluded to.

"*Master,*" Gaius repeated. "You were a slave?"

Cato was hesitant. A part of him wanted to run. He was near enough to the gate that he might have a shot. Certainly, once he confirmed his identity Gaius would turn him in. If he wasn't sent home, he would certainly be nailed to the cross.

"I..." Cato bit his lip, fighting with himself to speak the truth. "I was a slave, sir, yes." Cato finally admitted.

Gaius leaned in closer, now sitting next to Cato.

The boy seemed unsure what Gaius' attentions were at the moment, but he sat down, pulling his knees up to his chest as he twitched terribly.

"A slave then? Then might I ask, why come here? Why do you choose to join the army instead of running? There is so much going on across the country with Hannibal running amok, you might have found your freedom."

"Because!" the boy blurted out loudly, but then he quickly pulled himself back, lowering his voice as he answered Gaius' question. If he was going to be turned in, then at least he was going to tell the truth, maintaining his honor.

"Because, Rome is in danger, and while I may be a slave – *was* a slave, that doesn't mean I don't love the Republic as much as you."

"You don't say," Gaius was interested by the boy's demeanor and sudden maturity. He wanted to hear more.

"Rome is our heritage. Rome is our civilization. She is the internal light that guides all of us through the darkness that is the world that surrounds us – a world that breeds demons like Hannibal and his ilk. If Rome should fall, then all of us fall with her."

"You are a slave. What do you know about freedom, civilization and Rome?" Gaius asked, not accusing Cato, but his question was spoken out of curiosity.

"My father owned a large debt after his shipping company went bankrupt. He sold me into slavery when I was six to pay it off. I know – *knew* what freedom was."

"Then you could have earned that freedom back, eventually, when you paid off your price," Gaius pointed out.

"I couldn't wait. I saw their faces, my master and his clients. They were hopeless, as if they were waiting for death to come, and while they had it in their ability to do something, to fight, or send their sons to Rome, they did nothing, nothing but complained, or worried about how the war was effecting business. Worse still, after Trasimene, what little life was left in them faded. For them, Hannibal has already won. But," Cato looked up at Gaius with hard eyes, "I couldn't just sit back and do nothing. I had to do my part, even if I'm just a body, I still can wield a sword and die for Rome."

Gaius stood back to his feet, having heard all he needed. Looking back down at Cato, who gazed up at him with narrow eyes, half expecting Gaius to grab him and drag him away, Gaius only smiled.

"Then, Cato, you have attained your freedom. Now that you have it, don't fail me when we are facing Hannibal and his horde. Is that understood, legionnaire?"

Cato bolted to his feet with a wide grin and eagerly replied with a snap salute, "YES, SIR!"

"Then, you best be back to sharpening that sword."

Gaius left Cato, who did as he was told, grabbing his sword and the wet-stone, and continued putting a fine polish to the blade.

Gaius continued through the camp. He knew that Cato wasn't alone – men of all backgrounds: creditable, unlawful, the poor and the wealthy had come to the call. Each had their own reasons for being here, whether it was for immortal glory, steady pay; food in their bellies or, like Cato, idealistic patriots, Gaius knew that, while not ideal, Rome was better for it. The republic was not mindless, nor was it represented in its buildings, it walls or its government. He had learned – his faith in Rome restored that night Julia showed him the city he had always dreamt of, that she was worthy of his blood. It filled him with pride to know that he wasn't alone in his beliefs.

It was then that Gaius' overheard the sentry's horn blow, which resonated across the camp as the watchmen on the towers had spotted something over the rise.

Gaius hurried forward as dozens of officers rose from their beds, rallying their men to arms. The horn sounded again; no doubt they had seen a force coming towards the city.

Gaius climbed the walls and took his position next the century commander, eagerly asking, "What do you see?"

"I don't know yet, sir. My man saw something over the horizon," the commander replied.

"Are you certain?"

"The boy is young, but he has eyes like a hawk."

Gaius struggled to narrow his vision. It was dark, and even though the moon hung high overhead, he struggled to see what might have caught the watch's attention.

He tried to listening, but behind him the centurions were rallying their men, forming them into ranks. There was more than enough to hold the fort, but Gaius feared that Hannibal might be making a move for Rome – would he and his ill-trained soldiers be able to stop him from laying siege?

"Shall we hold men to arms?" the watch commander asked.

"Yes," Gaius answered after a short pause as he thought the matter over. It was then as he finished his word that he heard the faint sounds of marching. It was erratic, not formal and spread out over a wide area. But, slowly, with each passing minute the sounds of marching men carried over the camp.

"Send a rider back to Rome and inform the consuls that we possibly have an attacking force heading to the city. Tell them to wait for further word, but to seal the city gates and man the walls."

"At once, sir."

Gaius waited as he narrowed his vision, which was slowly starting to adjust to the darkness. Still, he could see barely anything but silhouettes against the blackened horizon. Eventually, those forms took shape as the men on the walls stood nervously.

"Sir, they look to be Roman!" the lookout with the bird-like vision called out, as he stood high atop the tower.

"Are you certain?" the watch commander called out.

"Pretty sure, sir."

"We know the enemy has been taking our weapons and kit since the first battle. This could be a trick," the watch commander uttered quietly to Gaius, who stood without saying a word as he studied the darkened figures that slowly moved nearer.

Gaius' eye opened wide with the sudden realization at what he was seeing. The banner of the Sixth Legion was carried before a small collection of men wearing Roman kit. At the head of the column was Valerius, who even with a thick grey beard, Gaius could have recognized anywhere.

"Order the men to stand firm, and have the first century ready. I'm going outside," Gaius ordered the watch commander as he was already rushing down the stairs.

"Are you sure that is wise, sir?" the commander asked, but Gaius merely repeated his instructions as he raced down from the walls.

A moment later, Gaius joined his men before ordering the gate to be opened. He couldn't take any chances. While that might have been Valerius outside, it did not mean that the old veteran wasn't a hostage, sent forth so an ambush waiting outside couldn't cease the moment and strike. Hannibal had proven his cunning, so Gaius was not about to make a mistake that would cost, not just the lives of his men, but Rome itself.

The heavy wooden gates were pulled open by a team of horses. Archers and spearmen stood high atop the walls, ready to unleash their anger on command, while several thousand men behind Gaius, stood in perfect formation, ready to repel any attempt to breach the walls. Gaius knew, however, if this did turn out to be a trick, he probably wouldn't have time to return to the fort. He had already ordered the gates sealed until he gave further instruction. If an attack did come, they would not be opened, regardless.

"Forward!" Gaius ordered with a strong voice, hiding much of his own apprehension. He prayed to the gods that it was Valerius, even if an ambush lies in wait. At least his old friend would be safe and alive, for the time being that was.

Once outside the heavy gates closed with a looming *thud*. He could see now that the men carrying the banner of the Sixth Legion had stopped several dozen yards from his position. No doubt if Valerius was with them he would not want to press too close, or fear that a nervous sentry might throw a javelin prematurely.

Two dozen paces from where the small group of soldiers stood Gaius halted his men and called out, "Friend or foe?!?" Immediately he felt like a fool. Any self respecting barbarian would say *friend*. It was, in fact the reply he got, and at once he recognized Valerius' voice.

Gaius swallowed hard, deciding against his better judgment that he should proceed. He doubted that Valerius could have been coerced into setting a trap, and if it had been any other man, he would have half the legion marched out to confront the uncertain threat. As it stood, he trusted his heart over reason. He wanted Valerius to be alive and well, nothing would up lift his spirit more than to see his old mentor again.

When Gaius finally saw Valerius clearly in the torchlight, he could hardly contain himself as he rushed out ahead of his men and embraced the legate.

"Valerius! I thought you long for this world," Gaius commented as he pulled Valerius back, who moaned with a bit of pain as his tired body had obviously been through quite the ordeal.

"Is this all the men you've brought?" he then quickly asked, gazing passed Valerius at the collection of two dozen soldiers, all badly needing a shave and clean clothes.

"No. I have several hundred more survivors with me. I kept them back in case the watch commander was jumpy," Valerius managed to reply with a smile.

"Call them forth," Gaius eagerly said, but he quickly placed his hand onto Valerius shoulder and steadied his words. "But, be mindful. Bring them in slow, to be safe. Understood, sir?" Gaius felt odd telling Valerius what to do, but the old soldier was wise, and experienced enough to understand Gaius' meaning without taking offense. He replied with a simple nod as he turned toward one of his men and relayed his instructions.

Back inside the fort, Gaius kept much of his men at arms and formed up. He wasn't taking any chances, not until all of Valerius' men had been accounted for, and disarmed. Thankfully, the old general and his remaining officers were understanding, and obliged to Gaius' orders.

"Quartermaster! Get previsions, clean cloths, medical supplies and anything else you can find, at the double," Gaius ordered as he and his officers tried to keep order as Valerius and the eight hundred men he had with him were kept in the center of the fort. Already his staff were trying to determine who among the men needed the most care, and from what he could see already, most, if not all were nearly starving – their bloodied kit, armor and cloths bloodstained, caked with week's worth of filth, that most of the men looked to be wearing rags.

Many of the men collapsed once they reached safe ground, while others threw themselves into the arms of waiting soldiers, balling like children. More, however, joined in the celebration that was quickly beginning to take hold of the camp, once it seemed the threat of attack had passed, while, already representatives from the senate were making their way to the Fields of Mars to get statements and firsthand accounts about Hannibal and his forces.

Gaius did what he could, but no matter how many orders he gave, he couldn't help the feeling that what he was doing wasn't enough. He had the food, medical supplies and all the needs the men could ever want, but the task seemed overwhelming. Valerius, to his surprise, had refused any services, as he directed care to his sickest men. The ordered madness would continue for hours on.

CHAPTER TWENTY-SIX

Gaius was smiling, something he couldn't remember doing for the past year as he watched his men celebrate long into the night. The whole camp was alive – spirits lifted for the first time since the war had started. Their brothers had returned home – not all of them, but enough to show the new recruits that they could survive.

Turning back from looking out the flap of his tent, Gaius grinned at Valerius as he moaned, once he dipped his head into a large clay pot filled with hot water. It had been three hours since the old veteran returned to Rome with his survivors, and this was the first time that he took any time for himself. His first concerns had been to his men, which Gaius and his officers rushed to attend too. The sickest and gravely wounded were rushed to the city, while the rest that were fit remained in the fort. Those that could find the strength remained with the recruits outside, enjoying their return with rounds of drink and bellies full of food.

Gaius watched as Valerius pulled his tattered and blood-covered tunic off, dropping it to the floor where the rest of his cloths had been piled, all of it beyond use. He could see in the flickering candlelight dozens of new scars, large and small lined his arms, neck and torso, while nasty welts and blisters had formed where bones had been fractured, leaving behind rough and dried skin that was hard as leather.

"You should have one of the doctors take a look at you," Gaius spoke as he took a seat at his desk.

"Blah, I've been through far worse, Prefect." Valerius grinned with a funny smile as he turned back towards his ward.

Gaius smiled. "Consul Paullus saw fit to promote me, until your return, of course."

"And I'm certain you are ecstatic at the prospect of taking orders from me once more," Valerius chuckled as he sat down on a stool that was placed near Gaius' cot, which he had already offered for him to use.

"The Wolves are, and always will be, yours. I'm just their keeper until your return," Gaius replied honestly.

"You've done fine without me, Gaius. I'm proud of you. Although, I must say that I'm saddened to see too many new faces among our ranks."

Gaius lowered his head, recalling those he'd grown up with – had trained with and called friends that were no longer with him. It seemed the whole world had changed in a blink of the eye that he hardly had time to reflect on what had already been lost before a new crisis began.

"Far too few have returned, after Trebia and," Gaius paused for a moment. "Valerius, what happened at Trasimene?"

Valerius did not reply, not at first, not before Gaius added to his question.

"You are the only senior officer to have returned. We've had trickles of men, here and there, but none as large a force as you've brought back. What happened – what went wrong?"

Valerius grumbled, not out of frustration by Gaius' question, or fear of recalling what had happened, but more from anger.

"It was that damn fool, Flaminius. Just like what happened at Trebia, Flaminius refused to listen to us, even though we feared Hannibal might be setting another trap. But he just kept marching us towards that damn lake."

Valerius rubbed his index finger between his temples before he started again. Gaius did not try to press him, even though he desperately wanted to know the details.

"Flaminius marched the whole army along the banks of Trasimene, hoping to cut Hannibal from retreating back into the woods, as he had done before. It seemed, for a time that the bastard had camped his forces around Tuoro, so we weren't worried about being out-flanked since it would take too much time for Hannibal to march his army out to confront us, if

248

he was indeed planning something. So, Flaminius set camp at the base of the lake, where we waited for morning."

Valerius took a moment as his tired mind struggled to recall the events of that day.

"When morning came, a heavy fog drifted in over the lake and encircled us. We saw fires still burning on top of Tuoro, so we thought there was no cause for alarm. At the very least, Hannibal might have used the fog to make a run for it. But that wily bastard had set the perfect trap, which we walked right into."

Valerius stood to his feet, throwing his arms out to his sides as he spoke with vigor, animating in detail what followed.

"By the time we realized that the fires we saw still burning were a ruse, Hannibal and his whole horde hit us from three sides. With our backs to the lake, we had nowhere to turn. Our formations were in tatters, and when the legion was on the verge of collapse, I saw hundreds of damn fools trying to swim across Trasimene, freezing, or drowning from the weight of their kit."

"We had reports that Flaminius died during the battle," Gaius pointed out one of the briefings he had read upon his return to Rome.

"I did not see it with my own eyes, but hope the bastard died shitting his pants. He led a lot of good men to their doom, just like that moron Sempronius had."

"What did you do next?"

Valerius ran his fingers through his matted hair, before he rubbed his eyes, trying hard to stave off his exhaustion, before yawning.

"I gathered what men I could and we pushed through Hannibal's lines. I started with five cohorts, but lost most during the attempt – more still on the march back to Rome."

"I should have been there," Gaius spoke more to himself than to Valerius.

"You had your orders and you carried them out as I had instructed. Don't dwell on matters that were beyond your control."

Valerius lied down on Gaius' bed. He tried to stay awake a moment longer, but sleep quickly overtook him before he could utter another word.

Gaius looked over at Valerius, who began to snore minutes after closing his eyes. He stood from his seat and careful walked over to the old legate and pulled the wolf-skin blanket higher across Valerius' shoulders, before stepping back.

Valerius looked ancient with his un-kept beard, now thick with grey. But, he didn't feel so young himself anymore. He had only seen and lived though half of what Valerius had gone through in the past few months, but, it was enough. He wondered painfully how the men, far younger and more inexperienced than he, how they might fair in the coming weeks.

All Gaius knew was, he would have to train his men hard if they hoped to survive Hannibal. He decided then, with drink still in their bellies and little hours of rest, that at first light he would rouse his men and drill them until the sun went down.

If the consuls believed strength through numbers was going to be enough, the Wolves would use knowledge gained through blood on the battlefield to their advantage. What may come, only the fates knew for certain.

CHAPTER TWENTY-SEVEN

The days had grown long and warmer as the summer sun rose higher into the sky, brining a welcome sense of calm and renewed hope as the distance between the year's previous events grew further apart. And while fighting continued across the breath of the republic, Rome was, at least safe, for the moment as Hannibal's army had been kept at bay.

Since the disastrous battles at Trebia and Trasimene, both Paullus and Varro, as co-consuls of Rome, had rebuilt the shattered remains of the senate's legions with new blood drawn from the ranks of Rome's allies, and her own citizens. The numbers were staggering. To date the consuls had gathered, trained and armed a hundred thousand men. It was the single biggest force the republic had ever gathered, and one of the largest the world had ever seen. With such facts, few in Rome felt the war with Hannibal could continue for more than a few more weeks, if that. When and if he decided to engage the republic's legions, his small force of barbarian allies would be swept aside like pebbles against the waves.

Since Valerius return weeks prior, Gaius had spent every day working his new recruits into a formable fighting force, which was comprised of survivors of both Trebia and Trasimene. No legion in the republic's army was better prepared, which in of itself, worried both Valerius and Gaius. From what they learned, few of the new recruits in the other legion camps around Rome had been trained nearly as hard, or primed for battle. It seemed that their respective officers followed the consul's thoughts, that size mattered, and not the man. Regardless, the new Sixth Legion was shaping up to the equals of those that had already perished. That in of itself gave Gaius tremendous pride, giving he had a large part in making them battle-worthy.

Rome was sending its legions off with style as the two consuls were going to march their combined armies through the city in grand triumph to celebrate their impending victory. And with just an hour before the first column was to enter Rome, thousands of spectators had already gathered, filling the streets in anticipation.

Gaius took the opportunity as his men had already been readied, and wouldn't be walking through the streets of Rome until the end – the famed and celebrated Wolves of the Sixth Legion had a place of honor, he walked, now towards Julia's home.

It had been several weeks since he had seen either her or Anthony, only in passing as Gaius attended some of Varro' meetings at his home. He had only a few words for either during those occasions, but had no time to reflect with either about the day he returned to the city, shortly after Flaminius' legions were massacred at Trasimene.

Then, unlike now, one would have thought the world was coming to its end. The city smelled of death: burnt businesses and homes lined every quarter of Rome, the bodies of hundreds of citizens stacked on overflowing carts – even the government brought to its knees. Now, life was as it had been. The city was alive with trade, business, entertainment and politics. Still, war loomed like a dark cloud. No one forgot that Hannibal was still out there.

Gaius walked into Julia's home. He did not see anyone, but he knew most of the house slaves would have been attending to their masters, who would be at the gathering near the forum. But, he knew Julia was still here. He had spoken to Anthony the night before briefly during a late night dinner with Varro and his officers, as he went over his expectations for the day's event.

Without waiting to be seen, Gaius continued forward, walking toward Julia's room, which was on the southern end of the large home, near the back, overlooking the garden outside. But as he neared her room, he could hear another person speaking, a man's voice who Gaius recognized as Paullus.

Easing himself into the next room, which was empty at the moment, Gaius listened carefully. He did not know why he was suddenly sneaking around. His visit was not unwelcomed, and Paullus had full knowledge of him and Julia's friendship. But, Gaius couldn't stand the thought, at this moment, to be between the two of them.

Julia was on the balcony, while Paullus was standing behind her, his hands resting on her bare shoulders as he spoke, low, but loud enough that Gaius could make out his words.

Anger boiled in the pit of Gaius' stomach. It nerved him to see Paullus' careful embrace around Julia, he didn't seem to be the titan he carried himself as around the senate. Here, with her, he was tender, seemly lighter in her presence. Gaius knew what that felt like – he longed to be like that around her once more.

"Do not fear, my love. I shall return in due time. The campaign will not take more than a few weeks, at the most," Paullus spoke in midsentence.

Julia seemed to listen to him, but her gaze was kept far beyond. Even here the jubilation in the forum could be heard, as thousands gathered to see Paullus and Varro' vast army.

"Are you so certain? Other men have gone, seeking a confrontation with Hannibal, and have not returned," Julia spoke with a tone of fear in her voice.

"Don't be so dramatic, Julia. The Republic has never gathered such men as the troops your father and I will be leading into battle. We outnumber the barbarian three to one. I don't think even Alexander the Great would have dared match iron with Rome's new legions."

"And when Hannibal falls, what then?" she asked.

"I suppose I'll be going to Africa, with the men to finish what Carthage started. But fear not, I will return in plenty time to be married to you, when the gods see it favorable, and have blessed this family and the legacy we shall create, together."

"I fear, Paullus, this army of boys and old men might not hold as well as you and my father believe. I fear, Paullus..." Julia's words trailed off as she seemed unable to truly say what was on her heart, nor was Paullus hearing any of it.

"Hush, my dear. It is not your place to think such things, not when they are well beyond your understanding." Paullus' tone was hard, but he held himself from speaking further, not before he steadied himself.

Paullus grabbed Julia and urged her to turn and face him.

"Or is it my abilities that you question?" he asked with a broken heart.

"I know nothing of military tactics or your abilities to lead men into battle. I only fear for my family – my father and brother's safety, and *others*, dare to me."

"Such concerns are not called for. The gods are on our side. I will not allow Hannibal or his ragged army to come within sight of Rome's walls. By Jupiter's sword, I swear it on my life!"

Paullus looked down at Julia, tilting her head slightly higher with his hand so that he may look into her eyes.

"When this is over, I shall return a hero, and then we shall be man and wife. That I promise you with my last breath, my dearest Julia."

She managed her best smile, and if Paullus had known her better, he would have seen that she still hand lingering doubts that could not be overturn with a few careful words.

Paullus knelt down and kissed Julia softly on the lips. As he did so, Gaius fell back behind the cover of the door, his heart racing, and his face flushed with bitter jealously.

As Paullus pulled away from Julia, he did not see Gaius as he briskly walked down the hall, heading towards the front of the house, and out into the courtyard.

Julia stayed where she had been, her sight once again fixed outside.

Gaius tried to steady his breathing as he glanced around the bend one last time. He wanted to leave. He couldn't recall why he had come to see her in the first place, and now regretted that he had ever come at all. But before he could step carefully beyond the threshold, Julia spoke.

"I know you are there, Gaius. Do not pretend otherwise."

Gaius sighed heavily before he stepped into view.

"How did you know I was here?" he asked.

She smiled. "From the smell of your armor: the scented oils you use. You smell better than most men, I must say."

Gaius blushed. It hadn't been the first time someone had said such to him. Now that he knew it gave away his position, he might have to reconsider his daily routine.

"I have not seen you for a while, well, at least privately. Why have you not come sooner?" she asked as Gaius joined her.

"I am sorry. I have been busy preparing my men. I would have like to see you more. I should have made a better effort," Gaius answered, a bit flustered, only telling half the truth.

"You do not need to make apologies, Gaius. I understand the life of a soldier better than you might give me credit. Your presence this afternoon is a wonderful surprise, that is all."

"I thought I should come and say goodbye before we march from the city this evening. I wanted to see you."

Julia took his arm and wrapped it around her own, glancing up at him with a warm smile, which Gaius hadn't realized how much he missed until now.

"Then, it brightens my day that you made the time to see me."

Gaius did not reply nor was she expecting him to. They both enjoyed these quiet times together without the need to fill the empty silence with unneeded conversation.

"Is it true what they are saying?" Julia broke the silence after a momentary pause. "Is the army truly as large as they say, and as powerful?"

"It is perhaps a bit embellished. However, it is the largest force Rome has ever fielded, and more are still expected to join us," Gaius answered.

"Will it be so easy to defeat Hannibal, do you think?"

"No, I doubt it will be," he answered honestly, a rare sentiment that he wouldn't share with anyone else.

Julia directed her attention high into the sky, watching as a group of birds flew over the city.

As Gaius looked at her, it seemed her mind was lost in another time as an odd smile, one that reminded him of the girl she used to be, crossed her face.

"Do you remember when we were children, and we used to play in my father's field? You were the brave hero – never a villain, and you were on a quest to find and save the princess from one of your stories. Even then you gave your all, never straying from your quest, regardless of the danger."

"I do remember," he answered with a smile. His mind never left those days far behind. Some days, when the world was hard and brutal, he would escape to those fantasies – reliving his youth with Anthony and Julia, wishing those times would never leave.

"It was only games, played by young children who thought nothing of the world or their place in it, I know that now. But too," she looked up at him, clutching him tighter in her grip. "I knew when I was with you, I was safe. Not just from practical dangers, but from anything. I knew you would never surrender under any circumstances, and that gave me hope."

Julia's eyes filled suddenly with sadness as she reached up and touched the side of his face, staring for a long while into his deep brown eyes.

"You promise me, Gaius, the day you left home that you would grow up strong, so you could protect me from the monsters of the world. I fear, no matter what my father or Paullus says, the coming days will be dark. Terrible things are going to happen, and I'm afraid, Gaius. I'm afraid what may happen to you. Just promise, even if it is a lie that you will come back for me."

Julia drove her head into his chest and wrapped her arms around his waist, waiting for his answer as she demanded once more, "Promise me!"

Gaius was silent for a moment as he held her, afraid to speak. But, like he did when he was a boy, he swallowed his fears and said what needed to be said.

"I swear it, my love. I swear I will always be here for you."

PART THREE

CHAPTER TWENTY-EIGHT

Late July

Gaius' attention was focused as he came within a hundred paces of his target, a pair of men on horseback racing away from him as quickly as their animal could run, impaired by its heavy load. One of them frequently glanced back, yelling to the other to push the horse faster, which was impossible.

Both were Carthaginian, or more so, dark-skinned Numidians that served Hannibal on his crusade, and these men were raiders who were part of a party that had attacked the outstretched Roman supply lines for going on a month now, since the legions left Rome.

The vulnerability to consul Paullus and Varro' vast army was apparent. There simply were not enough men to protect every stretch of road as the caravans that traveled it, tasked with feeding the legions, were under constant attack.

Hannibal had tried his usual tactics, which had worked for him against the previous legions sent against him. He kept his troops on the move, using the natural topography of the land to his advantage, and with fewer numbers, around forty thousand, he had been able to stay ahead of the legions that pursued him relentlessly.

Gaius and some of his Wolves had been recently charged with protecting the lines. It was not his preferred duties, but after the cavalry prefect had been injured during a previous encounter, he had been ordered to take the man's place until a suitable replacement could be found. And while Gaius preferred marching with the legions, he had always had a knack for horsemanship, which made him a quantified choice.

Gaius closed the gap between him and his target that he could see the terrified expression on the rear rider's face as he glanced back once again.

They had belonged to a group of a dozen other riders, but when Gaius' men broke them, they scattered. He'd given the order for pursuit, and to cut them down. At the moment, however, he feared that he was alone in the chase as he dared not lose momentum by glancing behind him to see if he was followed by his men.

Reaching back and grabbing one of the three short spears in a satchel behind him, Gaius quickly brought the weapon to bear, holding it high as he aimed, and waiting for his target to come within range. And when he narrowed the gap between him and the two Numidians to less than twenty-five paces, he let loose his spear.

The man in the rear looked back just in time to see Gaius throw his spear. He could do nothing to prevent the point from tearing threw his back, which was unprotected, save for a loose tunic.

Blood shot out his mouth from the force of the spear impacting through him, pushed him forward, which unbalanced the driver who lost control of the horse, which veered violently, throwing both men to the ground, hard.

Gaius' own momentum carried him past the two riders before he could rear his animal back around.

As he circled, he saw that both were down as the enemy horse quickly trotted away. The man he attacked lay still, his arms and legs bent and twisted, broken from the fall. It would have been painful if he wasn't already dead.

The second man lie a few feet from the dead man, lying face down in the tall grass, also not moving.

Gaius slowed his horse before hopping off. He wanted to check and make sure the Numidians were dead, even though neither man was moving.

Gaius removed his sword from its scabbard and slowly began to move towards the man he knew he hadn't killed. He couldn't help but notice the sudden quiet. He was in the middle of nowhere, in a large field with knee-high grass as far as he could see. He only heard the sounds of distant birds, and the gentle summer wind blowing through the field. Any other day, he would have taken the time to enjoy such calm and peacefulness.

Gaius inched his way closer to the rider. Suddenly, before he could check to see if the man was dead, the rider leapt to his feet and swung his sword in a violent arch that nearly took Gaius' head from his shoulders.

Gaius backpedaled quickly, keeping his own sword up in a defensive position as the man, nearly as black as the night sky, grinned at him with bloodied teeth, saying something to him in his native language, but it was only the word, *Roman* that he understood.

The Numidian was at least twice Gaius' age and the numerous crisscrossing scars that stood pronounced against his dark features, showed that he was a veteran of many battles, most of which he probably won.

Gaius regained his composure, realizing that he must have looked like a frightened child, and fell back into a fighting stance, as he had been trained.

He had killed before, at Trebia, and had trained against many skilled combatants in single combat, but he knew that a legionnaire's strength wasn't in one-on-one battle, but in a group: a century, cohort or a legion. The Numidian, on the other hand, had no quarrel about facing Gaius in lone combat. Still, an unwelcome and unfamiliar fear ran up from his stomach and spilled over him like a sickness.

Clearing his head, Gaius tried to bring himself into focus, not thinking about the man's obvious size, his scars, or the madness that stared at him in the man's bloodshot eyes.

"I wasn't planning on dying this day. I'm just letting you know," Gaius said with the best and bravest grin he could muster. It seemed to work as the over-confident warrior rushed, attacking first.

Gaius moved to his right as the Numidian struck high.

Easily the man rebounded from his first failed attack and came at Gaius with the same determination, countering with a wide horizontal swing that he must have hoped would throw the younger Roman off balance, but Gaius, to even his surprise, kept pace with the older man. He had done this so many times, both in practice and war that his reactions were second nature.

Parrying one blow, Gaius instantly felt the powerful vibration run through his hands, up his arms and into his chest, where his heart beat furiously. The dark-skinned man was powerful, but, he lacked form and proper control.

The larger and heavier sword hit Gaius' smaller gladius time and time again, but each time, he was wearing himself down as he was confident in his strength.

Gaius wished he hadn't, but he couldn't help but scream in pain as a wayward sword blow finally struck home, as the tip of the Numidians blade sliced just under his shoulder garment.

Blood drizzled down from the open wound as the Numidian couldn't help but laugh, as he said something that Gaius assumed was mocking in his native tongue.

Gaius ignored the sensation of his blood running down his arm, as well as the Numidian's mocking as squared himself for more savage blows.

Think, Gaius. You've faced bigger men than this one before, Gaius thought to himself. He was no small man himself, but there had been others larger than he during his training with the Sixth, men like his now dead friend Agrippa.

The Numidian attack again, yelling at the top of his lungs as he swung for Gaius' head, however, the blow came up short as the younger Roman dove out of the blade's path, and quickly rose back to his feet.

Gaius kept his distance from the Numidian who attacked once more, but again Gaius failed to meet his challenge as the man swung with the force to bring down a tree.

The Numidian screamed, yelling something fowl as his frustration was painted over his face.

Gaius smiled as he began to understand that this man had a short temper, and had difficulty controlling it. He wanted a fair fight, to prove he was stronger and better than his Roman opponent. But, war wasn't fair, as Hannibal had proven already, so Gaius played the part as he grinned wide, making sure to keep easy distance from the Numidian.

"Come now, old man, can't you keep up?" Gaius mocked, which the Numidian seemed to understand, at least the meaning from Gaius' amused tone.

The Numidian rushed forward with his sword held over his head, screaming with rage as he brought the blade down. Again, however, Gaius moved from the man's path.

Seeing an opening, Gaius struck quickly. The wound he caused was superficial, as he drew a line of red across the flat of the Numidian's back.

"You are too slow. You should have stayed in Africa and fought men of equal value as yourself, my friend." Gaius felt odd speaking as he was. It wasn't in his nature so rude, but, his tactic seemed to be doing its trick. With the hot summer's sun overhead, and the heavy sword in the Numidian's hand, he was beginning to sweat buckets as he struggled with each new attack, as his reactions lessened.

Again, with another murderous roar the Numidian lunged forward, but this time the man's fatigue was getting the better of him as his speed was drastically reduced. It was hot, and while Gaius was weighed down by his armor, he wasn't as bothered by the dry air.

As the dark-skinned warrior was sweating profusely, his grip on his sword loosened, held lower with each attack. His chest heaved with considerable effort, yet stood, refusing to withdraw his and fight on the defensive, to conserve energy.

Gaius saw his opportunity.

"You come to my land, my country, and bring war," Gaius yelled as he moved closer, waiting for his opening. "Why, to murder my people in a war not of our making? Your people are cowards, and will one day face judgment for the lives you have taken!"

The man did not like what he was hearing, obviously, to some degree he understood what Gaius was saying as sounded repeatedly what seemed like the same word, none of which Gaius understood. It did not matter, regardless; Gaius was done with this fight.

As the heavy Numidian sword came crashing down, striking the earth with a savage blow, driving nearly a full foot into the soft soil, Gaius dodged a moment earlier as the blade came rushing past him. He danced around his opponent and saw his opening: the Numidian's exposed ribcage, where Gaius drove all twenty-four inches of his sword into the Numidian's chest.

The Numidian screamed in agony, baring his teeth like a caged beast as Gaius' sword was quickly withdrawn from his torso.

The man tried to strike at Gaius with what remaining strength he had left, but again, the Roman easily ducked under the counterattack.

Dark crimson blood poured out from the wound, which the man's hastily tried to cover with his freed hand. Gaius had missed the heart, which he had been aiming for, but the angle prevented him from dealing a quick blow. No matter, his opponent was done, both of them knew it.

The Numidian began to stagger as his color turned a ghostly shade of choky blue. An artery had been severed, that much Gaius knew as his opponent seemed to be no longer aware of where he was standing.

For a moment, as the man dropped his sword, Gaius thought about leaving him as he stood – let the man bleed out. But, he could not bring himself to do so.

Moving carefully toward the Numidian, Gaius aimed the tip of his sword for his opponent's throat. Slowly, but effectively he drove his sword into the man's gullet. The act was easy as the Numidian's eyes opened wide.

The Numidian's eyes rolled back into his head as he tumbled over, falling onto his back where his body twitched violently for several long seconds, before finally he was still.

Gaius breathed deeply, seemly taking his first breath in a full minute as he stared down at the man he killed. He felt nothing, to his own surprise. It was not like Trebia, as he had been horrified by battle and seeing his brothers floating down the icy river. He had done as he had been trained. He bested a superior foe in combat, but he felt no joy in the act, or pity for the man.

A moment later four Roman riders trotted up behind Gaius, happy to see the two dead warriors at his feet. Right away they congratulated him as the leapt down from their horses, wanting to hear the details. Gaius, however, said nothing beyond ordering his men to mount and ride back to their patrol. A moment later, looking down at the men he'd killed, Gaius pondered the action a moment longer, as he wondered if these men left anyone to their name, far from the foreign soil they had invaded.

It did not matter, Gaius decided. He was content to let them rot under the sun, and be eaten by the birds then to ponder these men's lives a moment longer.

As the sun moved over the horizon, Gaius and twenty of his men, all of them tired from a weeklong patrol, safeguarding the supply-lines, were finally in sight of the Roman camp, much to their relief.

The consul army had been moving from day-to-day, tracking Hannibal and his forces for weeks now. Now they seemed to have cornered him near the town of Cannae, which Gaius knew had to be a bad sign for Rome, as the town hosed an important supply depot.

Gaius did not know the logistics at this time, but he figured that Hannibal must have taken the town purposefully. At least now Rome knew where he was.

As Gaius observed briefly during his short ride toward the Roman camp, the plains surrounding Cannae offered neither side any advantage – it was flat, mostly featureless with a few low-lying hills covered by dried grass. Gaius hoped the field, if battle was soon to start wouldn't allow Hannibal to try his tricks. A pitched battle was what Rome had been seeking, and now it seems they've gotten it.

Already thousands to torches lit the Roman camp, making it look like a small town among the sea of stars, which were just now starting to break through the night sky as the sun disappeared below the western horizon. A few miles away he could just barely make out the glow from Hannibal's camp and while considerably less bright, it still stood as a stark reminder of the apparent threat.

"I guess Hannibal has finally stopped running," Maurus commented as he hadn't turned his head from Cannae since they reached the plain.

"So it would seem so," Gaius replied.

"A shame really. If we were going to just give him Cannae and all the supplies within its walls, we could have spent the last few days doing something better with our time than patrolling the supply caravans. Bloody ridiculous," Maurus snorted his frustration.

"Indeed," Gaius replied. He felt the same but did not voice his opinion as openly as his subordinate. He was just thankful to be back among his people, and happy that he hadn't lost any of his men during the deployment. They had been in three engagements, counting the skirmish this afternoon as Hannibal's raiders had been picking off any foraging party and supply convoy they could find. The toll had been heavy on those unprotected as one hundred thousand men needed mountains of food and water to remain affective.

The rumbling in Gaius' stomach reminded him that he needed food as well, so he did not prolong his ride toward the camp a moment longer.

Hours later Gaius had been ready to bed down for the night once he rejoined the rest of the Sixth Legion when he was called by an aide who had been instructed to tell him that his presence was requested at a gathering of senior officers. Now, with the full moon hanging high over his head, Gaius walked towards a series of large tents that had been erected in the center of the camp.

"Going my way?" Valerius called from behind him.

"It is to the viper's nest, then I suppose we may journey together," Gaius replied with a wide smile.

"It is good to see you back. I trust all went well?"

"Nothing that couldn't be handled with a good sword and a fast horse, which I have both," Gaius replied. "It would seem that you've had troubles of your own."

"Indeed. Hannibal took Cannae two days ago, and the grain storage we had in there. As a result, we've put our men on tight ration. I'm afraid what is arriving by caravan isn't enough to sustain us for very long."

"It is good to know that my work was for nothing," Gaius sneered with a mocking tone. "Aren't the consuls going to confront Hannibal?" he asked.

"We've tried, but that snake won't come out of his hole. For now, he seems bent on standing between us and breakfast. In the meantime, his riders continue to harass our foraging parties, apparently hoping to starve us out of food and water."

"Then, what are the consuls planning?" Gaius asked.

Valerius laughed. His distaste for politicians was legendary, but Gaius did not know if his laughter was out of disrespect, or if there was meaning behind it.

"Well, normally the consuls would lead their own respective legions, but since this is a combined army, they share command on rotating bases – swapping command like two children sharing toys. Paullus has been cautious. He probably doesn't want to strain his reputation by getting this army wiped out. While Varro is brash, trying to force Hannibal's hand, and get him out from behind Cannae's walls."

"I'm afraid to ask – whose turn is it to lead tomorrow?" Gaius wondered.

"Varro, I'm sorry to say."

Gaius did not know what to think. He did not understand the Roman system as well as Valerius. He liked Varro well enough – he was the father of Anthony and Julia, and had always treated him with respect. However, Gaius was concerned. Varro was not a military man, but he was a career politician, businessman, and land owner. Gaius knew the truth well enough: it was fame and glory that both Varro and Paullus sought. If they defeated Hannibal, not only would their future interests be assured, but their names would live on forever, and generations to come would celebrate their victory and their decedents. But, waiting for an enemy that refused to budge while their own men slowly starved wasn't the way to victory. The food shortage might cause one or both of the consuls to act foolish, Gaius feared.

Even before Gaius stepped foot into the largest of the command tents he could hear the heated debates, as if the army had been turned into a small example of the senate. And in many ways, it was just that. There were more officers from the ranks of the senate than there were real ones, and most of the tribunes were the children of wealthy senators who sought advancement for their kin.

Most of the yelling was coming from the center of the room. Gaius could see through the densely packed bodies that the room had been divided between two parties: those in support of Paullus, and those that favored Varro.

Gaius could see Anthony from where he stood, as he was behind his father, standing tall and proud. However, Gaius knew his friend well enough to see the subtle discomfort as his eyes darted from person to person, as the arguing had reached its boiling point.

What was supposed to be a strategy session had quickly escalated to a distressing debate over the fate of the army, and the actions it should take in the morning.

Anthony broke from his father's side once he saw Gaius enter the room. "It would have probably been best if you had stayed beyond the camp's walls, protecting our supplies, my friend. At the very least, you wouldn't have to endure this," Anthony commented once he joined Gaius.

His tone, as it typically was, was in good humor. But Gaius could see the stress beneath his smile. It had taken him some time getting used to seeing his boyhood friend in the uniform of a soldier, no less one of high rank. He carried the title of senior tribune, even though Anthony had no military experience; he commanded thousands of men and officers, most, if not all of them with more experience than he.

"Well, at the very least we don't have to spend the whole summer tracking Hannibal across the damn country," Gaius replied as he tried to put a positive spin on the predicament the army was facing.

"True, I suppose," Anthony attempted a smile. "Oh, I nearly forgot." He pulled out from underneath his tunic a sealed letter, before he handed it over. "This came for you today, from Rome, from my sister. I dare say that it is thicker than the note she sent me and my father," Anthony grinned as Gaius took the letter from him, trying his hardest to not seem too eager.

"Thank you. I shall read it when I have the time," Gaius replied as he careful tucked the letter away.

"I'm sure you will," Anthony laughed.

Both men's attention was turned when they heard the sound of a jug breaking against the floor. It had been thrown by Varro, who cried out, "This is ridiculous! That bastard has cut us off from our supplies, brining about the real possibility that this army may starve to death before we have faced the enemy in the field. That is, of course, if we don't die of thirst first, as the continued attacks on our water bearers makes it impossible for us to reach the Aufidus river. And now, you suggest that we divide our forces into two camps." Varro had the support of most of the officers in the tent, who voiced their agreement, demanding that Paullus and his supporters heed their master's call to arms.

"That is why we must split our troops, to better protect our foraging parties so we aren't forced to withdraw from the field," Paullus rebuked, sounding calmer than his rival and soon to be father-in-law.

Varro looked tired, as if he hadn't slept for days. Gaius recognized the signs. The old senator wasn't accustomed to military service. It had been decades since last Varro had worn armor, no less commanded troops into battle, and even then, never under these circumstances.

"The liability of our sizes has become our weakness," Paullus added.

"Our size is our strength!" Varro cried, slamming his fist against a nearby table. "To separate, as you have suggested will weaken our position here. Already Hannibal's cavalry have been emboldened to strike at our forward lines, coming just a few feet from our ramparts. I can't afford to give him opportunity to try something even bolder."

Gaius was conflicted as the two sides continued their argument. He could see the wisdom in both, but he also knew that if the water problem wasn't solved, starvation wouldn't be an issue. If the army had to retreat because of supplies, the flank would be exposed to Hannibal's forces. Weakened men from lack of food and water would die by the hundreds. Suddenly, Gaius wondered if ancient kings such as Xerxes, who brought a million men to Greece hadn't faced such issues that threatened his invasion.

"Hannibal must be confronted, now!" Varro cried out. "I will take our legions out tomorrow and present ourselves for battle, as it is my right by law!"

"And if he does not stand, as he hadn't yesterday, then what will be done?" Paullus asked, sensing the worst.

"Then, we shall storm Cannae and take back what is ours," Varro replied, which brought a roar of approval from many of his supporters.

"Do not be such a fool, Varro!" Paullus yelled as he tried to be heard over those that stood with his opponent. But years of debating in the senate had taught the old senator how to win the audience to his side.

"We cannot face Hannibal in the open. With the river to one side, the hills to another and a force of this size, we won't be able to maneuver. We risk being enveloped!" Paullus pleaded as he tried to point out his military experience, but Varro and his supporters weren't having any of it.

"Encircled! We outnumber the barbarians three to one. He doesn't have the manpower to envelop our entire line, nor does Hannibal's barbarian allies have the discipline to stand and fight in a pitched battle. They will buckle under our weight. By dusk, the ground will be littered with the dead of Hannibal's horde, and Rome will again be safe," Varro protested.

"Well, there you have it, my father the great general," Anthony commented with a sneer.

"Hannibal may not fight tomorrow, so everyone might be getting all worked up over nothing. The day after, Paullus will command and he will have to act. Perhaps then a better solution will have presented itself," Gaius commented.

"Tell me, my friend, if you were Hannibal, a man that probably knows us better than we know ourselves, who would you rather fight – Paullus or my father?" Anthony asked.

Gaius sighed as the arguing continued for hours more. Neither side was willing to break from their standpoint, as both Paullus and Varro believed they had the winning strategy that would end the war. Both men knew what was at stake, but Gaius wondered how much the prospect of fame and immortal glory played into either man's thinking. Win the day and Varro wouldn't need Paullus and his money to rise higher in the senate, which for Gaius meant, while distant, there was the possibility that he might not marry Julia to Paullus.

Paullus on the other hand already had great power and wealth, but not the support within the senate. While popular during war, in peace he would be faced with an uphill battle to see any of his measures passed if Varro stood against him. The two families might be at odds for generation, if one man over the other defeated Hannibal in the coming days.

However, the other side to that coin, Hannibal somehow defeating both men, was a future that was more frightful. Both men would lose everything, if they survived, but Rome might be the ultimate victim if these men did not find a way to work together, for the benefit of the republic, or all might be lost come morning.

CHAPTER TWENTY-NINE

Both Gaius and Valerius stood before Anthony, who had summoned both men. It was well past nightfall and the long meeting between Paullus and Varro had come to a conclusion, with no meaningful results.

While Anthony did not outrank either man, as son of Varro, co-leader of the vast army sent to crush Hannibal, he carried his father's authority and had been tasked with issuing his orders. Gaius could see that it troubled his friend, as he sat behind a long desk, surprisingly small before the two veterans.

Anthony looked as if he hadn't slept in days as large droopy bags hung under his eyes, which were blood-shot from having spent too many hours going over paperwork inside the dimly lit tent. Gaius wondered when the last time Anthony ate as the man looked ten stones lighter.

Anthony cleared his throat as he reached for a rolled up parchment that sat among a stack of documents and clay tablets.

"My father is reassigning a portion of the Sixth Legion, three cohorts to the town of Canusium. We will be using it as a secondary supply depot and hospital for wounded, after the battle. I expect you and your men to hold the town against any possible Carthaginian counterattack," Anthony said as he handed the orders over to Valerius.

"Understood," Valerius replied, his words calm and collective, as always. However, Gaius' mouth hung open, dumbfounded by what Anthony had just said.

Valerius nodded without saying another word before he turned on his heels and started to leave. But, Gaius remained fixed at his spot, staring down at Anthony, angry by what he had just done.

Valerius said nothing to Gaius, knowing full well what his pupil was going to say. So, he left the two boys alone.

"What are you doing?" Gaius demanded.

"Canusium is important to our efforts. My father needs good men that can be trusted to safeguard the town," Anthony replied, sitting back down in his chair.

"Your father did not issue these orders, did he?" Gaius suddenly realized as he stared down at his friend, who was silent for a long while.

Anthony took a deep breath. "The orders to hold Canusium do come from him. But, the decision to send you is my reasoning," Anthony admitted.

"Dammit, Anthony! Why do this to me?"

Anthony bolted out from his chair and slammed his fists down upon his desk.

"What do you expect me to do?" he cried out. "You were in that meeting. You heard my father speak. Those damn fools will follow him to the gates of Tartarus if he asked them, which is right where he is taking this army."

Anthony took a deep breath before he continued, this time his voice low and calmer.

"They underestimate Hannibal. They all have from the first day of this war, and no one, my father chief among them will listen to reason. He believes that he can win through numbers. I fear, however, that will be our undoing."

Anthony closed his eyes as he placed his hands over his head, holding his face sorrowfully as he sighed deeply.

"I've seen this day in a dream, for years now: the ground littered with the dead of our countrymen – our heads mounted on spikes, and the parts of our body stacked so high that the sun was blocked out. Even the river had turned bright red, running with the blood of our people. Doom is upon us and there isn't anything that can be done about it."

"Anthony, it is only a dream."

"I wish it were."

272

Anthony reached under his tunic and pulled the broken half of the clay medallion he had worn since that day, now years past when Gaius left home. He looked down at it, a sad smile on his face as he rubbed it with his thumb.

"Do you still wear your half, Gaius?" Anthony asked without looking up.

"Of course I do. I have never taken it off."

"Then you remember that day outside the arena, the day the old man told us the story of Lupus – well, more telling it to you. That was one of the happiest days of my life, even after what we saw later that evening. I still cherish those memories. Things were much simpler back then. The world made more sense to me when we played in the fields, pretending to be heroes, as if it were in our power to change the world." Anthony sighed heavily, "It is a cruel fate to grow up, isn't it my friend?"

"Those days were good. But all boys must grow into men."

Anthony looked over at Gaius, staring at him for a long while before he spoke again.

"I am a coward, Gaius. I do not belong here, leading men such as you. You are the man, the soldier, Gaius, not I. I have always admired you for your courage and strength, even when we were children. I know you let me win many of our bouts, and I think I loved you more for that kindness. But even then, I wasn't you. I did not have your heart, and I know I will not live to see and do the things you have already done. You have to live, my friend. When this battle is over, Rome will be at risk – Julia will be in danger. She loves you with all her heart, as I know you love her. You were always there for her, and for Rome. You have to protect them both."

Anthony stepped around his desk and reached out, taking Gaius' hand into his.

"You have to swear to me, my brother, that you will protect her – my sister, from men like Hannibal. You have to take her far from here if it seems the city will fall. I ask that you promise this to me...please, Gaius, promise," Anthony pleaded, his words heavy with sorrow as he stared with saddening purpose into Gaius' eyes.

Gaius lowered his head, but only for a moment as he struggled to say what Anthony wanted him to say.

"I swear it, Anthony. I swear on my honor that I will protect her. But, you do not need to fear. Neither you or I are going to fall."

Anthony nodded before he hugged Gaius, holding him tightly.

Gaius couldn't help but feel that Anthony was saying goodbye to him, even as he attempted to agree with him that all would be well.

Some hours later Gaius stood alone on top the wooden walls that surrounded the Roman camp. Within, a hundred thousand men slept, and for the most part they were unaware of what tomorrow was going to bring, if indeed Hannibal accepted battle when Varro marched the army onto the field. But, it would not matter if they were aware. Most wouldn't care about the fuss the officers and nobility had made, nor would many have understood. All they needed to know was their enemy was out there, less than two miles away, and tomorrow, politics aside, they would finally have their chance to face Hannibal and his horde, believing they would win a great victory, one that would be remembered for all time.

Gaius wished he could think as simply as many of the men under his command. The logistics, the tactics, the men that claimed to lead this army, it gave him terrible headaches. He wished the world worked the way it used to during the classical age. Why send so many out to die, Roman and Carthaginian when those that started this fight could face one another in the field, and settle their difference in single combat. It was simple and honest, and would save countless thousands – fathers, husbands, sons and brothers from having to be unleashed on one another, so that other men may grow powerful.

The burden and guilt of knowing that so many of his people weren't going to go home was what got under his skin. He wanted to give his men more than a bloody death from a battle that should never have been fought. They deserved more – they deserved long and happy lives: to have and watch their children grow, get into trouble, see their children have children, and then to die, in bed, surrounded by loved ones. That was peace. That was happiness. Not this.

But the world did not work so. Instead, Gaius had to do everything in his power to ensure his men's safety. He had to train them hard, and teach them to kill without a second's thought. They were soldiers and all had sworn an oath to the republic.

Gaius stared up at the star-filled sky. Its beauty was the one true thing that felt natural; a small comfort at least. He wondered, however, gazing up at the heavens, why the gods toyed with men. Why they took such joy in seeing their children tear each other apart for little or no gain. How better the world would be if the gods had never existed.

Suddenly, Gaius remembered the letter that Anthony had given him earlier in the evening.

Removing it from under his tunic, he carefully broke the seal. Right away, as he opened the papyrus, Julia's scent enveloped him, which caused him to close his eyes and picture in his mind's eye her touch against his bare skin.

He carefully read each word by the torchlight, studying each sentence with meticulous care.

Dearest Gaius,

It troubles me that we are apart for so long. I miss you so...more than my simple words can express. I know we have said much to one another and have spent a great deal of time together, but it is still not enough. I long for your touch, the warmth of your body against mine, the touch of your lips. I know that for whatever reasons the fates have conspired to keep us apart, and that I'm destined to marry a man I can never love as much as I love you. But, I can't curse the gods either. I cannot bring myself to hate them, for I'm grateful for the time we shared together – what it has meant to me. I cannot pretend that I understand everything that is going on in the world, why you must be away from me in body, but not soul. But each day away from you brings tears to my eyes. I fear what might be, what darkness might lie over the horizon. I'm frightened for you, Gaius. I'm fearful that you won't come back to me. I can't live without you, and that scares me even more. Please, Gaius, please come back to me. I will always be waiting for you, my love.

Be well and be safe.

Eternally,

Julia.

Gaius heard someone coming towards him. He quickly folded the letter and placed it back under his tunic. He didn't bother to turn around, he didn't care who might be walking towards him, as he only wished to be left alone.

"It is a beautiful night, don't you think, Prefect?"

Gaius turned sharply when he realized it was Paullus standing next to him, before he quickly saluted the consul, but he was stopped as Paullus raised his hand quickly and said, "No, please, no formalities. I only want to stand here and enjoy this wonderful view with you, Gaius. Is that all right?"

"Of course, sir, if you wish," Gaius replied as he turned back and looked out over the far horizon, towards the town of Cannae and the glimmering torchlight of Hannibal's encampment.

"You are close friends with Varro's son, Anthony, and his sister, Julia, are you not?" Paullus asked after a short pause. He seemed to hesitate in asking his question, as if he had been afraid to even utter a word.

Gaius looked over at Paullus, puzzled, knowing that the consul already knew the answer to that question. But, Paullus kept his eyes fixed on the horizon, seemly not particularly looking at anything.

"Yes, sir, I've known both of them since I was a child."

"Then you are close to them?"

Paullus spoke softly, differently than Gaius had ever heard him speak before.

"I would like to think I am," Gaius answered simply.

"I've only known them for a short while. When I was first approached by Varro and offered to marry his daughter, I was hesitant. I always, foolishly I will admit, thought I would marry for love, and not political gain. But when I first met her, I knew then that all my apprehension was for naught. She is intoxicating. I could never have imagined that a woman such as her could exist; it is enough to make you –"Paullus paused as he looked for the right words.

"To believe in the gods and all the possibilities unseen or unspoken," Gaius added.

Paullus smiled as he glanced over towards Gaius.

"Yes, exactly. When I'm around her, I feel that I can fly, or scale the tallest mountains – that I can be a better man. I don't know how to properly express it. I wish I had been born a poet. Oh, how I envy you Gaius. I would have loved to have known her as long as you have, to share as much as you two. I've seen the way she is around you, how comfortable you make her feel. If only I could make her feel the same." Paullus sighed heavily. "I know that she does not love me the same as I do her, but how I wish to just have the chance to be with her longer, to build her a better world. But I know she doesn't love me. She will marry me, of course, as is demanded of her, and maybe in time she may come to care deeply for me, but love..." Paullus shook his head, fearful of his own words.

"Could you live as I, Gaius?" Paullus asked as he turned to him.

"No, I could not, sir," Gaius answered honestly.

"You are a good man, sir," Gaius spoke honestly. "She knows that, and will love and admire that man, as long as you stay truthful to yourself, and do everything in your power to make her happy, beyond material wealth. I understand her enough to know that she values certain qualities, such as honor and truthfulness more than anything you could ever buy her. She will love a man that embodies these things."

Paullus smiled as he let his mind drift for a moment, thinking long on Gaius' words. He then turned and looked over at him before he placed his hand down onto Gaius' shoulder.

277

"Thank you, my friend." With those words, Paullus turned and headed back down the stairs, before he disappeared into the camp.

Gaius remained where he was for a moment longer as he stared back up into the heavens and again watched the flickering stars high above him – his mind a hundred miles away, back in Rome, with Julia.

He reached back into his tunic and pulled out the letter she sent him. He read it again. He needed to remember her, to see her in his mind's eye. Her words, which expressed her true feelings for him was all he had left.

CHAPTER THIRTY

The dust obstructed Anthony's view as much as it choked his throat. He could barely see more than a dozen feet in front of him. His men, who had formed along the right flanks, had already faltered, as had the entire army. Carthaginian soldiers were now mixed with his own troops, as discipline had failed. He tried as best he could to keep order; to try and reform his men but his words were drowned out by the screams and fighting of men all around him as his men were being cut to pieces.

The battle had started promising, he had to admit. The mass of Roman bodies hit the smaller forces of Hannibal, while the Carthaginian general had sacrificed his Celtic soldiers in the center, which began to falter when the superior Roman formations advanced on them. However, Hannibal's s cavalry overwhelmed the Roman counterparts, as the center continued to advance once the Celts had begun to withdraw. Unknown, the Romans fell into a trap as Hannibal's center had created a gully, which the legions were trapped.

It was impossible. There was no way that Hannibal could have tricked his enemy for a third time, not when Rome had poured all its resources, and had finally gotten a pitched-battle. But, Anthony soon learned that Hannibal's forces, with years more experience and dozens of victories, while outnumbered, equaled any thousand Roman soldiers.

Anthony had gotten word that Hannibal's horsemen, his Carthaginian and Numidian riders struck the rear, completely enveloping the whole formation – trapping a hundred thousand men like cattle.

As the Roman frontlines, which were too tightly packed, were encircled, no one could retreat, no less form a proper defense. What orders might have reached Anthony's own men, was lost, its messengers killed, or the officers that would have issued them already dead. Now, after five hours, those that were left were being sucked into a whirled pool of men and metal, grinned to blood and bone until the ground was littered with Roman dead.

Anthony knew that fleeing was no longer an option. That time had come and past. Now, he, like his portion of the army was trapped on the far right flank. He was thankful, however, to not be stuck in the center. At least here his men could stand and die on their feet, with sword in hand, like true Romans, and not wait for their turn to fall.

Anthony knew he was not the best swordsmen, despite what training he had received, but he did his best, standing before his men, trying to give them encouragement. He wondered if Gaius would have done any differently.

At times it had been difficult for Anthony to determine friend from foe. Not only had the dust blocked his view, but many of Hannibal's men were equipped with Roman gear and armor, stolen from the previous won battles. They used these tools to their fullest affect as they drove through the Roman formations man-by-man.

And then, out from the thick cloud of dust Anthony thought he saw a face that was strangely familiar. The barbarian, bare chested was massive. He was older than his father, but was built like a mountain, shaped by decades of killing. Anthony watched as this man, in single combat struck down Roman after Roman as if they were children: their heads flying from their shoulders, or bodies cut in two as the man had the strength of a titan.

Anthony wondered if this man wasn't a demon, called forth from Hades. *Did Hannibal have such powers?* He wondered as the man murdered soldiers in droves, never tiring as he slowly worked his way over towards him. It was then that Anthony suddenly realized that the monster was coming towards him. He had been distingue by his black-brimmed helmet and long red cape, indicating that he was an officer, and one of wealth as his armor was adorn with ivory and gold.

Anthony called to his bodyguards, but they were already dead, or engaged in their own battle for survival.

He gripped his sword firmly in his hands, while raising his shield, hoping that the wood between he and the barbarian would be enough to save him.

His eyes were locked on the giant as he slowly came towards him. He carried two swords, both caked with the blood and bits of flesh, which dangled from the edges of the blades.

The barbarian grinned widened as he stood ready. Anthony could do nothing but shiver as he decided against his better judgment to attack first.

He charged forward, roaring as he loud as his lungs could bear, but what fear he hoped it might have struck in the heart of his opponent had done nothing.

His single thrust of his sword was easily deflected by the barbarian, who then slammed his second sword down against Anthony's shield.

His arm felt like wax as his shield was torn from his grip and cast aside like a piece of useless plywood.

The barbarian did not counterattack. He stood before Anthony, looming over him as he stared down at him, his teeth grinning with delight.

Anthony tried to attack again, but his effort was stopped as the man grabbed his sword arm and squeezed.

Anthony screamed as his wrist was being crushed under the man's impossibly powerful grip, until his sword dropped from his fingers. And then, the barbarian twisted, snapping Anthony's hand, at the wrist before he let him go.

Quickly, even before the pain set in, the barbarian rammed his fist into Anthony's face, shattering his nose as blood gushed, splashing out across the barbarian's chest.

Before Anthony could comprehend what was happening, the barbarian continued to beat him, slamming his closed fists across his face time and time again. Upon the forth strike, Anthony fell from his feet – his vision blurred as his faced was layered in blood and grit. He did not think he could ever stand again, but, with all his strength Anthony struggled back to his feet. However, as quickly as he tried, he fell back down on his backside as the world was quickly becoming one big haze, where no single sound could be sorted from another.

It was in this haze that Anthony suddenly remembered where he had seen this man before: the imagine of Calfax, the gladiator that had haunted him for years after he had seen what he was capable of in the arena, filled him with panicked fear.

"Calfax?" Anthony whispered as he looked up at the man that stood over him.

Calfax smiled.

Calfax grabbed Anthony by his hair, lifting him up effortlessly. He was like a limp doll in the powerful gladiator's grip. He didn't even bother to struggle against him, nor could he even if he still had strength.

Calfax stared at Anthony for a long minute before, he dropped his long sword to the ground; its blade sticking out of the blood covered, dried dirt.

With his freed hand he reached around Anthony's neck and grabbed the broken half of the clay medallion that was now hanging freely outside of his armor. He seemly admired what he was seeing, perhaps even wondering where the broken top-half was.

With one easy yank, the chain that had secured it around Anthony's neck, broke, even as he fought against him trying to take back the medallion, his last act.

Calfax let Anthony go.

Anthony wanted to reach out and take back the medallion. If he was going to die, he wanted to die with it around his neck, but his feeble efforts were in vain.

Calfax closed his fists around the medallion, holding it as he obviously decided to keep the memento of the easily won victory on the plains of Cannae. And then, without a care or even a second's thought, he then grabbed his sword and pulled it out from the ground, and as carelessly as a farmer slitting the throat of a pig, he brought the tip of his blade to Anthony's neck, and drew the full five feet of the iron across the young Roman's throat, slowly.

There was so little force behind the cutting that, Anthony, as he bled, arms and hands down by his side, knelt down on two knees, stared straight ahead, taking his last struggled breaths, fighting for one more moment to stay alive, Calfax stepped around him and continued on with his killing. In those last few moments, Anthony's mind returned to his childhood – his time with Gaius and his sister. His last thoughts of happier times – how he wished he could live in them forever.

Before his last breath escaped his lungs, he hoped he had made the right choice in sending Gaius away. He prayed with his last gasp that the gods would protect his sister, his last family from the very real monsters that now would be free to strike at Rome.

A moment later, as the world around him grew silent, his eyes closed as the last drop of his blood flowed out from his neck. He was gone, spared having to see the slaughter that would continue for hours more.

Varro stood within the ranks of his army. He was surrounded by hundreds of his men, yet, never before in all of his life had he felt as alone as he did now. Dozens of officers ran up to him, each one relaying reports from the battle, which was now taking place on all sides. His army, all eighty thousand plus men were totally surrounded with nowhere to run. He couldn't fathom how this could have happened. The battle was going so well. He had every advantage, and most of all, strength in numbers.

This was impossible, or so the thought ran through his mind over and over again.

His men eagerly demanded to know what to do – what they could do, but Varro had shut himself off. He simply didn't know what he could do. He wasn't a soldier; he had no brilliant tactics or strategies that would save the day. He could hardly think straight; barely comprehend what had happened to his army – all the books he had read about famed heroes of the past: Alexander, Leonius, Romulus, Agamemnon and what strategies they might have used to salvage this defeat, escaped him.

"Console Paullus, where is he?" Varro called to the nearest officer.

"Sir, as I said already, we don't know. You're the only ranking officer on the field that we can find, or know that is still alive," the man cried out.

"Dammit Paullus, dammit, where are you?!?" Varro couldn't help but cry out to himself. He suddenly wished he had listened to the man the night before.

"We...We have to reform ranks. We have to push against..." He was a loss for words. He couldn't think straight and no matter what he said, it wouldn't have made a difference. He could barely tolerate the screaming of his men any longer as he watched the distant line of marching enemy soldiers draw nearer to him.

Varro' eyes opened wide as he watched one of his own men slit his throat, killing himself, over waiting for the approaching Carthaginian army. That man was not the only one to do so either as Varro saw panicked men fall onto their swords, or ask that their friends to kill them where they stood. Other men held stronger, pissing and shitting in their pants, waiting endless minutes to die, but still determined to meet their end on their feet. A few of the braver, older veterans called out, saying prayers and demanding that they stand and fight – *take a few of the bastards with them so that Rome will have fewer barbarians to deal with tomorrow*!

"My son, where is my son?" Varro called as loudly as he could. "Anthony!" But no one had an answer for him, at least one that he wanted to hear.

"Sir, we can still try to get you out of here if we act now," the officer said as he tried to bring Varro out of his stupor.

"My son, where is he? Tell me Flavius, where is he?"

"Sir, we've already reported, he is dead...Now, we have to act before it is too late."

"No, Anthony...my dear boy. No..."

As he watched the Carthaginian army near to his position, he knew what he had to do.

"May all of you forgive me," Varro said more to himself than to any man near to him, as he drew his dagger out from behind his back, and raised it quickly up to his throat.

"Sir - No!" Flavius tried to stop him, but even before he could reach out, Varro rammed the knife through his own neck.

He slumped off of his horse, falling to the ground, still alive, but not for much longer.

No one came to him as he fell. He just lied there, bleeding as he stared up at his men that were all around him. Their fate was already decided, it would only be a few more minutes before they were all dead as well.

Then too, Varro' eyes closed to the world; to the failure that he had created. Only history could judge him now.

Across the plains of Cannae much of the fighting had stopped as Hannibal stood on top his horse, standing on one of the far hills surveyed the battlefield. Only a few pockets of survivors continued to challenge his men, who were now superior in numbers, and bloodlust. He had only the faintest smile on his face. He did not enjoy seeing so many brave souls dead at his feet; more bodies then he had ever seen gathered in one place that, the birds that circled over head by the hundreds, would certainly eat to bursting, for weeks to come. Yet, he couldn't help but feel a sense of accomplishment and pride. He had won a victory that would forever be remembered in the chronicles of warfare, which by each new day was closer to not being written by a Roman's hand.

"The Republic is broken!" Hasdrubal cried out with joy as he rode up and stood beside his general.

"Are they?" Hannibal asked as he refused the offer of wine that his officer attempted to pass over to him, as the two stood looking out over the battlefield.

"Do not be so doubtful, general. You have won a great victory! How proud your father would be of you. Now, there is no force of man or nature that stands between us and the gates of Rome. And when we arrive, we will make the Senate eat our shit as they lick our asses. They will give you their kingdom and the entire world shall know that Carthage is again the sole power in existence."

Hannibal glanced over at his friend, not rebuking or agreeing with his statement. It was true, he knew that there was nothing left standing between he and Rome. What men had escaped would not be enough to mount an effective defense of the city. He could have the capital in a matter of days. But still, as he turned his head back towards the battlefield, the sense of joy and excitement that his men showed was not evident on his face.

"There are still Romans out there who have escaped our trap. I want them found and dealt with," Hannibal finally spoke; his words ice cold even in the growing summer heat.

"That will be done. I will put Calfax and his men on the task at once. But shouldn't we ransom some of the survivors we find?"

"No. I want our Senate to see my resolve. Find me the Roman elite, living and dead. Tear their wealth from their bodies; their rings and anything that represents their authority and collect them. Do not melt them or pass them out. I want them all. I want them delivered to those old fools on the first ship out of Italy. Is that understood?"

"That will take some time. That is a lot of rings to collect from the battlefield."

"I know. You best get started."

"And, what about the survivors that aren't of the Roman elite?"

Hannibal stared at his man for a long time before he finally answered.

"Use your imagination."

Hasdrubal smile widen as he took a long swig from the wineskin before he kicked his horse, and raced down towards the battlefield. Already Hannibal's mind turned towards the future, which for him, was strangely uncertain.

Rome was defeated and left open to him. What was stopping him from marching his army to its gates now?

Nothing...yet, he was hesitant, despite his victory this day there were still many uncertainties he was fearful of. He knew this enemy – Rome, was a hydra. He had severed its head so many times all ready - its body was far from dead, that he knew, even as he watched the last vestiges of survivors slaughtered to the last man; no quarter given. Rome would, however, rise again. This fact vexed him without end, even upon his great victory.

CHAPTER THIRTY-ONE

It was quiet, almost too quiet. Gaius had always hated silence, he needed activity. The sounds of a city or the steady breeze of a warm summer's day, as farmers worked their fields – the sounds of their pick axes breaking through the earth, curing up rocks, dirt, with the songs of birds overhead. Here in the nearly abandoned city of Canusium, it was eerily still, as if everyone knew a terrible storm was brewing over the hills. Only a handful of the town's people had stayed behind. A few stubborn farmers and store owners, or those that simply had nowhere else to go. Tens of thousands had already fled to Rome, or the southern most cities. But in truth, there wasn't anywhere people could go, north, south, east or west. The enemies of Rome were everywhere, or so it seemed.

Standing up on top of the high stone wall that surrounded the town, Gaius looked out towards the east, towards Cannae. He and his men had come to this place two days ago, on orders to make ready for any casualties that might come this way once the battle was won. He knew it was an excuse. There was no real reason to expect any Roman casualties to come this direction, not if the battle was indeed won, not when the main army's camp had all the needs for those wounded. And if not the camp, then the city of Cannae would suffice.

Gaius wanted to be at Cannae more than anything. He had no real wish to be in a battle against Hannibal, not after surviving Trebia. Still, he wanted to be with the army. He wanted to be doing more than babysitting a small and unimportant settlement as this. It was his right as a soldier of the republic to face his enemies head on, and not be sent away on the eve of Rome's greatest victory, or its greatest defeat.

A part of him hated Anthony for what he had done. Why he had sent him away. It was unprofessional to put his personal feelings before his duty as an officer. The Wolves deserved to be at Cannae. They had fought, lost and suffered as much as any two legions since this war had begun. Still, however, something in Gaius' old friend's eyes told him a different story. It wasn't as if Anthony was afraid of battle. While he wasn't nearly as seasoned or as trained as he, Anthony was no coward, Gaius knew that. It seemed as if he had seen something, perhaps a vision of what was to come in his dreams; that something horrible was coming, and that he needed Gaius away from it; for Rome, for himself, for Julia.

He knew the reasoning, but failed to understand its meaning. Now going on two full days, there had been no word from the army. The battle should have started by now. However, there had been no dispatch or wounded coming in from Cannae from the time he arrived at Canusium, till now. If there was a victory, then Rome would have sent word. Even if the battle was a defeat, then still word would have arrived about what actions the men stationed here should take.

Even the worst imaginable defeat couldn't have been that suffered.

Gaius could not take it anymore as he had spent the better part of the day pacing back and forth along the high walls, looking out over the rolling brown hills that surrounded the town, waiting, hoping for any sign from Cannae to reach them. He was done waiting. If he had to ride out to Cannae on his own, he would. But before he deserted the army to seek his answers, Gaius figured he had better ask permission first, and see what came of it.

As he walked down the crowded streets towards the building that Valerius had chosen as his headquarters, the roads were mostly filled with bored and frustrated soldiers that had little to do, other than sit out in the hot sun and speculate among themselves why they were here, doing nothing.

They, like he, needed to know what was going on. Many were not happy about missing the battle, victory or defeat they just wanted to be where the action was. Some watched Gaius as he walked by them, he could tell that they wanted to ask him for any updates, if he knew anything, but most hesitated, seeing that he was obviously rushing towards the headquarters.

Truthfully, for the whole fourteen minutes that it took him to cross the town he was trying to think of a million and one excuses that he could make up so that Valerius would authorize him to take men to the battlefield. When he finally reached the building and stepped inside, into what had been the home of one of Canusium's wealthier citizens, he saw Valerius in the back room, in what had been the dining hall. A dozen aides were with him, all going back and forth taking care of the various orders that Valerius was issuing out. He had scouts out in the field, shift rotations for men on the walls that needed taking care of, management of the food stocks, and over a thousand men that were bored with nothing to do but listen to each other's fears and doubts about what was happening.

Valerius glanced up and saw Gaius standing in the doorway. To even his surprise, Gaius never got the chance to say anything - use one of his reasons for why he should take some men to Cannae. He had a good argument ready, but Valerius just looked back down at his maps and started speaking.

"I want you to take the first cavalry cohort to Cannae. Find out what the fuck is going out there, and report back to me once you have some answers. Is that understood?"

Gaius perked up, standing a bit taller as he was loss for words. He hadn't expected his old mentor to issue such an order.

"Yes, sir. At once."

Gaius turned quickly and raced out of the manor and towards the army barracks that housed the men he would be taking with him to Cannae. It took him less than five minutes, and when he called forth the eighty men that he would be taking, they all eagerly leaped to their feet, grabbed their gear, and raced off with Gaius.

The distance between the city of Canusium and Cannae was covered by Gaius and his men fairly quickly. They had left Canusium in the morning, and now with less than an hour before night fall, he could see the surrounding hills of Cannae before him. And immediately, he knew something was wrong as he could see thousands of birds circling over head, further towards the plains that were set between the city of Cannae, which was where Hannibal had based his army, and the Roman camp.

He kicked his horse, demanded that it run faster as he needed to get to the far side of the hill and see for himself what he already knew: a battle had taken place. But who had won? The knot in his stomach gave him early indications that it wasn't his side.

It was very hot and the smell of dead and putrid flesh hit him hard as he rounded the bend, following a narrow paved road that was cut in between two daunting hills. And then, when the fields of Cannae came into view, Gaius' mouth opened wide as he and his men stopped dead in their tracks.

For miles, further than he could see with his naked eyes, laid the bodies of tens of thousands, all stretched out, and clumped together like stacks of logs, as if an entire forest had been cut down.

Banners, flags and standards of the various Roman cohorts, units and entire legions stuck out of the ground, between the fallen dead. Birds, thousands, more than Gaius had ever seen before flew down from the sky, landing between the dead, filling their bellies with putrid human flesh; even wild dogs had come down from the hills and walked among the Roman dead as well. None fought one another, there was so many bodies that they could feast for months without worry of hunger.

Gaius and his men slowly trotted into the battlefield. Along the outer edges they could see the severed heads of their countrymen stuck on pikes, a clear warning set by the barbarians that were under Hannibal's command.

A number of Gaius' soldiers, mostly his newest recruits, could not stand the sight or the smell as they dropped from their horses, and puked their guts out. A few men leaped down from their animals and helped those few that couldn't bear to look at the carnage any longer, as more than a few of them were openly crying now.

Gaius paid little attention as he continued forward, eventually leaping down from his horse as the animal could not go any further through the thick carped of dead men.

He looked around him, barely sure of where he could go. There were so many bodies that he couldn't avoid stepping on pieces of men, entrails and globs of blood that had pooled, soaking into the earth before drying under the baking sun.

He hated the faces of the dead. Most, nearly all had their eyes open, mouths wide as the look of share terror had filled their expressions, before they had died, slowly, painfully, clumped together with the men before them, beside them, and behind them. Many of the dead were nude, or near nude. The Carthaginians and their allies would have picked the dead clean of anything useful: armor, weapons, coins, jewels, even body parts such as tattoos and heads to be displayed as trophies.

Gaius had a rough estimate where Anthony would have been positioned. He needed to move forward and find him. He knew it was impossible to find one man among the countless thousands. It did not matter - he had to at least try.

He could see, as he worked his way deeper into the body laded ground a few hundred people also walking among the corpses. Most of them were women, and most were sobbing openly. Gaius knew that these women would have been the wives, mothers, sisters and other relatives that had followed the army. They would sift through the remains of the dead looking for a familiar face of a loved one, hoping that they could find them so that they might give them a proper burial. It was morbid and a tedious task, but these women would stay here for as long as they could - weeks, even months picking through the stacks of dead, trying as hard as they could to find those men they had loved; only now, most of the dead looked alike.

A number of other people were also among the dead. These people were mostly men, and were human scavengers. Their task wasn't as mournful as the women that he saw. They searched through the bodies looking for whatever they could take, at least what the Carthaginians had overlooked. It appalled Gaius, these people were the filth of the earth, but it wasn't illegal either. They were common when any army of size marched to battle. They would stay miles behind the lines, just waiting to see who won the fight, and then, would move in and pick clean the dead of anything remotely valuable.

"I never thought I would live to see such a thing," Maurus, who stood behind Gaius, said as he gazed across the battlefield.

"Send a rider back to Canusium and inform Valerius of what happened here. Also, start breaking the men into teams of four. Have them search among the dead and try to find any survivors if they can," Gaius spoke, but not looking back towards his young officer.

"How long do we look?" Maurus asked.

Gaius only glanced back at him. "For as long as we can."

"And what about you? Where are you going?" Maurus asked, but Gaius did not answer as he started making his way deeper into the sea of broken and bloodied bodies.

A few minutes later as he glanced down at the various faces, most if not all staring up at him, eyes glazed over with death, he saw what looked like a large pile of hands, arms and fingers that had been collected into a dozen stacks, each nearly five feet high. For a moment, he wondered, as he looked at the gory scene, why the Carthaginians would have done this; what purpose it might have meant. Then, it dawned on him. As he looked closer many of the appendages that had been cut off were ring fingers. Each officer, tribune, legate, quaestors and senators, they all wore rings. There were hundreds of them, if not thousands in the army before the battle had started. Gaius realized that Hannibal had probably had each ring collected and cut off from its owners' hands, dead or alive. The wealth alone would make any one man rich for the rest of his life.

After a few hours, long after the sun had gone down and night had filled the sky, Gaius finally gave up his search. He hadn't found Anthony, his body nor his head. He could see how the battle had went as he stood, alone, on top of a sloping hill as his men continued with their work, lit by torchlight, as they worked their way in a grid pattern through the carnage below.

He had found survivors, a few dozen so far, and that he was thankful for. Valerius was sending a cohort of men and wagons, which would take all night to arrive, but at least these men wouldn't die amongst their brothers. But as he stared down at the flickering fires that guided his men's morbid work, trying to find signs of life among the many dead, he broke down, finally.

He had failed; he had failed to find Anthony, his oldest and dearest friend. All he could think about now was, how little time they had spent together, how much he wanted to say to him now, but never had the courage to say before.

He didn't know what he was going to say to Julia, how he could possibly tell her that both her brother and father were dead, slaughtered nearly to the man, and by a weaker army no less.

He cried, not just for Anthony, not just for Julia, or for his own father, or the men down below, and those that had died in the past year alone. No, he cried for them all, letting out years of built up anger, sorrow and pain flow out of him.

From this day on, Gaius, the boy that had dreamed great things once - believed in the greatness and superiority of his beloved republic, was not the same man any longer. He had grown up, forever changed by what he has seen, and lived through. Above all, he craved justice for what had happened to his people, and as the gods as his witness, he would see it served.

CHAPTER THIRTY-TWO

The Senate hall was empty, save for one man who sat alone on one of the stone benches that ran around the two marble seats that represented the chairs of the consuls of Rome. It amazed Fabius Maximus how empty this place was; how utterly quiet it was. The bulk of the senators that would have typically spent the afternoon debating without end, were in the field. Only a few dozen had remained behind, leaving much of the city's affairs to him, as the elected People's Tribune. He wished he was out there now, with the army, which he had received reports had discovered Hannibal at Cannae.

Now, he waited like the whole city for word about the victory that was certain to come. Yet, Fabius' mind was lost; adrift among a sea of doubt; left to govern a body that stood frozen with fear to the possibilities of just *what if* the two consuls and their unstoppable legions weren't enough to crush Hannibal?

That question had plagued Fabius from day one. He didn't want his fears and frustrations to get the better of him, so he didn't act on his thoughts and call to question the republic's chances of survival if indeed Hannibal was victorious.

His mind still drifted to the past. How many different ways this conflict could have been avoided if he had the chance to lead; he did not seek any grand title, of course, a rarity among his own countrymen, not to mention his family. But, he wondered what choices he could have made differently if given the chance. He knew it mattered not to dwell on the past. That could not be changed. It was the future that mattered now.

Fabius turned his head as he heard a far door open, followed by the soft footsteps of another man, a fellow senator by the name of Marcus Brutus Nero, walk towards him.

Fabius stood to his feet and watched the elder statesman as he slowly approached him with uncertainty in his stride.

Fabius could see the parchment in his right hand, which was held down low by his side as Nero's eyes wavered, as he neared the tribune.

"Word from Cannae?" Fabius asked eagerly as Nero stopped just before him and raised his hand, holding it out for him to take.

"Read for yourself," Nero spoke; his voice trembling.

Fabius took the note and read its words very carefully. There wasn't a lot written on it, as it had been issued with haste, before being sent out.

The document was written by Valerius, Fabius observed, which read:

Senators of Rome, I regret to inform you that the armies lead by Consuls Lucius Aemilius Paullus and Macro Julius Varro have been destroyed, nearly to the man by the forces of Hannibal and his allies. I and fifteen hundred survivors that had been sent from the battlefield prior to the beginning of the campaign are the only substantial force left in Italy. My men have found several hundred survivors and we are currently on our way back to Rome, in hope of beating Hannibal, whom I assume will be marching towards the city to lay siege. I urge the Senate to make preparations for the defense of the city if I do not arrive in time with my army.

Claudius Augustus Valerius, Legate of the Sixth Legion.

Fabius slumped down, falling back down onto his seat as he dropped the document that Valerius had sent, onto the senate floor.

"How could such a large force be defeated, and so quickly and utterly?" Fabius asked more to himself than to Nero, who stood before him, his head hung low.

"I...am gathering my family, and what belongings I can bring, and leaving the city within the next three hours. More of the senators are joining me as well. I advice that you make preparations to do the same, Fabius," Nero said with a heavy heart; his words filled with shame.

"What? What do you mean you are leaving the city? And who else?" Fabius asked shockingly.

"It does not matter who else, only that it is important that we leave, at once."

"And abandoned Rome to the barbarians?"

"What else is there for us to do? What do you think Hannibal will do to us once he reaches the city? If we do not capitulate to him, he will pull down the city walls, and have all of our heads. He may do so just out of spit once we've surrendered to him."

"Surrender!" Fabius bolted to his feet. "You read Valerius' letter. He is coming even as we speak."

"And who will arrive here sooner do you think, Valerius and his fifteen hundred, or Hannibal and his forty thousand? What do you expect us to do, Fabius? Even if Valerius and his legion reach the city in time, it can't be held with fifteen hundred men, and what city cohorts we have left."

"I will not surrender or give this city to Hannibal, not without a fight."

"A fight! We have been fighting, Fabius, and we have lost – we've been slaughtered time and time again."

Nero reached over and placed his hands onto Fabius' shoulder, speaking to him with a quieter voice.

"We've done all that we could. The city will fall, but we can still save the Republic if we exile ourselves to our furthest colonies; to Greece, with the rest of our legions. In time, we can force terms, and return, and retake the city. But, not if we all die, staying here, trying to defend...what - stone walls and temples?"

"And what of the people, Nero? What of those that you and I are charged with protecting? And what of the men who have already died? You want me to abandon their memories to save our skin? No!" Fabius pulled away from Nero and shoved his finger in the older senator's face.

"If Hannibal or anyone else wants Rome, then they will have to take it from me by force! And as Jupiter as my witness, I will kill any man not native to these lands that tries to set foot in these halls. Go, and get yourself and your family to safety if you must! I will not stop you. But, I will not join you either. Even if this city should fall, then someone should be here to see that it was remembered."

Fabius said nothing else as he walked away from Nero, already pulling off his senatorial robes as he exited the hall.

Outside, as Fabius departed, Nero could already hear the rising panic as news of the defeat at Cannae had reached the plebeians, as quickly as it had reached his ears.

He didn't stay any longer as he rushed out of the senate house, and towards his estate. He had packing to do. He just hoped he made it out of the city before the mob tore it down first.

CHAPTER THIRTY-THREE

Three hundred men out of nearly ninety thousand still alive, after having survived the worst military defeat in the republic's history, Gaius could barely comprehend that fact, and would never have believed that such a disastrous blunder could have happened if he had not seen it with his own eyes.

He had spent two full days at Cannae sifting through the carnage of twisted and battered bodies of his countrymen. Of course, there were thousands of Carthaginian, Gallic and Numidians, Spanish and any number of other tribes that supported Hannibal, bodies on the battlefield as well. Hannibal had paid a heavy price for his victory. Out of his forty thousand men he brought to the field that day, he lost some nineteen thousand, or so early estimates have been determined. Rome's losses were greater, however. While Gaius knew that tens of thousands probably survived the battle, as most were either captured or scattered, what remained of Rome's legions was broken as an effective fighting force from this point forward. It would take weeks, maybe even months to regroup the scattered men; blown to the four corners of Italy like leafs in the wind. Even then, the survivors would have been battered, bruised and beaten. Most would no longer be fit for duty. He wondered, as he rode over the open country, the high full moon over his head, alongside a group of twelve other riders, what the state of Rome might be now.

After the battle at Lake Trasimene, the city had erupted. Hundreds had been killed in rioting, thousands more wounded, and a quarter of the city burnt to the ground. What would the people do now, knowing that the most powerful army the republic had ever gathered had been crushed? Who could they turn to? Certainly not the fractured senate, which left over a hundred of its members on the battlefield, dead, their hands and fingers stacked like winter logs. Even the two consuls, gone, and presumed dead, or at the very least, captured. What was left of the government would probably be divided, ready to surrender in hope of saving themselves.

He wasn't sure what to think or what to do. He had dug through hundreds of bodies looking for Anthony, or at the very least, Anthony's father, Varro. But he had found nothing. As far as he knew, he could have stepped on them a dozen times over, for the bodies looked the same after days left to rot under the hot summer sun; bloated, bruised, bloodied, and torn to pieces from weapons, animals, or by the fact that thousands of men had walked over the corpses.

There had been witnesses to the battle; scholars, writers and civilians hoping to see something memorable. They had told that, in the first hours everything seemed to be going Rome's way. Hannibal's front lines, mostly Gaul's; a people that hated Romans as much as the Carthaginians, sustained heavy losses as the center formations broke under the superior numbers of the legions. When the center fell back, Rome thought it had victory. The officers blindly ordered their front ranks forward, chasing after the fleeing barbarians, unknowing that they were heading right into Hannibal's trap.

No one had thought it possible. The army had been raised to force Hannibal out into the open; to engage a proper army on equal terms so that he could not use trickery or deception to win the day. Yet, Hannibal knew the Romans better than the Romans did. He knew that the two consuls and their lackeys of senators, and noblemen, would want to cease the advantage, and push the lines forward without thought to the whole battlefield. And when that happened, Hannibal only had to sit back and wait.

As the Roman front advanced, Hannibal's left and right flanks swung around the whole formation like a mythical bird closing its wings around its prey. The army was so large, and tightly compact, that even when the calls went out to reform, it was too late, as the ranks could not move or adapt to the changing battlefield.

Hannibal's cavalry closed the rest of his master plan. They broke the Roman horsemen, scattering them. With them gone the rear was exposed and cutoff from any chance of retreat. The witnesses said after that it was just a matter of time; hours longer, as those still alive up till this point, were compacted shoulder-to-shoulder with barely an inch to move.

Gaius recognized it. It was a mirror image of the Battle of Marathon, hundreds of years before, when the Athenians defeated a larger Persian army. Hannibal clearly knew his history as well, and had made use of that knowledge.

Gaius couldn't imagine being in the battle. He wasn't even sure if he could have survived it. Because of this, he was confused. Anthony, as angry as Gaius had been with him for sending him away, had saved his life. Anthony had not robbed him of a glorious victory, and most certainly, not a glorious death. It was a slaughter, plain and simple, and as far as he knew, Anthony had paid the price for his father's arrogance.

Hannibal's army was still out there, somewhere. More than likely it was heading towards Rome, to lay siege to the city, and either force terms from the senate, or sack it. Even though there were probably more survivors from Cannae, and certainly other legionaries scattered around the countryside, Valerius had ordered Gaius to pull out and return with what survivors he had found, those that could be moved, and weren't beyond helping, and head back to Canusium to regroup with the only organized, and combat effective legion left in the country, the Sixth.

They broke camp and quickly began to march back to Rome, hopefully getting there before Hannibal's army. After that, only the gods knew what might come next. Fifteen hundred men, a few thousand city guards, and whatever civilians might be armed was not enough to stop a prolonged siege for any given amount of time, no less stop an entire army from burning Rome to the ground. No matter the facts, it was not going to stop these men from getting back. Gaius had made a promise that he would protect the city and Julia, who remained within its apparently safe walls. If Rome should fall, he would get her out of the city, out of Italy if he had too. Her safety was his sole priority.

The night was tranquil with only a slight easterly breeze that cut through the tall grass to disturbed the stillness. Gaius rode, scouting ahead of the main column. They had to hurry back to Rome, but Valerius had chosen a longer path to avoid coming in contact with the bulk of Hannibal's forces. As it were, they had not seen or heard any signs of his forces, until now.

Gaius halted his horse and raised his hand, signaling for his men to also stop. He felt for just a moment that he had heard something, a noise, a yell perhaps, carried over the wind.

His men looked around eagerly trying to see in the moonlight if they had been spotted, or if they could see any enemy presence, but the fields were empty of anything or anyone.

Gaius waited for a full five minutes until his ears again caught something, which he knew was a man's scream, carried by the wind as it changed direction, cutting across his position. It was very faint and distant, coming from the west. Some of his men had also heard the same sound as they looked over at their commander and waited eagerly for his orders. Gaius just nodded to them as he dismounted from his horse and quietly, but quickly, started to make his way towards the noises, which grew louder as he neared.

The Romans stayed low as they reached a raised hill that was over a mile from where they left their horses. Only five men were with him, the rest staying back to watch the animals and cover their rear.

When they near the top of the hill they knelt onto their knees and crawled to the edge of the incline. And even before Gaius reached the top of the hill, he saw the glows of camp fires burning, and the continuing screams of men that were mixed with joyful laughter.

"Those are our boy," Cato, one of Gaius' men, a burly centurion said as he stared down at the camp.

Gaius focused his eyes, leering through the darkness and into the well-lit interior of the camp that lie at the bottom of the hill. Scattered throughout he could see Roman soldiers, some being tortured, all captive; tied back-to-back with other legionnaires, while others seemed to be forced to fight each other as if they were gladiators.

"Those can't be the rogue gladiators, do you think?" Cato asked.

"I would bet a year's pay that they are. We've finally found the bastards," Gaius answered, his blood boiled at what he was seeing. Even from this far the screams and sights of his countrymen resonated heavily on his soul.

He caught sight of one group of gladiators as they stood around a long wooden table. They all seemed to be in a drunken stupor as they talked loudly, placing bets and jeering as one of their comrades dragged a Roman soldier towards the gathering rogues.

The Roman seemed young, perhaps no more than seventeen. Most of the soldiers that fought at Cannae were of such age, as that army had been put together hesitantly.

The boy screamed as he fought hard against his two captors as they dragged him over to the table. The two gladiators, however, were bigger than the Roman, so his efforts were for fruitless as they forced him down onto the wooden slab where the two men strapped him down onto the table with a set of buckles. The table was big enough that the boy's arms were easily held out to either side, with only his hands dangling off the corners; his cries serving to encourage the gathering of fifteen gladiators as they laughed and taunted the young man.

The two men that had dragged the Roman to the table, after secured him, backed away, joining their comrades. A third man approached the boy; the Roman was already peeing and shitting himself as he begged for mercy, but his amused captors would not have any of it.

Gaius then watched as the third gladiator raised a very large mallet, one that would normally have been used to slaughter pigs or cows.

The crowd grew more anxious as they waited.

As the young Roman was yelling, continuing to beg for his life, his cries echoed over the crowd that cheered as the large hammer was slammed down onto the back of his ankles.

Even from his distance Gaius could hear the sound of bones breaking. A number of his men also squirmed as two of his soldiers drew their swords and seemed ready to charge down the hill. Gaius had to quickly reach out and grab Cato's arm, stopping him from going any further. The old soldier reluctantly eased back, but not wanting to watch anymore as the young Roman's second ankle was broken; and with each bone that was shattered, the surrounding gladiators cheered louder.

The torturer moved up the Roman's thin body as he slammed his hammer down onto the boy's legs, then his hands, and then his arms, and finally down onto the lower back, crushing his spine; the boy had already stopped screaming as he lost consciousness seconds earlier. Then, when the torturer had broken nearly every bone, he slammed the bloody blunt down onto his head, which split in a splatter of gore like a small melon.

The gladiators roared with excitement as the boy's lifeless body was removed from the table and carried off, thrown into a pile of a dozen other brutalized bodies. As this was done, the gladiators that had won their small bet, guessing how long the Roman would last before he passed out from the pain, collected their earnings from their comrades. Then, a moment later new wagers were placed as the same two gladiators returned with another Roman. This one was older and more defiant as he fought against his captors, spitting and swearing in their faces.

Elsewhere, in the center of the camp, around a series of fires were small stakes the height of a man. Strapped to them were more Roman soldiers. Some had already been burnt alive, while others were still in the process of being cooked, as their agonizing screams carried over the camp, mixing in with the rest of the prisoners own cries. A few others that weren't dead yet were being cut to pieces, body part by body part, starting with their fingers, ears, nose, toes and genitals, which were then stuffed into the Roman's mouths, muffling their agony.

The biggest sport that the gladiators had put on was mock games. They had dug a small pit into the earth and had forced twelve Roman's into the arena. Each man was nude and was given six daggers to fight with. The Roman's were hesitant at first, refusing to reach for the daggers as they stared at their comrades, wondering what they could do. No doubt they had been offered their lives if they should fight, and be the last man standing. But still, few of the men would kill their brothers as a number of them refused to take up the daggers, even if it meant their own deaths. Unfortunately, not all of the soldiers stood united as some did rush over to the weapons in the dirt, and turned against their brothers.

"How many of our men do you think are down there?" Cato asked as his enraged eyes watched the madness below him.

"Hard to say, perhaps a couple hundred; certainly enough for them to keep this up for a few more hours," Gaius answered.

"We are going to do something, right?" another soldier asked; he already had his gladius out, seemly ready to charge down the hill and take the camp all on his own if given the order.

Gaius turned away from the rogue camp and looked over at his men, who gazed at him eagerly.

"Cato, get back to the horses and ride back to our lines. Find Valerius and get him here, as quickly as you can."

Cato smiled as he nodded his understanding before he slowly crept back down the hill, then darted off into the darkness, running as fast as he could to where they left their horses.

Gaius turned his thoughts back to the slaves down below. He hoped that he wasn't too late to save most of those men. He wished he could have found the camp hours earlier, but no matter, he was going to do something about what he was seeing even if he had to storm that compound on his own.

Forty minutes later, Cato returned with Valerius and another detachment of riders. Gaius had returned to where he had left his horse, having left two men behind to keep an eye on the gladiator camp.

"Any changes?" Valerius asked.

"None so far. The gladiators haven't noticed our patrol or my men watching over their camp," Gaius replied, still keeping his voice low even though they were a quarter mile from the camp.

"What about numbers, theirs and our prisoners?" Valerius then asked as he was already working out a plan in his head.

"We have a more accurate count now. From what we can see, there are at least three hundred and thirty of our men down there give or take; probably more that we can't see. As for the gladiators, most likely no more than two hundred, maybe three, but most are drunk, and a few others already asleep from what we can see. I've noticed women as well, runaways most likely."

"Defenses?"

"It is a basic camp, not much of an outer wall, no trenches, sparse lighting, and a dozen watchmen from what I can tell."

"And no sign of any Carthaginians?"

"None - These gladiators act alone, apparently."

Valerius raised his hand to his chin and settled his fingers over the rough stubbles as he thoughts briefly to himself. He could see in Gaius' eyes, and the eyes of those men around him that they were eager to get down there and do something to save their captive comrades, but he knew too that any action on his part would not only put his legion, what little he had left in danger, but it would slow their march back to Rome as well. He had to reach the city before Hannibal's army did. There was no way the city would hold without his men behind its walls, nor was there any way they could hope to engage a larger force out in the open, which is what he may be forced to do if he came behind Hannibal's lines, if the city was already besieged. But Valerius sighed, knowing too that there was no way he was going to leave Romans to die to such a horrid fate as the ones that the gladiators were given them.

"We will have to do this quickly," Valerius began. "I will take the first cavalry cohort along with two century's of infantry and ride to the north of the camp, and attack in one hour. You, on the other hand will have to take your men, a dozen, no more, and sneak down into the encampment, and eliminate the watchmen. We cannot allow those bastards to raise any alarms as we're approaching. We only have a short time. The sun will be up in four hours, and I want the gladiators dead or scattered, the Roman prisoners secured and put with the rest of our column, and all of us back on the road to Rome by sunrise."

Gaius smiled.

"Don't worry. We'll be done long before that."

Valerius grinned as he turned and got back up on his horse, as did the rest of his men that had followed him.

"I'll see you on the field then," Valerius smiled as he turned and rode off.

"Come on, we've got gladiators to kill," Gaius said as he ran back to the hill that overlooked the camp.

CHAPTER THIRTY-FOUR

The killing within the camp had not subsided since Gaius and his soldiers had first discovered it over an hour ago. He, along with a dozen men had made their way down the surrounding hills, and was so far undetected. He had informed his men what Valerius had instructed them to do, and not a one of them had questioned the orders. Each had eagerly followed into the lion's den, so to speak.

He and his dozen troopers had removed their armor and most of their other gear, opting for stealth over protection. They had muddied their faces and arms and took with them only their gladius' and daggers. Gaius then broke his men into four groups, three men each, and gave them their assignments. So far, as he and his company moved along the outer perimeter of the camp, they had not been spotted by the few sentries they saw.

Most of the gladiators were still celebrating their games, using the captured Romans for their amusement. Gaius had seen what these men were already capable of, and ever since he had found the estate that had belonging to Decima Felix Titus some weeks after the battle of Trebia, he had prayed to the gods to give him the chance to track these men down and expense justice on them. Even the Gaul's, Spanish or the Carthaginians did not treat Roman prisoners as these men were now. They would at least have the decency to kill them outright, or at the very least, torture these men with a purpose, to learn more about their enemies. No, these gladiators took special care to showcase their hatred for Rome and its people. He doubted that even the gods of the underworld could be so cruel.

As the screaming within the camp continued, Gaius was about to get his first chance to spill the blood of the gladiator bastards, as he inched quietly towards two sentries, which spent more time talking to each other than keeping their eyes out towards the surrounding darkness.

There was only the moon light overhead and two torches behind the sentries to illuminate the area. Gaius was, however, moving within the shadows of the fence, which concealed him entirely.

Maurus, who had joined Gaius' group came from the opposite direction. He couldn't see him, but knew if they timed it right that they would be able to attack the sentries from their blind sides. Then, Gaius caught the glint of white in Maurus' eyes as he saw that he was in position. He had a few extra feet to cover before he could attack his target, so he would have to lead, putting himself in danger for just a fraction of a second before Maurus could drop the second sentry.

Don't fuck this up, Gaius thought to himself as he moved forward, down low in a crouch as he held his dagger out before him and inched his way to his target.

He waited as the furthest sentry took a swig from the jug, which blinded him for a moment before he leaped up and attacked the closer of the two.

Gaius didn't make a sound, save for the sudden ruffling of the grass under his feet as he charged forward.

The first sentry barely had time to react before the sharp point of Gaius' dagger tore through the back of the man's neck, ripping out through his throat.

The man tried to scream but no words left his mouth as bubbles of blood and gargling mutters of death could be uttered.

The sentry with the jug quickly realized what happened as he dropped the vase, which shattered on the ground, then attempted to reach for his sword. However, his head was suddenly jerked back as a second dagger, Maurus' was thrust over and over into his lower back.

Both of the sentries dropped to the ground nearly at the same time before the two Romans quickly grabbed the dead bodies before any of the nearby gladiators saw what they had done, and hid them between the fence and shadows, before both quickly darted into the camp.

Gaius and Maurus, plus Cato ducked behind a series of small tents that were set near the outer perimeter. They waited a moment to see if there was any sudden call for alarm, but after a full minute, they heard no change, just the screaming of Romans and the joyful laughter of the gladiators. They then quietly moved through the rest of the camp.

As Gaius reached one bend, he stopped and put his back up against the side of the goat skin tent. Maurus quickly darted over to the opposite side and also put his back up against the next structure. Between them were two drunken gladiators that stood no more than thirty feet from either of them. They were talking to one another, as one of the men was peeing on the ground, seemly making a joke about his ability to write his name with his piss, which the other gladiator thought was hilarious.

When the man was done, they turned and continued towards Gaius and Maurus' direction, passing a small wine skin between each other.

Gaius had his sword drawn and attacked the man that was drinking. The sudden shock of iron ripping through his guts caused the man to spit out a mouthful of wine, which was quickly followed by blood.

The second man hadn't any time to react either as Maurus plunged his sword right through the man's chest.

They let the two bodies' fall where they lay as their blood mixed into the already wet mud, before Gaius and his party quickly continued forward.

A short time later it was Cato that got the next kill, as the three came across a man that stood over a large water barrel, and as the man dip his head down into the water Cato stepped behind him and thrust his sword down into the back of the man's skull. The gladiator's body hemorrhaged as his death grip held onto both sides of the barrel. It was only when Cato removed his sword did the man finally fall down to his knees; his dead weight knocking over the drum in the process.

With that last gladiator dead, Gaius had a clear run to the pit that several dozen Roman prisoners were being held in. They were attached to one another by a series of ropes. Most of them seemed in good health as they were apparently waiting their turns to be tortured, but hadn't been harmed beyond that.

One of them noticed Gaius as he hid down low behind a stack of looted crates, taken from nearby towns. The soldier, from what Gaius could tell looked to be an officer, perhaps a centurion, who looked for a long few seconds before he realized that the mud covered man was one of his countrymen. '

Gaius held up his finger to his lips and singled for the man to remain quiet, as he wasn't the only Roman to have noticed him by now.

The centurion nodded and with just a glance of his eyes indicated that there was a guard just out of Gaius' sight.

Gaius inched forward just enough to poke his head around the stack of crates and saw that one of the gladiators stood guard in front of the pit. He was awake, but seemly just barely, as he had to use the long spear he held to keep himself propped up.

Another guard sat by the far corner asleep; a spilt clay jug lying next to his feet.

Gaius indicated for Maurus to take care of the sleeping man, while he positioned to take out the standing sentry.

Cato covered their rear.

Gaius felt his heart racing as he neared the standing man. He heard only a faint gushing sound behind him as Maurus ran his knife across the sleeping man's throat. He didn't wake, but sat where he had been, seemly still asleep, despite globs of thick blood running down his chest.

The sentry before Gaius yawned, which Gaius used to his advantage. However, as he rose to attack, the gladiator heard him and instantly reacted.

Years in the arena had given the man an uncanny ability to react quickly, as he shifted his stance just enough that the tip of Gaius' sword missed his neck by a fraction of an inch.

Gaius knew he had ruined his opportunity. The guard would yell and engage him, and even if he managed to kill him, it wouldn't take much effort for more of the gladiators to come running. Thankfully, on any given day, save for this night, the gladiator might have been an equal match. Unfortunately for him the man was so drunk that he lost his balance, as he had dodged Gaius' first and failed attack that the gladiator tripped over his own feet, falling face first down into the mud, which thankfully prevented him from sounding the alarm.

Gaius didn't give the gladiator the chance to rise back to his feet. He slammed his left foot down onto the man's back, pinning him to the ground, and then shoved his sword through the back of his head. After a moment the dead gladiator stopped moving, allowing Gaius to forcefully withdraw his blade. As he turned, Maurus and Cato were already cutting the Romans free.

Gaius hurried over to the centurion that had seen him first and cut the man loose.

"We didn't know anyone else had survived the battle. Who are you?" the man asked as Gaius helped the officer to his feet.

"Gaius, prefect of the Sixth Legion, and we weren't at Cannae. We were reassigned the night before," Gaius answered as he helped free the remaining soldiers.

"Well, I guess that explains that then. I hope there are more of you on the way."

Gaius smiled as he handed over one of the dead gladiator's weapons to the centurion.

"Oh, quite a bit more. Do you think you and your men are up for a fight?" Gaius asked.

"We are, sir."

Each of the Romans that were with him grinned, and while all were weak and tired, they were indeed ready for some payback.

"Good. I have more men freeing other prisoners and eliminating the sentry posts. A cohort of horsemen will be coming through this camp in about fifteen minutes. When they do, I need you and your men to attack with anything you can find; your teeth and nails if you have too. Kill as many of these bastards as you can – no mercy for any of them. You hear me, soldier?"

"Oh, we hear you, sir," the centurion smiled.

Gaius was about to turn and head off, but the centurion grabbed his arm and stopped him.

"Wait, sir. You have to free the consul. The slaves are keeping him alive for Hannibal, but I'm sure they'll kill him the second your men show up."

"The consul? Which one?" Gaius pondered. For a moment he silently prayed it might be Varro. Perhaps then, he might be able to get some answers to what happened to Anthony, or if he might still be alive, perhaps in this very camp.

"Consul Paullus. He was gravely injured in the battle. We managed to get him out of Cannae and were attempting to flee back to Rome when these gladiators ambushed the column."

Gaius sighed silently to himself, disappointed that it wasn't Anthony's father, but Paullus instead.

"Where is he?"

"Towards that damn arena they set up…killing my men. I don't know which of the tents he is being held in, or what his condition is."

"*Near the bloody arena*, we'll never make it there undetected," Maurus pointed out. Indeed, they would have to expose themselves to even get within a hundred paces.

Gaius looked around and noticed that the man he had just killed wasn't all that different, in appearance than himself. Most of the gladiators in fact, those they had already killed were dirty, bare chest or wearing looted Roman armor, and carrying weapons and gear from the legions. Hell, many of the gladiators were Italians.

Gaius walked over to the man he killed moments earlier and rolled his lifeless body over. He had worn a legionnaire's helmet and fur cape and simple trousers. Both Maurus and Cato saw what Gaius was planning as he stripped the dead gladiator of his things and put them on. They too followed his lead and took clothing and items from the other dead man before they were ready.

"Remember, when you hear our signal, don't let any of these bastards out of here alive," Gaius turned and said to the centurion and his men.

"And the signal will be?"

Gaius raised his finger up and held it.

"When the screams you hear now, end, and are replaced by the slaves that is your cue."

Once Maurus and Cato were ready, Gaius turned to each of them.

"Spread out, and try not to act too professional," Gaius asked with a sly grin. "And if anything goes wrong...well, let's just make sure nothing goes wrong, okay?"

Both Maurus and Cato acknowledged that they understood before the pair split and stepped out from the shadows and walked freely among the rebels.

Maurus walked to the far right, while Cato took the left position. Gaius walked down the center, all three moving as if they weren't in the same group, but keeping a safe distance from each other that they could react quickly if something should go wrong.

Gaius grabbed a nearly empty clay wine jug that a sleeping gladiator had sitting next to him. He began to walk as if he had been drinking all night, nearly tripping over his feet with every other step, to further sell the as he kept his eyes low between taking drinks of his wine as he staggered over towards five men. After a moment, they turned their attention away from him and continued on with their conversation, one of them actually nodding as Gaius passed them.

Gaius breathed again as he looked back. Both Maurus and Cato got by easy enough without even a second glance. He couldn't help but grin as he saw that Maurus flirted a little with two women that he passed by, perhaps getting too into his role.

Before long Gaius was out in the middle of the camp, walking among and through the gladiators' ranks. For a moment, as two of them came his direction; a nude Roman soldiers between each of their arms as they dragged him, kicking and screaming to be tortured, Gaius nearly went for his sword and attacked those men. He knew, however that he had to ignore it and allow them to continue with their murderous entertainment a little longer. He hoped that the kid could last a few more minutes before help eventually came.

All around him now was the carnage he had only seen from afar. The smell of overcooked human flesh nearly made him empty his stomach as he had to struggle not to look over at the burning rows of his countrymen, but it was hard not to.

Gaius looked as a group of gladiators poured oil over one Roman soldier, the man actually spent the whole process cursing and swearing at his captures, calling them every name he could think of. The Roman seemed more angry than afraid, and even as they tossed a burning torch over to his feet, flames engulfing his body, the man was still yelling vulgar words of resentment between his agonizing screams, as his body was roasted.

The biggest mass of people was centered on the makeshift arena. A lot of plundered money was passing hands as the gladiators spent hours placing bets on the Romans they threw down into it. From what he could tell, a fight had just ended, with only one man still alive - a lone Roman, bloodied and covered head to toe in mud was pulled out and tossed back into the holding pin. The man, like many of the other Romans had a blank stare on his face; others shook horribly, even causing self inflicted wounds to their bodies as they clawed into their wrists, trying to cut their arteries.

Finally, Gaius saw where Paullus might be as a series of small tents, not to different than those he had seen all over the camp, were before him. But at first glance he couldn't tell which might hold the Roman consul.

Gaius glanced over his shoulder. It was difficult to see either Maurus or Cato among the larger collection of gladiators, but he found them as they kept pace with him. He nodded to them and indicated to the tents. They each replied back with the same gesture as they started their way over to him.

There were no discernible features to any of the tents as each were made out of the same leathery material, nor were they set up in any particular pattern. Some tents faced Gaius, as he scanned them with his eyes, while others back ends were to him.

He moved closer, trying his hardest to be quick, but not seem too obvious. Then as he walked around one seemly uninteresting structure he then heard what sounded like a woman, one that was yelling in Latin.

Through the thick skin he listened as best he could.

"Haven't you done enough to us? He is dying! Leave us alone!" Her words were broken as Gaius only understood about half of what the woman was saying, as the outside noises were too loud. And then he heard what sounded like a hand slapping across flesh, followed by a louder, more assertive voice.

"Shut up, woman, or I shall have my men do away with you!"

Gaius caught sight of Maurus and Cato and nodded to them.

They hurried over to his position as he walked around the tent and saw a man burst out.

Two guards stood outside, staying at their post as the tall gladiator that had exited rushed out of sight a moment later.

Gaius turned back and indicated with just his fingers to Maurus and Cato that there were two targets, and that he would deal with them.

Gaius raised his wine jug and poured its contents over his face and chest. Then, he took a deep breath and moved, pretended as best as he could that he was seriously drunk. He staggered out in front of the two gladiators that stared at him as he wobbled, muttering to himself as he was seemly having a conversation with an invisible partner. The two gladiators laughed as they glanced over at each other, still unaware as to whom Gaius really was.

He turned and faced the two guards and smiled. As he staggered over to them Gaius threw out his arms as if he was going to give each man a big hug.

"Brothers! War, isn't it beautiful?!? Here's to our great victory over Rome!" he bellowed at the top of his lungs as he moved towards the two guards, about ready to take another long swig from the wine vase.

Before Gaius reached the two men, however, he tripped over his feet, stumbling forward, falling between the guards and into the tent where he landed onto his stomach and purposely broke his clay jug.

Inside, a woman screamed as Gaius' lump body collapsed on the floor. The two gladiators, each of them smiling entered behind him.

"I think you have had too much to drink, brother," one of the gladiators said as he reached down to help Gaius up off of the ground.

"I'm not your brother, slave," Gaius, his drunken expression now totally gone as he turned onto his back and shoved the broken handle of the jug into the gladiator's throat.

The man staggered back, falling against the side of the tent before he fell to his ass, his hands gripping his throat as he tried in vain to stop the gushing blood that came out of his neck.

"You bastard!" the second gladiator yelled, but before he could draw his sword, Maurus appeared behind him, thrusting his own blade into the man's lower back, before letting him fall dead to the ground.

"Move the bodies in here, quickly – and silence that one," Gaius said as he stood back to his feet.

Maurus grabbed the man he killed and dragged him further into the tent, stashing his body in the corner while Cato walked over to the still alive man in the far corner and quickly pushed his dagger into the man's chest, killing him instantly.

"Good, get back out there and stand guard," Gaius then ordered before he turned and faced the woman, who sat on the ground, her back pressed up against the side of the wall.

"Who are you?" she cried out, still panicking.

Gaius raised his finger to his lips and indicated for the woman, who looked to be in her early twenties, to be silent. He could see right away that she was a slave, as her brand was easily seen on her right shoulder. She was perhaps the body slave to Paullus, loyal to him to a fault, which would explain why she had remained by the consul's side all this time.

"I am Gaius, and I'm a soldier of Rome," he answered, his voice low and calm as he moved over towards the frightened woman, whose spirit seemed to lift when he revealed himself to her.

"Who are you?" he asked as he took her hand and helped her off of the ground, before moving her aside so he could look down at the man that lay on the ground, covered by a bear's pelt.

"I am Claudia. I'm the property of Consul Lucius Aemilius Paullus," she answered as Gaius examined the man that lay under the blankets. His face was swollen and bruised. He had several gashes on his cheeks and forehead as well, and as Gaius lifted the blanket he saw that the man had been cut up pretty bad. He clearly had a temperature as buckets of sweat beaded down from his deformed brow. He doubted that he would live more than a few days, if that. If he didn't get Paullus back to Rome, and soon, the state would be without one of its most important leaders for the foreseeable future.

"This is Consul Paullus?" Gaius asked just to make sure.

"Yes. He was injured during the battle. His men escaped with his body. We were attempting to get to Rome, but these..." She seemed lost for words as the woman knelt back down to her knees and started crying.

Gaius turned and tried to comfort her, and to keep her quiet. He couldn't afford to draw any unwanted attention, not until it was time to move.

Then Gaius heard Paullus utter something as Claudia's sobbing brought him around.

"Sir, be still. I'm here to take you back to Rome," Gaius said as he stood over Paullus.

With his one good eye he leered up at Gaius as if he was trying to place his face, as it was covered with flakes of mud and grit, as well as beaded drops of blood and wine. And then Paullus' eye widened ever so slightly as he seemed to recognize him.

"Gaius?" Paullus muttered in a low, barely audible voice.

He tried to raise his hand up and touch Gaius' face, as if the physical contact would convince him more that what his eyes were seeing was really real.

Gaius took the consul's hand and held it.

"Yes sir, it is me, and the whole Sixth Legion is with me as well. They'll be here shortly, and then we can get you out of here and back to Rome. The city will need you, so you have to stay strong and hold on as long as you can."

Paullus closed his eye as a single tear ran out of it.

"No...Rome..." His words were spoken with considerable effort, but Paullus' forced them out. "...needs you. Julia needs you, Gaius...you must...you must protect..." And then he was gone, slipped back into unconsciousness.

Gaius took a moment to compose himself as he looked down at the most powerful man in Rome. He felt helpless.

Carefully putting Paullus' limp hand back under the covers of the warm blanket, he turned back towards Claudia and spoke.

"Here," Gaius reached behind his back and removed his dagger, which was sticky with blood, and handed it over to her. "Take this, and if anyone other than me or a Roman comes into this tent, kill them. Do you understand?"

"I am just a slave?" Claudia commented as she reluctantly took the dagger.

"Not tonight you are."

Claudia nodded as she held the dagger; its weight feeling strange in her hands.

"Thank you," Claudia said before he left.

"Don't thank me right now. We aren't out of this yet," he answered truthfully before leaving her and the consul alone once more.

"Was it him?" Maurus asked as he stood to the right.

"It is. Be ready. If what our man said was true, when Valerius attacks, they will come and kill Paullus the first chance they get."

"Just the three of us, against all of them?" Cato asked, the veteran sounded nervous.

"Is that a hint of fear I hear in your voice, my friend?" Maurus asked with a chuckle.

"Up yours, brat! I will kill more than you this night, which I promise you."

"We'll see about that, old man," Maurus sneered as he rested his hand on the hilt of his sword.

Gaius knew that the time was fast approaching. If everything went according to plan, which he assumed it had, since life in the camp handed changed with a sudden alarm, then all the sentries would have been terminated, most of the Romans freed, and any second now

Valerius and hundreds of men would come storming through the camp. And then, the true slaughter could begin.

The only problem was, Valerius was late.

CHAPTER THIRTY-FIVE

"The old man gave us one hour, right?" Maurus asked as he started to fidget some as he noticed that a few of the gladiators had glanced over at them, staring longer than he was comfortable with.

"I know he isn't as quick as he used to be, but he is coming, right?" Maurus nervously asked again.

"Just shut up and do your fucking job," Cato bellowed as he stared-down any man that glanced over at him.

Gaius on the other hand remained silent. His eyes were fixed on one gladiator that walked with a group of four other men. He then realized that this man was the same that had exited out of the tent, before he had killed the two guards that had originally been posted here.

"Oh no," Maurus muttered as he watched the man stop in his tracks, and turn towards the three Romans.

"Be calm. I will deal with this," Gaius uttered under his breath.

"Where is Dougal and Torin? I told them not to leave their posts," the man called with a rough Greek accent.

The gladiator was very tall, muscular, badly scared and twice Gaius' age. More imposing was the fact that this man was built like a bear. There didn't seem to be an ounce of fat on his body, which had been harden by decades of battles won in the arena. And for a moment as the man and his escorts neared, Gaius thought that he recognized him as well.

And then, when the gladiator was near enough, Gaius' eyes widen as he saw around the man's neck, dropped down over his bare chest among other tokens, a clay medallion. But it wasn't just any medallion; it was the very same one that Anthony had worn since the day the story of Lupus was told to the two friends.

His eyes flashed red when he saw the medallion, knowing what it meant: this man had killed Anthony and took the bond that represented a brotherhood of two boyhood friends.

"I said..." the gladiator tried to say, but Gaius roared as he drew his sword and rushed the tall man, whose eyes opened wide with surprise.

Gaius heard between his blood rage the name *Calfax* as it was yelled by one of his escorts as Gaius spilt first blood.

Calfax just barely heeded his man's warning as he stepped back, but not far enough as Gaius' sword ran across his stomach.

The blade went deep, but not deep enough to cause any serious harm to him. He had had worse, far worse, and in time it would just be another scar to add to the many hundreds more that crisscrossed his body.

"Bloody hell!" Maurus cried out as he and Cato each drew their swords and rushed forward, joining Gaius as they attacked the four other gladiators that tried to protect Calfax.

As Calfax withdrew from Gaius' first assault, the nearest gladiator that had accompanied him stepped up. He swung wildly which forced Gaius to cancel his attack on Calfax.

The second strike came quickly but Gaius easily deflected the gladiator's horizontal strike that, when his sword, a weaker Greek weapon was pushed aside, Gaius spun in the opposite direction and struck low as the tip of his blade sliced cleanly through the back knee of the first gladiator.

The man screamed as all two hundred and fifteen pounds of him dropped to the ground like a rock. Gaius then easily drove his sword down into the man's shoulder, angling the blade so it tore through his vital.

The flesh was soft and the iron of his blade easily pierced through the man's dark skin and as Gaius withdrew his blade, blood gushed out, squirting all over his face, chest and arms. He then turned towards Calfax who had drawn his own sword, two of them in fact. He didn't care that Maurus and Cato had engaged the remaining three gladiators, or that their fight had gotten the attention of dozens of other men, who at first were a little confused to who was attacking their leader.

"You killed him!" Gaius accused as he moved towards Calfax, who now grinned at the younger Roman.

"I've killed many Romans, boy, and I don't bother asking any of them for their names," Calfax stated.

"His name was Anthony, and he was my friend!" Gaius attacked, but his violent blows were blocked easily by the senior fighter.

Calfax didn't counterattack. He was enjoying the Roman's rage, seemly feeding on it as Gaius' abandoned years of training, discipline and careful practiced form. He just wanted blood.

"I will take back what is his!" Gaius bellowed again as he rushed in, swinging his sword in a series of deadly arcs that failed to get through Calfax's decades of practice, and hundreds of won battles.

"Oh," Calfax started to laugh uncontrollably as it dawned on him what Gaius was blabbering about. "It is this you are talking about?" He indicated to the medallion that had fancied his eyes at Cannae, the very one he had taken off from Anthony's still warm corpse.

"He was a weak one. Young and suckle. He should have been sucking on his mother's tits than pretending to be a soldier," Calfax mocked, which infuriated Gaius even more as he rushed forward, trying to bring the bigger man down with brute force, but Calfax struck, his blade ripping through Gaius' right upper arm, forcing him to rear back. Stubbornly, Gaius attacked again, and once more Calfax cut him, this time across his back.

The cuts weren't deep enough to keep him down, but it was enough to further break Gaius' concentration, weakening what advantages he might have had to stand equal.

A large crowd had gathered. They knew that their leader, the best among them would want to deal with the young and arrogant Roman himself, so instead, most turned towards Maurus and Cato who desperately tried to hold their own against an increasing number of opponents. If the gladiators had rushed they could have killed the two Romans easily, but they thought that the three were just escaped prisoners, so to them this was just another game to play. So, they would break them down like a pack of wild dogs hunting, waiting for Cato and Maurus to grow tired; their reaction times slower, and then move in for the kill.

Gaius had fucked up. He knew it now and two of his best men were going to pay for his mistake – for his blind rage and momentary madness.

"Your man, he shit and pissed himself as I ran my sword across his throat. I've faced better Romans before, but what I've seen in recent years, shames me as to how far your kind has fallen," Calfax taunted as he circled.

"He was no coward, nor were any of my people you slaughtered, slave! They were too young to wear the armor of the legion - they were just boys - boys who childhoods you and your kindred stole when you forced this damn war upon my people." Gaius' strength seemed to be failing him, but he found enough to stay on his feet and stand against Calfax.

"Brave words, boy, but Rome is not innocent, nor are its people. Your damn Republic has stolen everything from me and many more like me; our lives, our loves, our honor and dignity!" Calfax's words grew angrier as he started hacking away at Gaius' defenses. Each savage blow felt like hammer strikes against Gaius' weakening arms.

"I will slaughter your men, your women and your children for as long as the gods allow me too, until I no longer draw any breath. I will see every last Roman dead, your wretched Republic destroyed and every last stone in your filthy city torn down. I will make you *all* pay for everything you and yours have done for generations, starting with you!"

Gaius' wrist shattered under the onslaught as he screamed in agony, not so much out of pain, but in knowing he was done – defeated by a man more powerful and skilled than he could ever hope to be.

His sword lied by his side as Gaius dropped down to his knees, cradled his aching wrist. He glanced around him for a moment as all sound seemed to be muffled. He saw the growing crowd of gladiators as they cheered for Calfax, and roared as new opponents stepped up and challenged the two other Romans.

Gaius watched, unable to do anything as one gladiator snuck up behind Cato and thrust his sword through his lower back. His screams were silent even though Gaius could see that his mouth was wide open, but he heard nothing.

Another man attacked Cato from the front, pushing his spear into the Roman's chest, and then withdrew it only to thrust in once more.

Cato was still alive as he dropped to the ground, his bloodied face staring up at Gaius, seemly calling out to him.

Gaius turned his eyes towards Maurus, his oldest friend within the Sixth Legion. He fought one man, sword to sword, but failed to see the second man in time as he cut into Maurus' lower back, which sent a stream of blood squirting out from the wound as Maurus turned and jammed his sword into the man's face.

A second strike came from behind once again, this time piercing into his upper left shoulder. His sword fell from his grip the moment the enemy weapon was withdrawn from his flesh.

Another man rushed forward and kicked Maurus across his face. He fell down to the ground as a group of four men started beating him violently with their feet, roaring with cheers and laughter as they did so. Neither Cato nor Maurus would be allowed to die quickly. Their torment was going to go on as long as the gladiators saw fit.

Gaius then turned back and looked up at Calfax who was walking over to him as he was rested down on both of his knees. And for a moment as he stared at the old gladiator, he felt as he had when he was a kid, after watching this same man slaughter five other opponents with hardly any efforts on his part. Calfax was born for killing. It was his art, and he was a world class master.

"You were not the best I've fought, Roman, nor were you the worst. I hope that may give you some comfort before the end, my young friend," Calfax said as he readied to run his sword across Gaius' neck.

As the end was about to come, Gaius could feel the air changed from the murderous joy of the gladiators, to one of panic. Something was happening, not near enough for him to see, but everyone knew something was wrong as men started yelling, then screaming, and then finally, dying in droves as the ground rumbled as five hundred Roman horsemen came charging through the camp.

The gladiators tried to react but most turned and ran the second they saw the first horsemen tear through their ranks, tents and any other object that was set before them. And then, large groups of Romans, the freed prisoners clutching whatever they could find, roared as they dog-piled anyone that was unfortunate enough to be in their way.

Calfax was distracted long enough that Gaius acted quickly, and despite the pain he was in, he leap to his feet and charged headlong.

Calfax didn't have time to react as his swords were knocked free as Gaius collided into him, carrying him several feet before the two men slammed into the side of a nearby tent. The supports weren't strong enough to stand against the two men's combined weight and momentum. It collapsed around them, but it was Gaius who was able to get out first.

He quickly staggered back to his feet as the fabric enveloped Calfax, who struggled to free himself.

Gaius frantically looked for a sword, but settled for a spear that was lying on the ground instead. When he grabbed it his intention was to turn back and run it through Calfax's body, but he couldn't as another gladiator ran towards him in a drunken charge – yelling at the top of his lungs.

Gaius impaled the man easily, but under his weight the spear broke as he dropped to the ground.

Another gladiator was about to attack Gaius, who was now defenseless, but before this man could, he was struck dead center by a javelin. The force alone threw the man off of his feet as the long iron shaft stuck out of his chest.

Gaius turned as he heard his named called by the Roman that had just saved his life. The rider tossed him a sword as he snatched it out of the air. By now, however, as he turned back to where he left Calfax, the man was gone. For a moment Gaius thought about racing after him, but his thoughts quickly returned to the mission at hand.

He ran over to where both Cato and Maurus lay. Maurus was already on his feet, standing over Cato who was screaming in agony.

As Gaius looked down at his officer he didn't know if the man would survive the next hour. So, there was no time to waste as he signaled for a group of riders to come over to him.

Seven in all arrived and quickly dismounted and awaited orders.

"The consul, he and his slave are in this tent. Get both of them out of here at once. And take both Cato and Maurus with you," Gaius yelled, relaying his orders over the chaos that had erupted all around them.

"I am fine. I can stay and fight!" Maurus pleaded, even though he had his hand held over the gash across his stomach, which was still oozing blood.

"No, you are not! And you are not staying here either in this condition. Now you have your orders. Get the consul out of here - Now!"

Maurus didn't argue as he was helped onto the back of one horse, while Cato's body was dropped over the rear of another. A moment later the slave Claudia exited the tent escorted by a Roman, while two other carried Paullus' body between them.

"Go! And do not stop for anyone until you have made it back to our column!" Gaius yelled as the riders reared their horses and galloped back towards where the battle had started from.

Gaius stood for a moment longer, watching and making sure that the riders had gotten out of the camp, or at least as long as he could see them before they were enveloped by hundreds more horsemen and infantry on the ground. Then, he turned towards a group of two dozen men, some freed soldiers, others belonging to his legion and rallied them as he and they ran off, their destination, the cages that held the rest of the captured men.

The battle had been sudden and many gladiators were already dead, but it was far from over.

CHAPTER THIRTY-SIX

Valerius stood in the shadow of one of the rolling hills that surrounded the gladiator camp. The full moon was hung behind the encampment. He strained his eyes trying to fix on any one target, but even with the light of the moon and the surrounding torches, it was difficult this late to identify any particular individual. This concerned him. He wondered if it wasn't just his age catching up to him. He recalled in his youth that he had eyes like a hawk. However, none of his nearby men who also kept an ever watchful eye on the camp could see anything that might indicate that his plan had been exposed. The screams of his countrymen, however, could easily be heard. This was the only real indication that his plan had not been foiled.

As Valerius glanced over towards his awaiting men – a hundred horsemen and two hundred heavy infantry, he could see in each of their eyes their desperate anticipation to race down the hill. They had suffered too many defeats already and had seen too many of their countrymen die at the hands of Hannibal's army. They wanted – no, needed to bloody their swords, and with each new chorus of cries emerging from the camp, Valerius had to urge his men to be patient, just a little while longer.

He had seen many horrors in his long life; too many battles and too many wars, death and mayhem were nothing new to the old veteran. This, however, was different. The very thought of fellow Romans, the survivors of Cannae being tortured to death for sport, by lowly slaves, was unbearable. If it were in his power, he would race down the hill on his own and slaughter them all, to the last with his bare hands. However, just getting on his horse some nights was a challenge. He knew that one way or another, this was his last war.

Finally, Valerius knew it was time. If all went as he had planned, Gaius and the dozen men that went down there with him should have removed the outer guards and made ready the attack from within. If not, he knew, as capable as his men were that they didn't have the manpower or time to spare to take the whole camp if it were defended. The sun would be rising soon, within the next two hours and he doubted that there were enough captured Romans down there to keep the gladiators occupied past morning. So time was not on his side.

Now was the time to act.

With only a whisper Valerius turned towards the nearest officer, a boy, too young to be a centurion, and gave the word for the men to mount their horses and make ready.

The message was quickly relayed from man to man.

Slowly and with as little noise as possible, save for a few words from the horses as they were mounted, Valerius and his single cavalry cohort began their slow and careful march over the hill and towards the gladiator camp, which was under a mile from their current position. They would shock the enemy with speed, while the infantry swept in behind them and slaughtered the stragglers.

He didn't order his men into a full gallop, not yet. He led from the front, spreading his men out wide. Their horses moved steadily in a parade pace. Always he kept his eyes ahead, expecting every minute the horn to sound, warning the gladiators of his riders approach. Yet, after the first quarter mile he heard nothing save for the continuing cheers and screams that carried for miles in all directions.

Within a half mile Valerius increased his speed, which was followed by his men. Now the ground started to rumble ever so slightly as the clattering of armor and weapons fill the blackened horizon.

His heart started to race. He felt young again, filled with the anticipation of the charge. He hadn't done this in so long. This was how his men were supposed to fight – their enemy straight ahead – no tricks or traps, just man and iron.

The outer walls were now in sight and even his old eyes could see clearly now, in near perfect detail. As he had hoped and expected, Gaius had not failed in his given task. Not a single gladiator sentry was in sight. The whole camp was undefended.

With a thunderous roar Valerius cried-out as he drew his spear and held it straight out in front of him, as he kicked his horse into a full gallop. He outpaced the rest of his men for a fraction of a second as the horsemen cried out, drew their weapons and charged at full speed.

A moment later, an alarm did sound as there was no hiding the fact that the gladiators were under attack. Only now it was too late to mount any kind of proper defense.

The low makeshift wall couldn't stop the horses from leaping over it, or breaking right through it.

Valerius remained out in front of his men, ahead of them by a few yards as his horse leaped feet first over the wall. He was smiling like a boy as he saw his first target, a lone gladiator, a dark skinned man who froze with panic in his eyes as he saw the still screaming Valerius come right at him.

Valerius struck before the slave could do anything to defend himself.

As the man's head split, the spear rattled terribly in his hand, which nearly caused him to lose it; he held on, however and continued forward, never stopping as more and more slaves ran out in front of him.

Those he did not kill outright, his horse slammed into. With its weight and momentum, dozens of slaves were trampled by the wall of horsemen that followed Valerius.

Blood spattered across his face as his blade cut across another man's throat. This time, he did lose his spear as the blade, which had quickly become dull and useless stuck as it hit bone.

Quickly he drew from behind him one of three smaller throwing spears. It didn't take long before he found another target as he threw the spear at a woman that had charged at him; a small dagger in hand. His aim was true as the long shaft of the iron tipped tore between the woman's breasts.

No sooner than he had thrown the first spear did a second man run up beside him, trying, or more so hoping that he could trip the horse and force Valerius down to the ground.

Valerius thrust, the spear just barely managed to clip the man across his face, tearing deeply into his left cheek. It wasn't a killing strike but he went down all the same.

Valerius had his last weapon in hand just a second after he released the spear. Now, however, deeper within the camp the gladiators were starting to rally. The early, easy victories were now harder fought as he caught sight of a number of his men go down; either their horses tripped, or they were hit by a well aimed arrow or spear throw. Still, not all the gladiators were willing to fight as large groups were running, most weaponless as they ran in the opposite direction of the Roman horsemen.

He caught sight of one large group of fleeing slaves; a mixture of men and women who raced towards the northern walls, and for a moment he thought about given chase. He could easily catch them and drop three, maybe even five of them before he had to veer off. However, the group stopped dead in their tracks as a larger party of tattered, beaten and tortured freed Romans ambushed them.

Valerius smile widen as he watched his countrymen, after having seen their comrades mutilated and tortured for hours, carried out their vengeance on their jailors. Those few with weapons hacked at the wall of panicked bodies while the others dog-piled the rest, beating them down, man and woman alike with their bare hands or whatever they could find on the ground. A few Roman's died in the process, but their numbers were too great to be stopped. And across the camp the scene was repeating as the gladiators soon found they had nowhere to run.

Valerius caught sight of his next target, a lone man who looked more like a child that couldn't have been older than fifteen. More than likely he was a runaway slave that had joined this army. At the moment Valerius did not care about the boy's age or the frightful terror that was in his eyes, as he glanced back, while still running as fast as his young legs could carry him.

Valerius yelled something. He didn't really know what he had said in the heat of the moment as he took aim while in a slow gallop. It just came naturally. He wasn't typically a person, at least in his age to taunt his enemies before he killed them. However, in his carelessness, caught up in his youth as he bore down on the running boy, he failed to catch sight of the real threat.

Just as he was about to unleash his spear, Valerius' grip on his weapon was suddenly knocked free as he felt a very sharp and extremely painful sting hit him right in his arm pit.

The old veteran yelled in agony as he knew from experience that an arrow had struck him just above his armor.

In near full gallop he wasn't able to hold onto the reins of his horse as he fell head first off of his animal and tumbled onto the mud and blood soaked ground where the arrow that stuck out of his armpit snapped from the impact, where the head was pushed deeper into his body.

The pain seemed to numbed as his face was caked with mud, but as he rolled over onto his back, the moment he tried to move his arm, all he could do was scream out again.

Before the gladiator could hit him again with a second well aimed shot, the man was impaled three times by Roman spears, as a group of riders saw Valerius go down and instantly redirected their attacks to defend their leader.

Two men leaped down from their horses and covered Valerius with their shields without hesitation to the danger they were putting themselves in. Right away a number of arrows and spears hit their shields. Clearly they weren't the only ones that saw Valerius go down. If his men hadn't acted as quickly as they had he would be dead already.

Soon the two were joined by a dozen more. They created a wall that was impenetrable.

Two men appeared behind Valerius. Worry in their eyes they pulled him out from under the Roman's that shielded him. He seemed a bit dazed as he stared up at his officers who continuously called out for him. It was only then did he realize that they were trying to get him to respond, to gauge how hurt he was. With the arrow shaft broken none could see where he had been hit, and the large cake of mud that covered him obstructed any signs of blood.

One of the officers signaled for a horse and rider to carry Valerius out of the battle. He suddenly felt very embarrassed at his vulnerability. His people weren't supposed to see him like this and every second they spent trying to safeguard him, they put themselves in more danger as the battle continued around them. More so, however, he felt ashamed. He had lost his mind in the heat of the battle. He had trained his Wolves for years to not give into their natural desires during combat and remain level headed, but for the first time in many decades, he had returned to his youth – those foolish years of his brash arrogance that had wounded and eventually killed his best friend Julius, Gaius' father, when he was too stubborn and believed he was immortal. But he was not young anymore and his slower reaction and diminished senses had finally caught up to him.

He slumped over the horse's back, barely aware that he was up off of the ground. Another Roman had the horse's reins tied to his own. A few moments later the sounds of fighting became distant. And a minute later Valerius was unconscious.

CHAPTER THIRTY-SEVEN

Gaius walked among the dead and dying. Hundreds of slaves, not all, in fact, most weren't even the gladiators he had been hunting for so many months. He hadn't even imagined there were this many people in the camp when he first saw it. The bodies, men, women and even children, choked the ground. Those that weren't dead, but badly mane, were put to the sword. A dozen men went about that ghoulish work, a few taking more joy in it than he would have liked to see out of his people. A number of the gladiators were dead as well, but their numbers seemed fewer than the typical slaves they had killed, and those still alive, held captive now. Some had managed to escape the battle, fleeing into the surrounding hills. He wanted to give chase, but he didn't have the men to spare, or the time. As long as they weren't heading towards the main column that escorted the survivors from Cannae, he had to let them go. His main concern now, as he looked down at the dead, was finding Calfax. He hoped that the old gladiator had been among those to fall. So far, he could not find him.

He knew Calfax was not among the hundred or so prisoners that had surrendered, and he prayed to the gods that he hadn't escaped. But with each passing hour he feared that might have been the case. Regardless, the deed was done. Calfax's army was broken, a minor victor among so many defeats.

The sun had rising some time ago; the warm morning air did not bring comfort. Despite this victory, time was still against Gaius and his men. Hannibal's army was still out there, superior in just about every way, and while he still had a fifteen hundred men at his command, they were badly outnumbered and hampered with the protection of the survivors of Cannae, and now those Romans they had saved hours ago. They had to set off quickly before their battle was discovered by Hannibal's scouts. Rome, the city was still in danger. With that fact still lingering in his mind, Gaius had no time to order a proper burial for the Romans killed here this day, not even his own men who died during the raid. So, he had ordered, without Valerius' consent that the bodies of the dead Romans be piled and burned. What rights they could afford he had given. As for the slaves, they would remain where they fell; food for the circling birds that waited eagerly for this army to move on.

Gaius caught sight of Brutus, one of the few senior officers he had seen since last night. He was running up towards him as he walked among the dead, still glancing from right to left, looking for the old gladiator leader of this defeated band.

"Gaius!" Brutus called as he neared, carefully working his way between the bodies. Gaius could hear the urgency in his voice as his name was called out again.

"I know, I know. You can tell Valerius that I will have the men marching within the hour. We are only cleaning up and still gathering survivors," Gaius called out even before Brutus, nearly out of breath had reached him.

"No. It is not that. I'm here about Valerius. I've been trying to find you."

"What of him?" Gaius asked eagerly.

"He was wounded during the raid. Badly, I'm afraid."

"What?"

"Yes. He took an arrow under the arm. We managed to save him before anymore damage could be done, and evacuated him from the battle. But I'm afraid," Brutus was nervous to finish his sentence. "He is hurt badly. I do not know if he will survive."

Gaius instantly forgot about his search for Calfax's body as he walked past Brutus, demanding, "Take me to him."

A temporary camp had been established to gather the wounded, prisoners and the survivors before they were to march and link up with the main body of the legion. Gaius worked his way through the collection of bodies that stood, most cheerful and bolstering about the victory. His men stood shoulder to shoulder with the survivors, sharing stories, offering water, wine, food and clothing, while doctors and orderlies took care of those who had been wounded during their imprisonment, torture and then battle. Those that could not walk were loaded onto wagons, while the prisoners were chained together, and waited for the long march back to Rome. A number of men, his fellow Wolves and the survivors cheered and patted him on his back as he walked threw them. He had freed them, and all were eternally grateful for his efforts. His thoughts were, however, only on where he needed to go.

Every possible horrific image filled his mind as he walked towards the small tent that had been erected to keep Valerius safe and away from prying eyes. When he finally neared, two men stood guard. They quickly stepped aside and opened a path for Gaius to enter. He was hesitant, however, as he stood before the tent flap, glancing over at one of the two men with a worried look. The man lowered his eyes, which too were filled with dread. Gaius then stepped forward.

Inside, Valerius was thankfully awake and alert. He was laid down on a cot, his armor stripped from his body, his chest and arms covered with dried blood and sweat as a doctor was knelt down next to the general, examining the wound.

Valerius cursed the doctor as the man dug into the wound, which had to be cut wider so that the arrow head and splinters of wood could be extracted. The whole process was worse than the arrow tearing through his flesh in the first place.

"Dammit man! Is it too much to ask that you hurry up?!?" Valerius bellowed as the doctor, knife in one hand, tweezers in another dug through the open wound. Now and again the old Greek would drop a bloody piece of wood into a cooper bowl that lay near him.

"If you would hold still, general, I could finish faster," the doctor grumbled as he grabbed another piece and dropped it into bowl. "It serves you right for falling off of the horse and shattering the arrow like you did. Next time, you need to be more careful."

Gaius' tensions lifted as he watched and listened to the banter between Valerius and the doctor.

"Yes, yes, I shall take your advice," Valerius muttered between long swings of wine, which did little to ease the pain.

The doctor turned and looked up at Gaius as he walked over towards him. Before he left, he leaned in close and spoke low, so not to allow Valerius to hear.

"When you are done with the general, I would like to speak to you outside. But do not be too long. I have to get him ready to be moved."

"Understood, doctor, and thank you," Gaius replied as the doctor stepped past him and exited.

"I want a status report. How did the rescue go?" Valerius asked as he forcefully tried to lift himself so he could see Gaius more clearly.

Gaius took a deep breath before he dared to speak. Seeing his mentor like this, lying down on a bed, bloodied and in obvious pain was a serious blow to his perceived images of the man. His own father, he had remembered being frail and weak as his sickness was slowly eating away at his youth. But Valerius, he was always strong, as powerful as an ox. He seemed invincible – a steward of Rome's unlimited power. But now, it pained him more than anything he could recall to see that image shaken as it was now.

"Ah," Gaius struggled to begin as he stepped over towards Valerius and stood at attention. "We killed or wounded at least two hundred of the slaves, while sustaining twenty-eight casualties on our end... ah, twenty-nine, including you. Seven dead and four more we aren't sure will survive the day. We have over sixty prisoners, most runaway slaves, a few of the gladiators."

"Which means some of them escaped, I assume?" Valerius grumbled, annoyed that he wasn't able to kill or capture all the gladiators as he had hoped.

"Yes. I believe so. I thought it best to not order a pursuit."

"Good, I don't won't our ranks to be thinned more than it is. And, what about the men we rescued? How many did we manage to save?"

"We freed forty-four. Nine were killed during the battle; five more have died since from wounds. Almost all of them are wounded in one way or another."

"And those already dead before we arrived?"

Gaius hesitated again, but quickly answered.

"As far as I can tell, they tortured and killed around four hundred, perhaps more. We can't really tell in some cases, since there isn't much left of them." Gaius sighed heavily before he spoke again, "If only we could have been quicker."

"We did what we could, lad. Don't blame yourself for not being able to change what couldn't be changed."

"I..." Gaius stopped himself from speaking further, but Valerius, even in his barely audible state could see that something else was bothering his pupil.

"What is it?"

"Their leader – the leader of the gladiators, his name is Calfax. I knew him...well, not personally, but I knew of him...He killed Anthony."

"You friend?"

"Yes. He killed him at Cannae, and when I found out that it was Calfax that had done it, I acted without thinking, putting not just my life at risk, but everyone's – the whole mission. It was my fault. I fought him when I should not have, and lost. Calfax is not among the dead or captive. He is still out there - somewhere...I should have -"

"Enough!" Valerius blurted out, not angrily, but loud enough that it forced Gaius to snap back to the here and now, and not dwell in the memories of what happened hours ago.

"You made a mistake. You allowed your emotions to get the better of you, and yes, you could have cost us our victory." Valerius smiled even though it hurt him to do so. He knew he was just as reckless, last night, and in his youth, and it had cost him a great deal. "But we did not fail and there are men out there that are alive because you acted when you did. The slaves are broken, and even if this Calfax is still alive, he is no longer a threat to Rome or its people."

"We do not know that," Gaius added.

"No, I suppose we do not. But what is done, is done. Learn from your mistakes and pray to the gods that they might look after the souls lost because of it. All you – *we*, can do, is move on. Rome is still in need of us. And right now, you have to get these men back to our city, if we are going to defend her while we still have a city to get back to. Do you understand?"

Gaius stood taller.

"You're orders, General?"

"Break camp and regroup with the column. We have to reach Rome before Hannibal does, or both the city and we will be caught out in the cold with our asses hanging in the air."

"I won't allow that to happen. Not ever." Gaius saluted Valerius, who just grinned as his young officer turned and left him.

Outside, the doctor was waiting. Right away Gaius recognized the grim look on his face. He knew he was going to bare bad news.

"How bad is he?" Gaius asked, speaking first. The silence would have just killed him.

"Not good, I'm afraid. I've removed the majority of the splinters, but more than a few fragments are still lodged. They aren't what concern me, however. I was unable to remove a large piece of the arrow head."

Gaius gasp as the doctor paused and allowed his words to sink in.

"I'm sorry. But when he fell from his horse during the battle, he accidently pushed the arrow deeper into his chest, too far for me to remove it without killing him."

"What, will happen to him?"

"Infection will set. His blood will be poisoned and then, he will run a temperature. Eventually, the fever will kill him."

"How long before that happens?"

"It is hard to say. I've seen men live days, even weeks. It will depend on how strong the he is. But in the end, it will kill him. I'm sorry. I know how close you two are."

Gaius was silent for a moment as the doctor's words sank in. Again he found himself forced to hold back his emotions, but every fiber of his being wanted to break down. First his father, than Anthony, and now Valerius; he just didn't know how much more he could take.

"Does he know?"

"Of course, but he won't show how it is affecting him. He's as tough as they come. I will do what I can to keep him comfortable, but his fate is in the hands of the gods now, and I don't think they have much mercy for our people, not these days, anyways."

"Thank you, doctor. I won't keep you any longer from your duties. Prepare your patients. We will be moving within the hour."

"Yes, sir."

As the doctor left, Gaius had to rest his hand against one of the poles that support Valerius' tent, to collect his thoughts. He couldn't, not now, not when there was too much to do, allow his emotions to get the better of him. So, he took a deep breath, straightened himself, and continued onward. His work in the coming days would have to sustain him. When it was done, perhaps then, and only then, would he allow himself the time he needed to grieve.

CHAPTER THIRTY-EIGHT

There was a thick fog that hung over the city as Gaius looked upon Rome and its outer walls. He stood along one of the many hills that dominated the surrounding countryside, staring with interest through the thick haze, trying to catch sight of anything that might seem out of the ordinary. He half expected to see the city surrounded by Hannibal's army when the high walls first came into view. But, here and now, four days since the battle with the gladiator army, and nearly two full weeks since Cannae, he saw nothing, or no one, literally.

Typically, during this time of the year the roads that led into the city would have been packed with people, carts and wagons bringing with them all sorts of good from around the republic. Despite the war, commerce continued, but Gaius saw nothing, save for the wet and empty roads in all directions. Even the river and ports were devoid of any traffic.

He had sent out scouts in all directs, and when they first reported back to him hours ago that they saw no sign of Hannibal's army, he sent out more and told them to go further, and find any signs that his army was here, or had been.

He simply couldn't trust his eyes. The banners of the city-watch were still hung high over the walls, indicating that they still controlled Rome. However, he couldn't trust that either. As far as he knew, with no army, save for the city guards, which were only good at keeping the peace on the streets, not fighting wars, the city fathers could have turned Rome over to Hannibal instead of waiting out a prolonged siege. He found that hard to accept, but anything was possible, and the *all clear* signs on the walls could merely be a trap to lure in what remained of Rome's armies.

Finally, after nearly an hour one of the riders he had sent to the city came racing back towards his direction. It was Avitus, Gaius could see. A few minutes later he was with him and quickly began to relay what the city guards had told him.

"The city is clear and still in our hands," Avitus began to say the second his horse stopped. "We still control the city from what I've been told, but there are only a few thousand guards along the walls. They are stretched to the limit. And were they glad to see us."

"What of Hannibal?" Gaius asked. He was still concerned about marching his men into Rome. With thousands of soldiers, wagons, supplies, and hundreds more wounded men from Cannae and the gladiator camp, it would take him hours to get the whole column into city. The last thing he wanted was to be caught between an approaching Carthaginian army and Rome's outer walls.

"They said that they have seen nothing of him. A few scouts here and there, but no army within miles of Rome."

"Nothing?" Gaius asked shockingly.

"Yes, sir, nothing - in fact, no one seems to know where Hannibal is right now."

"General!" Another soldier called from behind Gaius. It took him a moment to realize that it was he that was being addressed. With Valerius off of his feet, the legion and its survivors fell to him, so his men addressed him accordingly. He wondered if the title, if he should be allowed to keep it, would ever fit right on him.

"Soldier?"

"Consul Paullus, he would like to speak with you, sir."

"Very well. Tell him I will be with him momentarily."

The trooper nodded and saluted, then turned back and raced off back towards the main column.

"Return to the city and inform the watch captain that I will be brining in our men, through the east gate. Tell him to have a list of needed watch posts, so I can get our men on the walls the second we are in the city," Gaius commanded Avitus, who too saluted with a quick and eager, "Yes, sir, General," before he turned his horse and trotted back down the paved road; disappearing a moment later into the thick haze.

Gaius walked through the long formation of his army. He was among the wagons and carts that carried the legion's supplies, as well as the wounded, sick and injured. Paullus' wagon, which was draped so to protect the consul from the elements, was in sight. Right away Gaius saw Claudia standing outside the wagon. She smiled the moment she saw him.

He had come to welcome her pleasant greetings whenever the two met over the past four days. She was lovely and had caring eyes. Her long brown hair signaling her Greek heritage was pulled back in a pony tail, still matted and dirty from her ordeal. Her clothing, a long drab dress was still stained with blood, most of it from the consular as she tended to him after Cannae, and still now.

Gaius admired her loyalty and devotion to Paullus. She could have abandoned him weeks ago, or could have joined Calfax and his other freed slaves, but she had remained and nursed Paullus during the worst of times.

"General," she greeted Gaius warmly.

"You choose to walk and not ride inside with the consul?" Gaius asked as he stepped up to her and accepted her warm reception with his own wide smile.

"Oh, I've been stuck in there for days. I needed to stretch my legs. Besides, I'm eager to see Rome again." She ran her hand through her hair, seemly a bit vain about her appearance before she spoke again. "Is it true that Hannibal isn't anywhere near here? I've heard rumors amongst your men."

"It would seem. But, I still have men out there making sure that he isn't near to us. Regardless, be ready to move quickly once the order is given. Now, is the consul free to speak to me?"

"He is. But do try to keep it short. While he would not act it, he is still in a lot of pain and very weak."

"I promise to make it quick. And, I'm sure with your loving care, the consul's recovery will continue."

Claudia blushed as Gaius walked past her and over to the rear of the wagon that carried Paullus. Two guards stood, ever vigilant outside. Each stepped aside as Gaius pulled himself inside.

Paullus lay on a floor of the wagon, covered with several thick blankets. He was awake and was seemly reading over a stack of clay tablet; each one, the various reports from the quartermaster and cohort centurions about the status of the legion.

Gaius would have preferred that the consul rest since he had regained consciousness and his fever broke two days ago, but Paullus needed to keep himself busy and feel like he could contribute something to this ragged army. While the law dictated that Paullus could have taken command of the legion, even in his current state, not once had he made such a request. He allowed Gaius to make all the decisions, despite that he knew Valerius was no longer fit for command. The consul just wanted to be brought up to speed on what had been happening over the past two weeks, nothing more.

A part of Gaius was thankful. While he did not want command of the Sixth like this, the thought of another man, other than Valerius giving the orders, was strange and unwelcome.

Paullus managed a smile, or as best he could when he saw Gaius. His face was still badly bruised as large purple welts had formed over the cuts to his forehead and cheeks. One eye was totally shut, and fresh cuts above it indicate that the legion doctor had been bleeding him, so to lessening the swelling before it risked his eye. The other cuts to his body had already been stitched up, but the consul still had very little feeling in his legs and feet, and his left arm was nearly useless. He may never regain its use again, or so he had been told.

Gaius could see in his one good eye that Paullus was in a lot of pain, but he had insisted that most of the medicine be used for those soldiers worse off than he, so he endured as best he could and tried to keep his mind active.

"General," Paullus said, still being formal despite his more relaxed attitude he for some reason tended to show around Gaius. He was in the field still, so Paullus kept his soldierly manner raised until everyone was in the city and safe. "I've been told that your men have not found any traces of Hannibal or his barbarian allies."

"It is true, sir. And we've made contact with the city guards. They've confirmed as much."

"Then I assume you will be marching the legion into the city and take up defensive positions along the wall then?"

Gaius noticed that Paullus didn't make it an order, but addressed his words as a question. He was still very new to this, given so much responsibility over so many lives. Paullus certainly knew this, but seemed to trust him to do what needed to be done without having to state the obvious.

"I will be, sir."

"Good. You must insure that our march into the city is done quickly, but calmly. We cannot afford to be caught between the city walls and Hannibal, if he should show up."

"Of course; I've already begun preparations for the march into the city, even as we speak."

"You'll also want to meet with the Senate as soon as possible. You may represent me in my stay. When I am set in my estate and capable, I will receive them. But until then, I will be placing you in command of the soldiers inside the city, and those that are already under your authority."

"Sir, Is that wise? I am not senior, neither here in this legion or in the city. Certainly an older and wiser officer should take command of Rome's defenses." Gaius was humbled and troubled at the same time by Paullus' command that it should be he that carries out Rome's defense.

"Do you feel that you are *not* up to the task, Gaius?" Paullus asked as he raised himself up a bit on his elbows.

"No, sir, I am more than ready, if that is your orders."

"It is."

"Some might argue it, however," Gaius added.

"Not with this." Paullus reached over, squinting in pain, which nearly caused Gaius to step over to him and help, but he held back as the older man grabbed a sealed roll.

"If anyone, and there will be more than a few that will give you trouble about you taking command of the city's defenses, show them this. The Senate will back it up." Paullus handed the document over to Gaius, who took it and carefully stared down at Paullus' crest, which had been sealed in wax.

"My orders are in writing. No one will dare cross you, not until the threat has passed."

"Yes, sir. I won't let you down, sir."

"Very good. I won't keep you from your duties any longer. You are dismissed."

"Consul," Gaius nodded and was about to turn and leave Paullus, but he quickly called Gaius again, low and barely auditable.

"Sir?" Gaius had the feeling since he first came that Paullus hadn't summoned him just for a report or to give him some last minute orders.

"Will you go see her, Julia, when we are back in the city?" Paullus asked.

352

Gaius hesitated for a moment. He had thought about little else over the past few days when he had a moment to his own thoughts.

"I – I doubt I will be able to for some time. I must see to the city's defense and coordinate with whatever officers remain within Rome," Gaius answered, speaking the truth, but also knowing he was avoiding the fact that he didn't want to face her, not just yet.

"I understand. I..." Paullus paused again, "Don't think I could see her right now either. Not like this. Not after everything..."

"I understand, sir," Gaius replied as Paullus turned his head away from him, seemly more frail and weak than ever.

It pained him greatly to see the man as he was, broken and beaten. He could see in Paullus' eyes the weight and guilt he carried on his shoulders. He lost the army, his army. Death might have spared him the torment of knowing that. But he had lived when so many tens of thousands had not.

Neither man said more as Gaius turned and left, leaving Paullus alone with his own doubts and painful thoughts.

CHAPTER THIRTY-NINE

Gaius had walked through the gates of Rome four times in his life. Twice it had been jubilant; the city was new to him and full of wonders. He thought he could have lost himself it its majesty. But now, like before, after the defeats at Trebia and Trasimene, the city was foreign to him – a ghost of brick and marble. Those few thousand city guards that had remained behind, those that had not abandoned their posts and fled with their families had long faces and tired eyes. The return of the Sixth Legion and the survivors of Cannae were not enough to give them hope, as the long column of soldiers marched through the gates in the pouring rain.

Gaius tried as best he could to monitor the long march into the city. He had sent one cohorts in first so that they could take positions along the walls, while leaving the last two outside to protect the rear. He had set up an unbroken chain of communications, starting five miles beyond the city limits, to his current position. If even a hare was spotted, he would know of it within ten minutes. The walking wounded, sick and mane were then allowed into the city once he was certain he had set up a strong defense. He made sure that his prisoners were brought into the city through a different gate. He couldn't afford to have them making any trouble, or more so, the Roman guards wanting to exact their built-up aggressions and fears on those men, not until each had been debriefed for whatever information they could reveal.

After, Gaius assumed that all of them would be tortured and then crucified – placed outside the city walls as a warning to any future slave that may think of siding with Hannibal. Unfortunately, while Gaius would have preferred to have stayed with his men until every last one of them was safely inside the city walls, he had been hounded continuously by officers and aides to the senate. Their questions were endless and asked with such frequency that he barely had time to answer one before another was asked.

Always the questions were the same: Where was Valerius? Where was Paullus? What of co-consul Varro – did he survive as well? Who was in command of the Sixth? When the various officers finally accepted the realization of the truth, their concerns were more relaxed. They wanted to know how the Sixth had survived Cannae. Had they encountered Hannibal or knew of his whereabouts? What of the gladiator army? Was it still a threat? On and on for hours, the bombardment continued without end.

Between the interrogation, Gaius had some of his own questions answered. He learned that a few thousand men had survived Cannae, and had managed to make it back to Rome over the past two weeks. However, most of those men had since deserted, gathering their families and meager possessions and fled, along with a full two quarters of Rome's population. Those that remain were placed along the walls, and what was left of the civilian population, mostly the very young and very old, were drafted or had volunteered to defend the city. They were given what training they could and kitted out, and then placed on the walls. Even if they could not fight, it was hoped that with enough numbers, if Hannibal and his army should come, he would think twice about directly attacking Rome.

To his surprise, the central core of the Italian peninsula had remained loyal to Rome, which gave hope that with time more men could be levied to rebuild the army. However, some cities had deserted to Hannibal after word spread about Cannae, such as Capua, which sent shivers through the minds of every Roman. If such a great city could side against Rome, who might follow next?

The senate, which had already lost dozens of members during the Battle of Cannae, was in tatters. A third of its body had fled as its members had taken their wealth and families to other boarders – where, Gaius couldn't imagine, as Hannibal seemed to be everywhere and anywhere. But everyone, the senate and the people alike, knew that Rome was a target. Its fall would symbolize not just the end of the war, but the end of the republic as well. What would follow - cowardice or not, not many wanted to face the day after the Rome crumbled.

Order would have to be reestablished and Gaius hoped with Paullus recovery that it could begin soon. However, right now no one was very optimistic. By the time the rain had finally stopped falling and the sun was well past its zenith, Gaius had given the order for the rest of his men outside the city to be brought in. He would keep dozens of riders outside, as they scouted the surrounding countryside for days still to come. But for the first time in a very long time he was able to breathe.

He felt weak in his knees and suddenly very hunger, but more so, unbelievably tired. When he was certain that there were no more officers seeking him, and if there were, he didn't care, Gaius walked through the empty city, taking his time. His final destination was the army hospital that he had sent the wounded and sick hours before.

As he walked through its halls, checking on the still recovering wounded, he took the time to stop and chat with those that were able to speak. Those that couldn't, he tried as best as he could to reinsure them that they were safe and back home. It took hours more for him to see everyone, and he grew more tired as a result. It didn't matter as he had one last person he needed to see before this day was done.

Valerius' was kept in a separate room. Gaius had strict orders to his guards that the general be left alone. Those that had pestered Gaius all day weren't allowed within ten feet of him. If they dared the squad of guards, each men of the Sixth would have gutted anyone that tried, regardless of rank or privilege.

Gaius stepped into the small room. Right away he could feel the musty heat, not from the torches that burned along the walls, but from the temperature that was slowly cooking his mentor from the inside.

Gaius wished that Valerius' condition would have improved over the last four days, but that was wishful thinking. Valerius was going to die and despite the old man's stubbornness and willingness to live, there was nothing that could be done for him.

It was only a matter of time now.

Gaius inched around Valerius' bed trying as best he could to be silent. He wanted to say something but found he could not form any words. Valerius looked to be asleep so he didn't want to bother him with needless details about the day and the happenings in the city.

There was a pile of soaked rags, both covered with blood and sweat that rested next to the bed. The old veteran's body glistened in the torchlight, and despite his body temperature he shivered under the wolf pelt blankets. Gaius almost broke down then and there, but he wasn't given the chance as Valerius opened his eyes and turned his head, staring up at his pupil before a small trickle of a smile formed in the corner of his mouth.

"Are the men safe and in the city?" Valerius asked, somehow finding the strength to speak.

Gaius grabbed a stool that sat in the corner and placed it beside the bed, before he sat himself down on it; his joints cracked. It was the first time in days that he was actually free to get off of his feet and rest, even for a moment.

He stared down at Valerius with heavy eyes. Taking a deep breath, he replied, "They are. We all made it inside without any loses."

"You look, terrible. You do know that?" Valerius grinned, which caused Gaius to laugh as he ran his hand through his thick and matted hair. Only then did he seem to realize that it had grown longer than should have been allowed.

"It is not befitting of an officer in my army. But I bet this new rustic look will drive the girls crazy. Wait until you show them the scars," Valerius smiled before he fell into a coughing fit, which lasted several painful seconds before it subsided.

"You're not looking all that good yourself, old man," Gaius replied with a comforting grin.

"I've been better, that is for sure."

Gaius tried to smile but Valerius could see he only managed it with considerable effort.

"How are you?" Valerius then asked.

Gaius paused as his mind processed the question.

"I have men along the walls, guarding each gate and passage into the city. I've kept forty riders out beyond the city limits, scouting for any signs of Hannibal. And-"

"No," Valerius cut him off before he could speak further. "I asked - *how are you*?"

Gaius sighed deeply as he lowered his head and answered, speaking words he never thought he would hear himself say out loud.

"I'm afraid…" Right away, he felt ashamed that he had admitted that to Valerius. However, the old veteran rose higher in his bed even though it pained him to do so. He listened carefully as Gaius felt compelled to continue on. "I'm afraid of what is to come, that I will fail the men, the city and you."

"You've already proven yourself. You have no one to answer for. Gaius, you've faced your enemies and have lived. You've protected you're men, and have brought them home safely."

"Not everyone."

"Bah! You cannot hold those deaths over your head. We are not gods. We cannot pick and choose which of us lives, and who dies."

Valerius reached out and took Gaius' hand in his own, holding onto him tightly.

"You are like a son, to me. You always have been. I will leave this world knowing that my boys are in the best of care. You will keep them safe, and when the time comes, you will lead them once more into battle. Men will die. Battles will be fought, won and lost, but always they will have you. And they will look to you now with the same eyes you've looked at me."

"And if Rome should fall?"

"Then it shall fall. But not because good men such as yourself gave up."

He laid back down, flitching painfully as the arrow that was still lodged in his chest, pinched deeper into his body.

"You are more a man than I could have ever hoped to be. At your age, I cared nothing about the future, my duties or the affection of those I commanded. I've had time to look back at my life, the mistakes I've made, the promises I've broken and the loves I let get away from me. If I could, I wish that I could go back and smack the boy I used to be, and demand that he wake up and live - not for the moment, not for the next conquest or battle, but just to live and enjoy what little time we have. It is too late for me now, and when I look back, the only joy I can find, was the hand I had in raising you, Gaius."

He shifted his eyes up, which were watering now as he stared at Gaius, who leered over him with equal sadness in his gaze.

"I can never replace your father, nor would I try. But I can take pride, like he would have in the man you've become – greater than he or I could ever hope to have been."

"I don't know if I can continue on with this," Gaius admitted.

"You will...I can see it in your heart that you don't know how to quit. Forget what you can't change – move beyond the past. There will be a world after this war, and while you may never forget what you've live through, have seen or have done, you will at least live beyond it."

Valerius reached out, holding his hand out and waited for Gaius to take it, which he did.

"Find what has the most meaning for you, Gaius, and hold onto it – protect it, and in the end, your life will be full. Don't let your end be like mine. Let your life have meaning, like your father's did."

Gaius lowered his head and whispered, "I love you, Valerius."

"As do I, my son."

Those would be some of the last words Gaius would ever share with Valerius, as he remained with his old friend, his mentor and second father for the next four days, before finally, Valerius, the last great Roman veteran of another era finally succumbed to his injuries. The following morning after his passing, the whole of the Sixth Legion stood out on the Fields of Mars and burned their beloved father's body, and when the act was done and the final words said, Gaius left his men and found himself walking through the city streets. Rome was slowly coming back to life once it was confirmed that Hannibal, for reasons only known to the warlord, had forsaken laying siege to Rome, and instead set up camp at Campania.

Rome was spared and for the first time in months, everyone, citizen and soldier alike took a deep breath and thought to what next was to come – how to rebuild and regroup. Gaius, however, couldn't share in the same joy. His mind and heart were trapped elsewhere.

When he found himself coming to a crossroads, one which led nowhere in particular, and one that would take him to Julia, he was vexed as to which he should take. He had not seen her or sent word to her about his return. He couldn't face her and say to her that her father and brother were dead, and he couldn't tell her that their deaths would not be avenged because he failed to kill Calfax.

It wasn't until he actually reached the iron gates that he realized he was standing at her doorstep.

When he knocked, the front gate was answered by the same old house slave that had greeted him each time he had visited in the past. He peered through the eyehole. Quickly the old man opened the gate, and with wide eyes he called out, "Master Gaius, you are alive!"

"Is the lady of the house present?" Gaius asked, keeping his own voice low.

"She is, and my lady will be most grateful to know that you are okay," the slave said eagerly as he escorted Gaius to the main building.

"How is she?" he asked, feeling foolish to even mention it. How else was she supposed to be with her father and brother dead? Even Paullus had stated that he would not be seeing her.

"She is, troubled. I'm afraid that the last few weeks have weighed heavily on her young mind, sir." The slave stopped and turned towards Gaius, and spoke lower. "Many have urged her to leave the city. She knows that her father and brother are gone, and that she is in danger here. Truthfully, I wish she had heeded their advice. But, I believe she has remained here, holding out hope that you will come for her."

Gaius wondered for a moment how much the old man actually knew about the two of them. Probably everything he figured.

He took a deep breath before he followed the slave into the house. Once inside, however, the old man didn't have to announce Gaius' presence as Julia was already in the room.

His heart sank to the floor the moment the two of them saw each other. She had been crying, that much he could tell at first glance, and the moment her eyes fixed on him, she started once more.

"Gaius!" she called as she rushed over to him.

Both fell into each other's arms, Julia's hands digging into his back as she uttered his name again, holding onto him as tightly as she could.

The old Greek slave politely back away and headed back outside to continue his nightly duties, leaving the two of them alone.

Julia dared herself to look up at Gaius, who felt a bit embarrassed at the moment. He hadn't bathed in days, or had the chance to change his armor and clothing, which was dried with flakes of dirt, girt and mud which was still mixed in with globs of blood. The rough stubbles on his cheeks were sharp and probably not comfortable to feel against her soft skin, but Julia didn't seem to care as she kissed him passionately.

"I thought...I heard that everyone died," she cried as she buried her head into his chest once more.

Gaius inhaled the sweet aroma of her oiled hair as he kissed her gentle on the top of her head.

"Tell me this is real, Gaius. Tell me you are really here. Say something to me, please, so that I know you are not an apparition," she pleaded.

Gaius pulled Julia back so that he may look into her watery eyes, and as he did, he tried desperately to talk, but his words failed to escape his mouth in the way he had hoped.

"I...He…is gone...They are all gone..." Months, weeks of being the harden soldier, strong for his men, for his friends and peers, finally gave way as he collapsed into Julia's arms, falling down to his knees as he sobbed, crying harder than he had ever done in his whole life.

"I could not save them! Anthony...Valerius...I could not save any of them!"

Julia grabbed hold of Gaius, pulling him closer to her as he let go. She held him for a long time as he let out all of his built-up emotions, safe and finally alone with her. She cried with him - for him, but for the moment, she knew she had to be stronger than he. He needed her – he needed her to just hold him, which she would.

CHAPTER FORTY

"He sent me away. He sent the whole legion away just to protect me," Gaius said quietly as he looked down at the broken clay medallion in his hand.

It was hours, perhaps even days later, he had no sense of time right now. He was alone with Julia, she in his arms as both sat on the floor, sitting before a large fire that crackled as its bright flames, which warmed the pair. He was clean shaved and nearly back to normal, or as normal as he could be. They hadn't had to say much to each other; words weren't needed between the two, for both knew what the other suffered. They just needed to feel each other's hearts, that both of them were alive, still warm and breathing.

They both had cried and allowed their emotions to flow feely without hesitation or judgment as they had embraced, and had made love, and now only wanted to be near the other for as long as they could extend this time. In a sense, they only had each other in the whole world, and nothing was going to break them apart now, no matter the rules, traditions, and arrangements, or by the force of the gods themselves.

"He did it so I could come back to you - so I could protect you as I had promised all those years ago."

Julia pulled herself into Gaius' arms, closer as he spoke to her as a lone tear ran down her face as she listened to him.

"I went back to Cannae and looked for him, for as long as I could, but I could not find him. I could not give him the rights that he and all those damn fools deserved."

"He knew what he was doing," Julia said softly. "He followed his father like a good son should, and fought to protect his country like every man should."

"And he died for it. They all died for nothing. They were led by foolish men, even those with the noblest intentions. In the end, we are no safer now than we were before...I should have been there."

"Maybe so, Gaius," Julia looked up at him, rubbing her hand over his still youthful features. "But he sent you away, not to save you or to protect me, but because he loved you as his brother. He could not change his fate and he knew that. But he knew he could spare you a similar end."

Gaius clutched the medallion tightly in his fist as Julia's words sank in. He then bent down and kissed her, which she returned with a passion before she rolled over, facing him and again shared the same breath as he.

"I love you more than life, Gaius," she uttered softly as she ran her hand over his bare chest. "And I know you will leave again."

He tried to say something, to deny it, but she stopped him before a word left his mouth.

"Nothing that happens from this point onward will ever change what we feel about each other."

Julia took the medallion away from him and carefully placed it back around his neck, until it rested against his chest where it belonged.

"You will come back to me when this is over. I know you will. And until that day, I will be waiting for you."

He kissed her again as he lowered her down onto her back. This would be his moment, the one he would live for – the one that would sustain him and allow him to see the war to the end.

For her, he would come back, no matter what.

CHAPTER FORTY-ONE

"Gaius," Claudia greeted Gaius with a wide smile. She was less formal than she should have been with a person of his status, being that she was a slave and he now a general, a legate promoted as commander of the Sixth Legion. He, however, did not care for social edict, least of all when he saw her warm and loving smile. She was his friend, regardless of her class, and he greeted her as such as he embraced her with a long and meaningful huge.

"Claudia, it is good to see that you are well," he replied as he knelt down and kissed her youthful cheek. He realized that this was the first time that he had seen her cleaned and in proper cloths. She was very easy on the eye, long brown hair and blue eyes. But Claudia had been raised into slavery, so the only alien aspects about her, were her features and not her accent or manners.

"It does my heart good to see you in better spirits, general," she grinned, which caused Gaius to blush when she addressed him by his rank.

He stared down at her and smiled, perhaps looking at her a bit longer than he should have. She really did look different, but she didn't seem to mind his long glare.

"I never got the chance to thank you. I mean, really thank you for what you did for me and the consul." She looked up at him, who was considerably taller than she. "What you did, I do not think others would have done. I thought I was going to die there. I should have."

"I did what any good Roman would have done," he replied, not wanting to take too much credit for what he had done.

In his eyes the operation was still a failure, to some degree. Calfax had escaped, Valerius had died as a result of the battle, and hundreds of Romans had been tortured and murdered. He didn't think he would ever let himself off the hook for that day, what he could had done differently – acted sooner to save more lives.

"Perhaps, but it was you that saved us. And for that, you have my gratitude, and love."

Gaius smiled at her, accepting her words.

"Claudia, could I ask you something personal?"

"Of course."

Gaius hesitated. He thought that perhaps he shouldn't ask his question on second thought, but he saw, as she looked up at him, waiting eagerly for him to ask that she wanted to hear him.

"While you were in the camp...well, it was filled with runaway slaves, many like you, young women. They had their freedom, even for a short time, yet, you stayed with the consul when you could had left him – ran away or joined the slaves if you so wished. Why did you stay with Paullus, despite that it could have cost you your life?"

Claudia crossed her arms as she lowered her head and thought about his words.

"To be honest, Gaius, I did think about it...many times. But I couldn't...I couldn't leave, Paullus...I..."

Gaius observed that Claudia had not called Paullus by his title, as she should have. Her words seemed to trail off as her mind returned to those days, now weeks past. She looked as if she was going to say more even though she seemed afraid to continue, but she didn't have to as Gaius placed his hand on her shoulders, easing her nerves.

"It is okay. I understand."

She smiled and escorted him towards the rear of the house. When they turned the corner they walked into a large room. Gaius saw Paullus right away as he was standing near the far corner, near the balcony. He was dressed, shaven and cleaner than Gaius had recalled seeing him, and as he turned and faced them once Claudia had announced Gaius' presence, Paullus smile with a big grin as he limped over towards the man that saved his life.

Gaius met Paullus halfway, not wanting the man to injury himself further by trying to make the journey to greet his guest.

368

The swelling around Paullus' face had gone down considerably, and he had even managed to gain back some of the weight he had lost. Still, Gaius knew that Paullus should have remained in bed a few weeks longer. However, he obviously wanted to make the effort.

"Consul, it does my heart well to see that you are up and about," Gaius said as he took Paullus' hand once it was extended.

"And it feels good, I assure you. In fact, it feels amazing to be alive."

Gaius noticed Claudia smile as she listened to her master's cheerful words as he escorted Gaius over to a series of plush chairs.

"Wine, breed, fruit?" Paullus offered with a gesture of his hand as Claudia helped him down into his chair.

Gaius made sure to sit after the consul had before he politely declined the display that was set out before him.

"I am sorry to hear that Valerius did not survive his wounds," Paullus then said, his voice filled with genuine sorrow.

"As am I; he will be missed by the Sixth," Gaius replied.

"He will be missed by all of Rome. While I did not know him as well as I would have liked, I always liked that he spoke his mind, and seemed to know more than he let on. He properly could have been consul himself if he hadn't distanced himself from Rome and politics as much as he had."

"He loved Rome, but detested its politics. His end came as he had wanted, in battle, among his men."

"I'm afraid very few men such as he is left. This war has claimed many of our city fathers, and greatest generals. Rome, and this war will be passed to men such as you, Gaius – our youth."

"Rome has you, sir."

Paullus smiled as he shook his head before taking a sip of spice wine that Claudia had poured him moments earlier.

"No. I had my chance, and I failed. It is hard for me to admit, but I was as foolish and brash as my predecessors were. How many of our brave sons could still be here if better men than I had led them? Instead, I marched them to their doom. I'm done with politics and the army. I will sit the rest of my term as consul out, and let Rome be as it will be. My service is done."

Paullus seemed a bit sadden by his words, but Gaius could see in his eyes that he was indeed tired. His brush with death had been it. He wasn't afraid, Gaius felt, but the very thought of having to go out there again and face Rome's enemies, must have terrified him. He didn't blame him.

"Then, what will you do now?" Gaius asked.

"You know, I really don't know. I never wanted this life to begin with. But family legacy is important to our people, so I was expected for this life. So I had to follow it. Perhaps now, maybe, I will marry and grow something useful. I have – had a farm that I enjoyed a great deal, until Hannibal burnt it down last year. I think I will rebuild it next summer and start anew, start a family and just grow old and fat." Paullus had a funny smile as he words drifted off, as his mind was already in that field working under the hot glare of the sun, planting and cultivating the land as his children ran about, enjoying their freedom.

"I think that is wonderful...A worthy goal indeed."

"But, do not worry, before I go, I will make sure that Valerius' Will is honored in the Senate. His wealth, his lands and the Sixth Legion will be yours, as he had instructed. Congratulations, General," Paullus said with a raised goblet.

Gaius nodded his thanks. He couldn't bring himself to say it out loud. He never wanted this, and did not expect it. Valerius had never made any mention of his plans after his death.

Gaius assumed the Sixth would be given to another officer that was appointed by the Senate, or handed to one of the senior officers within the legion – those still alive. But times had changed and very few capable and experienced officers were left at this point, so there would be no argument over who was now appointed the command.

"Tomorrow," Paullus continued, "the Senate will appoint Fabius Maximus as dictator."

"Really?" Gaius asked surprised. He knew that politically a dictator was only appointed in the most extreme of crisis, and even then, it was very rare.

"Yes. It will fall to him to begin a new campaign and try, somehow, someway, to win this war. At least those fools in the Senate won't be able to undermine him, and with no consul, including me to second guess him, perhaps we may survive this after all."

Paullus put his goblet down and leaned in closer towards Gaius. A big smile appeared on his face as she stared at the young general. "However, I did not bring you here to fill you in on dreary politics or current events, Gaius."

"Oh? Then why did you summon me?"

Paullus stood up to his feet even though it seemed to cause him some pain.

"You saved my life that day when it would have been easier to ignore what you had discovered."

"Consul," Gaius said as he shook his head. "It was not just I, and really it was nothing."

"Oh? Saving my life was nothing?" Paullus asked amused.

"That was not what I meant," Gaius replied nervously.

Paullus laughed.

"I meant; I did what was required of me, as a Roman, a soldier and an officer of the Republic."

"Please, Gaius. I know more than a handful of men and officers that wouldn't have tried what you and your men did. You should had left us to our fate and returned to Rome. You exposed your men to uncertain dangers, and perhaps even put the whole legion at risk. Hannibal could have arrived at Rome's walls before you had, or there could had been a larger force in the camp...There were any number of *ifs* and *buts* that could had gone wrong. But you acted quickly and without thought to your own safety. I don't think many men could have done as much, least of all without thought to the reward you would be given by saving a consul of Rome."

Gaius wanted to say more, deny what Paullus was saying, that he believed more men, all men, all good Romans would had done the same. He saved his arguments and allowed Paullus to continue.

"But, since you did save a consul of Rome, you should be rewarded. I would like to offer it myself. Name it, anything, and it shall be yours, Gaius."

"Consul, you've already granted me the Sixth Legion. What more could I ask of you?"

"Those were Valerius' wishes. And frankly, there is no one else that could command the Sixth at this point. Regardless, I would request that you ask for something, anything that your heart desires."

Gaius glanced over at Claudia. She stood near the far corner, a big smile on her face as she listened, seemly sensing his uneasiness.

"Your friendship would be all that I ask," Gaius stated.

"Bah! That is already yours," Paullus replied as he sat back down and stared at Gaius for a long while. Clearly he wasn't going to let him leave his house until he made an honest request.

After a long moment of silence, Gaius actually laughed as a funny thought crossed his mind. Paullus smiled and ask, "What is so funny?"

Gaius shook his head as he remembered the first story that Valerius had told him many years ago.

"Nothing of great importance, sir, only that my father, a very long time ago found himself in this same predicament when he stood before a superior officer who said he would grant him anything he wished."

"Oh? And did that officer do such?" Paullus asked.

"Yes, yes he did."

"And may I ask what that was?"

"My father asked for my mother."

Paullus looked confused as Gaius elaborated on the memory.

"She was a slave and property of the camp prefect. My father and she had falling in love prior, and he wanted to marry her. Of course, the prefect was not too keen on letting her go, but he felt compelled to comply nonetheless."

"Well, I do hope that you don't ask for Claudia. I would have issues parting with her. I do not think I could get dressed in the morning without her there to help me figure out which arm to put through my tunic first," Paullus chuckled, which caused Gaius to glance over at her. He saw that she was blushing.

He noted that she would have been a fine prize, and if he asked, Paullus probably would give her over to him. But at the moment, as he had told the brief story about his father, Gaius knew what he had to ask for. It was the only thing in the world that he truly wanted. He knew, however, that his words were about to cause a great deal of pain to the man that sat across from him, and that scared him a great deal. Not because he feared what Paullus might do or say, but that he actually liked the man a great deal and the thought of hurting him pained him greatly.

"Consul," Gaius' voice grew serious as he stared back at Paullus. "You ask what I want – what you want to reward me for my services. Then, I ask only one thing."

"Ask and it shall be yours?" Paullus said enthusiastically.

"I want you to release Julia of her marriage vows."

Paullus' expression changed suddenly. He was no longer excited at the prospect of Gaius' request as he looked at him for a long while, not saying a word, almost as if he had not heard what Gaius had asked for.

"What do you mean?" Paullus stuttered.

"Varro, her father is dead. The political and financial gain you would have attained no longer has meaning."

Paullus stood to his feet and stepped away from his chair. His back was to Gaius as he placed his hand to his forehead, seemly lost for words.

"You asked me what I desire the most, consul. It is she. I love her, and I always have," Gaius added, now standing to his own feet. He felt like he had dug himself a hole that he could not get out of. However, he had said what he needed to say.

"And she loves you, I suppose?" Paullus asked, not facing Gaius. His words sounded cold and bitter, almost to the point of rage.

"She does," Gaius answered truthfully.

"Have you shared her bed?" Paullus asked, his words becoming colder.

"Sir?" Gaius was hesitant to answer.

"Answer me!" Paullus cried out as he turned sharply and faced Gaius.

"We have."

Gaius felt sick, suddenly, when he watched Paullus expression of frustration and anger change before his eyes. He seemed weaker and sad by this realization as he stepped further away from Gaius.

Gaius felt like he was betraying the man – tearing out his heart right then and there. He desperately wanted to say something that could ease the consul's mind, but he knew that no words could.

"Why...why her? I would have given you anything, Gaius – armies, wealth and power. I would even promote you as the next consul of Rome if you so asked. I would have set you and your descendents up for generations to come. Why her of all women?" his words weren't spoken so much as statements, but almost as a bribe.

"Because, there are no other women, there never has been. I've loved Julia my entire life, and she loves me. She is all that I crave in this world, nothing more. I do not make this request likely, but I need her as I need air. The blood in my body aches for her. I'm nothing if she isn't with me, in body and soul."

"You know what she means to me! I've confided to you what I've never spoken to anyone before, and this is what you do to me!"

"I do not mean to create mistrust between us. Your friendship does mean a great deal to me."

"Do not -" Paullus wasn't able to finish his sentence as his emotions had gotten the better of him. In his still weakened state he fell into a coughing fit as he dropped to his knees. Both Gaius and Claudia tried to rush over to him, but Paullus raised his hand and cried out, "Don't! Both of you get out of my sight! NOW!"

"Master..." Claudia tried to say as she looked on, a few feet behind Gaius.

"I said, leave me!" Paullus cried out again as he spit out a mouthful of blood. He had exerted himself in his anger, but Gaius' words had hurt him more than his still healing wounds, that much was painfully clear.

Gaius turned away from the consul and placed his hand on Claudia's shoulder. She was already beginning to tear as she desperately wanted to run over to Paullus and help him, but Gaius urged her to leave him be.

"I am sorry, Paullus. I truly am," Gaius said before he left him alone, who had falling down to the floor, now rested his back up against the wall; his hands over his face.

"Take care of him," Gaius then said to Claudia once the two were outside.

"I'm sorry, Gaius," Claudia tried to say as she wiped away her tears.

"No. You have nothing to be sorry about. I did not mean for any of this. I just had..." He couldn't even finish his own words. He felt it best that he just leave now. "Be safe, Claudia," and then Gaius left.

CHAPTER FORTY-TWO

Gaius stood among a dozen officers. This was only the second time he had ever stepped foot inside the senate house of Rome. The last time it had been when the war with Hannibal had started and back then, which seemed like a decade ago, the senate was confident in its resolve and its ability to crush the upstart warlord that had taken a tattered army of barbarians across the Alps, and crossed into Italy; however, a great deal had been lost since that day – entire armies, tens of thousands of lives, both military and civilian alike – more than the republic had ever sustained in its entire history. Lesser countries would have fallen under similar circumstances, and in fact, only days prior the senate was debating whether or not to call for terms with Carthage.

Rome would have given up much of its territory – everything gained in the last war and then some, yet the senate did not give into its fears and instead turned towards another man to guide Rome from the crisis.

Gaius had seen many men, consuls and generals alike that vowed to win the war, but all had come from the same cloth – rich, influential, aristocratic individuals that sought personal glory and fame. Paullus had said the day prior when Gaius had spoken with him, Rome's fathers were dead and it was left to the sons to usher in a new era. If they did not many feared that this nation would not survive another generation, no less another war; so, in response the senate and people had put its trust into the hands of Fabius Maximus.

Gaius had met him years before, the nephew of Varro that had seemed bent on irritating his uncle during that first dinner many months now past. Maximus had been outspoken then, a freethinker with radical ideas that did not, and in many ways still did not sit well with the social elite of Rome. But like Gaius now, Maximus was a changed man. He too had lost a lot, seen too much and now expected a great deal from those men he was going to lead.

The senate had just finished granting Maximus the title of dictator. He would be the sole power in Rome – a king in everything but name. He commanded the armies, navies and the political powers of the republic. What he said, no man could question. It was a dangerous gamble, one that the republic had tried desperately to avoid. The return to the old kings was every Romans greatest fear. But at the moment, there was no other choice. If Rome was to survive it needed to speak with one voice until the crisis had past and the war won.

Gaius stood towards the rear with the other officers listening to the closing statements from the various senators that applauded the decision to appoint Maximus as dictator. There was no real point to their speeches. The choice had been made and there was little need to justify why Maximus was the right candidate for the title. These men were merely playing the political game that Valerius had said he hated so much about the republic – covering their own asses and positioning themselves to benefit from Maximus' new position.

He ignored much of what they were saying as one speaking stood and gave his speech, followed by thunderous applause and cheers as Maximus sat quietly, smiling and nodding his thanks to each speaker. No, Gaius' eyes had been locked on Paullus who sat in the left stone marble seat of the consul – the second seat still empty as Varro' place had not been filled.

Paullus had already stated that he would be staying out of politics and so far, it seemed he was doing just that. Beyond a few choice words earlier in the proceedings the consul had little to say about the historic events of the day.

From time to time Paullus would turn and look over at Gaius. He could still see the anger in Paullus eyes when they stared at each other.

Gaius didn't know what Paullus might do. He had not granted his request to release Julia of her marriage vows, and in fact, if he wanted he could drag Julia to the courts and force her to marry him, or perhaps even take away all of her father's wealth, land and holdings for her violating their contract by having an affair with another man.

Gaius knew he should never have admitted that the two of them had slept together or shared a relationship. However, it was hard for him to lie to the man's face when he knew the truth anyways. Truth be told, he didn't regret anything he had said. It did pain him that he had hurt the consul, but he had to say what he felt in his heart. It seemed pointless, now with everything he had seen and lived through to continue to hide his love for her in the shadows – allowing proper Roman edict to stand in the way of expressing his true feelings.

When the last senator finished his long speech and sat back down, Maximus stood up and stepped out onto the senate floor. He was dressed in his finest white robes with a dark red tunic underneath. He stood quiet for the moment as he allowed the room full of senators to finish their applause before he spoke.

"We have suffered a great deal, we Romans have. Our lands have been tainted with barbarian filth. Our farms burnt, our cities raised, our citizens driven to the four corners of Italy, and our brave soldiers massacred by the thousands. And for what I ask you – for the personal glory of one man – Hannibal?"

The mention of Hannibal's name brought a chorus of jeers from the senators. Maximus just raised his hands and signaled for everyone to be silent.

"You have sent forth many of our city fathers to face this threat, and very few have returned alive. We have burned and grieved for too many of our greatest men since this war has started. We have lost entire armies, not once, not twice, but three times. And now you ask me where will we get more? How will we find new bodies to fill the ranks of our brave legions, and how will they be able to stop a man that most believe can't be defeated?"

There was another chorus of rumbling from the senators as they acknowledged Maximus' questions.

"If this Republic is to prevail and endure the years to come, we must cast off our old ways – our old system and beliefs, and embrace a new doctrine that will usher in a new era for Rome. I have already set plans in motion that will, within the coming year, restore our legions to fighting strength. No more will our armies be filled with the social elite and those privileged few to own land. I am inviting all Italians, not just Roman born, to join our ranks regardless of property. Even the lowest peasant and beggar have the right to defend his country."

The senate began to rumble disapprovingly, but Maximus ignored them and continued on with his speech.

"All personal debts will be wavered for those that choose to serve in the army."

More rumbling followed that statement.

"I will issue orders for able bodied slaves to be freed and drafted into the legions. And no longer will these new legions be led solely by the wealthy elite, but by those men who have already proven that they have the experience and strength to fight and win battles, regardless of class or upbringing. And no more will our soldiers be made up of children and old men, draftees or seasonal soldiers. Our armies will be comprised of professionals, experienced officers and men of fighting age. Terms of service will be twenty years, with reward upon retirement with land and citizenship."

Gaius glanced over his shoulder at the gathering officers that stood with him. They all looked at each other with the same amused expressions on their faces as the senators, all whom had thrown their support behind Maximus, now seemed troubled by his words. While they expected military reform, they hadn't expected this. In a single speech the dictator had thrown away hundreds of years of social edict.

"Rome can no longer look only to her own benefits. We, the whole of Italy and our holdings beyond these boarders are at risk. We must become a single nation and not just a single city among many nations. Those cities around us have been loyal during this war despite Hannibal's calls that they should rise up against us, yet despite what they are threatened with few have sided with him. It is because of these brave Italians that we are still here today. I will no longer ignore these facts as my predecessors had chosen to do. Any that join our legions will be granted Roman citizenship, including a movement that will soon include all the central Italy!"

A loud chorus of jeers and boos roses up upon his last statement. Maximus smiled at those that were openly trying to rebuke him, but he had more supporters among the senate that forced those that were most outspoken to sit down and be silent. He, however, seemed to care little about what those few men were saying as their words could not drowned out his own.

"We will no longer try to battle Hannibal openly. Our armies have faced him four times, and each time they have met with utter disaster. Instead, we will, as I have suggested in the past, will avoid conflict with his army and instead focus all of our attentions on breaking his overstretched supply lines, his support from his barbarian allies, and his native country. Under the leadership of Scipio the Younger, he will lead our legions to Spain and crush Hannibal's means of supplying his armies here in Italy. I have already recalled four legions from Greece to aide in this effort, and with the new legions we will be raising in the coming year, Hannibal will have no means to carry out his campaign against the people of Rome and the Republic. He will be trapped here in Italy, too weak to fight, but still too strong for us to meet head-on."

"It is cowardice!" Gaius heard one senator yell at the top of his lungs.

"And it is foolish to send more of our sons out to be slaughtered in meaningless campaigns that will accomplish nothing!" Maximus rebuked. "I will no longer see our brave soldiers used for your political gains and shortsighted ambitions," Maximus' words grew harsher as he seemed to be speaking directly to the man that had cried out moments ago and those like him.

"We are fighting for our very survival. It is this Senate that only a month ago had abandoned its post – leaving our people to the vices of our enemies. Yet, it is the brave officers and men of our legions, such as the Sixth," Gaius felt a sudden since of pride that Maximus had just mentioned his men, "that stood upon our city walls, waiting for Hannibal and his army. And while that army never came, I know that they would have stayed and fought to the last man – not for you, senator – not to protect your wealth or even to save this house, but to safeguard their families, this city and its legacy. It is they that I will turn towards – it is they that will carry the Republic out of these dark times, not you, senator, nor even I."

The murmurs within the collection of senators seemed to diminish. Some of the men that were outspoken against Maximus' new policies glanced nervously towards Gaius and the other standing officers in attendance. Gaius realized that Maximus more than likely wanted them here so that they may hear his words personally, and of course side with his renewed strategies. If he had the full support of the army, no one would dare challenge his new doctrine for the republic.

"We are at a crossroad, gentlemen. We have stood against the storm – not always united, but still we share the same resolve. Rome will not surrender, not to Hannibal or his ilk, now or ever. I do not promise you a quick victory or that there will not be more bloody battles to come. But I do promise you victory in the end. And when we have attained that victory, not just over Carthage, but the whole world will know of the power that is Rome and our beloved Republic."

Maximus' last words got the reaction he was hoping for. His supporters, the majority of the senate stood to their feet and applauded him, cheering his name as if he had already delivered on his promises.

The senate chambers would not quiet down for several long and loud minutes, when it finally did Claudia stepped next to Gaius and spoke into his ear.

"Gaius, the consul would like you to stay. He wishes to speak with you once everyone has left the chambers."

Gaius looked at her, seeing her nervousness as she relayed Paullus' message to him, and nodded his understanding.

She stepped back as he turned his gaze toward Paullus, who was standing like many of his colleagues, applauding Maximus' speech, yet his eyes were on Gaius as he stared at him for a long while.

Sometime later Gaius stood alone near one of the large support columns. The last of the senators, aides and officers had left moments ago leaving just him and Claudia, who stood in the far corner near the front entrance, and Paullus, who was still seated in his consular chair. He wasn't looking directly at Gaius, not yet as he seemed to be deep in thought.

Gaius, despite the uncomfortable silence stood poised waiting for Paullus to say what it was he had to say. When it seemed that Paullus had made his mind up he stood uncomfortably out of his chair, still aching from his wounds that slowly were healing day-by-day, and started over towards Gaius who stood taller, at attention, ready for whatever Paullus was going to say to him.

He could not read Paullus' face as he neared him, walking with a heavy limp, but still making the effort to look strong. He did not know what to expect or what he might do if Paullus demanded that he should keep Julia and planned still to marry her. He would not let that happen. Not now. Not after everything he had lived through. He knew without a doubt that if those were Paullus' words that he would take her away from Rome – somewhere far from this place beyond the reach of senate and Hannibal. He just didn't want it to come to that.

And then Paullus spoke, not with anger, but still stern and direct.

"I did not agree to marry Julia because I desired political favor from her father, or to further my own career. I agreed to marry her because I loved her. I always have, since I first laid eyes on her years ago when she was still a child."

Gaius wanted to say that he regretted making that comment that that was Paullus' only reason for entering into the agreement in the first place. He hadn't meant for his words to come out as it had. However, he kept his mouth shut as Paullus continued.

"I may not have known her as long as you have, but that does not change how I feel about her, Gaius. I have cherished what time I have shared with her, even as little as it has been. And I dream of what life we may yet have left to live, together, as husband and wife."

Paullus' expression changed suddenly as his voiced lowered, as he suddenly found that he could no longer look Gaius in the eyes.

"However, I knew then – I've always known that her feelings towards me were not returned. I had hoped that with time she could see me in the same light as I see her. Yet, I know

383

now that her heart and soul had always been entrusted to another man, a man that not even my wealth, power and influence could stand against."

Paullus looked up at Gaius with heavy eyes.

"I am glad at least that it is you, my friend that she loves. I do not know of anyone better."

Gaius did not know what to say or what he should. He just stood staring at Paullus, seeing that the realizations that he was letting go of someone important to him was perhaps the most difficult thing he ever had to do.

"I will release Julia of her marriage vows as you asked, and give you my blessings for your union, Gaius."

"Thank you," Gaius replied, which brought only a sad nod from the consul before he turned to leave.

"Paullus," Gaius called. Stepping over to him, he stood before Paullus and placed his hand onto the consul's shoulder, and spoke softly.

"I am not of noble birth, or do I pretend to understand Roman edict or social standings as much as you, my friend. But I do understand what it is to hide my feelings for another person, but are not able to express them. I know how much it hurts, how far you would be willing to go to be with that person, even die for them."

Paullus looked confused by Gaius' words, but he listened regardless.

"Claudia," Gaius indicated towards her with his eyes. Paullus too looked back at her, who stood quietly watching the two men speak, unknowing that the subject had turned toward her.

"She stayed with you when you were injured – defended you against your captives even at the risk of her own life, and never once while you were unconscious did she leave your side. She did not do this out of servitude or loyalty. She could have left you. She could have been free. But she stayed, no matter the risk. She stayed because of you, because she loves you more than you could possibly know."

Paullus looked back and stared at Claudia.

"But, she is a-"

"A slave," Gaius finished Paullus' own words. "My mother was a slave, but that did not change the fact that my father fell madly in love with her. He didn't care what others would think, or how it might reflex on him. He only needed to know that he loved her, and she him. Everything else, it doesn't matter."

"I..." Paullus struggled to speak, but he hesitated for a moment as he kept his eyes on Claudia, seemly seeing her in a new light. "I did not know this."

"We seldom do, until it is pointed out to us. Build your farm, my friend, and be happy. This is your life. Live it as you want to – with whom you want."

Gaius turned and left Paullus alone. He hoped as he left that some good would come from this war for Paullus. That he would heed his advice and forgo all judgment of other and follow his heart. He deserved at least that much – a real chance to share his life with another that care for him as much as he loved Julia.

When Gaius turned back one last time, he saw that Paullus was now standing with Claudia, speaking with her, not as a master but just as a man speaking to a woman as he held her hand. A small tear ran down her cheek as she listened to him with a warm smile. Gaius didn't stay longer to see what happened next. He didn't have to as her smile was all he needed to know.

He had what he wanted. He had Julia for himself. No rules, status, obligations or family could stand in their way now, save for one thing – his duty to Rome.

CHAPTER FORTY-THREE

There was a bitter chill in the air. Fall was coming quickly, but Gaius didn't mind, not one bit. He stood on a balcony looking out across Rome. The moon hung high overhead and the gentle breeze. For the first time in a long time he felt comfortable with this city. Nothing grand had happened since his return. Hannibal was still out there somewhere, and Maximus' propositions were still in its early stages. But he was perfectly content.

Gaius smiled as he felt Julia's arms wrap around his bare chest as she stood behind him, kissing him on his shoulders as she pressed her naked body up against his.

He returned her kiss as he placed his hands over hers and caressed them.

It had been several days now since Gaius had spoken with Paullus. The consul had been true to his words and had already released Julia of her marriage vows. She was his now, finally and there was nothing or anyone that could stand between them.

"What vexes you so that you leave the warmth of our bed?" Julia asked as she rested her head between his shoulders.

"Tomorrow I leave for Spain," Gaius answered.

"You worry about the deployment then?" she asked.

He turned and faced her, making sure that he kept her close to him, in his arms.

"I worry about leaving you. After so long, we have nothing to hide from – the chance to finally," Gaius paused as he thought about what a future with he would be like. He hadn't gotten very far in his daydreams, which he had always believed were just fantasy. "I don't know really. I don't want to leave you here alone, again."

"I have waited this long to be with you, Gaius. I can wait longer if I have too."

"It could be years. There is still much that needs to be done before we can be sure Rome is safe, no less actually winning this war. I'm afraid what might happen in that time, that I may not --"

She placed her index finger over his lips, politely asking him to be still.

"What may come may come. We can't dwell over what we cannot control."

"But I could control it. I could ask to remain behind and help Rome in some other capacity. The Fifteen Legion will be left behind to protect the city. I could take a up post with them."

Julia smiled as she shook her head.

"I know you, Gaius. You cannot leave your men in the hands of another man. You cannot stay here while others are sent to face whatever may be out there waiting for them. You love this city and the Republic too much to just stand by and not protect her, as you have always tried to protect me."

"I love you more."

Julia placed her hand over Gaius' heart and stared up at him.

"Perhaps so, but we both know it isn't the same. Out there, beyond our borders lies your destiny, and you need to see it through to the end. I will always be right here waiting for you to return."

"But I may not return at all," Gaius added as he lowered his head.

"Then, if we can't be together in this life, then the next. It will change nothing."

Julia buried her head into his chest, wrapping her arms around him as she held onto him tightly.

"Just never forget what you have to live for," she whispered. "You will come back to me, I know it."

PART FOUR

CHAPTER FORTY-FOUR

Mago had been on a long journey since last he spoke with his brother. He had spent a short time in Italy just before Cannae where Hannibal had crushed the consular army of a hundred thousand men. It had been one of the proudest moments in Mago's life seeing so many Roman's dead. But, soon after, as Hannibal's staff urged him to march on Rome and take the city, he had refused – failing to cease his great victory.

Hannibal then sent Mago back to Carthage to request more men, so that he may finish the war in Italy and bring Rome's walls crashing down.

Mago had with him the rings and other markings of the Roman senate and elite – thousands of small pieces of gold that had been stripped from still warm corpses following Cannae. When he stepped foot in the senate, for the first time in his life, Mago threw the rings onto the senate floor for all the leaders of Carthage to see with their own eyes what Hannibal had accomplished.

He spoke passionately about what he witnessed – three consuls dead, hundreds of thousands of Roman soldiers killed – whole settlements and communities destroyed, Italy was Hannibal's.

Mago expected, with his words the senate to bow to Hannibal's wishes and rally their swords. The only question would be, how many soldiers should they send? However, that question never came.

When Mago finished his speech, those within the senate, enemies of Hannibal who had grown jealous of his success turned against him as they called him a warmonger – a tyrant and a traitor for instigating the conflict with Rome in the first place. It sickened Mago. These men were merchants and businessmen that cared only about money, and not the pride of their nation. And, before he knew, the whole senate had rallied against Hannibal, calling his actions a crime as they turned their attention towards protecting Carthage's interests from Rome, namely its territories in Spain.

Hannibal would not get any reinforcements as he hoped. Rome's walls would remain strong and still standing, and he, as he began to lose support from his Gallic allies, was trapped, as his opponents under the leadership of the Dictator Fabius Maximus refused to confront him in open battle.

It was an embarrassment! Mago left furious as he was refused the chance to return to his brother after he was ordered by the senate to take up command in Spain, and make ready for a new Roman offensive. And so he had been for the past five years, trapped, freezing his ass off, holding firm against the Scipio, a man unlike any Roman he had ever encountered – one that fought more like his brother.

Now, Mago returns to Italy with terrible news. He races to tell his brother in no short order that Spain had fallen – New Carthage had been taken by Scipio, and that Hannibal was now cut off from his only reliable source for reinforcements and supplies. However, Mago would not get the chance to deliver his terrible message through words - just symbolically as small bag was thrown by a Roman horseman over the high walls that surrounded Hannibal's camp.

The bag was found momentarily by a Carthaginian soldier who read the notation that it was a message meant for Hannibal. He raced as quickly as he could across the camp to his leader's tent where he presented the bag to him.

As Hannibal unfurled the string that sealed the bag shut, the smell alone indicated to him what it was, just not who.

A moment later, Hannibal pulled the severed head of his brother, Mago out from the bag; his white eyes rolled into his skull; his neck dry of blood with only a note attached to the base, pinned into the flesh indicating the sender – *Scipio*.

Even Hannibal's bravest men shuttered when they heard him scream in agony over the loss of his beloved brother.

If there were any doubt to the long term outcome of the war, Hannibal's army had lost all hope of claiming another smashing victory against their bitter rivals upon Mago's arrival. Little did they know, they would all be going home soon.

.

CHAPTER FORTY-FIVE

"Julia," Gaius whispered to himself as she began to fade from his dream, as if she had never existed.

Gaius opened his eyes as he heard his name being called by a familiar voice. Someone had just walked into his tent and stood just beyond the sleeping area separated by a thin curtain. For a moment as he lay, not moving, desperately hoping to recapture the exquisite image of his beloved, he wished the intruder would leave. However, his name was called with more urgency for a second time.

"It is time for you to wake, my friend. I know you can hear me, so there is no pretending otherwise."

"I do hear you, though I wish I had not," Gaius finally replied with a low mutter as he forced himself to rise from his cot, tossing his wolf pelt covers to the ground.

"Just give me a moment."

"As you wish. I'll go outside and tell the war to wait for a couple more hours," the man replied with a sarcastic yet friendly tone. Gaius actually managed a faint smile.

As he stepped out from his small sleeping area, he looked up at his officer, who smirked at him, as if he was in on a joke that Gaius had no knowledge of.

"What is so damn amusing?" he groaned at Maurus, who stood in full armor, admirably cleaned and polished - he might have been on parade.

"You look like you were dragged under your horse," Maurus joked.

"I'm fine. Do not give second thought of my appearance; just a rough night's sleep. The damn sand fleas and such," Gaius lied as he walked over to a large copper bowl in the corner that was filled with cool water.

He dipped his hands and splashed the water over his face, and rubbed his aching shoulders and neck. He repeated this for several minutes until he removed the foul smell of the forsaken country from his flesh, for the moment.

"How are the men?" Gaius asked as he reached for a clean cloth and began to wipe down his naked body.

"They are fed, armed and marching out onto the field as we speak," Maurus answered, as he walked over to the far side of the tent. A wooden mannequin stood, holding Gaius' black leather armor.

"By the gods, Maurus, why did you let me sleep so long? You're my chief centurion."

"I felt that you needed rest, at least an extra hour. We need your mind clear this day, above all others. Besides, what good is being your chief centurion if I can't attend to things on my own without you looking over my shoulder?" Maurus answered with a warm grin as he tossed Gaius his tunic and belt.

"Regardless, I should have been awakened." Gaius sighed as he dressed. "Are they nervous, the men?" He then asked.

"More excited, I would have to say. It has been seven years of war, which I would rather forget. We've waited a long time to reach this point. I can hardly believe it myself. I wonder where the time has gone, if home is even like we remember it."

"I'm sure it is the same as we left it."

"I do wish one thing, though," Maurus said as he walked over to where Gaius' helmet lay, on a nearby table, as Gaius buckled his armor in place.

"What is that?"

"If this is to be my last day on earth, my only regret is that I couldn't have died on my own soil," Maurus answered, sounding uncharacteristically moody as he turned with the helmet in hand, and walked back to his commanding officer.

"The gods decide such things, my friend. However, I do believe you will get the chance to see home again after this battle is done." Gaius' words were encouraging, but he too seemed to have a slight hint of doubt in his voice.

"And what of you, do you think the gods favor you such that you will see our homeland?"

Gaius hesitated to answer at first as he considered Maurus' words. He did not want to seem uncertain, as the two of them had survived so much that the prospect of dying now would have been aggravating.

"I believed the god of war, Mars will have plenty of blood this day. That much is certain. However, if he wants mine, he shall have to fight for it." Gaius managed a wide smile as he slammed his palms down onto Maurus' shoulders.

"Look to the heavens and praise the gods, my nervous friend. We still breathe and shall continue for a long time to come. I'm sure that both of us will live through this day. We will go home. We will marry beautiful women who will tend to our every need. We shall drink long into the night recalling tales of our victories, while our children grow together, bored stiff of those stories. Of this, my friend, I am sure as I'm sure the dawn will bring a new day. But when that day comes and death's hand reaches down for us, far from now, we will leave this world with honor and pride, and shall rejoin our fallen brothers as heroes of the Republic."

"A wonderful paragon that would be," Maurus smiled widened.

"Indeed it is – one worth living for."

Maurus walked over to Gaius, holding out a helmet that was capped off with a bright red feather crest, which signified his rank. He carefully placed it onto his head and laced the straps in place, preparing himself for what lay beyond the folds of his tent.

"Enjoy this day, Maurus for there will never be another like it in our lives. Today the sons of the Republic walk on the soil of our bitter enemy. Today we will avenge the losses we have sustained in this war. Carthage will finally know our pain, tenfold." Gaius' voice was firm as Maurus smiled, placing hands at the entry to the tent. The warmth of the morning sun entered, illuminating the interior. Already the organized chaos of the barracks filled Gaius' ears.

"Then, Legate, sir, let us not waste a moment. We would not want to disappoint our enemies by being late for the battle, now would we?"

Gaius rode into the main camp, which lie several miles to the east of his legion's barracks. His destination was a series of large interconnecting tents that served as the headquarters for the army's commander. Waiting outside were a dozen legionaries, who stood guard despite the intense heat, poised in their full armor and kit. One of those soldiers, a centurion with a scarred face, walked over to Gaius and grabbed the reins of his horse as he stopped a few yards from the tent.

"Sir, the legates are assembled and are awaiting you," the centurion quickly spoke as Gaius leaped down.

"And, what of Scipio, has he arrived?" Gaius quickly asked, fearing he may be delaying the assembly.

"No, sir. He is still surveying the men, but is expected back at any time now."

"Thank you, Centurion."

The inside of the tent was spacious and lit well, with oil lamps burning. It was also surprisingly cooler than outside, which was a welcome relief as the African heat did not agree with him.

Everywhere Gaius noted the splendors of a proper Roman home that a nobleman couldn't seem to leave home without. He found it amusing that many of the prefects, tribunes and legates he had served under would not begin a campaign until their creature comforts were attended to. Although he hadn't dared say it beyond a few whispered jokes around the campfire he figured he was just too used to sleeping under the stars and living out of a pack to care much about these luxuries. A sharp sword, good armor, bread in his stomach and a sky to look up at was all he desired.

He admired, however, the fine plush furniture, expensive marble tables and exquisite statues of various gods and champions of eras long past that adorned the inner living areas of the command tent. The smell of fresh fruit laid out in gold and silver bowls on top of the various tables, mixed with the aroma of scented oils filled his nostrils, drawing him toward the sweet treats. A few slaves went about their daily chores, completely oblivious to the war outside.

His destination was back toward the rear, where a second section had been built into the main living quarters. This area was the war room where the officers were gathered, waiting for their commander to arrive.

As Gaius parted several layers of silk veils that separated the living quarters from the war room, he saw a dozen officers standing around a long, rectangular wooden table that had a leather-hide map stretched out across it, detailing the entire region where this army was camped.

"Legate Gaius, it is good to see you've joined us. I'm pleased to see you managed to get out of bed on this momentous day," one of the Roman officers joked as he greeted Gaius with a warm smile, a full cup of wine in his left hand.

"It is good to see you as well, Avitus. And I'm simply amazed to see that you aren't drunk, yet. How will you be able to command your men with such a clear mind?" Gaius replied with his own grin as he took the man's hand and shook it.

Avitus was one of the old commanders, a burly man who had survived every battle of the war. He commanded two legions – frontline troops that had fought across Italy since the war began. He had never been popular under the old guard – too different, too connected to his men, having risen through the ranks, now going on some thirty-eight years of service to the republic. Men such as he had become favorites of the new leaders of Rome – they were very nearly the only seasoned commanders left after the disastrous Battle of Cannae, now five years past.

"Oh, give me another hour, my boy, and I shall not disappoint you," Avitus bellowed with his characteristic laugh.

"Perhaps you should have stayed in bed and allowed real officers conduct this battle," another general by the name of Cassius spoke up, not even trying to hide his contempt for Gaius.

Cassius was an officer from the old guard: wealthy, proud, and descended from a long line of equestrians who had not agreed with the transitions that had been made to the army in recent years. He believed that only noblemen had the right to hold command, and Cassius was not alone in his stance to maintain the old ways, even if their resistance nearly destroyed their country.

"Yes, well, I had to rise and make sure you and your men don't turn and flee from the battlefield yet again," Gaius replied, which brought a sneer from Cassius, while several other officers, including the foreign Numidia commanders, chuckled.

Gaius ignored Cassius and those like him. Neither he nor his *Wolves* had to prove anything to anyone. They had stood on the wall of their city after Cannae, when there was no army left to defend the capital, while so-called Roman noblemen, such as Cassius, fled.

"I grow tired of these strategy sessions Scipio continues to insist on," Flavius, one of the younger officers complained as he stood over the table.

"You know how Scipio likes to remind everyone that he is in charge," Claudius Nero spoke. He was a few years older than Gaius, but was fairly new to the campaign. He had avoided much of the war at his Greek estate, overseeing his family's wealthy shipping business until no longer able to refuse the call to arms or, more likely, the chance for immortal glory.

Gaius didn't bother to listen to the bickering between the old and new guards' obvious dislike for one another, which continued without pause. He was standing on the far side of the table, surveying the map that was laid out before him, focusing on the particulars of the army's formation and the terrain.

There was nothing inventive about the battle plan. It was surprisingly simple, one that did not rely on numbers, terrain or hidden surprises.

This was done less for their army, but to hamper its opponent, which often had defeated superior forces with trickery and deception. Out here, on the flat ground with nowhere to hide, the two armies faced one another, an advantage Gaius was certain would bring them victory.

Carefully positioned across the map were two sets of wooden figures. The blue characters represented those of the Romans, while the red were the Carthaginians. The enemy lines were made-up of infantry, three formations deep and nearly half a mile long. Two cavalry units were placed on either side, with a unit of reserves in the rear, while Carthage's elite soldiers, veterans of Italy, were also in the rear. This was the formation that the generals believed the enemy would assemble.

Rome's numbers equaled that of the enemy – two cavalry units to the side, with infantry in the center. However, Scipio had changed the formation of his infantry, splitting them into cohorts' number close to five hundred men, creating gaps between the formations, which ran three lines deep and across.

Lack of mobility had cost the republic deadly in the past, so it was hoped that this time the army would be able to adapt to any situation that may arise once the fighting began.

The Numidians, who had begun the war on the side of the Carthaginian, stood to the right of Rome's line. He did not trust them so he needed his men to perform beyond expectation if he hoped to break through the Carthaginian cavalry.

He needed to flank the enemy, encircle and attack them from the rear while the main force pushed into the center. It was a tactic that had worked for centuries and one that had been used successfully against his people five years ago.

The officers' attention turned to Scipio who had finally arrived. Saluting, the men went silent, their eyes following Scipio as he rounded the table and took his place.

"Gentlemen, you must excuse my tardiness. I will not spend more time than is needed. I know that each of you is eager to get onto the battlefield and win this war for the Republic," Scipio said as he stood before his officers.

"It has been a long and costly endeavor to reach this point, hasn't it my friends? Each and every one of us has lost much: men, family, land and wealth. I've picked each of you for your past valor," Some of the old guard couldn't help but sneer at Scipio's comment, which he let pass.

"Today, we will make Carthage know what we as a people have endured in this war, a war that was not of our making. We will make them suffer as we have. And our victory today will not just end this war, but it will send ripples across the world to all those who would dare raise arms against the Republic. Today is the first day of our nation's destiny."

Scipio began to reposition several of the blue and red figures, anticipating how he believed the opposing army would react.

Gaius studied Scipio as he carefully laid out his strategy to his generals.

Scipio was an unassuming man who hardly exhibited the qualities of a great leader. He was only ten years older than Gaius; twenty-eight.

Like everyone in the room, Scipio seemed much older than his years, maybe more so as his hair had already begun to recede from his scalp and several deep wrinkles settled under his tired eyes. And while he was still able and ready to fight, Scipio's eyes told a somber story of a man that was tired of war and death, which included his own father, who died in the opening stages of the war now seven years past.

He had led his legions through Italy, to Spain, into Greece and now finally to Africa, the home of Carthage. His strategies had turned the tide of the war. But even he knew that no Roman living or dead, had beaten the Carthage army led by one man, Hannibal. That fact weighed heavily on his shoulders and on each man in the room as they listened carefully to every word.

Gaius had been deep in his own thoughts, staring down at the wooden figures, picturing in his mind how the battle might play out, and did not notice that Scipio had finished his briefing.

Standing silently Scipio stepped back from the table, looking at each officer intently before speaking again.

"There were times when each of us had given up hope and doubted that we would live to see such a day as this. We watched our brothers, our sons, our fathers taken from us. We bled at Trebbia, at Trasimene and at Cannae. We fought and died on our own lands, but not anymore. We are here, on the doorstep of our enemy, and one way or another, this army will not return home until this war is over and that bastard Hannibal knows the bitterness that we feel. Or by the gods, I will march to Carthage and pull down its filthy walls with my bare hands."

The officers nodded their agreement. They knew that this battle would be remembered for ages to come. This was their moment, their chance to right all the wrongs that had befallen their country. Seven years of tireless war was coming to an end.

Scipio walked around the table as each of his generals' eyes was glued to him.

"Like our forefathers who drove the last Etruscan kings from our homeland, and those who kept the northern barbarians at bay for all these centuries, we, today, shall etch our own names into the altar of our beloved Republic's history. The world will know that no nation, now or ever shall equal our might; that no matter the losses or the cost, the Roman Republic shall forever burn the brightest in the entire world."

Scipio embraced each of his officers as friends and comrades alike, as if it were the last time he would see them again. He preferred speaking to them as equals, even if some in the room did not respect him for it.

Gaius was one of the last that Scipio approached, purposely so.

"You stood alone on the walls of Rome, my friend, when all others ran away. I know that above all other men in this room I can count on you and the Sixth the most. Help me win this war, Gaius, and we can all return home to those we love."

"Victory or death," Gaius replied.

"Victory or death."

CHAPTER FORTY-SIX

More than an hour later, Gaius stood alongside a number of officers, including Scipio astride his white horse, surveying the Carthaginian lines, which stretched for several miles. The strategies laid out during the meeting had changed very little. For the most part, what he saw was what he had placed on the map. Gaius hoped the general's foresight would prove just as fruitful when the fighting started.

"Well, I guess it was too much to ask for him not to show up, or just surrender," Commodus, one of the generals beside Scipio commented with a smirk.

"By the gods' man, do not say such things. Not when we've come all this way," another officer spoke.

Each man chuckled lightly before Scipio put his heels to his horse's side, urging the steed forward as he spoke.

"Come; let's see what our esteemed colleges have come to say."

He and his men rode the short distance onto the field of battle to meet the Carthage contingent. The two armies were separated by five thousand paces; only the cracked and scorched earth separated them, which soon would run red with blood.

The two groups stood poised for a moment, staring at each other, sizing up the opposition before Scipio broke rank and trotted toward the enemy riders. One of the Carthaginian officers did so as well.

Gaius and the other Romans remained where they were, but they would still be near enough to hear the conversation between the respective generals.

Gaius had to narrow his eyes to get a better look at the Carthaginian commander across from Scipio, as the two men stopped their horses a few feet across from one another. And after a moment of close observation, it dawned on him that the officer could only be Hannibal Barca.

Hannibal had become the most feared individual in Roman history; a man who had single-handedly brought the republic to its knees, killer of tens of thousands. Gaius had never seen him in person until now, although he had faced the general's army once before.

During the long cold nights in the Roman camp, soldiers around the fire wondered if Hannibal was a god, for all that he had accomplished in such a short time. He seemed to be conjured from every man's worst nightmares: cold, calculating, deceptive and cunning to a fault. It was hard not to admire him. He may have given Alexander a challenge worthy of history.

Hannibal was not what Gaius had expected. Rumors had been many: He was a giant of a man standing fifteen feet tall. He wore armor fashioned by the gods rendering him indestructible. He had the gift of foresight, so that he knew in advance how to defeat any army that was sent against him, and that his sword possessed the souls of every man that Rome had slaughtered in its history. Many more legends had surrounded him, but what Gaius saw now, seated on horseback before the most celebrated Roman general of this era, was not the villain he had pictured.

Hannibal was no small man. He had a large build and broad shoulders; clearly he had trained to be a warrior from birth. Despite his fame among his own people, he was not dressed in the attire of an officer or nobleman but was far less expensive and impressive. He was covered by a simply-made leather chest piece, which was worn and badly scratched from decades of use. He wore no helmet; numerous scars lined his bald head and rough face. His horse was no different than the animal that his senior officers rode. His sword, which was longer than a Roman blade but made from the same Spanish iron, hung low on his left hip. It seemed generations old, and had probably been handed down from father to son.

Most noticeable, and perhaps the only truth among the rumors, was that he only had one eye. His right eye, having been lost, was covered by a black leather patch: proof, at the least, that he was indeed mortal.

To Gaius' surprise, he found that Hannibal was not the cold bloodthirsty monster as had been described: horned head, breathing fire, harden scales on his flesh, dragon wings, standing the height of five men. He was a man, to be sure. He could see in his posture and carriage the same confidence and sense of duty and honor that Gaius had admired in many men. What hatred for Rome and its people that boiled deep down in the recesses of his soul, could not be seen – but was surely just below the surface.

Hannibal broke the long awkward silence first as he tilted his head in a respectful manner.

"It is an honor to finally meet you, General Scipio," he spoke in perfect Latin; his voice easily carried over the desert floor.

Scipio had no kind remarks to exchange with his rival. He moved his horse back and forth while Hannibal remained still. What this display of power was doing to Scipio's mind, Gaius could only imagine. If it was apprehension, Scipio did not show any signs.

"What are your terms?" Scipio demanded, louder than Gaius had ever heard him speak before this day.

Hannibal smiled at Scipio's blunt speech.

"You have come a long way. Many soldiers have given their lives to defend your Republic; bravely, I might add. There is no need for us to sacrifice the lives of our men further – not today, and hopefully never again."

Scipio smiled as he reined in his horse and learned forward over his saddle, crossing his arms over the pommel.

"You wish to surrender then?"

Hannibal managed a faint smile. "No. I only convey my government's terms."

"Then enough with your pitiful pleasantries, I grow bored. Let us finish this tiresome conversation and tell me your terms," Scipio repeated.

Gaius could plainly see Hannibal's officers' displeasure at Scipio's disrespect. They held their place however, a few feet behind their general and dared not interrupt the proceedings.

"My Senate has issued the following terms for Rome: To end the war between our nations, once and for all, Carthage offers Rome full control over the Spanish territories, plus Sicily, Sardinia, and a guarantee that neither I, nor my country, will ever again raise arms against Rome or its allies, directly or indirectly. Along with these terms, the Senate agrees to pay your Republic an annual sum of fifteen million aureus for the next ten years," Hannibal seemed to force his words between his gritted teeth as if someone was forcing him to say them against his will.

Scipio's smile widen as he positioned his horse closer to Hannibal before he gave his reply.

"My dear general, Rome already controls these lands. We took them, from you and your brother, or has your memory faded in your waning years?" Scipio let his mocking words sink in before he continued.

Hannibal grunted at him with contempt, but maintained his composure.

"My army is at your country's doorstep. I think, general that I will bring my terms to your Senate personally, once I have razed Carthage to the ground, and disbanded this excuse for an army you have brought to meet me."

Hannibal leaned closer to Scipio. "You forget that my army lies between you and Carthage," Hannibal replied with an icy glare.

"Oh, it does, does it?" Scipio replied.

"You would be foolish to sacrifice your life, and the lives of your men. Do you do this in an attempt to defeat me on my own soil for the sake of glory or reward? If so, don't be a fool, Roman, when needless bloodshed can be avoided. What my government has offered you are more land and wealth than your Republic could have hoped to achieve in a hundred years. Take the offer and remove your forces from my country with the satisfaction that you have won. Your celebrity is assured."

"Oh, my fame will be earned when you rabble has been ground into the dirt, general."

"Hannibal smiled. "You know who I am. I doubt that you have brought anything I have not faced, and crushed, before," Hannibal sneered.

"And you know who I am. When you are defeated, I will have earned more fame and wealth than I can imagine. It will make me immortal in the eyes of my people. However, that is not why I refuse your offer."

Scipio drew closer to Hannibal, his words low and hard; the bitterness in his voice conveyed the anger of millions who had suffered since Hannibal started the war years ago.

"You brought this war to my people, to my homeland – and for what? You have killed so many, entire villages, cities, generations of people, and for what?"

Of course Hannibal did not answer.

"You came to my homeland for your own glory, which was fueled by hatred against a people who never offended you personally. You destroyed much, and have taken many lives, and none of it was for your people, your country, or for justice - only for your selfish ends. You are a monster, Hannibal, whose terror will end today. I will destroy your army, and with it, your legacy. There can be no other way to end this war."

"Then that is how it must be."

A smile appeared on Scipio's face as he sealed the fate of his men. He stood, higher in the saddle, as he presented Rome's official response to Hannibal's terms.

"General, I'm afraid that on the behalf of the Senate, the People, and the Republic of Rome, I cannot accept, in good conscience the offer that your government has proposed."

Hannibal sneered with an annoyed grunt as he pulled the reins of his horse, forcing the animal to turn as he prepared to rejoin his troops.

"You are either brave, or very foolish. History will decide which."

Scipio turned and rode past each of his waiting officers who followed one-by-one. However, Gaius noticed that one of Hannibal's men had not turned and joined his general, but remained seated on his horse, staring at him with a sinister grin – dangling in his massive fist was an object that he recognized immediately.

Gaius' right hand flew down to the hilt of his sword at the sight the clay medallion that dangled on a leather string between the soldier's fingers, seemly taunting him with it. However, after a few seconds, he steadied himself, slowly taking his hand off of his sword. To draw it while the Carthaginian and Roman generals were still on the field would have violated the brief truce.

"My dear friend, it has been so long since last we met," Calfax's voice was harsh and mocking. His Latin was bad, every word spoken as if it were an insult.

"Look at you; your desire for revenge must be overwhelming. You can barely contain yourself. But that pitiful sense of honor is standing in your way isn't it? You want this back, don't you? It was your friend's after all," Calfax mocked as he moved his horse nearer to Gaius.

"This is the way it should be, just like in the arena, two warriors standing against one another – not with forty thousand me between us ready to tear each other apart. Don't you agree, Roman?" The very word, *Roman*, was said with so much hatred that Gaius' skin crawled.

"Strike me down, young Roman. It is easy. Put your hands down on that sword and draw it. Take my life and have your revenge upon me. Forget all of this. Forget your duty and sense of honor, and just kill me – you know you want it this way. Let these fools fight, their struggle means nothing compared to ours."

Calfax waited as he threw open his arms, exposed his powerful chest, inviting Gaius to attack.

Despite his hatred for this man, Gaius did not give into his darker instincts and lash out.

"You are no fun, not like he was." Calfax gestured to the clay medallion. It hung around his neck, among other trinkets that had belonged to other Roman lives he had ended.

"He whimpered like a baby when I slit his throat," Calfax said. "I trust when you face your end, you will have more courage than he did?"

Gaius leaned in closer to Calfax. He wasn't going to play the gladiator's games any longer.

"On the field, to the south, I will be there. I will find you, and we will finish this once and for all," Gaius finally spoke as he dug deep to draw on as much courage as he could find. His words, thankfully, were firm, because Calfax's presence was terrifying. The man feared nothing and no one. Gaius knew he had to be strong before him; the old gladiator could smell fear like a dog and would exploit it without hesitation.

Calfax's smile widened as Gaius turned his horse and galloped back towards the Roman lines.

"Then on the field it shall be, Roman! On the field!" Calfax cried out several times, roaring with laughter.

This battle had a whole new meaning for Gaius. While Rome needed to defeat Hannibal to move beyond the man's legacy, he needed to face the gladiator to avenge the savagery of the man's own sins.

Live or die, he would find him and thrust his sword into the man's chest. This he vowed with every fiber of his being. This he would do even it took his last breath.

CHAPTER FORTY-SEVEN

"What do they call this place again?" Maurus asked.

"Zama - They call this place Zama," Gaius finally answered as he glanced over at Maurus, who squinted under the heat of the sun.

"As good as any place to die, I guess. I wish it was cooler though," Maurus replied.

"I think you already said that earlier," Gaius smiled.

"Did I? Did you have anything encouraging to say to me?" Maurus smiled as glanced over at his old friend.

Gaius shook his head and grinned, amused by Maurus' nervousness.

"Well then, perhaps you should say something inspiring for the men. They look uncomfortable right now."

"You know I hate speeches," Gaius growled as he looked over his shoulder at the gathered horsemen behind him; his Sixth Legion. However, he knew that Maurus was right. They needed to hear him, now. The waiting for the call to charge had drawn out too long.

Before Gaius could turn his horse around to address his men, Maurus grabbed his forearm and asked, "This is the last battle, isn't it?"

"It had better be, or I will ride out to Carthage myself."

The eyes of the Sixth followed him as he broke from his formation among the other officers and rode out before the first rank. The air was quiet with only the sounds of the horses to disturb the peacefulness of the empty plains. Then, in the distances a loud horn sounded, carrying over the far horizon. It was a signal from Scipio's lines to stand ready. Soon the final blow would come to signal the attack.

"Wolves, listen to that!" Gaius raised his hand into the sky and indicated towards the sounding war-horn. His men gazed upward, looking towards the cloudless sky, not seeing anything, but understanding what he was indicating to.

"For too long we have traveled across the breath of our Republic to lands none of us had ever seen before. And for longer our nation has been under the boot heel of Carthage, in not just this war, but those our fathers and grandfathers fought before us. I was, like many of you at Trebia. I faced our enemy as Hannibal slaughtered our brothers. I was there at Cannae and saw the piles of our dead left out to rot in the baking sun. I've seen the horrors and atrocities that Hannibal has committed against our people, and I've lost brothers and fathers in this war. We all have."

Gaius stared into the faces of his men. All of them now, each and every one he knew. They, like he, were the survivors that had lived, fought and bled in the long war against Hannibal and his horde. Each man listened to him with full attention. Everyone man knew what this day meant, but so too they knew who they were going to face.

"I can see it in your eyes. I have heard it during the silent nights. You fear what lies across this valley and the man that leads this army against us." Many of Gaius' men grumbled disapprovingly, which caused him to smile. "You fear Hannibal as all Romans do. You fear that the gods have forsaken us and have blessed this man with immortality and foresight."

The rumbling between the men grew louder and angrier with each new word.

"We are just another long line of walking dead, only we don't know it yet. This is what you believe, isn't it? We should turn around and run, or at the very least, have the decency to fall on our swords. For Hannibal cannot be defeated. He is better than any million Roman sons – is he not?!?"

A chorus of voices rose higher, louder and angrier. Gaius' smile grew wider as his words rose higher, carrying over his men.

"Well, I tell you now, what they say is fabrications! Hannibal has never faced this army – these men – my Wolves before!"

The men cheered louder, which was mixed in with enraged laughter. Gaius allowed his men to carry on for several seconds longer before he continued.

"Romans," his words grew lower now. "We have suffered greatly; not a brother here hasn't been touched by the sorrow that this man has brought to each and every one of us, but here today, all of Rome has come united and will cry out in one voice, the Republic shall not fall, now or ever!"

The men of the Sixth Legion roared with excitement as Gaius rode back and forth in front of his men.

"When the signal comes, we will ride out and face the enemy. We will engage them and slaughter them to the man. We will ride behind Hannibal's lines and cut his veterans to pieces, and when that is done and this war is over, he and the whole world will forever know the name of this legion, and tremble with fear!"

The roars of the Wolves carried over the whole battlefield. All sides, Roman and Carthaginian could hear them, and perhaps wonder was this the day that the unbeatable Hannibal would finally be defeated?

"Very inspiring," Maurus said with a cheerful smile as Gaius rejoined him. "A bit melodramatic, don't you think?"

"Whatever works, my friend," Gaius replied with a wide grin.

The Sixth remained still a bit longer as Gaius could feel the anticipation build. Across the field, beyond the haze of the sun, he could hear the roar of his enemy, the echoes of the powerful elephants and the beating of Carthage's drums.

"I am coming home, my love," Gaius uttered to himself as he drew his sword, which was followed by the thousands of men that stood in formation behind him. And then, carried over the distant horizon he and all the Sixth heard it, the final horn blow – the signal to attack.

"For Rome!" Gaius roared as he kicked his horse and raced across the desert – the whole of the Sixth charging behind him.

CHAPTER FORTY-EIGHT

The cavalry charge was intense. Gaius had never been in one so large and this furious, as over five thousand men collided with a thunderous clap of flesh and iron. The sounds of men and animals screaming as they were being chewed to pieces with deadly efficiency was overpowering, yet Gaius stayed poised as he rode through the first wave of riders that had charged headlong into his men. Now, the charge had ended and both Roman and Carthaginian were mixed together in a deadly duel – the victor would break the other's lines and ride around to the main center, enveloping the army and claim victory. It was a simple tactic that was devoid of any trickery or surprises. The battle would be decided by the merit of the men, their equipment, training and experience.

Blood splashed across Gaius' face. He couldn't avoid a mouthful of the salty, cooper taste of his opponent's gore going down his throat. He had learned a long time ago to ignore the strange unnatural taste as his sword cut across the face of one horseman that charged towards him. For the moment he was with a group of a dozen or more Roman riders, but with each savage micro battle among the greater engagement, men fell or were pushed further into the melee.

For all the tactics and training he had received in his life, none of it meant anything, not in the heat of battle. He could call out if he liked, but his words would easily be drowned out by the sounds of battle. So, Gaius worried about one thing at a time, one opponent at a time as he moved, still on his horse through the Carthaginian ranks.

He had lost count how many men he had killed or wounded. He himself had already sustained half dozen cuts to his body, but thankfully his superior armor protected him from anything too serious. Most men he shoved his sword into didn't even see him. It was the nature of the conflict. With so much dust and chaos surrounding the battlefield, men just pushed and thrust into anything that moved either before them, or to the sides. It was becoming hard to distinguish friend from foe, and these were only the early moments of the battle. It was only when the tip of his blade met resistance, and then the splatter of blood that Gaius knew he had actually killed someone. Soon, however, most of the riders on either side of the battle had dismounted, either because their horses were struck down, being as they were a bigger target than the man that rode them, or forced down.

Out from the dust and clamoring of bodies Gaius saw him, the only man among this enemy army he had been searching for, Calfax.

The former gladiator seemed to notice Gaius at the same time. They were both still on their horses, less than fifty paces from one another. For just a moment their eyes locked, and then Gaius roared as he encouraged his horse to charge.

Calfax soon did the same as the two men galloped through the fighting that was taking place all around them, and readied to face the other, picking up where they had left off.

As Gaius neared the man he had faced only once before, that night, five years prior, just days after the battle of Cannae, he could see the horrors in his mind's eye that Calfax had overseen in his camp – the murdered and tortured Roman captives that he had tried to save. Those images had forever stayed with him, haunting his nights, pushing him to the brink of insanity at times. He swore some nights, as he lay awake in his bed that he could still smell and taste the cooked human flesh of his countrymen. What Calfax had done was inhuman. His hatred for everything Roman boiled over into the rage that had sustained the old man for decades. When he was finally given the chance to break the bonds of his slavery, he did not seek freedom, but revenge for the injustice that his Roman captives had done to him for more years than Gaius had been alive.

Whatever past crimes Rome had done to Calfax, it had been paid for, ten times over. Yet, even in victory, Calfax's bloodlust didn't end. He found new and ever more interesting ways to slaughter his former masters, regardless of status, sex or age. If you bore the eyes, the hair, skin or blood of a Roman, you were his target. But it was the death of his beloved childhood friend Anthony that had haunted Gaius the longest.

He knew without a doubt that Anthony had died at Calfax hands - the man wore the medallion that had become the symbol of two boy's brotherhood – a lifelong promise that they would always be there for one another, fight and defend the other from anything, man or monster. Gaius wanted that broken half of the medallion back more than anything, and he was just seconds away from rejoining the two pieces.

When he was within range, Gaius threw himself forward, off of his horse and right at Calfax, who had no time to react as the younger man's body hit him with all the force and speed that Gaius had been traveling before his daring leap of faith.

The two men fell to the ground. Gaius hit hard, landing on his side and rolled several more feet before he finally stopped.

The hard earth beneath him did nothing to cushion his fall, but his armor had saved him from any serious injury beyond the gash to his head as his helmet was knocked free.

The old gladiator fell onto his back and rolled once before he stopped.

As Calfax stood to his feet, it was painfully clear that he had broken several ribs on his right side, but despite the pain, he stood his ground and reacted quickly as Gaius charged at him once he was back on his feet.

Gaius' blows came savagely. Years of built up rage poured out of him as he struck at the old gladiator time and time again. He forwent any form and any practiced training, and just attacked with all the force his younger body could bring.

Calfax, with decade's worth of experience expertly dodged or blocked Gaius' savage beating, but the younger Roman was, for the moment, too quick for him to counter against.

The two men covered several meters in a matter of seconds since the first blow had been struck. Both ignored the battle that was happening all around them. Neither man cared at this moment which side was winning the battle even though both knew what should happen if one faction should faultier and collapse.

The world was only them right now, which was just as Calfax wanted – this was his arena – man to man with only one possible outcome.

Gaius charged again, swinging high, hoping that the tip of his finely crafted sword, the very sword that had once belonged to Valerius, would make contact with Calfax's throat. However, the experienced warrior dodged the oncoming attack with ease, and then quickly struck low.

Gaius felt it, a fast and painful sensation as the tip of Calfax's slightly longer sword sliced right across his lower thigh.

Instantly, he felt the weight on that leg gave way, but he forced himself to counter balance and remain standing. Calfax, however, had a clean shot if he took it. Gaius' defenses were down for a fraction of a second, yet, the old gladiator did not attack. He instead stood back and allowed Gaius to regain his footing and level his defense.

With a wide smile on his face, Calfax spat a mouthful of dust to the ground, and leered at Gaius with an amused smile.

"You have improved since our last encounter, Roman," Calfax said in as good Latin as he was able.

Gaius just snarled at him as he attacked again with the same determination as he had previously shown, but now, Calfax had regained his own form and easily held, despite the punishment that Gaius unleashed with each savage swing of his sword.

Calfax was playing with him now, or so the thought had accrued to Gaius as the veteran warrior blocked, and seemly teased the younger man. And with each swing of his sword, his speed lessoned and his strength slowly began to fade with fatigue.

"You make easy mistakes, young one. The same mistakes I've seen many better warriors make in the arena," Calfax observed as he deflected another blow from Gaius.

Gaius screamed out in pain and frustration as Calfax cut him again, this time his sword slicing across the other leg, against his lower calf.

He tried to close the gap and use his shorter range to his advantage, but Calfax slugged him directly in the face.

Gaius' nose broke under the direct hit as his blood mixed with the sandy dust drizzled down into his mouth. Calfax just grinned as he repositioned himself and waited.

"Try again, Roman - attack with a broader stance."

Another charge was met with another cut, a deep gash to his left arm, and then a second even quicker slice to his lower back – the sword tip tearing through the leather armor of Gaius' chest plate.

He dropped to the ground this time as his vision began to blur. Calfax stood like a monolith over him, teasing him with just his eyes as he waited for Gaius to stand up again.

"Why...are you like this?" Gaius uttered. He wasn't even sure if his words could be heard; however, Calfax actually leered in closer and replied.

"Why? I was like you once. I fought for your Republic, in many battles. Sparta allied itself with Rome against the other Greek city states...I was proud to wear that armor, but I saw that Rome used us as cattle – using our lives to weaken the enemy before they attacked. So I deserted and went home, but your Rome tracked me down. They burnt my home," Calfax's words were become angrier as he moved towards Gaius, who was only now started to get back to his feet.

"They raped my wife before my eyes, and then slit her throat as my children watched. When they were done, the bastards sold my children into slavery, as well me. But I became gladiator, and then all of Rome cheered my name."

Calfax attacked this time. Gaius tried to hold his ground but the older man was surprisingly faster, stronger and now enraged with the memories of what Rome had done to him long ago.

Calfax cut into Gaius' sword arm. The blade sliced deeply into his bicep, which splattered blood across the already soaked battlefield.

Gaius had no time to even scream before another savage attack hit him – this time Calfax's blade cut across the side of his neck. He had only managed to turn just enough that the blade didn't tear more than an inch into his flesh, but still, the damage was done.

"Rome made me better – a better fighter than I ever was. And for that, I thank you. For it has given me the means to slaughter your kind for years now."

Gaius couldn't lift his right arm as it dangled down to his side; his fingers just barely gripping the hilt of his sword as he back stepped, trying to put some distance between he and Calfax, who advanced slowly on him.

When Calfax attacked again, seeing that Gaius was all but done for, his sword found flesh two more time, and on the third attack, even as Gaius' blood continued to flow out from his numerous wounds, Calfax slammed the butt-end of his sword up against the back of his skull.

Gaius slumped forward, falling to his knees, but still strong enough that he didn't drop completely to the ground.

Calfax circled him, as he did not get up – did not seemed capable of getting up as he bled and breathed heavily – his eyes staring up at the superior warrior as Calfax stopped before him and looked down at the young Roman that had challenged him.

"You, young one, represent everything that I hate about your people – what you have done to me. You may win this war, but you will not stop me from fulfilling my destiny. I will never stop until I see your city and its people burnt from this earth and blown to the wind, never to be remembered."

The image of Julia flashed across his mind as Calfax said his last words. He had sworn long ago to protect her from the monsters of the world. And while that promise had been made by a boy who dreamt of myths and legends, Gaius had found that monster, and he was very real.

He had failed to live up to his promise.

Unable to move or raise his weapon to defend himself, Gaius was going to give in. He sat where he had falling, on both his knees before Calfax, but somehow, Gaius found what little strength he had left, and spoke.

"I pity you, gladiator. I'm sorry for what we did to you." His words were barely audible, but Calfax seemed to understand them good enough as his expression changed suddenly to confusion, and then pure rage.

"I am sorry for everything we did to you."

Calfax stared at Gaius with a dumbfounded expression on his face, as his mouth closed and his eyes seemed to widen.

For a moment, Gaius saw the old man for who he was, what had happened to him, and what he had been forced to endure. He seemed ancient; a warrior from another era when men lived with honor and dignity.

He could see through Calfax and knew that he had once been a man very much like himself - a man that had loved someone as much as he loved Julia. But that man was gone now. He had died the day his wife and children were taken away from him. He was something else now; a product of Rome's own dark soul.

"And, I forgive you," Gaius finished.

Then, that small moment had past. Calfax's anger boiled over as he leered down at Gaius and cried out with a bellowing voice, "I do not want your pity, Roman! I just want you to die!"

Gaius closed his eyes as Calfax raised his sword up over his head and readied to plunge it down into his chest. In his mind he saw his beloved, smelt her, felt her and held onto that

421

image as long as he could before he drew upon what little strength he had left. And then, as he opened his eyes once more, just for a moment, through the thickening of the dust fill smog, he saw the white wolf, standing, poised, looking at him for just a moment before it was gone in the rising heat.

Before Calfax's final blow could come, Gaius suddenly rose to his feet, his right arm, which had dangled uselessly down by his side, shot forth and plunged the tip of his sword into Calfax's chest.

Calfax's eyes opened wide as he looked down at the ivory handle of Gaius' sword sticking out of his chest, shocked and amazed by the sudden realization that Gaius had faked his apparent weakness, but had kept just enough strength in reserve and bought his time, knowing that he was desperately overpowered and outclassed by the seasoned gladiator.

And then, Calfax's grip on his sword faltered as he looked up and stared into Gaius' eyes, as he pushed his sword even deeper.

Gaius reached with his freed hand and grabbed the clay medallion that hung around Calfax's neck, and with on good tug, he ripped it off from the gladiator's neck.

"This does not belong to you," Gaius said as he broke the leather strand that kept the medallion in position.

And then, with one forcefully tug, Gaius withdrew his sword.

The old gladiator's eyes rolled back into his head as he slumped down onto his knees, still staring up at the young Roman that had bested him, gazing with puzzlement, and then, fell face first into the dusty sand that lay beneath his feet.

Gaius dropped to his knees, no longer able to stand as his wounds had finally gotten the better of him.

He looked around as he heard the sound of a distant horn blowing, and for a moment he thought that it might have been a Carthaginian rallying cry. But, then he heard it again and realized it was coming from his men – his Wolves had broken the Carthaginian lines and were now pouring through their ranks as those that still lived, turned and ran.

He would not see the end, but he knew what its outcome would be. Rome had won, and his men had succeeded as the backbone of Hannibal's army had been broken, seemly at the same time that Calfax's own heart stopped beating.

Gaius closed his eyes and allowed his world to slip away from him as his men all raced pasted him, onward towards Hannibal's rear, which was already engaged with the main Roman front, but would not break as Rome had at Cannae.

Soon, the sounds of the battlefield left him. The world around him became quiet as he returned to a better place, a home he had not seen for many years now – a distant house, alone in the hills surrounding by lush green fields – a place he remembered from his childhood.

When his feet touched the road that led to the far off estate, he saw her, Julia, standing watch for him as she had done for five long years.

Oh, how he marveled her at beauty – how he craved the touch of her lips and longed to hear the soothing sounds of her voice. He had longed for her his entire life, an impossible dream that had come true. She was his soul, his reason for living each new day, and for her, he would always protect her from the monsters of the world, even at the cost of his own life.

Unlike in his dreams each night, this time, however, Gaius did not wake up. He did not hesitate to keep walking forward until she was in his loving embrace once again.

His war was over. Now his life could begin – a perfect dream made real.

End

ABOUT AUTHOR

Christopher is a native of California, having lived most of his life in Sacramento. He has a passion for anything science fiction and history related. Considering himself an armature historian, Christopher has studied Roman history exclusively for the past twelve years. *Swords of Rome* is his first Roman publication – the first book in a series of Roman theme stories that meant to cross the breath of the Republic era through to the Empire, centering on many of Rome's most celebrated heroes and events, starting with the Second Punic War.

Christopher has worked in the video game industry for the past six years for two independent game studios in his hometown of Sacramento and London. He has also worked for several websites dedicated to video game journalism. In 2013 his sci-fi book series, *Conquest of Heroes* is scheduled to be released through publication with Double Dragon Publishing.

Printed in Great Britain
by Amazon.co.uk, Ltd.,
Marston Gate.